MINERVA'S FOX

MINERVA'S FOX

A NOVEL

KRISTINA BAER

TWO HARBORS PRESS
MINNEAPOLIS, MN

Copyright © 2015 by Kristina Baer

Two Harbors Press
322 First Avenue N, 5th floor
Minneapolis, MN 55401
612.455.2293
www.TwoHarborsPress.com

ISBN-13: 978-1-63413-293-0
LCCN: 2014922901

Distributed by Itasca Books

Cover Design by Alan Pranke
Typeset by James Arneson

Printed in the United States of America

For George

CONTENTS

PART 1

BROOKTON UNIVERSITY

1969–1970

Minerva's Fox

Archibald Billings Library: The Reading Room Fresco, Campus Guide, Brookton University, p. 22.

In 1860, Brookton University alumnus Archibald Billings donated marble from his quarry in Danby, Vermont, for the construction of a library on the campus. Billings, a classicist, stipulated that the building be modeled after the Tempio di Minerva in Assisi, Italy, and that the university commission his son, Michael Billings, to paint the fresco on the domed ceiling of the library's reading room. Michael Billings completed Minerva, Goddess of Wisdom *in 1864.*

Shield and spear in hand, Minerva stands on a mountaintop gazing into the distance. Her presence in the fresco makes the connection clear between her role as patroness of the arts, commerce, medicine, and defense, among others, and the library as the repository of learning. The owl on her shoulder, a symbol of wisdom, fixes its wary regard on a red fox peering through the grass into the reading room below, amber eyes alight, lips upturned.

September 26, 1969

"Makes you wonder, doesn't it?" Clean-shaven, with longish brown hair curling over the collar of his khaki parka and blue (gray?) eyes, he glanced up at the fresco, then looked at me.

"In a way, yes. I know about the owl and Minerva. And Billings's interest in the classics. But the fox?" He looked familiar, but I couldn't place him.

"There's an old story—something to do with Archibald Billings, naturally—about a pet fox, one he rescued from a trap." Gray eyes, yes. A little anxious, certainly attentive, they took me in.

"So the Archibald Billings Library fresco is a memorial to Archibald Billings's pet fox?"

"A bit of a stretch, I agree." He glanced at the students working nearby and lowered his voice. "Maybe you've seen the other ones around campus—the foxes carved out of stone and wood?" He leaned closer. "Rumor is, Billings belonged to a secret society, like a fraternity. The fox was their mascot. The members all became big donors."

"Money for other buildings?" Obviously. All universities like Brookton counted on their wealthy alumni to fund their construction projects and their endowment.

"Right. All signed with a fox."

This, at least, sounded plausible. Too plausible?

He stifled a smile and held out his hand. "Jack Nelson. Second year. French."

It was like playing charades with someone who gives away the main clue: I'd seen him at the department meeting the week before. "Malorie Ellsworth."

"First year. French." He filled in the blank with a grin that banished the guarded look he'd worn just a moment ago. He was almost handsome.

"How's the Hughes course going so far? The translations?"

All first-year students took the Old French course, so why did his question make me wonder what else he knew about me?

"Marie de France this week." I gestured in the direction of the stacks. Would he take the hint?

"If you have questions—about anything—here's my carrel number. It's downstairs, near the elevator. We should have coffee sometime." He scribbled on a piece of paper and handed it to me.

I glanced up at the fox. That smile. And the eyes. The eyes seemed to follow me. Perhaps it was true that Billings had had a pet fox. Whether he had or hadn't, the fox's presence in the painting had an unsettling effect. In its ambiguous expression, I read a warning.

I'D BEGUN the doctoral program in French at Brookton University confident of my language skills. Thanks to my French grandmother, I was fluent. A doctorate in French would prepare me to teach in a college or university. But so far, graduate school seemed like *terra incognita*; everywhere I turned, I seemed to trip up. I kept reminding myself that I was working in a field I knew and loved. So what, exactly, was the problem? This much had become clear to me: every professor conducted his class (there were no women professors) according to a set of unspoken rules supporting his own particular approach to the works we studied, an approach we were expected to discover on our own according to clues tossed out like breadcrumbs to koi in a pond.

Just that afternoon, at the end of the Old French seminar, William Hughes had taken questions. I asked if he could recommend background reading, information about Marie de France, for instance.

Hughes set his pipe down and leaned toward me, his lips pursed. "This isn't the nineteenth century, when everyone put out floods of personal information. Even then, who cares, really, what Baudelaire had for breakfast? Anyway, Miss Ellsworth, even if we discovered that Marie de France kept a daily diary—and found the thing—it wouldn't matter. You see, the text is all we can know. It's all we have." He pushed back from the table to write these last two sentences on the board. Sitting across from me, Patrick Lane caught my eye and winked.

I wasn't the only one who felt out of place.

AFTER SHARING a room for four years at Alden College, I was relieved to have a single room on the second floor of one of the graduate dorms. It was minuscule, but it had everything I needed: a single bed, a built-in closet, drawers, desk, bookshelves. And an illusion of solitude: a rowan tree stood outside the window.

Just as I began to take my privacy for granted, Danielle Delavigne, another first-year French student, began to drop by to compare notes on our assignments. This soon became an annoying habit since she rarely completed any of her own work.

The way to avoid Danielle's visits appeared the day I found the Old French dictionaries in the reading room stacks. Nearby, I discovered a single desk tucked into an alcove. Thanks to a buffer zone of shelves, it was probably the quietest, most secluded study space in the library.

So far, Danielle hadn't tracked me down.

As I skimmed the latest assignment, a selection from a lai by Marie de France, words formed phrases that quickly shaped themselves into a dramatic scene: a dying stag confronts the hunter who has mortally wounded him. I managed to translate the Old French version without too many interruptions to look up words. As in the original Anglo-Norman, nouns and verbs bumped into one another without the connective tissue of conjunctions, adjectives, or adverbs.

It had the feel of an incantation. How had the original sounded when it was read or recited aloud? I could imagine a wide hall, its walls hung with tapestries, heated by an enormous fireplace. A single figure standing before a group seated at a long table begins his recital—half spoken, half sung, to the accompaniment of a lute.

As I closed my notebook and bent down to reach my book bag, I felt his hand on the middle of my back. Just a touch. Still, a touch. I stood up fast, bumping into the desk and knocking the lamp over.

How had he found me?

I couldn't force a smile. There was probably a way to let him know I had chosen this tiny space because I didn't want to be disturbed. Was that really so much to ask?

"Jack . . ." I heard the edge in my voice and gave up.

"Sorry I startled you. Coffee? Or a drink?"

I wanted to beg off. Not that there was anything wrong with him, exactly. Only that he seemed too sure of himself, too sure of me. I could still feel the pressure of his hand on my back. My hip throbbed where I'd bumped into the desk. *It's only coffee.* I eyed the pile of dictionaries. "Ten minutes?"

"I'll wait." He waved in the direction of the lobby.

Re-shelving took longer than I expected. I wondered why he hadn't offered to help. Maybe if I hadn't been so abrupt?

Fifteen minutes later at the check-out desk, I looked around the lobby. *Maybe he left.* Then I heard him call my name. He stood just outside the front door.

"So how did it go?"

"Parts still don't make a lot of sense. It's so piece by piece, you know?" The urge to take back my words was so strong I blushed.

"I could smooth it out for you, if you want."

"I'll do a clean copy, give it another go. If it still seems rough to me, perhaps later?" I sounded as irritated and defensive as I felt. Was that so unreasonable? I wanted not to depend on anyone but myself for my work. It was beginning to seem as if my attitude was the exception, and Jack's and Danielle's was the rule.

"Later's fine."

WE WAITED for a table at Tony's, the restaurant and bar down the street from the library. Smelling of stale beer and patchouli, and blue with cigarette smoke, the place didn't have much going for it except proximity to campus and a liquor license.

Jack told me about his thesis topic, Lamartine's late poetry. He'd given a paper about it in a seminar that day. His mouth twisted with annoyance. When we got to our table, he explained. "Ellis had to catch a train. He takes off early on Fridays. Someone's usually left hanging. My turn today."

Ellis Jacobs, the department's expert on the French Romantics, smoked a cigar, affected a pageboy haircut, and wore a cape.

"Will you get to finish next time?"

"Most likely he'll ask me to read my conclusion." He shrugged. "Reading the whole thing to the others doesn't matter to me. It's Ellis's opinion that counts."

I couldn't read his expression, couldn't tell how he really felt. His flippant tone made it impossible to know if, or how much, he cared. I leaned toward him, straining to hear him over the background noise. Laughter, clattering dishes, music from the jukebox. The din was louder now than it had been when we arrived.

"I said I'm looking forward to seeing Lamartine's letters in France. Next year, probably." Eyes narrowed, he tilted his head back. "You look so worried. Don't be. Once you get through this year, you'll know the ropes. It's not so hard, really. Especially when you get past your field exams and start work on your dissertation."

Patronizing, again. Maybe he didn't realize it. Or maybe he just didn't care.

Patrick and some of the other first-year students came in. I waved. "Do you know anyone else in my class?" I asked Jack.

"I've met Danielle. Patrick, I know. I went to Yale, too." His voice had an edge. His lips tightened. A reaction to Danielle, or to Patrick?

"Do you want to meet the others?" I stood and picked up my jacket and bag.

Jack checked his watch. "Some other time. Catch you later?"

SITTING BESIDE Patrick in the booth, I thought about Jack's attitude about the way things worked at Brookton. Was it indifference? After everything he had told me about his dissertation, I had no idea at all why he had chosen Lamartine, or if he even liked poetry. He seemed more interested in the poems as artifacts than as art. And what about Lamartine himself, the writer and the politician—and France's first Romantic poet?

"He's been watching you." Patrick pretended to peer at me through binoculars.

"And you know this, because . . . ?"

"Because I watch him."

I brushed some crumbs off the table. "Apparently you know each other."

"In a manner of speaking. Let's just say we didn't run with the same crowd up there at Yale." Patrick sat up very straight, lifted his chin, and looked down his nose at me.

"I just met him, Patrick."

"Well, he *is* a snob. And he doesn't like people like me."

"People like *you?*"

Patrick exhaled a stream of cigarette smoke and leaned close to me, his voice inaudible.

"What?" I asked.

"I'm gay, babe."

"So?" If he had told me he was a Martian, that wouldn't have changed how I felt about him. Patrick was the only person I'd met so far who didn't pose as anyone but himself.

Anyway, I wasn't surprised. Somehow, I already knew.

Patrick sipped his beer. "So he's a homophobe. That's a laugh!" he scoffed. "He should know he's got nothing to worry about. He's not my type. Nor yours, I think." He put his arm around me. "He's got the hots for you. Or have you already figured that out?"

"I'm still trying to understand this place. All the unspoken rules. That's more than enough to keep me busy."

"Kind of a drag for you." He laughed. "But it won't keep us—you and me—from having some fun, right? Life is way too short to take it seriously all the time."

"Of course!" I kissed his cheek.

As I slid out of the booth, he handed me a sheet of paper.

"What's this?"

"The syllabus for Hal Rose's spring seminar. I took two: one for you and one for me." He managed a little bow in my direction. "I've read them all."

"Which means?"

"I can have fun—the second time around, you know, with both feet on the ground."

I glanced at the list.

"You look like you've seen a ghost—or an old flame."

I shook my head. "Neither. Or maybe both."

"Which means what, exactly?"

"*Le Grand Meaulnes* . . . I've read it. More than once. Just not in a class." Seeing it on the list was like meeting an old friend unexpectedly and knowing that there was a reason for everything. As if my grandmother were standing beside me, I heard her whisper, "*Il n'y a pas de coïncidence, ma chérie.*" No such thing as coincidence . . . Lightheaded from the burst of confidence and hope I felt, I could laugh off the fox's warning smile and my malaise. Maybe I had found firmer ground at last.

"You're in luck, then. You can read it again—only this time, you get to tell the rest of us what makes it so special!" He looked at me, laughing a little. "Do you think Fitzgerald read it?"

"Do you?"

"It's an idea. You know, *The Great Meaulnes*, *The Great Gatsby* . . ."

"Both outsiders, idealists . . ."

Patrick looked up, excited. "Both in love with an inaccessible woman . . ."

And Hal Rose? What would he make of this idea? I had been at Brookton long enough to know that Rose's thoughts on *Le Grand Meaulnes* would shape whatever I might have to say about it.

October 4, 1969

My mother carried a plate of sliced pears and toast to the table and set it down. "How did you make out?"

"Found it." I handed her my copy of *Le Grand Meaulnes*, its blue linen cover soiled, dented, and frayed.

She wrinkled her nose. "Mildew! Where was it?"

"In a box with some other books."

I showed her the endpaper's signature: *Malorie Granger, 1913*. My great-grandmother had given this first edition to my grandmother on her thirteenth birthday. At first, hesitant even to touch the smooth linen cover, my grandmother had worn gloves and kept the book hidden in the space between her bed and the wall, where her brothers wouldn't find it.

An envelope fell out onto the table. Yellowing around the edges, the glue on the flap cracked and peeling, it contained a strip of four black-and-white snapshots. Each showed a set of features that could only belong to four different people: a forehead and nose, an ear, two eyes, a mouth and chin. . . .

"Who in the world?" my mother asked.

"Louise and Pierre Lebrun, Ted Girard, and me. At the train station in Mâcon."

Together that day, waiting for a ride back to Flagy, we'd been bored and tired. Pierre had noticed the photo booth tucked into a corner not far from the ticket counter. We had just enough change to make four copies of this one strip. How had I ended up sitting on Ted's lap, wedged next to Pierre, with Louise sprawled across our laps?

"I haven't heard anything from the Girards since I got the wedding announcement. You know Ted is married?"

After the summer of 1961, Ted and I had lost our only link, the village of Flagy and our summers there. My freshman year at Alden, I played my recordings of Georges Moustaki, Léo Ferré, and Edith Piaf, projecting my own magic lantern show to keep my memories alive—Flagy's old church, the spring-fed *lavoir* at the crossroads, the ebb and flow of visiting kids, Ted and his gang racing on bikes around the village.

"Yes. I know."

As soon as I'd heard the news from my grandmother, I'd put it out of my mind. Ted and I had been friends. Nothing more or less. At least that's what I told myself.

"I've never read it, you know." She gestured at the book. A small muscle at the corner of her right eyelid jumped, like a switch flicking off. Or on. Her eyes narrowed; she looked away with a frown.

Something about her tone of voice, the way she hunched and tensed her shoulders, made me wait.

My mother still wouldn't look at me. "I just . . . couldn't. Something like that."

Half French, half American, she refused to speak French. It hadn't always been like this. As soon as she began to talk, she spoke French to my grandmother and English to my grandfather. This was so normal, so natural, that when she stopped speaking altogether, my grandparents sought help right away.

Their pediatrician had advised them to be patient. A week went by. Then another. Not a word until my grandfather decided, and persuaded my grandmother, that Lucie needed to hear and speak one language, not two, until she was old enough to choose for herself. As soon as they both began to speak English to her, her inhibition ended.

I suspected there was more to the story, for the simple reason that my own experience disproved the explanation: I had been speaking French, with my grandmother, and English, at home and at school, from the beginning, switching easily back and forth.

Although I didn't believe the family story that my first word was "Milou," my grandmother's nickname, instead of "mama," I knew that every French syllable I learned and spoke was a gift of love, mine for Milou, Milou's for me. Doubtless my mother felt jealousy—and perhaps even guilt that she felt jealous—and this was part of the difficulty between her and Milou.

"I do regret it, you know, not learning French. But I just don't seem to have any aptitude for it—or any other language, for that matter. That's probably the real reason I never read *Le Grand Meaulnes*." She poured more coffee for us both, speared the last slice of pear, and put it on my plate. "Apart from that, I'm glad it gave you a reason to come home for the weekend. Can you fill in the blanks a bit?"

I told her about the seminar on the novel, explaining my idea about working on *Le Grand Meaulnes*. She nodded and smiled, distracted or preoccupied. It was pointless to go on. Besides, I didn't have much to say about the course and hadn't yet decided how or what to tell her about my life at Brookton.

IN THE garden at noon, it felt more like late August than early October. My mother knelt at the far end of the border, taking one daffodil bulb at a time from the pile and placing it in one of the holes she'd dug. I picked up a tulip bulb, its skin so delicate it flaked off at my touch. It seemed a miracle that this compact globe contained everything the plant needed to begin its life, that it didn't question its own coming-into-being or concern itself with the challenges ahead. It was what it was, only that, an expression of supreme confidence.

"What's so funny?" Relaxed and smiling, she had a smudge of dirt at the end of her nose.

"I'm imagining what it's like to be a tulip bulb, all that power and beauty stored up, and the assurance you will turn out exactly as you're supposed to."

"Unless you happen to live in a garden next to a forest full of ravenous deer, that is. Then, your chances aren't so great. Maybe twenty to eighty?" She took out a handkerchief and wiped it across her forehead.

"At the moment, at least, they are none the wiser. Anyway, what do you plan to do about the deer?" We had lived in Long Meadow for fifteen years, from the time my father had been made partner at his law firm. The village itself and the surrounding countryside had changed little. The fields and woods with the deer, foxes, and other wildlife that flourished there appealed to people who didn't mind a two-hour commute into Manhattan or Philadelphia.

Less than ten miles away, developers were buying up failing farms and farmland to build bedroom communities, and there was talk about widening the main road into four lanes. As the woodlands and fields disappeared, the deer and other wild animals had to make the best of what was left, just like the die-hard farmers who wouldn't let go.

"Live and let live, I guess." Her laugh sounded more like a sigh. "I have bigger problems to worry about." The corners of her mouth tightened. In the harsh light, her face drew in on itself, hollow and sharp-edged. She turned to look over the newly planted bed. Her shoulders relaxed. "I hope it will be just as beautiful as your plan."

The bulb border I designed for her relied on periods of bloom that overlapped just enough that contrasting colors and sizes would mingle and blend. After a year or two, depending on the deer and the bulbs themselves, it would develop enough that she could add new bulbs or select perennials the deer wouldn't consume.

She hadn't yet mentioned the divorce. It hadn't occurred to me she might lose the house. The whole point of the bulb border was to give her something to look forward to, some hope in her future there.

While we made our lunch, I talked about my courses, other students, and my professors. "They take themselves so seriously.

Most of them can't hear—won't discuss—different points of view. Like the two department members who don't speak to one another. Not even in faculty meetings or oral exams. One wrote a review of the other's book, calling it 'specious' and 'inconsequential.'"

"Oh, my. Do they really talk like that?"

"I guess this kind of feud happens a lot. Milou has always said that reading a new book is like meeting a new person. Read with an open mind and heart. That's what I want to do. And it's what I want to teach. Battles over points of interpretation, quibbling about terminology, taking a hard line . . . not my thing."

"Maybe learning different approaches is the point? They're training you for a profession, right? Every profession has its own ways, its own lingo. Look at the jargon your father uses!"

"Exactly. And that's one of the reasons why I wanted to do this, not law school like him."

She shook her head. "I'm not saying you should just take it, you know. What about the other first-year students? What do they think?"

"Most of them seem terrified that word will get out they're criticizing a prof. Talking about books ought to be a conversation, not a contact sport. So far it seems everyone in the department is more concerned with piling up markers in some kind of weird power trip."

My mother fidgeted with her napkin, distracted. What difference did any of this make? The more I talked about my qualms, the more trivial they seemed. Was that the problem? How important was it all, anyway? Especially considering real problems—war, poverty, racism. Was my father right? Was I trying to "escape real life," as he'd put it?

She sighed. "I can't talk to anyone else, Malorie. You know that. You're the only one who understands what it's been like for me."

What about me, *Mom?* It seemed that no one, except me and my mother, knew about my father's drinking. Or what he did when he was drunk. It was as though we all—my mother, my father, and I—had made a terrible pact of silence.

Of course my mother depended on me. I was the only person she didn't have to lie to—about the broken furniture or the bruises. So I made myself hear her out. This was our unspoken agreement, the one that spelled out a role determined for me long ago.

"He called yesterday. To tell me he's having an affair. Can you believe it?"

I knew my father had a new secretary—"new and nubile," my mother had sneered.

"I want to talk to the lawyer to see if I can get any leverage from this. If he won't do something this time . . ."

"How close are you?"

"I want this house, and some alimony. That part's just until I get my business going. But that's all. Even *his* lawyer thinks I'm being reasonable."

My mother had worked as an interior designer briefly when she and my father first married. As soon as she made up her mind to divorce, she had begun to look for ways to start over.

"Can't you make your guy do something to speed this up?"

"Lawyers!" she scoffed. "He talked a good game, but I wonder whose side he's really on."

I pushed back against my own anger, horror, and exhaustion, letting her talk just to talk. My parents were like two fighters, torn and bleeding, each trying for the knockout blow. *When will this end?* Through the kitchen window, I saw the first cirrus clouds, signaling the storm that was on its way.

She looked at her watch. "Tell me more about you. The guy you want to work with—didn't you say he's interesting?"

How to begin? Would she even pay attention?

"Hal Rose. He's all right, I guess. He's in his thirties, younger than most of the others. Maybe not so narrow-minded. He wants me to switch to Proust and Gide. He says there're more opportunities, better thesis topics." How much of this made sense to her? Although she at least knew the names, she couldn't know anything about why it might matter—or how much—to change course now. "He's the one doing the seminar on the novel, why I needed to find my copy of *Le Grand Meaulnes*."

"What's the problem?"

"He makes me uncomfortable."

"Uncomfortable? How?"

"There are six of us in the class this term and only two women. He can't keep his eyes off the other one." I didn't say that the other one—Danielle—did nothing to discourage the attention, or that, to the contrary, the way she dressed, her body language, seemed to invite it.

"Oh." My mother put her sandwich down and brushed her napkin across her mouth.

"It's like I can't trust him to give me a fair shake. I think he'll play favorites." I swallowed some iced tea. Was I making too much of Danielle's appearance and behavior? She didn't dress that differently from most women students—jeans and shirts were the uniform. Still, she wore the jeans low-slung and tight; the tops were low-cut and clingy. Above all of this, her green eyes glowed, cat's eyes within a thick fringe of mascara and eyeliner.

"Who's the other girl?"

"Danielle Delavigne. We're in all the same classes. She rooms near me in the dorm."

My mother made a face. "He's married, right?"

"With a couple of little kids."

"It's as though when a married man hits thirty, a switch flips—like those gates in a horse race—and he can't help himself. He just has to play around. If you love him, you hang on until he gets his equilibrium back."

"That didn't work with Dad."

Her eyes narrowed. "Well, I did my best. Even after I stopped loving him. I thought I owed you that, Malorie."

We never talked about the drinking. We just went on as if it were normal, a pastime, like stamp collecting. The awful truth was that it *was* normal, and that's what made it easier to maintain the pretense that all was well.

Anger, hot and sour, burned the back of my throat. I swallowed some tea.

"Sorry. I need to figure out what I'm doing. Maybe you're right about Hal Rose," I said.

"At least you're not married to him."

It was such a bad joke that we both laughed.

My mother reached for my hand. "You can always find something else to do. You're only twenty-two. You have your whole life ahead of you. Think about the possibilities. What about a job in publishing in New York? With your language skills, you might be able to work for the UN. Or the Foreign Service? Your French is a means to an end. The end doesn't have to be a doctorate. Anyway, who knows what will happen? Wait and see!"

A gust of wind rattled the window as the rain began at last. I imagined the water seeping into the soil around the bulbs, the soil enclosing each one, forming a cushion against the hard frost to come.

I leaned over and kissed her cheek. "Sounds like advice we should both follow."

October 18, 1969

A book cart clattered down the next aisle. Someone shelving books on a Saturday morning? I tried to ignore it.

"Pst!"

Jack grinned at me through a gap in the stacks, then ducked out of sight. Immediately a hand-lettered sign appeared in the gap: "Fox hunt, anyone?"

I laughed.

Jack reappeared. He raised his eyebrows and cocked his head in the direction of the exit.

It was Saturday, after all. I'd just finished a long translation. I needed a break. Besides, I wanted to see the other foxes Jack had mentioned the first time we met.

I went with him to his carrel to pick up his camera. "It's just a hobby," he told me. "Around the campus, I've been taking pictures of some of the buildings at different times of the day. Mostly, I've been doing black-and-white studies of the stonework."

Like many American universities, Brookton had plunged into a building spree after the Civil War, when the neo-Gothic style came into its own. Here, as elsewhere, these buildings displayed the expertise of European stonecutters and sculptors.

"Sutton?"

"Especially Sutton." At the graduate college across the campus from the library, with its turrets and crenellations, the Sutton bell tower looked out of place, like a tuxedo at a picnic. But it was unquestionably a tour de force—of the carver's and sculptor's mastery of the play of light and shadow over limestone surfaces.

"Today, for a change, I loaded color film." Jack checked the strap around his neck, closed the camera case, and tucked it into his pocket. "One more storm, no more leaves. It's now or never."

Outside the library, drum rolls and rim shots echoed across the deserted common, as the marching band warmed up for a home game at the stadium a mile away. Jack pulled out the camera, adjusted the lens, and aimed at the tree line, where clusters of pin oak leaves carved the cloudless blue sky into a red and blue mosaic.

Since he had a part-time job as a tour guide, showing visiting students and their parents around the campus, he gave me the highlights as we crossed the grounds. "The boys all want to see the new gym, of course."

"And the girls?"

He laughed. "The library! They want to know how late it stays open."

"Come on!"

"Actually, the parents ask those questions. Mothers, especially. They also want to know about campus security. Fathers usually find a way to ask about parietal hours."

In 1967, Brookton admitted its first female undergraduates. This outraged some alumni, who canceled their annual donations in protest. On campus, during the first fall term, there had been panty raids and some harassment, but the disruptions didn't last long. Although it was still boys against girls, in numbers at least, coeducation, now a fait accompli, suited the students. Most of them couldn't understand the fuss about admitting women in the first place. It was what they were used to, after all.

Jack turned around, walking backward in front of me, lowering his voice as he gestured toward a plain brick building fronted by a white-pillared portico. "And this is the faculty club, where professors conduct séances to see who'll get tenure next." He smiled, as if uncertain I'd gotten the joke. "You told me you live near here. What about the rest of your family?"

"I'm an only child." My throat closed, as if I'd swallowed something the wrong way. "And, well . . ." I skimmed over the rest—that my father was a lawyer, my mother, an interior designer.

He glanced at me, waiting for me to fill in the blanks.

There was so much *not* to tell him—the drinking, the battles, the imminent divorce, everything I wanted to get away from. Once I started on all of this, where would it end? I shrugged and kept walking.

NEITHER OF us said anything for a while. The rhythm and pace of the drums quickened in the buildup to the trumpet fanfare that brought the players onto the field. When had he put his arm around my shoulders? When I turned to look at him, he pulled me closer.

"I'm an only child, too. My mom got pregnant in 1945, in July when my dad had leave on his way to Hawaii. He died there in February 1946, before I was born. Influenza." He removed his arm and ran his hand through his hair. "She never forgave my father for dying."

"She didn't want to remarry?"

He shook his head. "She went back to work as a nurse. My grandmother—my dad's mom—came to live with us until I went to high school. I didn't see much of my mom."

"I'm sorry." I wanted to ask him what it was like to live with these two women and their grief. And about his grandmother. Instead, I told him about my grandparents.

"They met in Lyon in 1919 when my grandfather enrolled at the university." My grandfather, Stephen Madden, decided to stay in France after the war to study botany, and he needed a French tutor. My grandmother had posted her name and qualifications outside his lab. "After they got married, they came to the States, to Vermont. He taught botany at Alden."

He nodded. "So you speak French with your grandmother?"

"Always, yes. And every summer, we used to go to France, to Flagy, where she was born."

"Is that near anywhere I know?"

"It's near Cluny."

"That's not far from Mâcon, but that's all I know."

Lamartine was born in Mâcon; the Lamartine archive was in the museum there. For the second time in a month, I revisited the train station. I saw Ted and Pierre walking away from Louise and me, their heads together, conspiratorial.

Jack was telling me now about his research plans. "Have to go to Mâcon, to the Lamartine archive. There's probably much more there—letters and such—than I know about. Who knows what I'll find?"

Jack had discovered a letter from Lamartine that had included the title and first few lines of an unpublished poem. Ellis Jacobs had told him right away that he had found his dissertation, that he should plan to go to the Lamartine archive, where he might be able to track down the rest of the poem. I wanted to hear more. Jack just smiled and changed the subject.

"What about your grandfather?"

"Milou—my grandmother—always says he was her worst student. He hired her, sight unseen, expecting she would be elderly, or at least older. She was nineteen, tall, blond, blue-eyed. For him, it was love at first sight. She kept trying to get him to focus on the lessons. He kept asking her out."

"At least he learned enough French to ask her to marry him."

WE HAD reached Desmond Park at the edge of the campus, where we sat for a while. Jack draped an arm over the back of the bench, his hand brushing my shoulder. "Go on."

"He wanted to be a painter, but ended up as a medic in the First World War. Whenever he could get away, he drew the plants he saw, mostly wildflowers. He always had a sketch pad with him. My grandmother has dozens of them, all filled with his drawings. He taught me to draw."

"Did you ever think about doing something like that?"

"When I was ten. For about a month. My father told me drawing was a nice enough hobby, but not practical. He wanted me to go to law school. I still sketch, though." I looked at Jack, thinking about his interest in photography. "What about you? Photography?"

He waved his hand, as if batting the question away. "Like I said. Just a hobby. And law school?"

"That didn't work out." I'd had an interview at the University of Chicago Law School, a standard question-and-answer conversation that went fine—until the end. On my way out the door, the interviewer, an assistant dean, had commented, "There are easier ways to find a husband, you know."

"What did you say?" Jack looked amused.

"Nothing." I had known that if I opened my mouth, I would be responsible for anything I said in response. "There was no point, really. If I hadn't already made up my mind that I didn't want to go to law school, his comment alone was enough to turn me off."

"And French. A doctorate in French? How does your father feel about that?"

My father had derided the idea. For once, I'd been ready for him. I brought up my grandfather, who had a PhD. But my father wouldn't—couldn't—let me score even that point. "Your grandfather is a scientist, not an intellectual snob," he had said.

As for my grandmother, who had taught French part-time at Alden College, my father dismissed her with a wave of his hand. "She's never pretended to be anything more than a French teacher. Besides, even with a PhD, you won't make any money."

"Sounds like a no-win situation." Jack looked at me. "So, anyway, here you are."

"Aren't you going to ask me how I won the war?"

"Sure . . ."

"As soon as I told him I had a full fellowship, he gave up."

"Practical. I see what you mean."

I could tell he wanted to ask me more questions. But I'd already told him much more than I meant to. "Let me show you something."

We took a path into a small grove of dogwood trees. At the midway point, I stopped. "We're almost there. Hold my hand and close your eyes." As soon as we got to the edge of the grove, I let go. "Open."

In front of us, we took in the oval of well-tended lawn ringed by tulip trees, dogwoods, and magnolias. Several couples with small children stretched out on picnic blankets, with baskets of food and toys beside them. Two squealing toddlers tore up handfuls of grass and threw them at one another.

Beyond the children, at the far side of the lawn, the dense red-gold canopy of a Japanese threadleaf maple shimmered in the sun. As the afternoon breeze ruffled the leaves, the tree's dark, undulating trunk and limbs came into view. I didn't want to talk anymore about anything, just to be in this spot, observing the boughs lifting and dropping, the interplay of light and shadow.

"The way it's placed, it's like a jewel."

"Watch." A few gauzy clouds drifted overhead, recasting the lawn into a tapestry of light greens and teal blues. As the tree's limbs rose and fell, moving like the wings of some exotic bird, the light caught its red-gold leaves, floating and fluttering against the deep shade of the tulip trees.

I heard the camera shutter click several times in rapid succession. Absorbed in finding new angles, different positions, it was as if Jack had forgotten I was there. I closed my eyes and breathed in the sun's warmth, feeling the clouds' shadows on my face.

"What kind of trees are those, the tall ones?" Jack asked.

"Tulip trees, my favorites, especially when they bloom in the spring. They're . . . elegant, almost classical, I guess you could say." I told him about driving to Brookton often in my last year of high school. "Mostly, I came down here to sketch." One day, I had been sitting under the Japanese maple, drawing the view up through its branches. I could see the canopy of the tulip tree just above and noticed how the feathery maple leaves seemed etched into its broad-lobed leaves. "That exercise taught me just about everything I know about foreground and background."

At that moment, jubilant cheers and thumping drums signaled the end of the game and a Brookton victory.

"What about our fox hunt?"

Jack looked at me. "What about it?"

"You were going to show me the other foxes, weren't you?"

He turned away, fidgeting with change in his pocket, his face hidden from me. "The story about Billings, the foxes, his group of friends . . . I made it up."

"You told me two stories. Did you invent them both?"

He cleared his throat. "Billings did have a pet fox."

"So the only memorial fox is the one in the painting?"

"As far as I know." He glanced at me.

"There was no fraternity of like-minded friends?"

"Nope."

Just when I thought I was getting to know him better, he slipped away from me, a stranger again. Why lie about something like this? That first afternoon, when we'd stood in the reading room talking about the fox, I knew his interest in it was genuine. Why not just invite me to take a walk? He didn't have to resort to subterfuge. I couldn't figure him out, but I didn't know my feelings for him well enough to confront him.

I kept my interpretation of the fox to myself.

A week or so later, Jack gave me copies of two photographs he took that day. One, a portrait, showed me in profile, looking into the distance, present but absent, wisps of hair lying flat against my cheek. In the other, the Japanese maple's glowing canopy draped over its sinuous trunk and branches, holding the light in the shadow of the tulip trees.

November 1, 1969

"Phone, Malorie!"

Six thirty. Just early enough for bad news.

Down the hall, outside the window on the landing, the frost-coated pines gleamed in the early light. Even before I put the receiver to my ear, he was talking to me. He must have heard me coming. "There's no deal unless she agrees to sell the house."

"Dad . . ."

"Understand? You tell her that. Exactly what I said." *Unnerstan'?* The slurring, the gurgling, throat-clearing sounds—drunk, of course. I hadn't talked to him since August; my mother had promised not to give him the dorm phone number. So how did he get it? Certainly not from Milou.

"Dad, I'm not talking to you. Not when you're . . ." *Drunk.* Even now, I couldn't say it. We never said it. Instead, we'd say something like, "Dad's tired." Or, "Dad's in a bad mood."

I heard the clink of ice in a glass. "I'm going to fight her and I'm going to win." The threat in his voice made him sound sober.

"This is between you and Mom, and your lawyers." My voice cracked. I couldn't feel my feet. Even my eyelashes felt numb. Did he know I was going up to Long Meadow, or was it just a lucky guess? My breath caught and I gagged. The riptide of their misery pulled at me, dragging me along with them, no matter how hard I struggled to break free.

When I got home, my mother's Saab, the driver's door open wide, blocked the driveway. I parked on the shoulder just beyond it. In the house, the cats cowered in a corner of the hall, eyes wide, tails twitching. I could hear my mother's voice, ragged with tears.

"Give you another chance? After what you did . . . ? No. No! If you come up here, I'll call the sheriff. . . . Yes, I do mean it. I'm hanging up."

The phone clattered to the floor. Both cats squirmed under the couch. I started toward the stairs. Something—a book?—hit a wall. High heels thudded like hammer blows through the house. The cats fled into the laundry room.

She made it to the bottom step and slumped against the wall. Her eyes glittered through a smear of mascara. "He's impossible, Malorie." She spat this out, curling her hands into fists. "I was just on my way out to get us something for dinner. I heard the phone, thought it might be you."

How many times had we played scenes like this? How many times had I arrived home—from school, from a party, from shopping—to find my mother in tears and my father sprawled in front of the TV in a drunken stupor?

"What has he done this time?"

Sinking down on a stair, folding her skirt under her, she rubbed her forehead, closed her eyes. "I can manage without him. And that's the problem. That's why he's fighting so hard." She shook her head in disbelief. "He'll fight me to the end because that makes him feel powerful." She patted her hair. "Do I look awful?" Her smile trembled. "You asked me what happened."

"Why don't you go wash your face? Change clothes? I'll make tea. Then we'll talk."

"I'm sorry, sweetie." Holding the railing, she made her way up the stairs, as if fearful of losing her way.

I put the water on and found a tray and a teapot. As soon as I opened the refrigerator, the cats came running, their fright completely forgotten. Maybe the divorce would have the same calming effect.

At least I would never live at home again.

By the time I set the tea tray down, it was nearly dark. The glow of a small table lamp played over the surfaces of the pewter pots on the mantelpiece. Wood-framed prints and a few of my grandfather's watercolors hung on the whitewashed walls. One of the cats stretched out on the couch beside my mother; the other lay on the floor in front of her.

"I don't know . . ." My mother lifted her hand and dropped it into her lap.

I couldn't read her expression.

"I can't remember what it was like to love your father. I know I did, once." She gave a soft laugh. "When we first met, that blind date . . ."

Alan Ellsworth had expected Lucie Madden to be dark and curvaceous. Like Arletty, the forties film star, he'd said once. Tall, blond, blue-eyed Lucie left him tongue-tied. The next day, when he called to ask her out, she turned him down. An hour later, he appeared at her dorm with a bouquet—three dozen white roses.

"So what happened last week?"

"He broke in on Wednesday when I was in New York and took the Duncan Phyfe table. And the chairs." Her voice shook. She had inherited the furniture from my grandfather. "He gave me that bouquet thirty-five years ago, and then this . . ." She leaned her head back, closed her eyes. "I'm beat."

"Dad called me."

"What did he want?"

"Before we talk about that, I'd like to know how he got my number."

"Not from me. I promised you. . . . He must have looked in my book the day he took the furniture." She leaned toward me, hands outstretched, pleading. "I didn't give it to him. I swear."

Even before I finished telling her what my father had said, she had pushed herself to the edge of the sofa, rigid, her hands clasped tight in her lap.

"I won't give up this house. As for winning—his winning—fat chance."

"When will it be over?"

"Soon."

ON THE way back to Brookton the next day, I noticed a new For Sale sign just off the main road. Beyond it, a boarded-up farmhouse faced a weathered barn and empty pastures. In a nearby cornfield, flocks of crows and starlings foraged, fat and lazy in the November sun. There was a faded peace symbol painted on the side of the barn. Above it, a dove in flight clutched an olive branch.

I found three messages taped to my door, all from my father.

I took enough change for three minutes and managed to get an operator who put me through right away. "You have a good evening, Sugar."

The phone rang a half-dozen times. He picked up; I didn't give him a chance to get started. "I know you broke in last week. I know you took Granddad's furniture. The divorce is between you and Mom. I have nothing to say to you. So don't call me again. Not here. Not at Long Meadow. Not at Milou's. If I ever want to talk to you, I'll call you. Understood?"

"Malorie, you don't—"

Yes, I do. I hung up.

November 14, 1969

Sitting alone, Patrick blew a smoke ring at me as I came into the graduate college bar. This was our routine: every Friday night, a group of us straggled in to smoke, drink cheap beer, and sing along with whatever happened to be on the jukebox. The beer, stale pretzels, dartboard, and ping-pong table—and the endless, pointless word games—were all we had to distract us from the grind of research and worries about the draft.

I had heard a few stories. There was the second-year student, a chemist, whose politician father worked his connections with the draft board. There were some whose draft numbers were so high that the war in Vietnam would likely be over before they were called—or so they hoped. Then there was Jack, an only child, a sole-surviving son. They wouldn't draft him. As for Patrick, he had told everyone he was 4F on account of a heart murmur. I knew the real reason. So did Jack.

Patrick slid over on the banquette, making room for me. As usual, he had on a blazer and chinos. Never jeans. He leaned close. "You smell delicious. Something French, I know, but what?"

"*Mitsouko*." I liked that he noticed, and that his compliment, simple and light, wasn't loaded with double meanings.

"All set for the department party?"

"What party?"

He poured me a glass of beer, slowly so that it didn't spill over. I didn't drink much, and then, only beer or wine. My father's example made me afraid of what alcohol could do.

"It's kind of a joke, actually. Someone suggested we have a dance party and dress for it. The catch is, it's a costume party. You get to pick your favorite era."

"And that *someone* would be?"

Patrick held up his right hand. "Hold the applause, please."

I listened to him enthuse about the costumes he'd culled from odds and ends left over from productions he'd directed at Yale.

"You're going to love your dress, I promise."

"There's one thing, Patrick."

"Anything . . ."

"No masks."

He looked at me in mock horror. "What do you think this is? Kindergarten?"

Danielle and the others came in then. Patrick talked up the party, throwing out his ideas for costumes. He ignored Danielle's smirk.

November 20, 1969

The day before the party, Danielle caught up with me on the way back to the dorm. She glanced at her reflection in a window and fluffed her hair. Dark blond shag, small hands, pointed nails. She looked like a Persian cat. "Did you know Hal Rose is married to Angela, that historian who looks like a flamenco dancer?"

"Oh?" If she was trying to mend fences, she could have spared herself the effort. I looked the other way, hoping she would take the hint.

Her eyes shifted in annoyance and she took a different tack. "I don't know how you can keep it up. The Old French translations bore me to tears. This is graduate school. Why bother? Anyway, Hughes doesn't even read them."

Before I could ask how she knew, she stopped in the middle of the crosswalk.

"I forgot—again. I have to pick up a prescription."

"Are you sick?"

"Just the Pill." She looked over her shoulder, as if expecting someone, and turned on her heel and headed back into town.

The next morning, having coffee with Jack between classes, I asked him if Hughes read our Old French translations.

"I guess so. Why?"

"Danielle told me he doesn't."

Jack rolled his eyes. "Wishful thinking, maybe? She's not very smart. Her mother has a connection here in admissions and pulled some strings. There's also a rumor about an affair at Smith. With a married professor." He shrugged. "That's the gossip, anyway."

Was I the only person who wasn't having, or hadn't had, an affair? In college when I told people I didn't do drugs or sleep around, the word went out that I was "uptight," a "straight arrow." My attempts to explain why only made matters worse. So I stopped trying.

"She'll probably leave by the end of term."

So what if Danielle left at the end of term? She was here now. I wondered if Jack knew she rarely did her own homework, skipped class often, and still managed to make passing grades.

"That's not the point. . . ."

His look told me all I needed to know. Maybe he was right. Maybe I should ignore Danielle. Still, Before I could ask how he knew she might be leaving, Jack stood and stretched.

"Off to the salt mines." He smiled. "I wouldn't worry about her, if I were you."

November 21, 1969

I dressed for the party in my room, then went out to the hall to look at myself in the full-length mirror. It was hard to believe the Yale drama department had discarded the dress. True, it was faded in places and had been taken in and let out more than once. Nevertheless, it looked barely used. Made of red taffeta, with a full skirt and crinoline, it had a wide patent-leather belt, a scoop neck, and three-quarter-length sleeves. Very forties. Perfect for Ginger Rogers.

I adjusted the lining of the crinoline and tightened the belt a notch. I didn't look at all like Ginger Rogers, but I didn't look like Malorie Ellsworth either. Who was this person and why did she feel dizzy? *It's just a party!*

"You're tall enough to wear this style," Patrick commented when I tried on the dress the first time. "And you've got the shoulders to carry off the scoop neck and the sleeves. It looks like it was made for you." He pleaded with me to wear the patent-leather high heels he had found in his collection. They, too, fit perfectly.

"If I wear them, we'll be the same height." I was five feet seven; Patrick, five feet nine. "That really won't work."

He frowned and stuck out his lower lip in a pout.

"Patrick, I checked. Ginger was five feet four; Fred was five feet nine. If we're going to be them, I can't be looming over you like a great blue heron. So it's ballet flats or bare feet. Take your pick."

He gave in with a gleam in his eye. "You win. But only because I'm bringing all my swing records. Be prepared!"

Tonight's the night.

I had waved and styled my hair in a shoulder-length bob. After I sprayed it and slipped on my flats, I took one last look. *Could I carry this off?*

NOT EVEN flickering candles and crêpe-paper streamers could disguise the department common room. It still looked and felt like the kind of place where people spent too much time taking themselves too seriously. I searched the room for Patrick. Although it was early, the floor was already crowded with students and faculty dancing to The Doors.

I heard Patrick laugh and spotted him across the room in top hat and tails. He, at least, looked like the person he was pretending to be. Pulling my full skirt around me, I squeezed through the crowd, passing Hal Rose and Danielle, who seemed oblivious to everything but each other. Rose was wearing a linen jacket, T-shirt, and jeans. Looking into his eyes, her lips parted, Danielle swayed from side to side, gold bangles gleaming against her black velvet dress.

Patrick swept off his hat and bowed. "May I?" At his signal, someone put one of his Benny Goodman records on the stereo, a fox-trot. People around us started to clap and whistle as he drew me out onto the floor. Soon, we had a large enough space to dance freely. And an audience. I felt Patrick's signal, preparing me for a turn. "You were right, Malorie!"

"About?"

"Not to wear the heels."

He released me into a tight pirouette and I felt the crinoline and the taffeta swirl. This was a dress made to be danced in and I was meant to be dancing in it.

The night we started dancing together, Patrick had slid a quarter into the jukebox to play the swing version of "I Got Rhythm." That time we had danced until the bar closed. One Friday night, he took me to a small dancehall he had found in Lambertville, not far from Brookton, where they had a good floor and a live band. He told me about touring with his parents, both professional dancers and teachers. "It's like dance is my first language."

As a partner, Patrick shared the music and what to do with it instantaneously. When I told him so, he had laughed. "What do you mean?"

"It has something to do with the way you hold me. Without clutching or grabbing, you show me what we're about to do."

He laughed. "Well, that's because dancing is a collaboration, not a power trip."

Someone changed the record. The Doors were back. Standing in the doorway across the room, Jack caught my eye and beckoned to me. Patrick had noticed Jack, too.

"Of course he wants to dance with you. Go on. I'm not greedy." His smile didn't make it to his eyes.

"I'm your date, remember?" When I turned to signal him, Jack was gone.

Jack and Patrick had one thing in common: their mutual dislike. I didn't have to ask. Jack had made his reasons clear. "He's gay, you know." His mouth had been tight, his jaw set.

"He told me. I don't care. I don't get why it matters to you."

"He's always on the make. He looks at me—even me—that way. And he's using you. Don't you realize you're his cover?"

"Patrick's fun and he's a friend. *My* friend." I waited to see if Jack had noticed the barb. When he didn't say anything, I figured he had made up his mind—then and there—not to let Patrick come between us. Not yet. For me, it was simple. There was no rule that Jack had to like Patrick, just as long as he didn't interfere.

At the edges of the dark lounge, just after Patrick left around midnight, a few people slow-danced to Janis Joplin. I went to find my jacket. As I was putting it on, I noticed Hal and Danielle in the middle of the room. Eyes closed, Hal swayed, one arm hanging loose by his side, the other draped over Danielle's shoulder. In her black velvet dress, Danielle merged with the shadows. Her skin glistened in the glow cast by the streetlight outside the window.

She moved closer to Rose, tucking her head into his shoulder. When the song ended, they danced on in the silence. I couldn't move. They turned away from me and sank down into a sofa that had been pushed out into the room during the party. Hal pressed his face into Danielle's neck. Her eyes flicked over his shoulder, looking straight at me. Hal's chuckle sounded like a purr.

Outside, the sky was clear, the moon almost full. I saw someone standing just off the sidewalk in the shadows. My heart pounding, I reached behind me for the railing, feeling my way back toward the steps.

"Who—?"

"It's me."

Why hadn't he spoken up sooner? Or waited for me inside?

"You didn't come back to the party."

"Ellis waylaid me. He wanted to talk about his conference paper." He took my hand. "Can I walk you home?"

We crossed the common, passing groups of students wandering in and out of the dorms, or sprawled on the steps, despite the cold. Competing stereos blared from open windows.

Jack's arm around my shoulders, tucking me into him, kept the chill at bay. Brushing against my legs, the crinoline raised prickles of static.

We stopped at the edge of the parking lot, just out of range of the hubbub. Distance distorted the music, shaping it into faint, tinny echoes. Their windows dark except for the occasional dull red of a security light, the classroom buildings loomed over us.

"What I missed is a dance with you." Jack turned toward me with a little bow.

Sliding his right arm under my jacket, he settled his palm across the middle of my back, fingers spread wide, resting his thumb between my shoulders where the dress's scoop neck ended. I felt his thighs against mine, faintly warm through the taffeta skirt.

Whistling a slow version of "Save the Last Dance for Me," Jack cha-cha'd in place, rocking his hips from side to side; the taffeta dress and crinoline rustled like fallen leaves swirling across the pavement in the wind, like brushes over the taut head of a snare drum.

December 19, 1969

At one o'clock the last Friday before Christmas break, I arrived at Hal Rose's office to go over my outline for my presentation on *Le Grand Meaulnes*. I heard Rose's voice, then Danielle's laugh. Wasn't he expecting me?

As I was trying to make up my mind—to knock or write a note and leave—Danielle opened the door. She turned back into the room and said something that made Rose laugh. About me?

Danielle reached into the pocket of her jeans and pulled out a plastic pot of Clinique lip gloss. Pink. First she dipped the pad of her ring finger into the container. As she began to apply the gloss to her upper lip with delicate patting motions, she watched Rose, whose eyes followed her every move. It was as though I had disappeared, as invisible to them at that moment as I had been the night of the party.

I hung my coat over the back of the chair facing the desk and sat down. As I went over my outline, talking to him from my notes, I could feel Rose's eyes. Was he even listening? Once, I glanced up at him. His lips were parted, his eyes unfocused. He had a pink smudge at the corner of his mouth. I stood, my heart pounding, my knees trembling. "I'll be right back."

In the lavatory across the hall, I turned on the cold water, splashed my face, and dried it. *I will do this. It's just a paper.* Back in the office, Rose held a handkerchief in front of him on his desk. The pink smudge had spread to his chin. He grinned at me. "Stage fright. Don't worry. You'll get used to it. The thing about imagining your audience naked? Forget it. Instead, imagine yourself as the world's greatest expert on the subject, and that anyone, anywhere, is fortunate you can spare the time to share your wisdom with them." He widened his eyes at me and laughed.

I forced myself to look him in the eye and felt the corners of my mouth stiffen in protest as I tried to smile.

He laughed again. "That's better. You're talented, Malorie, perhaps even gifted. You must know that." Casually, he picked up the handkerchief and wiped his mouth and chin. "You've got a pretty good start there. Why don't you tell me more about why you want to work on *Le Grand Meaulnes*?" He wiped his face again, checked the handkerchief, and shoved it into the front pocket of his jeans.

"It's a complicated story. I enjoy that." I could barely move my lips. My tongue stuck to the roof of my mouth. I couldn't think and my notes were no help; my mind had stopped, trapped by irrelevant details—the way the room smelled, the pile of papers perched precariously on Rose's desk.

"Of course." His smile, indulgent, dismissive, gave way to a sigh. "But maybe you're making it *too* complicated, so let's see if we can come up with an approach that might work better for you, hmm?"

Evidently I had convinced him I couldn't handle anything more complicated than . . . what? He would decide, and I would have to live with his decision.

He toyed with a paperclip. The bangs and clicks of the radiator behind him resonated in the quiet room, a crescendo that ended in a hiss of steam.

At last, he set the paperclip down, put his hands behind his head, and tilted back in his chair. "Here's the question: Is this really just a classic story of an adolescent who refuses to grow up? Someone who's so stuck in the past he's unable even to imagine the present? That would explain Augustin's love for Yvonne, yes? But then there's his relationship with François." Now his voice dropped. He raised his eyebrows and leaned toward me, about to clue me in.

Listening to him, I heard each word, formed the syllables one at a time in my notebook. It was like transcribing a foreign language. I glanced at his face, watched the tip of his tongue flick the corner of his mouth from time to time. And then it hit me. This wasn't about me or my ideas. It was about Rose's theory.

"François and Augustin's relationship is homoerotic, of course." He chuckled and shook his head: How could so many smart people have missed something so obvious? "Homoeroticism as a theme and a motif interests me a great deal. It comes up often in early twentieth-century fiction. Why do you suppose that is?"

I glanced at the ceiling, at the plaster rose in its center, the petals sharp-edged against the fullness of the opening bloom. Rose rocked back and forth, his arms again folded behind his head. He didn't seem to notice I had stopped taking notes or mind that I hadn't risen to the bait.

"These writers' attitudes reflect the *Zeitgeist*, you know, the feeling at the time, an *ambivalence*—the word itself means *two-sided*—about modernity. For some of them, the past and the future are equally seductive. They simply can't choose. 'The love that dare not speak its name'—homosexual love—is one way they treat this theme. Unrequited love is another. Both themes play out across *Le Grand Meaulnes*." Rose leaned forward, placed his hands on the desk, and nodded. Surely I saw his point.

When I didn't say anything, he went on. "So you can understand that this casts an entirely different light on Yvonne de Galais. And François. After Yvonne dies, when Meaulnes runs away again, you could say the novel has reached the only conclusion possible: Augustin Meaulnes cannot find fulfillment with a woman." He pulled out the handkerchief and wiped his mouth again. "Or with François, in the end. Fascinating, don't you think?"

I nodded. There was nothing I could say about any of what he had told me. We left it that I would take another look and rework my proposal.

IN THE student union, Jack had a sandwich and a cup of coffee on the table in front of him. I dropped my jacket and book bag on a chair and told him about Rose's idea.

"Sounds like the typical first go-round with him. Don't worry about it."

It was already two o'clock. To make his train connection to Boston, Jack had to catch the 2:30 bus to New York. We didn't have time to sort out why his attempt to reassure me felt like a brush-off.

"Is there something else?"

"I walked in on them."

"Who?"

"Danielle and Rose. I'm sure they'd just had sex."

"On his desk?"

"Or maybe the couch." Books, files, and empty wine bottles usually cluttered every horizontal surface in Rose's office, even the leather couch sagging against the wall. Today, it held only his jacket. The room had smelled of cigarette smoke and *Rive Gauche*, Danielle's perfume. And sex.

"Malorie, he's up for promotion this year. Why would he take a risk like that?" Jack wiped his mouth and sat back with a peculiar expression on his face, as if he were stifling a smile.

"The risk of having sex with Danielle? Or having sex with Danielle in his office?"

"The second, obviously." His tone of voice, clipped and emphatic, felt like a slap.

"Because he can." I reached for my jacket and book bag. "She cuts his class. She doesn't do any of the assignments. Does she look worried?" Heads turned in my direction. I lowered my voice. "Why should she? She knows exactly what she's doing. And how to get what she wants."

"You haven't eaten anything."

"Lost my appetite. Besides, I've got a paper to finish before I leave tomorrow." I got up and pulled my jacket on.

"Malorie!" He reached for my hand. His face was flushed. "So what if Rose is fooling around with Danielle? You told me you're excited about your paper. Can't you at least think about that, see if you can figure out a way to combine his ideas with yours? I can suggest a few things that might help, if you want."

He stopped, looked away, as if embarrassed. Was it because I'd made a scene or because he knew—or suspected—I was right and didn't want to admit it? I left him staring at his sandwich.

BACK IN my room, I had references to check and footnotes to finish. My stomach turned over at the thought. I hadn't had breakfast or lunch, but the idea of eating anything made me feel worse. I decided to walk to Desmond.

The door of the dorm slammed behind me. Someone called my name. I kept walking. The foggy, cold weather fit my mood. There was a slick skin of ice on the sidewalks and roads. I skidded once and slowed down. The low, flat sky, layered in gray slabs of cloud, promised snow.

When I first talked to Rose about working on *Le Grand Meaulnes*, he had listened and nodded with a knowing smile. "It suits you." Whatever he meant, what he had said felt like a pat on the head. Still, I kept going, explaining my idea.

When critics talked about the theme of disillusionment in early twentieth-century fiction, they usually mentioned *Le Grand Meaulnes*, published in 1913. Riven by his younger brother's death, Augustin Meaulnes can't let go of the past. Large-hearted, generous-spirited, impetuous, he refuses to grow up. Based on absolute values, his actions have dire consequences, including, at least indirectly, the tragic death of his young wife, Yvonne de Galais.

The first time I'd read the novel with Milou, I had been furious. I had never felt so strongly about a character. I told Milou then that Augustin didn't deserve to be the hero. "He abandons Yvonne.

She dies after giving birth to their daughter. How could he do that, Milou?"

"Did he know she was pregnant when he left her to help Frantz find Valentine?"

"No, but . . ."

"Why does he answer Frantz's plea for help in the first place?"

"Because he promised Frantz he would—no matter when, no matter where."

"So it was conditional, that promise?"

I began to see where Milou was headed. "No, but . . ."

"He keeps his word, doesn't he?"

"Yes, but he doesn't consider even for a moment that acting on his promise to Frantz might keep him from doing what's right for Yvonne. If he loves her so much, why doesn't he say no to Frantz?" And then I saw the connection and Augustin's tragic flaw. "So that's it. He has made promises to the two people he loves most, and there is no way he can fulfill them both." A classic double bind.

Milou nodded. "Remember, he leaves Yvonne in the care of François." She looked at me. "But even so, it's a terrible choice, one he *must* make. Because that's who he is."

"I see." I had looked down at the book in my lap, as if finding, there on the page in front of me, the explanation that began to form in my mind. Choices and their consequences. This was at least part of what made Augustin interesting.

I liked my idea, understood how it worked in the story, and didn't plan to give up on it—or Augustin. Where—if—Rose's idea about homoeroticism fit in remained to be seen.

IT WAS nearly time for dinner when I got back to the dorm. There was a message on my door. As soon as she heard my key in the lock, Danielle opened her door. "Your mother sounded upset."

I went out to the phone, put in a dime, and connected with the operator to make the collect call.

"Mom?"

"Malorie . . ." Her voice splintered and broke in ragged, gasping sobs.

"What's wrong? What happened?"

"Your father . . . last night . . ."

"Take your time, whatever it is . . ." *Whatever it is this time.*

I leaned against the side of the phone booth, trying to piece together the fragments as she choked them out. Something about a car accident. Black ice? "He skidded on black ice? Where?"

My father had been living several miles away in a rented house at the end of a narrow, winding road, a spur off the main road to Long Meadow. With no streetlights or guardrails, the road was hazardous in the dark, even when it was dry and clear.

"The car went over the embankment late last night. They found it early this afternoon." She got this out in one breath. *Like tearing off a Band-Aid.* She didn't say they found *him.*

"He had a broken neck. She went through the windshield." She sobbed again, calmer now. "No seatbelts, of course. You know how he felt about that . . . seatbelts were for everyone else." She cleared her throat, blew her nose. "There was some kind of meeting in the city. He must have stayed on for dinner. Of course he'd had a few drinks."

A few drinks. How often had I heard these words? Said them myself? *He was drunk.*

"What else?"

"Nothing. There's nothing else."

I wanted to hang up. "I'll be home tomorrow sometime, all right?"

"What about your paper?"

"I'll finish it tonight. Is there anyone who can come and stay with you?"

"One more thing." She stopped there. The silence lasted so long that I thought the line had gone dead.

"Mom?"

"I'm still here. It's just . . . the divorce came through two days ago." Her voice caught. "My Christmas present. I was going to tell you when you got here." She coughed and cleared her throat again. "What did you ask me?"

I repeated my question.

"I'll be fine. Just get here as soon as you can."

Will you *be all right, Malorie?* Had she asked, would I have told the truth? That I'd been holding my breath all my life? That I could breathe at last?

Most students had already left campus. The branches of the rowan tree clattered against the window of my room. I turned out the light and lay on my bed, watching the shadow play of the tree branches on the ceiling. I couldn't move.

I thought I knew the place where my father had crashed. When I began to drive on my own, he had warned me about the curve where the trees appeared to be right on the road, a hazardous illusion. What you saw from the car was only their tops: the trunks grew up from the bottom of the gully, forty feet below. The embankment there dropped sharply away from the roadbed. My father had told me that if I ever lost control of the car going into the curve, it would flip over and into the gully. Even the trees wouldn't stop the fall. "There are no second chances. So don't take any, okay?"

I shuddered.

Around nine o'clock, someone knocked. I got up and opened the door, squinting against the light. Patrick held out a container of yogurt, a spoon, and a cookie wrapped in a napkin.

"Bad news?"

"The worst. My father . . ." I couldn't go on.

Patrick set the food down and held me. "Do you need anything? Shall I stay?"

"Thank you for this." I picked up the food and tried to smile. "I need to finish my paper. Apart from that, some sleep."

I sat in the dark and ate the yogurt and part of the cookie. It was nearly ten when I turned on my desk light. I watched my hand reach for a fresh sheet of paper and wind it into the typewriter, as if it belonged to someone else. The room began to spin; a wave of nausea hit me. I put my head down on the desk.

Twenty-four hours ago, my father had been alive, laughing over a drink with his girlfriend, thinking only of the evening ahead with her, in the city. I could see his hands. He wasn't wearing his wedding ring. Now that the divorce was final, he was cutting his losses. So they'd been celebrating? Would he have married her eventually? Out of nowhere, I heard him laughing at me for thinking such a thing.

At one thirty, I typed my last footnote and went to bed. The storm had begun. Listening to the clattering branches, the bursts of snow against my window, I closed my eyes, imagining the rollers at high tide on Sandy Neck Beach, on the Cape. In the distance, a dark green wall of water loomed, moving toward me, its curl breaking into plumes of spindrift.

The wave streamed ashore, rippling over the sand, until its edge of foam subsided, inches from my feet, exposing shells, bits of seaweed, pebbles, sea glass, tiny animals torn from their underwater perches, gleaming reminders of somewhere else.

Milou's Story

December 30, 1969

To the northeast, storm clouds brooded over the mountains, blue-gray under the lowering sky. Milou dozed next to me, her head leaning into a pillow wedged against the window, a wool throw over her lap.

She had taken the train from Alden for the funeral. Expecting a church service, a graveside eulogy, and lilies, the perfunctory, by-the-book affair and mounds of evergreen branches heaped around the casket had surprised her. In the chilly room, the crowd of lawyers, their wives, and the staff had seemed ill at ease. Maybe they were trying to avoid all thoughts of the sordid affair that had brought us together that afternoon.

We had been spared lengthy speeches and amusing anecdotes reinventing my father for the occasion, as a favor to him and the firm. The senior partner's low-key remarks had conveyed a broad-brush view of my father's accomplishments: Alan Ellsworth had had a solid—if unremarkable—career. That was all. It was enough.

Afterward, we had driven back to Long Meadow, too tired to make small talk.

"At least no one mentioned the divorce," my mother had murmured.

Two days before Christmas, I had found a small, misshapen Scotch pine. I wrestled it into its stand, strung the lights, and hung a few ornaments. Milou came into the living room as I was filling the stand with water.

"It looks out of sorts. Like how we feel." She smiled. "Day by day, you'll see."

On Christmas Eve, I had started to make the *bûche de Noël* after lunch, determined to do it by myself, if necessary. But Milou and my mother needed something to do, too. Usually, making the traditional Christmas dessert occasioned storytelling and reminiscences. This time we had talked only about the task itself—or worked in silence. Later, we sat by the fire, listening to Christmas carols, our conversation hesitant, our words winking out like dying embers.

When I loaded the car that morning to drive Milou back to Vermont, the *bûche* sat untouched on the middle shelf of the refrigerator.

MILOU TURNED her head and craned her neck to look out the window. "What time is it? Where are we now, *chérie*?"

It was nearly noon. "Just a few more miles to the Thruway. I'll stop there so we can have coffee and something to eat. You can sleep some more. I'll wake you, don't worry."

"I'm fine now. Wouldn't you like company? We can talk."

"I can't stop thinking about Dad." "Dad" stuck in my throat. My eyes burned.

"Start with the first thing that comes to mind. Let it just float up." Milou leaned toward me and touched my face. "Everything is going to be all right, *ma biche*. Tell me."

"I haven't—hadn't—seen Dad since he moved out in August. He called me the night before I left for Brookton . . . so angry about Mom and the divorce. Then he called again in October. He wanted me to intervene somehow. I hung up."

"I am so sorry. . . ." Milou hesitated. "Your grandfather and I worried about him." She shrugged. "Lucie called me the day she got the papers. It was the first I knew about the divorce. Why didn't she tell me sooner?"

"Maybe she thought you would blame her." Only a month ago, I might have said, "She didn't want to worry you."

"*Mais pas du tout!* How could she? Over the years, we saw and heard things—especially the drinking—but we didn't want to interfere. We both knew how hard your father worked at first, before he joined the firm, to get his practice started. We hoped once he got settled, especially after you were born, he would change."

I didn't know much about my father's early life, or his first years at the law firm. I had memories of his "moods" and his "headaches"—that's what my mother had called them, telling me to steer clear of him when he was "like that." Until I was nine, he had left me alone; I had had no part in what happened between them when he was "like that." I couldn't remember why or how I, too, became a target, pulled out of bed sometimes, dragged down to sit on a chair next to my mother, listening, waiting, watching while he paced back and forth, accusatory, abusive, incoherent.

The first time he slapped her, knocking her down, I ran into the woods and hid until morning.

AFTER OUR Thruway stop, I looked forward to two more driving hours, two more hours uninterrupted by phones or daily tasks. I hadn't had this kind of time with Milou for several years. It was like being in France with her again.

"Shall I put the seat back?"

"I'm fine now, *chérie*." She patted my arm. "I'm enjoying this drive with you. Would you like to talk about *Le Grand Meaulnes*?"

After hours analyzing the novel's characters and themes, my delight in the story had faded. It was like knowing someone too well, when those traits and quirks you once found charming or intriguing become irritating. Since I'd left Brookton, I hadn't given the novel, let alone my paper about it, much thought. First the funeral preoccupied me, then just getting through Christmas.

"I want to, yes. The problem is I'm not enjoying it anymore. At all."

Milou shifted in her seat and loosened her scarf, releasing the fragrance of sandalwood into the car.

"*Que c'est joli, ce paysage,*" she said, as if talking to herself. "Such a pretty landscape. It reminds me a little of *la Sologne.*" With its marshes and fogs, *la Sologne,* the countryside in *Le Grand Meaulnes,* had the soft contours of a childhood memory, both familiar and strange. "Alain-Fournier chose the perfect setting. It's—how do you call it in English—a *paysage de rêves*?"

"A landscape of dreams, a dream landscape."

We were driving through a snow squall, the fringe of the storm that lay ahead of us. Not far from the highway, a small pond gleamed like polished jet. Pale curtains of snow swirled around it. Tied to a willow branch, like a promise of warmer days to come or a memory of those just past, a blue rowboat traced a languid arc across the surface of the water.

"You know the way ripples move when you toss a pebble into a pond? At first, close together, then farther apart, until they fade away?" Milou turned her head to keep the pond in view as we passed it.

Of course I knew. When I was little, she and I had often gone to the lake in Alden to toss pebbles into the shallows. The size of the pebble, its impact on the water, affected the size and the extent of the ripples.

"My father's death in 1908 was like a pebble cast into my life." Milou flexed her wrist, as if tossing a pebble. "In 1913, I was still caught in the ripples."

I could feel the small round stone roll off my own fingertips. The motion of the car and Milou's voice carried me into the story. Of course I already knew many of the details, how Milou, born in 1900, lived with her parents and three young brothers in Flagy; how, in 1908, after her husband's death, Milou's mother had taken the children with her to Lyon, where she found work in a silk mill.

"As you know, my mother gave me the copy of *Le Grand Meaulnes* for my thirteenth birthday just after it came out. The copy you have now." She smiled across at me. She had raced through it once, then started over, savoring every word. "I felt so close to Augustin Meaulnes—his fears, frustrations, determination were so much like mine. How could Alain-Fournier, a perfect stranger, create someone so similar to me? Yes, Augustin was a boy. There was that difference. But we were alike in so many ways. It was as if Alain-Fournier had written the story for me alone."

Augustin's loss—his younger brother's death, his memories of the mysterious estate he discovered by chance—helped Milou to understand how closely her grief for her father and her nostalgia for Flagy—her village, her own lost estate—were intertwined. Little by little she began to accept that she might never return to live in Flagy, and that, in any case, it would never—could never— be the place she remembered from her childhood. Lying awake, imagining the morning sun on Saint-Thibaut's tower, hearing the sound of the church bells and her father's voice as they walked to Mass together, she had cried herself to sleep.

"Augustin's search for the estate and Yvonne de Galais com- forted me in one way. His dream lived on, inspiring him despite his setbacks. That gave me hope, not a hope that was pinned to anything—or anyone—in particular, just a vague sense that my life would change . . . I would change." She wiped her eyes and smiled again. For a while, she seemed lost in thought. When she took up the story again, her voice was clear and strong, younger, somehow.

Augustin's experience had taught her a lesson—it was useless to dwell on what she had lost. She became determined that her life would be different from her mother's, who had no choice but to find work in the mill.

"At that time, I had to care for my three brothers, managing their homework, the housekeeping, and meals. And my own schoolwork, of course. Just like *maman*, I had no choice." Milou closed her eyes. When she continued, her voice sounded far away. "But I knew I wanted something more. So I took courses at the university off and on, during the war, and when I finished my *licence*, I found the job at the girls' *lycée* in Villeurbanne."

"Did you ever stop missing Flagy?"

She lifted her hands and let them fall into her lap with a shrug. "*Pas tout à fait.* Let me explain."

She had been seventeen. The war seemed finally to be drawing to a close. She had woken one morning feeling strange, as if she had forgotten something—a dream, perhaps? She finished clearing up the breakfast things after her brothers had gone to school.

Sitting in the quiet apartment, she had closed her eyes, let her thoughts drift. When she opened them, her eyes fell on her father's photograph, hanging on the wall across from her. How many hundreds of times she had looked at it, each time drawing strength and courage from it. This time was so different. She felt calm and content looking at him, his eyes gazing into hers. And then he spoke to her. She heard his voice as clearly as if he were in the room with her.

"What did he say?"

"'*C'est fini.*'" Her voice barely audible, Milou repeated, "'*C'est fini, ma chérie.*'" It's finished.

"I felt like a room swept clean, waiting for a new occupant. No longer homesick, no longer looking back. Augustin doesn't have that. And we can't know what might have happened to him had he been able to break with his own past. That's why François is so important in the story."

"François? How?"

Up to now, I had focused on François only in his capacity as Augustin's surrogate brother, who admires Augustin and yearns to be like him. He's too cautious, reined in by his prudent nature. Eventually, François outgrows this role, becoming Augustin's advisor and friend, who learns to accept his own—and life's—limitations and accommodates to them.

The thrill of the hunt didn't motivate François. Certainly, he went along with Augustin to help him, because he loved him, not because he was himself an adventurer. He accepted his loss, endured his grief, content to live in the present. He became a schoolteacher, just like his father. For him, *le juste milieu*—the happy medium—prevailed.

"You said Augustin inspired you. But it's François, not Augustin, who becomes a teacher in the novel."

"It seems contradictory, doesn't it? I did feel an affinity with Augustin, yes. But I recognized he couldn't free himself from his nostalgia. Who knows? Perhaps if we hadn't gone to Lyon when we did, I never would have left Flagy. But in Lyon, the shock of Papa's death faded, as did my grief and homesickness. *Bien sûr*, I still loved the place. I always will. But I grew up in Lyon. And I met your grandfather."

Thinking hard, I gathered the pieces, put them into place. For the first time I understood the larger role François plays in Augustin's story. Paradoxically, by settling for an ordinary life, he transcends the unhappiness and chaos Augustin's departure causes—in Yvonne's life as well as his own. A sympathetic witness, he grows up to be a teacher and a writer, Augustin's biographer.

At last, I knew what to talk about. The next step was to figure out how.

THE STORM that arrived in Alden after midnight wore itself out in a surge of gusting winds that rattled the shutters and drove the snow against the house. It was five thirty. The headache that had sent me to bed early throbbed behind my eyes.

Dad is dead. And buried.

It was like talking about a stranger, as if my father's death—and his life—had nothing at all to do with me. I didn't yet know how I could get beyond the fact of his death to sort through the facts of his life, to get to a new place where I'd feel safe from my memories.

My father, drunk, had crashed his car and died, killing the woman who was with him. I couldn't remember her name. Ann? Barbara? Married or single? Did her family live nearby? How would I feel if my daughter or sister died this way? What would that shock and grief feel like?

She couldn't remember what it was like to love him, my mother had said.

Had I ever loved him? There was something in the answer to this question, a key to something about me, yes, and about the future. And also about the past. Perhaps being able to ask it at all meant I might, at long last, stop pretending.

February 11, 1970

As they headed out of the classroom buildings into the quad, it was boys against girls, tossing handfuls of soft snow, jostling each other on the icy walkways. Their laughter floated away in puffs, like detached speech balloons.

Crossing the quad to the fourth meeting of my section, I pulled my scarf up around my face, ducking into it to avoid the wind. It wasn't just the cold that made my teeth chatter. I had the jitters and it seemed nothing—not my careful preparation, nor my enthusiasm for teaching—could calm them.

I knew what I knew and I had a plan for each session. But I hadn't expected the students to ask questions that got me—and them—off the track. Also, I felt I had to give them what they asked for. The second time a student interrupted me, I'd gotten flustered and tongue-tied, and lost the point I had been trying to explain.

"You'd think they were doing this on purpose."

Patrick laughed. "They'd have to know a lot more than they know, a lot more than you know."

"So what can I do besides freeze? I seem to have perfected that."

"First law of stage management: expect the unexpected." Patrick's way of handling the situation, to hang loose, worked for him. His theater experience made all the difference. "Lots of times, you just have to wing it," he said. "People forget their lines; someone misses his entrance, whatever. Teaching is like a show."

"Improvise, you mean?"

"Ta-da!"

"I'm better at painting by numbers."

Patrick nodded. "Look, try this: Next time a student ambushes you, repeat the question—as if you're just making sure you've understood it. That way, you give yourself time to think of an answer. You'll think of something. Then you can go back to where you left off."

"How many years do I have to practice?"

"You have to start somewhere. Just give it a try. You'll see." His smile of encouragement and support made me a believer.

This course, an introduction to seventeenth- and eighteenth-century French literature, was my first teaching experience. I'd been surprised to learn that the graduate program had no formal instruction in teaching techniques. The sink-or-swim approach seemed inefficient. Costly, too. How many parents realized the substantial tuition they paid covered part of the salaries of novices who were learning by doing?

Jack hadn't had any practical advice. After reassuring me that everyone went through the same experience, he told me that the next time would be easier. "Remind them they need to pass the exam. That's all they really care about, you know." He put his hand on my shoulder, consoling me. I resisted shrugging him off.

He thought I took teaching too seriously, that I should concentrate on my coursework. But to me, teaching was just as important. Until and unless I could find a balance, I wouldn't be satisfied.

AS SOON as I walked in, the students took their seats and opened their notebooks. The adrenaline jolt I felt only added to my jitters. During the first ten minutes, I summarized that week's lecture and explained concepts and terms the students needed to know for the exam. For this part of the class, at least, I knew I could count on their undivided attention—and no interruptions. As usual, I had the first hint of a bumpy ride when I opened the floor to questions.

"Miss Ellsworth?" Alice, a sophomore, sat in the center of the front row. She had asked the first question in the three previous classes, always in English. "I don't understand how we can call eighteenth-century writers modern. We're modern, right?" The lecturer had spent at least a third of his hour describing the modernity of writers like Montesquieu and Voltaire.

As I translated and wrote a short version of her question on the board, I heard the door open and close. When I turned back to the class, Joan Miller, the teaching assistant supervisor, stood in the aisle. She gave me a noncommittal nod and took a seat in the last row. *The show must go on.* I wanted to say something to break the tension. But what?

How to explain what "modern" meant to Enlightenment thinkers like Montesquieu and Voltaire? I repeated the question and began to answer—in French, as department policy required. The students looked at me, blankly. I glanced at Joan. If I decided to speak English, her evaluation of me, and my grade, would suffer.

Through the window across the room, I glimpsed two students on the snow-covered lawn. Just then, a Frisbee soared above the trees. The boys ran after it, flapping their arms. I thought I could hear them hooting.

"What does the word 'modern' mean to you?"

Twenty-four pairs of eyes snapped into focus—on me. The students straightened up. They were as surprised to hear me speaking English as I was. A couple of them ducked their heads to look at Joan Miller. They knew why she was there.

Alice raised her hand. "To me, it means new, different—usually an improvement over what's come before."

Other students shared their ideas freely now—in English. Leaning forward in her chair, Joan Miller frowned at me. I went to the board, translating and jotting the students' thoughts, building a general definition.

I took some time going over their ideas, pointing out how many of their suggestions had to do with change. "Anything else?" When I looked around the room, all I could see of Joan Miller was the top of her head. She was taking notes, and I knew they weren't about the Enlightenment.

Outside, one of the Frisbee players tossed the disk behind his back, laughing when it got caught in the branches above him, then dropped down and bounced off his head.

For the next ten minutes, just like the Frisbee flying back and forth outside, ideas about the lecture went back and forth faster than I could translate and transcribe them into French. But the energy in the room was palpable. For the first time, I understood why I wanted to teach: to have this sense of joy in a shared intellectual activity. I was surprised to hear chairs sliding, books shuffling, as students prepared to leave. Then I looked at the clock. We'd gone overtime.

"*Merci, tout le monde! Bon week-end! À mercredi prochain!*"

"MALORIE?" JOAN Miller hadn't moved from her seat in the last row. "Come on back here, would you?"

She finished making a note and looked up at me. "I know how hard it is to stick to the language policy, especially in these introductory courses. But, until they go to France, the only place these students get to practice their French is in class." She made a check mark on the form in front of her. It looked like a score sheet. My name was printed at the top.

"Another thing. You need to work on time management. Spending the entire period talking about one idea . . ." She frowned and shook her head.

I wanted to tell her how it felt to break free of the constraints and speak in my own voice, to help the students say what they knew and take their own ideas a step further. Instead, I defended myself. "I understand about the policy. I do make an effort to follow it. But if the students have questions about key concepts, what difference does it make if I explain them in French or Urdu?"

Joan Miller's eyes narrowed. She pursed her lips. "You're fluent, Malorie. Just use your French more, would you? I've given you a C for this round. Let's see how the next two go."

At last she stood up. She looked out at the snow falling on the quad. "I can't believe this weather. Summer can't come soon enough."

"DID YOU really say that?" Jack asked.

He pulled the loose end of my scarf over my shoulder and slipped it under the strap of my book bag. It felt to me as though he were reining me in. Is that what he thought? That I was out of line?

"I did." Why didn't he get it? The French-only policy made everything harder for the students, turned teaching and learning into a power trip. "Of course there's value in their hearing the language, but in a discussion section, they have to speak it, too. *That* is beyond them."

"Look, Malorie, can't you see you're just making it harder for yourself?"

"Not at all. If Joan had suggested a way to stick to the rules and while making sure the students understood what I was talking about, that would be one thing. *Just follow the rules* is idiotic."

The wind tugged my scarf loose again. This time, I pushed it into my jacket and zipped the jacket collar around it.

April 8, 1970

I tried not to anticipate how Hal Rose would react to my paper. He hadn't seen the final version, so he didn't know I wouldn't be talking about—or even mentioning—homoeroticism. I couldn't fake it. Furthermore, I was convinced—and would show—that François Seurel, not Augustin Meaulnes, was the novel's hero. Alain-Fournier had turned the glamour and drama of the romantic hero upside down, pointing us in a new direction.

We might admire Augustin's bravado, but in the end, just like François, we want to survive. We were not all moths drawn to ambition's flame. This was a new idea—mine and Milou's. Even the novel's title pointed this out: Like "great" in the title *The Great Gatsby*, "grand " in the title *Le Grand Meaulnes* was laced with irony.

"How did you figure it out?" Patrick had read the novel once in a course he'd taken at Yale. He'd thought then that Augustin was Alain-Fournier's version of a tragically flawed hero. "Rose's idea about homoeroticism—like you, I don't know. I don't really see what he's getting at. And if anyone should, it would be someone like me, no?" He patted himself on the back, then laughed at himself.

"After Milou and I talked, I realized that Augustin fits the mold of the idealistic, absolutist, self-destructive hero. We don't want to be like him, fascinating as he is. We admire him, yes, but we also pity him. And we wish he could adapt—grow up."

Jack listened, expressionless, when I told him about my idea. "You make a lot of good points about the differences between Augustin and François," he said.

"But?"

"Since Hal told you to look at the homoerotic aspects of their friendship and the theme of ambivalence, he expects you to talk about that. You don't have to make it the focus of your paper, but you need to include it somehow."

"*It* is the problem." A week ago, I told Rose I'd reached a dead end and asked him if he could give me something more to go on, you know, scenes or passages that illuminate this theme. He told me to keep looking. I did. And I didn't get anywhere. How can I discuss something I don't understand? Something that isn't even there?" I had done my best not to let Rose see my frustration. "Anyway, what exactly is wrong with my interpretation?"

"It isn't *wrong*, Malorie—at least not in the same way a fact can be wrong. Your ideas about the novel are fine. It's just that you haven't—you could take it a step further. Of course, it's okay to like the story, and the characters. But you need to stand back, to place the novel in the context of other novels written at the same time, to understand the larger issues the writers address, if only between the lines. That's why it's so important to take what Rose tells you seriously. He's just doing his job."

Jack sighed, as if I were being willfully obtuse. His expression, patient, forbearing, underscored his message, familiar to me by now: I needed to face the fact that no matter how good, insightful, or original my work might be, my ability to work with Rose mattered more. I needed his help—letters of recommendation, his professional contacts—to succeed.

But becoming a mouthpiece for Rose's theories, rather than discovering and presenting my own ideas, was a high price to pay—too high.

April 15, 1970

The morning of my presentation, I woke with a sore throat and a headache. Flu. Or at least a cold. Staring at myself in the mirror, I knew that no amount of makeup would hide the circles under my eyes or my blotchy skin.

"You look wasted."

Danielle stood behind me, scrutinizing my face.

I tried to clear my throat. "Just a cold." If the rasp I produced was the best I could do, how would I make it through my talk? I let the faucet run and scooped up some water.

"I'm sure Hal'll reschedule your talk if you ask him to."

"I'll be fine."

Danielle cut class or rescheduled presentations whenever she felt like it. That I was determined to give my paper, as planned, no matter how bad I felt, would never occur to her.

She put her cosmetics case on the shelf above the sink and leaned close to the mirror. She slid a band over her hair to lift it off her face and patted the skin around her eyes. "I wonder how I'll look with lines. Of course, I already have a few. Not that you'd notice, unless you're too close to be interested in lines." She smirked.

She moved closer and peered at me. "You have great cheekbones, you know? Have you thought about wearing your hair up, or even having it cut to show them off? Why hide your best feature?"

I tried to see myself as she saw me. I got my coloring from Milou and my mother—blond hair, blue eyes. I tanned easily. I'd always thought my nose was too long, until I grew into it. Still, every time I looked at it, I saw my father—this was his feature— so I ignored it as much as possible. The cheekbones seemed to be my variation on my grandmother's. Although I never would have admitted it to Danielle, I liked them fine. My mouth, too. Thanks to the magic of genetic roulette, I'd been blessed with my grandmother's full, uptilted mouth.

I combed my hair and brushed on some mascara, which did little to improve the wan mask I was wearing. The effort itself made me feel better. A blue turtleneck, a silk scarf, and gray slacks, laid out the night before, completed my costume. Except for Patrick, I was likely the only member of the class who would not be wearing jeans. Would anyone even notice? Bad as I felt, I knew the blue sweater would keep me warm in the drafty seminar room and the Hermès scarf, a gift from Milou, would bring her spirit close. I had to credit her somehow for the discussion that had given me my theme. That, Earl Grey tea, and an aspirin would have to do.

Patrick walked with me to campus. When I started to talk, he shushed me. "Too cold, too dry. Save it for class."

Outside the student union, he told me to go on without him. In the seminar room, Rose stood at the board, outlining his lecture and talking to Danielle, who leaned against the board, looking up at him. Absorbed in their conversation, they didn't notice me until I pulled out a chair. Neither said a word to me. I was too ill to care.

Rose finished and wiped the chalk from his hands. "Sit up here, would you, Malorie?" He pointed to the head of the table and went to the far end. Danielle sat next to him. Patrick arrived with a cup of tea; he greeted me with a casual salute and set the cup down on the table. "Break a leg!" he whispered. He sat to my left. The others drifted in and sat around the table in their usual places.

Rose led off with his remarks about Henri Alain-Fournier and how *Le Grand Meaulnes*, like Proust's *À la recherche du temps perdu*, inspired radical changes in the novel, in France and elsewhere in the early twentieth century. After the first hour, before the break, he answered a few questions. When the class reassembled, I let them settle, took a sip of tea, and began. I placed my paper on the table in front of me, but after the first few minutes, I put it aside, explaining my ideas and making my points from memory.

I glanced around the room. Everyone was taking notes—everyone except Danielle, whose hands were folded on the notebook in front of her.

Nearing the end, I swallowed some more tea. Patrick caught my eye and winked. Thumbs-up. Elbow on the table, her chin resting in the palm of her hand, Danielle appeared to be doodling. As for Rose, he was gazing up at the ceiling, inscrutable.

Too tired to ad-lib, I found the last page of my paper and read my conclusion. "Alain-Fournier knew his public well. He understood and shared their tastes and interests. His was a simple scheme, really. The theme of loss and disillusionment was a powerful and current one, so he used it. It was an obvious choice. And it works. It pulls us into the story. Once he has made us comfortable with this theme and with his characters, he changes course—and our expectations.

"If Augustin is the hero, his problem and how he works it out should by rights be front and center in the story. But that isn't the case. Augustin cannot put the past behind him, cannot accept life, messy and problematic as it is. So he loses. He doesn't grow up and suffers tragic consequences.

"And that is the point. In the character of François Seurel, Alain-Fournier takes a step away from the egocentric, destructive romantic hero. He lures us in with Augustin's story and character, then François takes over. Down-to-earth, empathic, generous François carries the day. François, a teacher, is also a writer, and Augustin's biographer.

"In François, Alain-Fournier presents a new hero for the new century, one who will tell its stories, beginning with this one, a cautionary tale."

"SO?"

"They clapped, Jack!"

By the end of the class, my eyes burned, as if I'd been up all night. I was in a daze. The applause surprised me. Rose's response came as a shock. What was going on? I knew better than to bring this up now. I needed time, and a clear head, to think over what had happened.

"Even Danielle?"

I nodded. "Even Rose."

Jack hugged me. Had I underestimated him? I knew he was worried that Rose would critique my talk on the spot and find fault with it for not addressing the assigned topic. I had prepared myself for Jack's "I told you so." That wasn't going to happen. I could relax.

"We're going for drinks."

"I'll buy the first round," Jack said. "With that crowd, that'll just get the party started."

On the way to Tony's, we didn't talk. I didn't understand Rose's reaction, his enthusiastic appreciation of my ideas. If he wanted me to deal with the theme of homoeroticism in *Le Grand Meaulnes*, why hadn't he at least brought it up himself? Was he just being considerate? Or was he waiting until he could talk to me in private, before I finalized my paper, to lower the boom? I could be sure of one thing: when I met with him, Hal Rose would tell me exactly what he thought about everything I'd neglected to talk about.

At Tony's, members of the seminar clustered around Rose and Danielle at several tables and booths at the far end of the room. People cheered and clapped when we arrived. Danielle looked sideways at Rose and slid closer to him on the banquette. I looked at Jack; he rolled his eyes. He went to the bar and came back with three bottles of Freixenet and some Perrier. He poured the wine and handed out the glasses. I served myself a glass of water.

"You're not drinking?" Danielle said this loud enough so that everyone turned to look at me.

I smiled and raised my glass to her.

"That's bad luck, you know, toasting with water."

"It's the thought that counts, isn't it?"

I had told Patrick and Jack of my decision to stop drinking. Neither of them had said anything—there were no jokes, no teasing. My father's crash and death were explanation enough.

So far, I hadn't had to turn down a drink in public. I was glad it was Danielle who noticed I'd declined the wine. I found it easier and easier to ignore her. It seemed there was no boundary she wouldn't try to cross.

SEVERAL HOURS later, empty appetizer plates, crumpled napkins, and a dozen bottles cluttered the tables. Besides Jack and me, only Patrick, Danielle, and Rose were left, talking over each other, incoherent. I leaned against Jack. My euphoria and the adrenaline rush after class had carried me through the first hour. I was bushed. And feverish.

"Time?" Jack put his arm around me and we both got up.

Rose tried to stand. "One last toast! *Santé*, Malorie! *Bellissima!*"

Danielle frowned.

"Don't let it bother you," Jack told me outside.

"Danielle's glare or Rose's bouquet?" My voice came out as a croak.

"Rose's send-off," Jack said. "As for Danielle?" He flicked his hand.

"I'm just feeling uncertain . . . confused, really. I want to hear what he thought—especially since I didn't say a word—not one—about what he told me to talk about. It's as if he didn't hear what I said."

"For starters, he's pretty tight," Jack said.

"That's hardly an excuse." I dropped his arm. I'd told him about my father's drinking, how I felt about it. Why didn't he get it?

"Just try to let it go for now. Go talk to him, maybe next

week? See what he has to say. Think about it like this: This is your first presentation, a major one, for the guy who's going to direct your dissertation. You'll have other chances, other papers for him. You'll learn how to 'talk the talk.' Give him—and yourself—a chance." He pulled me around to face him, holding my hands.

What Jack said made sense. But it didn't entirely quiet my anxiety over what, exactly, had happened that day in class. I hadn't set out to challenge Rose's theory, so I didn't care if he told me I'd missed the point—his point, that is. As long as he heard and understood my idea and found my presentation convincing, that would be good enough.

I tucked my hand into Jack's pocket and tilted my head back so I could see his face. "Let's not fight about Hal Rose."

"All right. I have another idea." He pulled me close and we walked, hip to hip, back to his room.

April 22, 1970

A week later, standing outside Rose's office, I hesitated before I knocked. I decided I'd let him talk. I wouldn't argue. Or interrupt.

"It's open!"

Rose stood and held out his hand to me across the desk. "Very nice job, very nice indeed," he said, smiling. He motioned for me to sit. As soon as I settled, he began to pace behind the desk, looking up at me once in a while, punctuating his comments with waves of his pipe.

"I'm interested in thematics, as you know. Some would call it an obsession." He laughed. "That's why I advised you to look into homoeroticism and Alain-Fournier's ambivalence toward the new era—he and Proust share that. In Proust, Charles Swann—a Jew and an esthete—is a magnificent incarnation of the same ambivalence. There are other writers—poets and playwrights, as well as painters and musicians—whose works inhabit the same space—what I call the gap between desire and reality.

"Augustin Meaulnes and François Seurel—their role reversal—reflects the same cultural theme: How better to show ambivalence toward the heroic ideal than to have Sancho Panza replace Don Quixote?" Rose's guffaw turned into a cough. He began to choke.

I grabbed his empty mug and rushed out to the lavatory. By the time I got back, he was sitting at his desk, fully recovered, it seemed. He took several sips from the mug of water I set down on the desk.

"I asked you to look at the homoerotic theme in the novel as a way to get a handle on the deep concerns shared by many writers and artists at the beginning of the twentieth century. There is an edge there between François and Augustin when they first meet, a point where the younger boy's admiration for the older one has many of the attributes of physical love, although these are never fully expressed." He tapped his pipe on the ashtray and smiled. "As they say in poker, you raised me." His eyebrows asked the question for him.

"I know what that means."

He laughed and cleared his throat. "It's curious, isn't it, that the *haut bourgeois*, Meaulnes, is thrown over by the *petit bourgeois*, Seurel, an ironic reversal if there ever was one. As you probably know, in real life, Alain-Fournier fell in love—love at first sight—with a young woman whom he spoke to once, maybe twice. There was never any hope of their being together—ever. They didn't frequent the same social circles. Far from it. She came from a well-to-do family; he was the son of a schoolteacher. In the novel, when Yvonne de Galais dies, it's François who carries her body out of the house; François, the witness who writes the story. As you said . . ." Rose looked down at his desk, thoughtful.

"Is there something else?"

He put his hands on his desk, palms down. "Your paper's fine as is. Just fine . . ."

I waited, expecting him to continue, expecting a qualification, something that would cut the ground out from under my main point. He yawned, stretched, and glanced at his watch.

"SO, HE liked the paper. He let you off the hook for ignoring the assigned topic. This is all good. What's the problem?"

"I'm not convinced he's leveling with me."

"Why do you think that?"

"I don't know, exactly. Intuition?" I avoided Jack's eyes. "I just get the feeling something else is going on, that he has some kind of hidden agenda."

"Come on, Malorie. Sometimes a cigar is just a cigar."

"I guess I'll just have to wait and see then."

By the time I dropped off my paper in Rose's box two weeks later, I had managed to put aside my misgivings. It was near the end of the term; I'd been too busy to dwell on my suspicions. During Rose's last seminar, I sat across from Danielle, who watched me, smiling faintly.

My irritation got the better of me and I looked her in the eye, catching her completely by surprise. It was too much to hope that she and I would never again be in the same class. At least we'd have the summer off.

Ardis

"Are you sure you can't come home for the summer?"

"Mom, please. I've explained this. Maybe you should think about going away, someplace where you won't think about Dad."

Depressed and bewildered, my mother had called me daily over the winter and spring. "It's not just the accident," she insisted. "My therapist says everyone goes through a phase like this after divorce."

"Dad is dead, Mom."

"That only makes it worse, don't you see?"

I didn't feel the same way and knew that if I told her that, she wouldn't understand. She ended every conversation the same way. "It would help me to have you around, you know."

It seemed nothing I said would satisfy her. I kept repeating my reasons for staying in Brookton: I had a part-time summer job teaching French at Brookton High. I would also be studying to take my first field exam at the beginning of October. I'd kept my room in the dorm for the summer. It was cheap and close enough to the library and the high school, so I wouldn't need my car much. And there would be no distractions.

Apart from that, there wasn't much to do in Brookton in the summer. Of course, I'd have plenty of company: most graduate students stuck around, catching up on their own research projects and complaining about being too poor to go anywhere else.

"Will you be able to come up for weekends, at least?"

I agreed to try. An occasional weekend away would be a welcome break.

At the end of May, Ellis Jacobs asked Jack to stay with his cats until September. Only three blocks from campus, the house had four bedrooms, a finished basement, and a large garden. And it was less than a mile from the high school, an easy walk.

Jack put his dinner tray down on the table across from me. When he finished explaining the house-sitting arrangement, he looked expectant, as though waiting for me to open a gift.

I waited him out.

"You could live there too."

What would it be like to live with Jack? Sure, it was a big house—big enough for me to have my own room, it seemed—but was that what he had in mind?

"Actually, I'd do just about anything to get out of the dorm."

He laughed. "Translation: you really want to live with me."

"That's not the issue." At least, it wasn't the only one. "My mom . . . I think you can figure out how she'll react to the idea."

"She might feel differently when she finds out we'll be sharing the house with three other people. We won't be living in sin. At least, not exactly." He grinned.

"Other people? What other people?"

"Matt, for one. He hasn't found a place yet." Matt, Jack's roommate at Yale and a mathematician, was working on a PhD. "Also, there's Ardis Summers and a friend of hers from San Francisco. They'll be driving out together sometime in June." Ardis, a painter, was Ellis's niece.

I described the house to my mother the next time she called, planning to introduce the house-sitting idea at the end. "It's a Victorian pile, with acres of mahogany, twelve-foot ceilings, a butler's pantry—complete with dumbwaiter. And a huge garden. Ellis rents it from the U. It's on the National Register, so they want someone living in it full-time, which is how Jack got it. Plus it's rent free, Mom."

"So you're going to live there with Jack?"

"And Matt, and Ellis's niece, and a friend of hers. That's five of us in a house that has room to spare. We'll even have an extra bedroom, if you want to come down for a visit."

"Your father wouldn't approve."

"Well, he's dead, so his vote doesn't count." I shuddered to hear his sarcasm and sneer in my tone of voice.

"Malorie!"

"Mom, listen. We'll share a house for two months. That's it. Jack goes to France at the end of August. Anyway, it's convenient to have a place so close to the campus. And to the high school." All of this was true, but beside the point.

What bothered my mother most, I knew, was that someone from Long Meadow, or from the law firm, might find out about my living arrangements. Hiding the details of our home life, protecting us from gossip, had become a habit, one she might never break.

"I don't want you to get hurt. You and Jack aren't even engaged." Her voice broke. "And I don't want you to spend the summer housekeeping for those two guys. You're not Wendy and they're not the Lost Boys. You know that, right?"

It was pointless to continue. I knew I couldn't convince her that Jack's proposal wasn't about free maid service or regular sex. "Could you just back off? Please? It's not worth arguing about, is it?"

"Just remember you can always come home. No matter what happens, your home is here."

The longing in her voice made me understand how much she believed this, as if to her, home wasn't home without me. Now wasn't the time to reveal that when I thought of home, Prospect Hill and Milou came to mind, not Long Meadow and my mother.

June 11, 1970

Ardis arrived at the end of my second week of summer school. Working in the kitchen, I had flashcards spread out on the table in preparation for the next day's review of foods, menus, and meals. At three o'clock, the front door opened and closed; someone crossed the hall in the direction of the kitchen.

"Malorie?"

I recognized her from photographs in Ellis's office. In living color, she gleamed. Her red-gold hair hung to her waist, catching the light from the hall window behind her. She could have stepped out of a Rossetti painting.

"Sorry to barge in like this." She had let us know she'd be delayed, but hadn't said for how long.

"I wasn't—we weren't—sure what day you'd get here." This sounded so much like a reproach that I tacked on what I should have said first. "I'm glad to see you."

She gestured at the front door. "The bell seems to be out of order. As usual."

"We should make a sign." Why hadn't we done this? It seemed so obvious.

"And lock the door." She threw her head back and let loose a throaty, full laugh, the kind that makes you want to do or say anything to keep it going. "Ellis—Uncle Ellis—blows off that kind of stuff. The last time I was here, the security system had been AWOL for months. It probably still is."

She was right. Ellis had told Jack not to report the broken system. Even when it worked, it went off at all hours, for no apparent reason. I got up and cleared the magazines and cutouts from the table, piling the flashcards in a shoebox.

"Don't stop what you're doing on my account. I've got to unpack the car anyway."

"I'm finished here and on my way out—to the library." I straightened the table and put a vase of roses in the middle. She stood there, watching me, looking a little lost.

"We set up the basement for you," I told her. "Sheets, towels, and so forth. If you need more hangers or anything else, help yourself. All the supplies are in the closet down there." I pulled a tagged house key from a kitchen drawer and gave it to her. We laughed as if we'd both had the same thought. Why bother with the key if we never locked the front door?

"I like that room."

"Oh?" Instantly I recognized my faux pas. Of course she knew the house.

"It's where I usually stay. I've even done some paintings, views of the plants—those hydrangeas—just outside the basement windows. The perspective—a cricket's-eye view?—makes me happy. I really like looking at things inside out. It makes you think about right side and wrong side, about who decides which is which. Don't you think?" She made air quotes around "right" and "wrong" and shrugged. "Like the Joni Mitchell song, you know?" This all came out in a rush, almost a sigh of relief.

I could see what she meant. The connection made me smile. For the moment, I forgot we had just met. "Jack and Matt will show up by five. I'll be back before nine. It's Matt's turn to make dinner."

"Really?"

I could tell she was looking forward to something more substantial than what would be on offer. "Don't get your hopes up. Matt's idea of dinner is grilled cheese sandwiches and a can of tomato soup. But you can count on precision-cut wedges."

Ardis giggled. "What do you mean?"

"He's a mathematician."

As if that explained everything, she nodded and smiled, then walked over to the sink to wash her hands. She lifted her hair off her neck and wrapped it into a knot that sat on top of her head without any help from a hairpin or barrette. I noticed her hands—square, capable-looking, disproportionate somehow in contrast to the rest of her, which was delicate, birdlike.

I picked up my book bag. "Is your friend waiting in the car?"

After a moment, she spoke to me, her voice so soft that I had to concentrate, leaning toward her to hear.

"I dropped her off in Chicago to spend some time with her family. She may make it out here for a visit before I move into the city in September." She shrugged; her voice trailed off. She looked at the floor, as if trying to decide whether—or how—to continue, then she met my eyes.

"She's a writer. A good one. She had a part-time job at the Free Medical Clinic in the Haight doing press releases and grant proposals." Two months ago, the friend had stayed late at the clinic. A couple of guys broke in, high on something. When she wouldn't give them money, they raped her and beat her up. Left her unconscious. A coworker found her the next morning. "The cops say they're looking." Ardis closed her eyes. When she opened them, they were shiny with tears. "They don't have much to go on. She didn't feel safe anymore, so I took her home. We had planned to get an apartment in the city."

Watching her expression as she talked was like watching the sunset fade. She seemed unaware of the feelings that flickered and died, revealed, then quieted, as she talked. I listened to the electric clock, humming, to the click and purr of the refrigerator, cycling, until the silence between us began to feel awkward.

She smiled. "Apart from my parents, you're the first person I've told about this. Thank you for that."

She turned down my offer to help her unload her car and walked with me to the end of the driveway. "I'm going to see if I can convince Matt to make us a few rectangles tonight."

"Now *that's* something to look forward to."

．

AT EIGHT o'clock that evening, Ardis and Matt stood side by side at the kitchen counter, making sandwiches. He handed her slices of bread; she spread mayo on them and added cheddar cheese. They turned when they heard me come in and burst into giggles.

"You won't believe this. . . ." Matt caught his breath. "Ardis has been explaining how she did these paintings, which got me started on my favorite topic. You know, Fibonacci . . ."

Ardis interrupted. "You'd never know English is our first language. Neither of us seems to understand a word the other says." More giggles. I couldn't help joining in.

Matt had developed an application of the Fibonacci sequence, a mathematical sequence where each term equals the sum of the two preceding terms. He hoped it would lead to a new form of computing, which itself was new enough; none of us really had a clue what he was talking about. As he went along, researching everything he could find, he had collected examples of the sequence in nature, music, and art.

"So we're talking, and I tell Matt about some of my paintings, especially the ones I did of the hydrangeas outside the basement window . . ."

"I asked if I could see them." Matt's hair stuck straight up; his face was flushed. He had a dab of mayo on the end of his nose. He couldn't have been more different from Jack—easygoing, quick to find the light side. Matt knew how to bring Jack out of his low moments.

"What he did is, he grabbed me, marched me down to the basement, and hovered while I unpacked the paintings."

Matt looked sheepish. "I scared her to death."

"Scared who to death, Matteo?" Jack's arrival launched a rerun of the story. "Can we see the paintings?"

Ardis gestured at the counter, where four small acrylics lay side by side on a black cloth.

"Wow!"

"You expected something abstract and large scale, right?" Ardis smiled. "I've been working in this format for a while now. But I'm thinking it may be time to try something larger."

The five- by seven-inch paintings showed the same view, differing from each other only in palette. The lack of a frame accentuated the patterns and glowing colors. "I had Monet's cathedral series in mind," Ardis explained. "I loved the idea of capturing the changing light through the same plants at different times of the day."

I looked at the light and shadow play and the different ways each painting showed the layers of intertwined stems, leaves, and flowers. "But in the Monet paintings, Rouen Cathedral is recognizable. It's such a famous place. In yours, you recognize leaves and stems—you know you're looking at plants. You might even identify them. At the same time, you focus on the patterns and colors for their own sake. Double vision?" As I talked, she nodded, as if keeping time with me.

Matt grinned. "That's what I said. Exactly. I also told her that the stems, the way they're articulated, grow in a Fibonacci pattern." He traced the branching pattern on the counter. "The best part? I've talked Ardis into coming to my lab to see what I am doing."

Ardis looked at him the way you might look at a brilliant, but harmless, eccentric.

"She thinks she can help me figure out ways to model the work I'm doing using drawings on tissue paper."

"At least maybe I'll get what you're talking about if you show me what it looks like—in real life!"

Over dinner, Matt and Ardis continued to talk about the Fibonacci sequence, what it was, what it meant, how it appeared and where—in plants (sunflowers) and shells (chambered nautilus) and, yes, hydrangeas. Matt started sentences that ran on in torrents of connected, half-formed thoughts; somehow or other, Ardis finished them. Together, the two of them lit up the room.

A pause jolted us, like a pothole opening in the middle of a highway, too sudden to avoid. We all just looked at one another. Jack leaned back in his chair, his eyes on Matt, who was staring, wide-eyed, at Ardis. "I'm not sure I can bear the thought of living with two of you!"

"Two of us?" Matt spoke as if he were repeating a phrase in a foreign language.

"You know. If Ardis becomes as obsessed with Fibonacci as you are, Malorie and I may have to take precautions."

"Such as?"

"Fibonacci vaccine?" This just slipped out. When the others burst out laughing, my neck prickled. I looked across the table at Ardis, whose eyes held mine, intent and reassuring.

June 23, 1970

I carried the sling chairs down the porch steps onto the lawn, one under each arm. Ardis had our sketchbooks and pencil cases and a tray with two glasses and a pitcher of iced tea. Sticky with dust and cobwebs, the chairs smelled of summer damp.

After we'd wiped the chairs, Ardis settled in hers and leaned forward, lifting her hair off her neck and draping it over the chair back. She looked up at the trees. There was just enough breeze to ruffle the leaves, enough to coax petals from the roses, whose early blooms were beginning to wilt, their fragrance edged with the smell of their decay.

The deep lawn in the back of the house had a border of old maples and oaks, their abundant canopies shading the entire area. How the roses survived, I hadn't figured out. Possibly the east-southwest sun exposure they got for part of the summer made the difference. The rest of the garden, mostly shade plants, offered different tones of green and blue. At times, sitting back here under the trees, I felt as though I were at the bottom of a lake or pond, looking up through the water at the sky.

"I love everything about my name except the sibilants in the middle. ArdisssssSummers—you see?"

I laughed too.

Ardis often launched into a conversation like this, the same way some people dive into cold water, plunging in fearlessly, without any of the hedging or hinting someone else might use to get the ball rolling.

"People can't tell where my first name ends and my last name begins. Also, it's so obviously a woman's name. It's hard enough to make it as an artist. The minute you identify yourself as a woman, it's like a force multiplier. People either don't take you seriously at all, or they look over your shoulder to identify the guy behind you. That's why I decided to choose one working name and stick with it, like Sappho. I thought Summers would do fine. But a friend thought it was too close to Summerson. . . ."

"Esther Summerson, *Bleak House*."

"Exactly. She's a wonderful character, but Dickens casts a long shadow and I want to make my own. The nice thing about Summer is that it could just as easily be a man's name. I can *pass*. Pretty slick, don't you think?"

She said this in a self-mocking tone, but her eyes were serious.

The plan was to do some drawing. Ardis had a new painting project in mind, beginning with sketches that would later become the basis for studies. I needed an afternoon off. It was too hot to prepare for tomorrow's class—it was a review session, anyway—or to walk four blocks to the air-conditioned library. So there we sat, sipping our tea, lifting our faces up to catch the fickle breeze.

"What about you?"

"What about me, what?" I sat up and wiped my face with the paper napkin I'd been holding around my glass. Cool and wet, it made my skin tingle.

"Tell me about your name."

I told her about my grandmother and the family tradition: Malorie was the given name of every firstborn daughter, beginning in the fourteenth century.

"That long ago? That's so cool." Ardis moved her chair around to face me. "Tell me more."

"It's like a fairy tale, in a way." Every time I told the story, I felt I was reaching back, holding hands with all the women who came before my grandmother, my mother, and me. "Malorie is the Modern French spelling of *maleurie*, an Old French word that means misfortune or bad luck. The first Malorie in our family was born during a battle between two landowners over property rights, vineyards to be exact, in Flagy."

"Flagy?"

"It's a village in Burgundy."

Even though the peasants weren't in the fight, the fight came to them, and they had no swords, no chain mail, to defend themselves. Many of them died, caught in the middle. Delivered by her father, the infant girl—and both her parents—survived, hidden in a *cadole*, a crude stone hut.

"That, at least, is the story that got passed down."

"Naming her *misfortune* seems odd to me. It's good fortune that saved her, right?"

"It's based on an old superstition: you give the child a name to ward off the evil eye."

Ardis nodded. "So your grandmother also is named Malorie?"

"Yes. And my mother. But everyone calls my grandmother Milou, her nickname. My mother had her name changed legally to Lucie when she was twenty-one."

"Why?"

"Sort of a rebellion, I guess." When I had asked my mother about this, she had made light of the change, but something about the way she had looked at me made me suspect this wasn't the whole story. I had pressed her; she had refused to discuss it further.

"If your mother didn't like to be called Malorie, why did she give you the name?"

"The long arm of superstition?"

"You don't have sibs?"

I shook my head. "An only, like my mother. I sometimes used to wonder if that had to do with my name. A kind of jinx, you know? But my grandmother had three brothers. So, no jinx!"

"Would you be the last Malorie, if you don't have a daughter?"

"At least in my own family."

"That's sad, isn't it?"

"Yes. But I can take some comfort in knowing that someone, somewhere, always picks up the thread and ties it to the next generation."

"What do you mean?"

"Thanks to first, second, and third cousins—someone will have a little girl and give her the name. It's the tradition that matters. Anyway, I don't have to worry about that. Yet." I relaxed back in my chair and closed my eyes.

I must have dozed off for a while. I opened my eyes and watched Ardis. Gripping a piece of charcoal loosely in her palm, like a brush, she made wide smooth strokes across the paper. As soon as she noticed, she turned her sketchbook to show me the portrait she had drawn. There I was, looking through a screen of palm fronds, gazing directly at the viewer.

"I look like I'm about to speak."

"I get the feeling you have many stories to tell."

"Why don't you take a turn?"

ARDIS HAD dropped out of Reed in '66, her sophomore year. A friend of a friend, a guitar player, rented a house on Haight Street, so she went to San Francisco to stay with him and his friends.

"My parents didn't freak out. I told them I wasn't running away, just taking a different road for a while." Both of them teachers and Democrats—"and peaceniks, of course"—they were activists at home, but they liked their jobs, they liked living in eastern Oregon, the feeling of being settled when everything else around them seemed so uncertain. "They'd never have dreamed of dropping out themselves, but they didn't object when I did.

"Anyway, I had a plan. I had been painting pretty seriously for a long time and wanted to continue in San Francisco, maybe take some classes—provided I could support myself. My parents came through for me—I never asked them, but they sent me a check from time to time, enough to buy more paper, or paint, or score some dope." She rounded her eyes and laughed. "I never told them about the dope."

There had been eight of them living in that house, busking or waiting tables by day, hanging out and smoking dope when they weren't working. "We were all pretty straight, considering. None of us wanted to overthrow the government," she laughed again, "and none of us were into experimental drugs. Now I know how lucky we were. No one ever sold us bad stuff. And none of us panhandled. My friend, the one I dropped off in Chicago, had some problems. But we straightened her out." She stopped, looked down at her hands, her eyes darkening, turning inward.

When she told me about her room, I closed my eyes and visualized the tiny attic, a kind of garret, with so little headroom that Ardis—who was only five feet two—couldn't stand up straight without bumping a beam or a rafter. The room's saving grace was its view out over the rooftops across Haight Street.

Sometimes she opened her window wide—it had a double sash, so she could raise the bottom and lower the top. Legs dangling out the bottom half of the window over the street, her head sticking out the top, she took in slices of the city and bay—peeks of the Golden Gate, the Marin Headlands, Telegraph Hill, the East Bay.

"It was a strange feeling, you know? I could look down on that mad street scene—hear and smell it, even—and then, just by shifting my eyes, look out over the bay, at the fog hovering in the distance, at the headlands—a different world. I liked that I wasn't really a part of either one."

LATER, WE walked to Desmond. Blank with heat during the day, the sky had begun to fade into amber-edged lavender. The air was heavy and still.

"How long have you and Jack been together?" Ardis put her hand on my arm.

"Since I first got here. We took this same walk." I explained to her about Minerva's fox and Jack's ploy.

"Didn't it bother you that he'd make up something like that?"

"I wondered about it, at first. He thought he'd been clever, that that would appeal to me." I shrugged. "I let it go, eventually, but I think about trust a lot. In any relationship, how can you be together with someone, really, without it?"

Ardis nodded. "I'm not sure I'm cut out to be in a relationship with anyone—male or female. I love my friend, the one in Chicago, but she's too needy. Emotionally and physically. I can't handle that. I guess I'm selfish is what it comes down to."

"Look how much you've helped her."

"Well, I can care about someone else, care for someone else, as long as I'm in charge. Even then, something always goes wrong, sets me off. It probably sounds melodramatic, but painting is it for me. At least for now. Like, the only emotional energy I can spare has to go into that. How else will I find out if I'm any good?"

"What about Matt?" Didn't she realize Matt was falling in love with her?

"The thing about Matt is that he's as obsessed about his work as I am with mine. We're on the same wavelength there. Love and relationships don't fit into our game plan. We're both working too hard, you know? Sure, we talk all night sometimes. I've never met anyone who can jump so quickly from one concept to another and end up with a new idea that pulls so many things together." She shrugged. "But that's it. Much better than sex, believe me. At least for me. For now." She glanced at me. "What about you?"

I knew girls who talked to each other, shared confidences and information about sex and their boyfriends. I never had. Couldn't. My habit of hiding what went on at home carried over into my life at school and at college. My resolution to stop pretending had retreated in the face of lifelong habit.

Being with Ardis was so different. Although I was unused to talking like this to anyone, her openness disarmed me. She seemed so sure of herself and how she wanted her life to be. Rather than reacting to things that happened, she took charge of herself, moving ahead, fearless. She was waiting for me to speak, but I knew—I felt—that it wouldn't matter to her if I didn't.

"I don't know exactly. It sounds strange to say that. But it's true. I really don't know how I feel about Jack. When we're together, it's like the closer we are physically, the farther apart we are." Jack made love to me with his eyes closed. I wasn't sure he even knew that I kept my eyes open. It was as though he wasn't really there.

"Sometimes, I wish he would just go away. His confidence . . ."

"You mean he's a know-it-all."

Of course that's what I meant. But I couldn't say it. Not even to Ardis. What did it say about me that I was in a relationship with someone who made me feel as though I were wearing a kind of emotional and intellectual straitjacket? I kept going. "Sometimes I can't imagine being with anyone else. But, for sure, like you, right now I'm not ready to commit to a relationship—"

"As in get married?"

"That, yes, or live with him." I bent down to shake a pebble out of my sandal. "I envy you, you know? You know who you are, where you're going. I don't really know what I'm doing, and I don't know why I'm doing it. When I first got here last fall, I thought I'd made the right decision. But now . . . I don't know. Until I get the *what* and the *why* matched up . . ." I listened to myself, heard the self-doubt in my voice, and wanted to take every word back.

"Yes?"

"I'm in limbo, I guess." Watching a butterfly emerge from its chrysalis once, I had wondered how it would feel to emerge as a fully-formed adult, free to be me, leaving behind the paralyzing confines of the past. How naïve. It wasn't just Jack, and the pressure of his expectations and needs. It was the frustration of not knowing any better now than I had a year ago what it was I wanted to do in life. Or even if it mattered. What would it be like just to drift? I couldn't imagine that. "At first, I thought my dad's death would make a difference, help me get unstuck. And it did, in a way, just not the way I expected."

"Give yourself some more time. You'll figure it out. It's like me. Sometimes when I've got a painting in my head, I discover once I've started I'm on completely the wrong track. So frustrating. But part of the process." She stopped in the path and craned her neck. We had just reached the tulip trees. "I've heard about these trees, but I've never seen one. How tall are they, anyway?"

"At least a hundred feet. But probably more."

"Just think of everything they've been through—the hurricanes, the nor'easters, the droughts. I don't know, maybe certain diseases and insects they've had to fight off. I guess someone must maintain them. Even so, they have to do the best they can. Seems like they're doing all right, doesn't it?"

Lying beside Ardis in the grass, looking up into the trees, I took comfort in what she said. The trees had taken it all in and here they were.

On the lawn, several small children lined up towels, pails, and shovels, pretending to be at the beach, while their mothers talked and watched, fanning themselves. They didn't seem to notice us as we walked by, as if, without children in tow, we were invisible.

I told Ardis about discovering the Japanese maple and about the hours I had spent sitting under it, drawing or reading. "Even now, it settles me down, just to come here."

"It's the silhouettes of the leaves, isn't it? If you focus on the edges, it's like they're holding or balancing slices of the background—the shade, the tulip tree trunks and leaves, the sky." Ardis held one of her hands up, looking at the branches overhead. "Interlace . . . what a challenge that is. All the intersections, each defining the space beyond."

As soon as she said it, I saw what she meant. "It is almost an optical illusion."

"I taught a class once, beginners. They just didn't get negative space at all, until I took them to look at an apple tree and had them draw the canopy. Until you can see it, you can't do anything, really. Without it, a painting is flat."

I looked at her. "Without it, there's no illusion."

She smiled. "It's a way of grounding you so you can grasp, visually, the place the painting occupies. All those intersections hold everything together. That's how I think about it, anyway. Endings and beginnings coexist, complete each other."

July 9, 1970

Some mornings I woke before dawn, tangled in the limp sheets. Ellis's two cats curled up in the middle of the bed, atolls in a percale sea. As soon as I rolled over, they stretched and yawned, the tips of their tongues flashing like pink beacons in the humid gloom.

On the other side of the bed, Jack slept on his back, his breathing light and regular. Once in a while, he muttered. Mostly, he lay still, hands by his sides, a million miles away.

The heat wave that had begun the first week in July showed no sign of relenting. Only Ardis didn't complain. The basement's stone walls kept her room so cool she slept under a blanket.

Each morning I walked to school through a cloud of blooming privet, hot tar, and car exhaust. By the time I arrived, gritty with tiny clots of smog, my clothes clung to me like a second skin. The students looked at me through half-closed eyes, as if I were somehow responsible for their misery.

Ardis made fresh lemonade daily. In the kitchen, in the early afternoon after my class, we sipped from iced glasses, fanning ourselves with the Japanese paper fans she had found in a box in the basement.

"They already think I'm behind the plot to ruin their summer."

"You're a witch, all right." She made a face.

"Six weeks down. Six to go."

"So there's hope, you see?"

Jack planned to leave for Paris at the end of August. He spent most days in the library, returning every evening hollow-eyed after scrolling through miles of microfilm. At the house, he was withdrawn, answering my questions in monosyllables. Sometimes I caught him watching me, his eyes wary.

"He's never lived with anyone but his mother, right?" Ardis nodded asked when I told her about the tension between us. "He's just sorting himself out. And he's under the gun."

"I was thinking it might at least distract him if I made a real dinner. For my birthday in a couple of weeks."

"Nice! Especially for us. I'll make a salad!"

July 31, 1970

The afternoon of my birthday, Jack came home early and sat at the kitchen table. To me, preparing a meal could be as satisfying as planning a garden. I'd learned from Milou how to balance flavors and textures, figuring out the specifics as I went along.

"It amazes me what you can do with food."

Melting butter for hollandaise sauce, I had my back turned. It had become something of a joke that I was the only one of us who knew anything about cooking. Only once had Matt hinted that maybe I could be persuaded to do it all. Ardis had come to my rescue, pointing out that I had a real job, as well as an exam to prepare.

"What about your mother?"

Jack shook his head. "My mother never met a can she couldn't open. And anything in a box is also fair game. In the summer, she grows peas and beans. Every year, in the window boxes on her balcony, she puts them in and watches them grow. Peas and beans. And geraniums, but I suppose you can't eat those."

"Actually, you can . . ." When I saw his face, I stopped. I wanted to say something to soften the edge, but what? I waited, hoping he'd tell me more without prodding. I knew very little about his mother and his life in Boston before Yale.

He came and put his arm around me. "You're the only person I've ever seen chop an onion or peel a potato. Can you believe it?"

I started to make a joke. The emptiness in his expression stopped me. "It's not as hard as you think." I picked up the potato peeler and showed him how to use it.

He was awkward at first, but it didn't take long for him to get the hang of it. "This may be the first time I've ever held an unpeeled potato, let alone peeled one. Where's my toque?"

"Not until you squeeze these lemons." I handed him the fruit and pointed to the bowl. "Lemon custard. For dessert."

"What happened to the cake?"

"Not in this heat. Besides, it's too humid for the one I had in mind." As much as I longed to make a vacherin, a birthday tradition Milou started when I was little, I knew the meringue would collapse into a rubbery mass that even whipped cream and raspberries couldn't salvage. For this birthday, at least, the custard would have to do.

It seemed cooler for a while. Except it wasn't. When I checked the thermometer, it was still over ninety degrees. But something had changed. Standing beside Jack as he squeezed the lemons, I wondered if the change was in us. Because we were cooking together? Because we were doing something I knew how to do and he didn't? Because it was so practical, so real, so concrete?

"What's so funny?"

"I'm having fun, aren't you?" I kissed his chin and began to beat the eggs.

Matt and Ardis came in with provisions for the salad. As soon as they got Jack involved cleaning the vegetables, the four of us worked in companionable silence, stepping around the cats, who were stretched out on the cool tile floor, watchful for tidbits.

IT STARTED as soon as we finished dinner. Jack's face was flushed—he'd had several glasses of wine. He had been telling us about an article he had found. "I can show the guy's interpretation is way off, and use his analysis to set up my main argument."

Matt nodded. "It's so much easier for you humanists: For you it's about interpretation. For us, it's so often about other things."

"You mean like addition and subtraction?" Ardis teased.

Matt and I laughed. Jack, confused, looked at them and refilled his wine glass. "So, I'm going to hammer the guy's view of the classical influences in the treatment of the life/death theme. Sure, Lamartine uses it, but it's a stretch to say it's a crutch. He's a good enough poet not to have to tip his hat to the ancients. Also, the guy overlooks the political side. That's a serious weakness in his argument."

Was it because I still felt the closeness of our time together in the kitchen that afternoon? Or because it was my birthday? Or something else? Whatever it was, I felt the laugh build until it burst out of control in a fit of giggles that got Matt and Ardis going too.

"What? What's so funny?" Jack's eyes narrowed; he clenched his jaw. We just laughed harder. He pushed back from the table, knocking over his wine glass. Gasping for breath, none of us said anything.

"You know—" It was too late to smooth things over. Reckless, I pushed ahead.

"What?"

"You are so set on beating up this person. Why? Why is that so important to you? He's dead, Jack. Can't you just make your point without setting him up? Do you really need a straw man?"

"That's enough, Malorie." His voice trembled and broke.

"Jack . . ."

"Enough." The slap of his hand on the screen door as he lunged through it echoed through the house. He kicked it shut behind him.

I FOUND him in the park under the tulip trees, staring up at the sky.

I knelt down. He took my hand and pulled me next to him. Together we lay back in the grass. The three-quarter moon, a Chagall moon, leaned over us, compassionate, consoling.

"I'm sorry."

"Me too." He leaned his chin on my shoulder. "I even dream about microfilm these days." He gave a short laugh. "I really have no idea what I'm doing."

"Is that because you can't see where this will end up? Or because you have so much left to do?"

"A little of both, I guess. I thought I'd be farther along by now. I have to finish before I go to Paris. One month. That's all I've got."

I rolled onto my side to face him. "You're doing the best you can."

Behind Jack, like guardians of the night, the tulip trees seemed to lift their branches to the moon. Their leaves fluttered, luminous in the light, a light just bright enough for me to see Jack's eyes, open to me for the first time, holding nothing back as we made love there in the grass.

August 19, 1970

Jack spent every day checking sources and refining his dissertation outline. Often he stayed until the library closed. Sometimes I stopped by his carrel to see him before I went home. He seemed dazed, in a trance.

He was falling farther behind, he told me. It seemed that every day he found yet another obscure European journal with yet another article discussing the minutiae of Lamartine's late poems. He couldn't help himself. He felt compelled to track down and read these articles, summarizing and cross-referencing them, connecting them into a semblance of coherence. He was determined to find the rest of the poem whose fragment he'd found in the letter.

Sometimes I talked about my students, sharing anecdotes I thought would amuse him. As long as I stuck to reporting what they said or did, he gave the appearance of listening to me. As soon as I tried to talk about my ongoing misgivings about my own performance, he would cut me off.

"You worry too much, Malorie. You're good. All you need is practice."

"That's just it, Jack. I don't know what to practice."

I believed that Jack's condescension was mostly an effort to mask his own insecurity and had stopped taking it personally. Still, I couldn't understand why he didn't get it: if learning to play the piano involved practicing scales, surely there were techniques I could practice that would help me learn how to teach. Hadn't anyone figured out a way to help novices like me?

The cats were sleeping on the floor by my chair, oblivious to my tone of voice.

"They assume I know how to do this. But I don't, not really. For instance, the kids need to speak more. Some of them are so shy. I wonder . . ." I felt his attention shift, like a current of air passing between us. When I looked at him, he was flipping through a stack of notecards.

I HAD skipped a period in July. This happened to me sometimes, so I didn't worry. Then another due date came and went. A week passed. Two weeks. I thought it might be the stress of teaching and the tension between Jack and me. I told Ardis, who talked me into having a pregnancy test.

"I can't be pregnant, Ardis. We're careful."

"Of course you are. That's why you need to have the test. So you can stop worrying."

When the doctor told me he would have the results in three or four days, I told him the same thing.

"Well then, try to relax." He leaned toward me, his expression open and reassuring. "If it's stress, you'll know soon enough. Anyway, if you're pregnant, it's early days. You have time to decide what you want to do."

"What I want to do?"

"If you're pregnant and you don't want to have the baby, I can help you. Or you can arrange for an adoption."

He was talking about an abortion. I didn't know what to say. I kept hearing my own voice in my head: *I can't be pregnant. We're careful.*

After the appointment, I went to the park. What was I going to tell Jack? I'd told him this was a routine checkup.

In the winter, after we had been together for several months, a graduate student we both knew dropped out—because she was pregnant. I knew the diaphragm wasn't fail-safe. My own doctor, the one who had fitted me for it, made sure I understood its drawbacks.

"What do I think we would do if you got pregnant?" Jack looked at me as if I'd just asked him if the earth really was round. "You'd get an abortion, no question. We'd find a doctor so that you could have a medical abortion. That is possible, you know."

I didn't ask him how he knew. I didn't care. His assumption I would agree with him bothered me. It was as if we were talking about having a tooth filled. "Do you think we might discuss it first?"

"I didn't mean to sound . . . " He shrugged, his eyes downcast. "But you agree, right?"

"Of course I don't want a baby right now. But having an abortion scares me. Because it's not legal, because there can be problems—even if you can find a doctor who'll agree to do it. There are other options, you know."

He wouldn't look at me.

I had to talk to Jack. But I didn't know how. We hadn't had unprotected sex, so the only way I could be pregnant was if the diaphragm failed. Would he blame me? What did it say about our relationship that I could even imagine that he might?

I walked home from the park. A block away from the house, I saw him waiting for me on the front steps. He ran toward me, picked me up, and twirled me around, urging me up the steps into the house.

Once we were inside, he started, his words tumbling out in a rush. "At last! Today, at last, I found out what all those mysterious references mean, the ones I've been tracking down."

I dropped my book bag and turned toward him.

"I've found another reference to that unpublished poem, Malorie. It's certainly one of Lamartine's last. Maybe even *the* last. I can't believe it. It's transcribed in a letter he wrote, a letter that's in the museum in Mâcon. What I can't figure out is why no one else knows about this." He shook his head. "Isn't that unbelievable?"

"It is, yes." I tried to smile.

Jack's shoulders slumped; his face fell. "What is it now, Malorie?"

What is it *now*? I heard a humming noise coming from somewhere in the house, felt it throbbing behind my eyes, and realized it was coming from a place inside me. Jack's mouth tightened. I realized I was holding myself, my arms wrapped around my belly. What is it *now*? His question echoed in my head, the space between us, a gulf electric with his irritation.

"It's just—you know. Of course I'm happy for you. Do you want to go out for dinner or something?" The strain of holding back, of wanting to make him hear me—to listen to me—made me dizzy.

"Look," he said, "it's going fine. You're well-prepared; you like the students. I've told you this before. You're too hard on yourself."

"Of course I'm well-prepared. I should know; I'm the one who's doing the preparing. And of course I like the students. That is just not the point, Jack."

"Malorie, don't . . ."

I needed to say something, anything, as long as it had to do with what he had found that day. I knew that was the only way to get back to a place where we could talk to, rather than past, one another. It was up to me, but I couldn't do it.

"Jack . . ."

He shook his head and walked out of the house.

August 25, 1970

I met Ardis in the park. "I can't imagine myself doing any of this." I held the crumpled brochure in my lap. It had a pink cover with "Prenatal Care" in blue splashed across it.

"What can you imagine, then?" She turned sideways to face me.

"Escape."

Ardis didn't seem surprised. "From here or from Jack?"

"From myself, most of all. I can't stand thinking about this anymore." Now that I knew I was pregnant, I would have to tell Jack. I had thought knowing the test results—positive or negative—would make it easier. I was wrong.

"Most of the time, delay just makes matters worse. Unless it's part of your plan."

"No plan. That's the problem. I also have to know how to say what I want to do."

After a sleepless night, I was no closer to a decision. Jack was leaving for Paris in two days. If only I could be sure he would listen to me. I feared he would not. And that fear paralyzed me. Distracted by the final preparations for his trip, Jack didn't seem to notice. Early the morning of his departure, we lay awake, not talking, not touching.

"I'll call you as soon as I can." Jack had sublet an apartment on the *rue du Bac*. He had joked that it had one of the three—or four—private phones in Paris. He needed a phone, in case something happened to his mother.

He rolled onto his side to face me, speaking softly. "This has been a tough summer. I'm sorry I've been so out of reach. I know how hard you're working now to finish your class and get through your field exam. I hope things will go better for you once that's behind you. When you can start working on your dissertation, you'll be fine."

I didn't point out to him that his own recent experience seemed to contradict this idea. Anyway, I wanted to believe him. But I didn't say anything, afraid that if I did, I'd talk about what was uppermost in my mind. I couldn't do that because I—we—needed his undivided attention. It was too late now. The time to talk, to sit quietly, to see if we could decide together what to do, had passed.

August 28, 1970

On my way to teach my class the next morning, I stopped at the student center for coffee. Usually the smell of brewing coffee revived me. That day, I felt so nauseated I knew I was going to be sick. Pushing through the crowd, I bumped into a student carrying a full breakfast tray. Everything spilled onto the floor, coffee, juice, scrambled eggs.

I bolted.

Shoving open the door to the restroom, I stumbled into the first stall. Even before I could latch the door, I bent over the toilet, retching. When the spasms ended, I felt worse. Shivering and dizzy, I ached all over.

When I felt well enough to leave the stall, I splashed cold water over my face. In the mirror, a stringy-haired stranger stared at me. I couldn't go to class looking like this. I'd have to go home, at least to change, and figure out what to do. Anyway, if I was sick, I'd be better off canceling for the day. My students would be better off, too.

A custodian, an older black woman, pushed a mop over the floor. She paused and spoke to me. "You'll be okay, honey. It's early days. Get some saltines. That always helps me."

Early days. Just what the doctor had said. Was it that obvious? The slacks I was wearing fit the same as they always did. I didn't look pregnant. And then it hit me. Morning sickness. That's what had tipped her off.

I called the school to let them know I was sick and went home. Dizzy and weak, I was glad to have the house to myself. Jack was supposed to call from Paris. I wrote a note to let Ardis and Matt know I had the flu, telling them to ask him to call back tomorrow.

The dull malaise that began after I'd vomited had become a throbbing pain. I turned on the fan and got into bed. I didn't want to move. Couldn't move. Couldn't think. *Should I call the doctor? Later.* The effort to climb the stairs had exhausted me. I slept all day, sometimes waking to the sound of my own whimpering.

Voices murmuring outside the door woke me around dinnertime. Ardis came in and sat on the floor beside the bed.

"What happened?"

I told her.

"What can I do?"

"Help me pack a few things and take me home?"

"Now or later?"

"Now, please."

August 29, 1970

Something held me, pinning me down, like the time a wave broke on top of me, raking me over the stony bottom. Then, I held my breath until the thrusting water flung me on the beach, choking.

Breathe!

Three o'clock.

In my own bed in my room in Long Meadow, I panted as the pain pulsed from my belly into my back and chest.

Tangled and damp, the blanket and top sheet wound around me. I rolled over and slid onto the floor. At my eye level, a pool of blood spread across the bottom sheet. I smelled iron and something else, something I wanted nothing to do with—something I wanted to have nothing to do with *me*.

Under the bathroom's harsh light, the blood streaking my thighs looked like primitive trails on the map of an unfamiliar place, a place I never wanted to visit. Spasms of pain throbbed through me, blanking out everything but the toilet seat.

Hugging myself, panting and whimpering, my breath whistling shrill in my ears, I felt the pain pressing down hard, as if trying to escape. I gave in, let myself go into it, made myself breathe into it. A rush of lightness went through me then. I heard—or thought I heard, it was barely audible—a faint splash.

I stood and ran water into the sink, soaked a washcloth and wiped away the blood. When I could bear to look at it, I could not imagine the almost-black clot lying still on the bottom of the toilet bowl as anything but what it was—the end of something that should never have begun.

I closed my eyes and flushed it away.

By the time I got back in bed, it was nearly four thirty.

ARDIS KNELT next to the bed. "Your mom just came home. I told her you had the flu."

"Time?"

"About ten."

"You know?"

She nodded and took my hand. "I know. Me too. Once."

I rolled over on my side so I could look at her. "What do I do now?"

"You need to see your doctor, to make sure everything is okay. I had some complications, a D and C."

"A . . . ?"

"Dilation and curettage. To remove some tissue that got left behind."

"Sounds . . ." This was more than I wanted to—or could—think about.

"A little, but not too bad. Anyway, it's better than the alternative."

"Don't tell me."

Ardis made a rueful face.

We both heard my mother on the stairs. Too late for me to pretend to be asleep.

"Malorie? The flu? Are you sure? Do you want to see Alison?"

Ardis got up. "I'll go make tea." She closed the door behind her.

"Not Alison." I tried to speak normally.

"I don't understand."

I gestured at the sheets and nightgown piled in the corner of the room. Her face went slack. She looked back at me. "Oh, Malorie."

I closed my eyes. The details could wait.

"It'd better be Dr. Stein, then." Her eyes fixed on mine, willing me not to argue.

Before I had gone to college, my mother had made the appointment for me to see Dr. Stein, her own OB-GYN. He had sat with me in his office, as if we were old friends, explaining his views on contraception. It was my right to decide when and with whom to have sex, he told me. As long as I was careful. "It's my job to make sure you are." His smile made it seem as if having sex with someone I wasn't (yet) married to was as normal as brushing my hair. "I'm sure single women will be able to get the Pill before too long. Just like married women. *That* will be a change for the better." He had beamed at me, as if he wished he could just wave a magic wand.

Married women had been able to get the Pill for a few years; single women, on the other hand, had to rely on the diaphragm—when they could find a doctor willing to provide it. When I left that day with the prescription for the diaphragm, Dr. Stein had told me to stop by to see him any time I had questions.

My mother looked at me, uncertain. "How do you feel right now? Dr. Stein will want to know."

I closed my eyes. "I feel sore, there's that part. And guilty. Jack . . . We hadn't been getting along. He doesn't know I am—I was—pregnant."

"What about the summer school? And the university? Don't your classes start soon?"

"I'll call the school later. Summer session ends tomorrow, anyway; someone else can grade my exams. I feel terrible about that, but it'll have to do. My classes start in two weeks. I'll be all right by then, don't you think?"

"I don't know. But Dr. Stein will." She looked away. "What about Jack?"

"I can't think about him now. I will. Later. When I decide . . . when I decide something." I heard Ardis coming up the stairs. "I need to talk to Ardis."

My mother felt my forehead. "You've got a fever, I'm sure. I'll see if they can fit you in today." She opened the door for Ardis, who brought in a tray with tea, toast, and a single cornflower in a bud vase. I tried to smile.

"You don't have to stay, Ardis. You should take my car back to Brookton. Park it in the graduate college lot and leave the key with Matt. I'll call him when I'm ready to pick it up." I bit off a piece of toast and sipped the tea. "Call me when you've got a phone in your new place. I'll try to make it to the city to see you soon."

Ardis leaned over and kissed my cheek. "You'll love the apartment I found."

"There's one more thing."

"Jack?"

"I want Jack—and everyone else—to think I've got the flu. Can you be sure to tell Matt? Just in case Jack gets in touch with him?"

"Don't worry."

September 2, 1970

Three days later, on the examining table, my feet in the stirrups, I listened to Dr. Stein's explanations, finding comfort in his tone of voice and his reassurance. Everything seemed normal, he told me. When he finished, he smiled down at me. "As soon as you're dressed, we'll talk in my office."

The office still looked and felt to me like a comfortable study. Medical reference books and journals were lined up on one set of bookshelves. In the other, volumes of poetry, art books, and travelogues shared shelf space with a collection of Native American ceramic pots. I set my bag on the coffee table and sat in one of the armchairs. I felt relaxed and drowsy. And relieved.

As soon as he came in, Dr. Stein took the armchair across from me. "Everything looks fine—a bit raw and swollen, but otherwise fine. It'll take a few weeks for you to get back to normal, but you're young, healthy, in good shape, so you probably won't have much more bleeding or discomfort."

He paused. "You'll need to wait, though, two months, say, before you have intercourse again." He said this in the same tone and with the same emphasis he had used to tell me my temperature and blood pressure were normal.

He flipped through his notes and pulled out a page that he attached to the top of his clipboard. "There is one thing, something you need to know—about possible repercussions down the road."

"Repercussions?"

"You may have had an ectopic pregnancy, possibly the tubal version. That's when the fertilized egg gets stuck in a fallopian tube and doesn't move on into the uterus. Many women miscarry when this happens."

"And later on?"

"You might not . . . you may have trouble getting pregnant again." Without waiting for me to reply, he continued. "There's no way to be certain, of course. I'm telling you only for future reference. I'm sorry. I know that sounds a bit vague. One day, when you decide to have children, you'll want to tell your doctor about this miscarriage, especially . . . especially if you have questions."

And that was that. I didn't think any more about it. I didn't worry about what it meant to have a miscarriage—any kind of miscarriage. I was too relieved. When my mother asked me, I told her only the part about being young, healthy, and healing quickly.

September 8, 1970

Within a week, I felt well enough to spend time in the garden, deadheading and pruning. I made lists of what needed to be done later in the fall. The pleasure of raking, pruning, and cleaning the beds gave me a comforting sense of clarity and renewal.

Late one afternoon, the phone rang just as I came in. I was sure it wasn't Jack—too late in the day, given the time difference. Ardis, perhaps?

"Patrick!" We hadn't really talked since the beginning of the summer when he left Brookton to work at a theater in the city. Several quick phone calls, moments he stole from the stage managing job he had, had been enough to tell me how much he loved being back among theater people.

"At last! I got Matt at Ellis's house. He told me you've had the flu. You don't sound so bad. What's going on?"

"It's been boring. But I'll survive." I needed to change the subject before I told him the truth. "What's up with you?"

He laughed. "I'm in love. This time it's forever, Malorie. I can hear your eyes rolling."

"So who's the lucky one?"

"Guy Davis, a set designer I met at a party. We started talking and haven't stopped since." He chuckled. "Well, there've been the occasional moments when we've found other things to do."

"I hope I can meet him, Patrick. Maybe when Ardis gets moved in."

"Sooner than that, probably. You know I'll be back at Brookton next week when classes begin."

"Yes, but I'm going to be here at home for a while. Doctor's orders."

"I thought you said you're okay?"

"A precaution. You know doctors. Anyway, is this just a check-in call?"

"I wanted to tell you about something I've sent you. You'll probably get it in a couple of days."

"A care package?"

"I wish it were."

"Sounds ominous." The dread I'd felt the night Milou called to tell us my grandfather had died came over me. As soon as I had heard the phone ring, as soon as my mother answered it, I knew it was bad news. Even though my grandfather had been ill for several years, even knowing he wouldn't recover, didn't blunt the force of that news when it came. Patrick's apologetic tone was enough to alert me. Whatever he had to tell me, I'd regret hearing it.

"It's a copy of the table of contents of the winter issue of *Literary Trends*. Hot off the press."

"And?" I leaned against the wall.

"Danielle's got an article in it. It's about *Le Grand Meaulnes*."

"Let me guess. It's about the hero."

"And that would be François, not Augustin. I managed to get a copy of the page proofs—from my friend at Columbia, who edits *LT*. All your reasons and many of your examples, if I'm not mistaken, and no attributions, except an acknowledgment of the seminar. I am devastated for you. And hate myself for finding it. But I had to send it to you. I figured it would be better for you to get it now. I feel like I'm stabbing you in the heart."

"That can't be much worse than being stabbed in the back, can it?"

"I am so sorry . . ."

"Yes. Me too. I can't say . . . I'll have to call you back."

When it arrived, I skimmed the article, tripping over my own words, phrases I had struggled with, trying to describe as accurately as possible the way the novel worked. Fury that Danielle had done this, disbelief that Hal Rose had been complicit, stunned me. I had to hand it to both of them. Only someone who knew my paper, such as Patrick or Jack—and Danielle and Hal, of course—would recognize my ideas lightly rephrased and repackaged in this piece.

Scholarly journals like *Literary Trends* typically didn't publish work by first-year graduate students. Although Hal Rose wasn't named as co-author, Danielle had cited the seminar in the first footnote and referred to him by name in support of her interpretation. It was clear that he had helped her to get the article into *LT*. How I wished I could show it to Jack. Even he wouldn't defend what Danielle had done, or Hal Rose's part in it.

I knew I had to decide—about Jack and about Brookton.

September 16, 1970

Ardis put the last box in the trunk of my car. "Call me?"

"Soon. I'll come into the city in a couple of weeks, after you're settled. Maybe sometime when Patrick is free."

"I want to meet him. And Guy, too, of course."

Ellis wouldn't be back from France until late September. Matt was in Wyoming visiting his parents. No one had seen Danielle—or Hal Rose—all summer, although everyone seemed to think they were together. Somewhere.

In the late-afternoon light, its windows deeply shadowed, Ellis's house looked abandoned. What had I expected, exactly? I had taken advantage of its proximity to the library and the high school. The house had done that part of its job very well. Even the house-sitting arrangement had worked out. Everything else was like the clutter in the corner of a room, waiting for someone to clear it out.

I needed time to understand what the publication of Danielle's article meant to me and what to do about it. The misgivings I'd had about Brookton a year ago had returned in force. Only now, they weren't just the product of my own uncertainty and lack of confidence. The way ambition seemed to drive everyone, I had been right about that from the first. No amount of explaining or reassurance that this was how it worked could change the fact that this wasn't what I wanted. Now that my leave of absence request had been approved, I'd have plenty of time—at least a term—to think over my options and make a plan.

I had *had* a plan, a good one, as well as hopes for a different life from the one I had known. I could feel Augustin Meaulnes again, my shadow. Like him, I'd watched my hopes and my commitments fail. What could I have done differently?

"That's it, then. Do you know you're the only part of this summer I don't regret?"

Ardis smiled. "What are you going to do about Jack?"

"I've written to him. No word yet. I don't have any illusions, you know."

September 24, 1970

"It's me." He had had to raise his voice over the static when he called the first time. Today, an echo gave each word the same hollow emphasis.

"Are you okay?" I'd had a letter from him the day before, describing his routine, his walks around the neighborhood, and the salesgirls in the Bon Marché across the street, who dressed and behaved like models or movie stars.

"Yeah, fine. Everything's fine. I'm calling from the PTT on the Boulevard Raspail. The phone in the apartment isn't working. Typical!" He made a noise. Scoffing or laughing? I couldn't tell.

I knew the French phone booths. A man as tall as Jack would have to hunch over to fit into a space meant for someone a half-foot shorter. Maybe he was leaning against the wall, his knees bent, looking out the door into the lobby. In order to call before the PTT closed at six o'clock p.m., he had to get there by five o'clock, at the latest. There was usually a line of people buying stamps, mailing packages, depositing or cashing checks, or placing calls to relatives or friends living abroad.

At this time of the day, there was often a delay making the connection to international numbers; all the overseas lines were busy. Besides, in France, making a phone call was still a complex transaction—at least for everyone who didn't yet have a private phone. It was eleven thirty a.m. in Long Meadow, late-afternoon in Paris. There, at five thirty, people were hurrying home, stopping along the way to shop for dinner.

"The library is a pain, as expected. I sign in, give them all the cards filled out for the books I want, and then wait hours to get anything. But I told you that in my letter. Did you get it?"

There was nothing quite like the Bibliothèque Nationale, France's national library. It had closed stacks and uniformed circulation staff like judges on a dais looking out over the bowed heads of laboring scholars, with pages who located and delivered books to them. Still, for all the library's inconvenience, to hold an original manuscript, or a first edition, made it all worthwhile. You were touching a page created long ago, perhaps hundreds of years ago, by someone like you, who grasped a pen and made a connection between his thought, the page, and—now—you.

In the month he'd been in France, Jack had written five letters. Just-the-facts-Mac letters, my mother called them when I told her they read like reports that could have been written by anyone, anywhere.

"It came yesterday, actually. What about mine? Did you get the one I sent last week?"

"That's why I'm calling. I hope you haven't finalized your leave?"

"The dean signed off yesterday."

"This is truly a terrible idea, Malorie. You need to get back to work and get through this year so you can begin your dissertation. Why waste a term?"

"I disagree. Anyway, it's too late."

"I really hoped I could talk you out of it." The echo made it seem like he was shouting at me. "Have you talked to Hal?"

"No."

"I just don't get it."

I looked out the window, trying to figure out how to get through this. Of course he didn't get it, because he could see only the ends—in my case as well as Danielle's.

"Let me see if I can make it any clearer. Danielle plagiarized my paper, Jack. The article she wrote will be published as her own work. I need to decide what to do about it. On my own. In my own way. Getting away from Brookton for a term will help me. This isn't about the *right* way or *wrong* way. It's about what I want.

I *want* to take time off. Besides, I really can't imagine facing her, or Hal, right now."

"Couldn't you at least go talk to Hal? Hear him out? There must be some explanation."

It was just like Jack to expect that an explanation, whatever it might be, would convince me to ignore what Danielle had done.

"Suppose I do go to Hal; suppose I show him—although he must know this—all the things Danielle used, practically verbatim, from my paper. Which she could only have gotten from him, by the way. Then what? What possible explanation can he come up with that will alter that fact? She submitted an article for publication that is not her work. I can't hold the *Literary Trends* editors responsible. They're victims in this as much as I am."

"Well, you can't go to the dean. There'll be an investigation. Danielle will likely be thrown out. And who knows what the repercussions will be for Hal. Have you considered that?"

"So?"

"Is that really what you want? Don't you want to finish your degree and teach? Don't you realize that if you expose Danielle, you'll only be hurting yourself?"

"You mean if I go to Hal about this or if I go to the dean first?"

"The dean. Look, if you go to Hal first and tell him you know about the plagiarism, you'll have him where you want him. He'll have to help you, especially if you let him think you plan to go to the dean."

Blackmail? I had a stomach cramp from the strain of sitting still, from listening and not reacting. I couldn't believe he would propose this idea; that, knowing me, he would expect me to take it seriously. I had to get off the phone. "I'll think it over. I've got to go now." I hung up before he could reply.

As soon as I put the phone down, I knew. However I might have felt about Jack once, there was nothing left, not even regret. Like festering thorns, my year at Brookton, and our time together, had risen to the surface, where I could grab and remove them and clean the wounds.

Danielle's article had given me the reason and motivation I needed to take a term off. The miscarriage and my conversation with Jack had freed me to leave Brookton for good. I had only to file an additional piece of paper to turn my leave of absence into a withdrawal.

This I planned to do as soon as I could.

September 29, 1970

"You're going to write to him?"

Her tone told me what she thought of that idea. Ardis was right. Breaking up with Jack by letter was a lousy idea. But I couldn't do it any other way.

"I'd rather tell him in person. But short of going to Paris, that's not possible. And I can't wait for him to come back. I've got to move on."

"This is about the miscarriage, too, isn't it?"

"In part. He still doesn't know I was pregnant. I can't explain this very well, but I realized we had nothing more to say to one another even before Danielle's article came up. At that point, I didn't know how to break it off. Then I decided I had to leave Brookton. All the threads, all the connections snapped at the same time. If I tell him about the miscarriage, he won't be able to help himself; he'll want to talk about it. I can't bear going through that. It's better that he not know and better that we split up."

"Because?"

"Because I know what he'll say and I can't bear to hear it."

"What?"

"That it's a good thing I miscarried because now we don't have to argue about what to do."

"That would be hard to take. From anyone."

"The other thing is I can't stay with someone who has such a dodgy sense of right and wrong. It was wrong for Danielle to plagiarize my paper, wrong for Hal Rose to turn a blind eye. If the only way to get the degree is to compromise everything I believe in, it's not worth it."

"Is that it?"

"Well, I can't stomach the idea of becoming a *cause célèbre*. Which is what I'll be if I report Danielle to the dean."

November 5, 1970

The day Ardis and I had decided to meet at the Metropolitan Museum of Art was clear and cold, an early November day when every traffic light, every street sign, every neon sign stood out in sharp relief against the buffs and grays of Manhattan's sidewalks and skyscrapers.

As I walked up Fifth Avenue, wrapped in the city's sights and sounds, my almost fourteen months as a graduate student seemed like an excerpt from someone else's life. If this were a novel, how the heroine dealt with the aftereffects of her miscarriage and her mentor's betrayal—this is now how I saw it—would make a fine turning point. What would the character do next? Where would she go? What life lessons had she learned?

I took in the roasted chestnut vendors, families with young children, and couples people watching. Maybe I would apply for a high school teaching job, or something in publishing. Or travel. I had inherited some money from my father, but it was held in a trust for my children. If I remained childless until I reached forty, the money would be mine. So I needed to find a way to support myself. My mother had suggested I find a lawyer who could figure out a way to break the will. But I wanted a clean slate. And no loose ends. I laughed. That sounded too good to be possible or true. It was, nevertheless, my goal.

Several passersby smiled at me.

I was going to talk to Ardis and to Milou. Surely I could come up with a plan.

ALL TWENTY-THREE of Monet's paintings of the village of Fresselines date from March and April 1889, when he stayed with a friend who had a house near where the Petite Creuse and the Grande Creuse meet. In the group are landscapes featuring the river and its surroundings, as well as close-ups of water rushing along past rock-strewn banks.

Waiting for Ardis, I walked through the gallery, taking in Monet's lavender, blue, and pink palette, unquestionably evoking spring. The brushwork was energetic and lush, as if he were trying to seize the landscape by the armful, or gulp it in, impatient to capture its essence. I sat on a bench across from *Rapides sur la Petite Creuse à Fresselines*. Without the context provided by the other, more general, views of the spot, you wouldn't be able to identify the place. Maybe that was the point: there was something universal, archetypal about the unbridled rush of the water across the canvas.

You could sense how much Monet wanted to express the feel of the water's surface, hectic and vital as it changed direction over the flow of the deep green current underneath. There was something inevitable and violent about the surging water, carrying everything with it, invincible, unstoppable, wild, and free, a powerful sense of its force.

"Malorie? What is it? What's happened?"

I couldn't speak. I was standing in the river, feeling the rush of water over and through me. Ardis sat and held me.

"This painting . . ." I felt as if I had found my way into Monet's mind, as if I could see the movement of the brush, feel him pacing, energized, as his eye and hand connected deeply with how he understood the river.

"What I like is the wildness." Ardis looked at the canvas; her eyes narrowed.

"It seems so intimate, though, doesn't it?"

"Intimate, yes. The close-up feeling. The thing is, there's nothing in the painting that tells us we're looking at water except that frothy surface. Those stones or clumps of plants along the bank of the stream—it's a stream, or a small river, right?—they look almost as agitated as the water. But, we know they're not water, because the perspective gives us a clue: the bank rises away from the edge of the stream, uphill. Still, it's as though once Monet got started on the water, he realized the textures of water, stones, and plants—at least in this place—were similar."

"It's the light. He talks about that."

We sat there for a while longer. We both knew the garden at Giverny and agreed that Monet's eye for the river water in motion, and the way it reflected the light, had shifted in his later works to focus on the interplay between the water lilies and the pond's calm surface. Nevertheless, Ardis agreed: Monet had captured a sense of the place, as if it were only here that water, light, plants, and stones could produce this effect.

Ardis took the bus with me down to Port Authority. We went to Nedick's and bought coffee to go. We had half an hour.

"You'll write to Jack soon?"

"Tomorrow. I'll have to get going on withdrawing from Brookton, too."

"Are you going to call Hal Rose?"

"No. Maybe I'll write him a Dear John letter, too."

Ardis smiled. "And then?"

I laughed. "Maybe I'll hibernate."

November 19, 1970

I didn't hear from Jack for two weeks. I had tried to let him down gently, blaming myself—my confusion and uncertainty—for my decision. I didn't know how he would react. Did it really matter?

As uncertain as I was about my future, one thing was clear. It didn't include Jack.

Then he called twice a day for several days in a row. My mother took one of the calls and talked to him briefly.

"More than anything else, he sounds worried. Call him; tell him you're all right." She shook her head. "No matter how you explained it in your letter, maybe he just wants that reassurance. Is that so hard to understand?"

"But that's exactly why I don't want to talk to him. I know it's over, even if he doesn't. Nothing he can say or do will change that."

"Since that's how you feel, it won't matter if you talk to him, will it? Maybe that will satisfy him and he'll stop calling. Would you at least think about it?"

"Yes. But only if you promise not to bring it up again."

I called Jack on impulse. If he wasn't there, at least I could tell my mother I'd tried.

He picked up on the first ring. "Malorie!"

"Just hear me out, would you? Everything I said in the letter is true. I'm not ready to have a full-time, committed relationship—with anyone. I need to figure out what I want to do, and all I know right now is that Brookton isn't the place to do it. I really need to find something else."

"Don't you mean *someone* else?"

"Please don't put words in my mouth. I've been feeling so disconnected from myself that I don't know who I am anymore. The Danielle article really got to me. I have to start over."

"The way I see it, you're quitting. Giving up on Brookton. And me."

You? Not a word of concern about me, then or now.

"Maybe you're right. Maybe I'll regret this later on. But that's something I have to find out for myself." There was the sound of a police siren, then an ambulance, perhaps nearby on the Boulevard Raspail. I imagined the traffic slowing, drivers wondering about the emergency, relieved it wasn't them this time or annoyed they would be late for dinner or a date. "Jack, please . . ."

I heard his breath catch, then silence, then the dial tone.

November 30, 1970

"*Bien dormi?*" Milou poured hot water into the filter of the Melitta coffee pot, careful not to overfill it. A pitcher of hot milk, a loaf of bread on a breadboard, a bowl of jam, and a butter plate sat on a tray next to the stove.

"*Sur mes deux oreilles!*" I kissed her cheek. "I don't understand how people can sleep on their own two ears. Do you?"

"Oh, you know . . . we French like to make things difficult." She laughed with me. "But, it's just as hard to figure out the English expression 'to sleep like a log.' Don't you think?"

As she moved from the stove to the cupboard to the refrigerator, Milou's slippers flapped against her feet and the tile floor. I smiled.

"What, *chérie?*"

"Wouldn't you like some new ones—new slippers?" I knew her views about replacing anything that still worked, no matter how dilapidated or threadbare. A brand-new electric coffee pot had sat in the same spot in the pantry, gathering dust, since the day it arrived, five (or six?) years ago. No one knew where its cord ended up. As for the Melitta pot, it was chipped, the handle glued and re-glued, and the original ceramic filter top was long gone.

She stood still for a moment. The sadness in her eyes made me regret teasing her.

"You know these are your grandfather's. They remember the shape of his feet so well. It's as though I'm walking in his footsteps."

Although my grandfather had died in 1966, my sophomore year at Alden, Milou always spoke of him in the present, as if he had just stepped out for a moment.

I carried the breakfast tray into the living room and set it on the coffee table so we could look out into the garden. It was sleeting now; occasional squalls blocked the view of the stone wall and the woods beyond. The birdfeeder hanging just outside the window swung wildly from side to side, and wind gusts plunged down the chimney, causing the fire to sputter and smoke.

During the night, listening to the wind, I felt comforted, safe in the familiar room under the eaves. Nothing had changed—the thick French cotton sheets that smelled faintly of lavender and fresh air; the creaking of the bedstead's wooden slats whenever I turned over; the goose-down duvet, its linen cover cool to the touch. Once, when I was little, I had seen a clutch of young goslings nestled under their mother. From then on, under the comforting weight of the duvet, I thought of them, safe and warm, just like me.

I remembered other times over the years, lying awake in this bed, looking into the dark. It had always felt the way I imagined a nest might feel. I knew now there was more to it. The house was so much a part of Milou that it had become an extension of her very being, as if her spirit filled its every nook and cranny.

She was telling me about her plans for the day, about a neighbor who usually took her shopping. "Even if he feels like it, I won't go. Not in these conditions. Besides, the stores will probably open late and close early. I heard on the radio there have been power outages. And flooding. Anyway, the storm isn't supposed to last more than a day. There's nothing I need that can't wait."

I followed her gaze out into the garden. The sleet had changed to snow, now swirling thickly around the house.

Milou turned to me. "So, here we are, my darling. Just the two of us, snowed in for the day . . ."

Her tone of voice, just like the Monet painting, released me. The tears came, softly at first. When I sobbed, Milou held me close until I caught my breath.

"*Pauvre petite. C'est terrible, le chagrin.* But I know you. And I know life. However much it hurts now, it will get better. *Promis, juré!*"

I smiled at this expression, an approximate equivalent of "cross my heart and hope to die!" From the time I was a little girl, Milou had spoken these words of assurance, as if they were enough to guarantee the future. And always, I took heart.

"Take your time, my darling. There's no rush."

She knew I had dropped out, but I hadn't told her much else. As I put into words my disappointment, my doubts about myself and my work, Milou nodded. After a while, it felt as if I were hearing the story for the first time myself. I began to see my fears and my missteps in a new light.

"I rushed into the decision to go to Brookton. I know that. I liked the idea of it, yes. And I didn't want to go to law school. It was time for me to go, especially with the divorce going on. I couldn't stay.

"I really didn't know much about what I was getting into. There is no comparison between Alden and Brookton. None at all. I could do the work, and I was beginning to enjoy the teaching. But most of the time, I felt like I was being brainwashed, having to spout ideas that weren't mine in a jargon I didn't understand— that really made it hard."

"What about that friend of yours? What about Jack?"

"It's strange. There are so many things about him that I like . . . that I liked, I should say. He's intense and smart. He's passionate about Lamartine, especially about tracking down things no one else knows. But I figured out he didn't really want to know me better. There were times when I felt like just another item he wanted to fit into his scheme of things.

"He knew his way around. He seemed confident, at ease. Of course that appealed to me, since I was mystified most of the time. As I got to know him, I couldn't understand how he could accept the games and the artificiality. And the way he could always make the ends justify the means. Then I began to have questions about my feelings for him."

Milou squeezed my hand.

"I thought about calling you."

She looked at me, puzzled. "Why didn't you?"

"I didn't want you to worry, and I wanted to try to figure it out for myself, you know?"

Milou nodded. "I need to move around. But I want to keep talking. Let's just put the food away and get some more wood for the fire."

I WENT through the kitchen and out into the garage to get the wood. Once, the garage had been a small barn with a hayloft, sheltering a cow or two and chickens. Now, Milou's Peugeot, a workbench and tools, a freezer, and the woodpile occupied most of the available space.

I selected several logs and put them into the canvas carrier. As I walked back to the kitchen, passing behind the car, I saw a chickadee lying on its side in a puddle of water that had seeped under the garage door. I put the wood down and picked the bird up. It shuddered and opened its eyes, looked at me, and nestled into my hand.

"Milou!"

She came to the door. I held out the shivering bird to her. "Can we find something to put him in? Until he dries out?"

Milou got a berry basket from the pantry and lined it with a soft clean cloth. She made a nest of cheesecloth and patted it into place. As soon as I set the chickadee down, it gave a loose strand of the cheesecloth a little shake and peered at us, seemingly unafraid.

"I feel like Thumbelina." The story had always appealed to me.

"But she rescued a *hirondelle*, yes?"

"A swallow, that's right."

Milou and I had read the Hans Christian Andersen story together many times, in French and in English. With every reading, I dreaded the ending more, to the point that Milou stopped before the swallow's flight out of Thumbelina's life. Looking down into the basket, where the chickadee had settled down, I knew it was too early to tell if it would survive its misadventure.

After Milou called her neighbor to reschedule their shopping trip, she came back to the living room. The fire was burning evenly again, thanks to the fresh supply of wood. I placed the chickadee's basket on the hearth, close enough to benefit from the warmth, where we could keep an eye on it.

"I had a letter from Isabelle last week. She doesn't write often, but when she does, she always writes pages and pages. I can hear her voice. After I finish one of her letters, I feel like we've had a good visit!"

"Is everything okay?"

"Oh, yes. I'll let you read it yourself, if you'd like."

"Can you tell me the highlights?"

"The biggest news is about making plans for Jeanne's *centenaire* in August. They're already starting to plan it, to make sure people who live far away can come. Jeanne has never met Ted's daughter— her only great-grandchild—so she hopes they'll be there. They named her Annie, after Ted's mother."

I didn't know what to say. Until hearing this news, Ted's marriage had been something I knew in a disconnected kind of way, like the periodic table. It had nothing to do with me, with my life. The news about Jeanne's hundredth birthday celebration, and that Annie might be there with Ted, made it as real as the small bird sitting in the basket on the hearth. I could easily imagine Ted racing his bike—no hands—down Flagy's narrow main road when we were kids. And I saw the sunlight on Saint-Thibaut's tower. I even imagined I could hear the bells of Jeanne's goats. They were real to me, too.

"What is it, *chérie*?"

"It's odd to hear about people I know, people my age, who have children. Since the miscarriage, I've thought about it. The idea of having a child. I had such a crush on Ted that last summer. So did Louise. But you knew that, didn't you?"

"I guessed, yes. But you didn't want to talk about it. I understood. It's possible not to talk about some things, even with people you trust. It's not that they're secrets, exactly. It's that if you talk about them, you can't dream about them anymore."

"I don't know if anything would have happened if we'd continued to see each other in Flagy. Ted was like an older brother. You know, to kids our age then, a three-year age difference is huge. Why are you shaking your head?"

"Jeanne and I spoke of this. We felt the same way about you and Ted, hoped you might marry. You can't imagine how we both longed for the connections to Flagy to continue in your generation. What better way than for the Granger and the Girard grandchildren to marry?" She gave a little laugh and shook her head.

"What?"

"I'll never forget the day he brought you back to the house, after you fell off the fence. Jeanne and I were thrilled—of course we were sorry for you, that awful gash on your leg—but we were happy because we both thought this accident of yours was a sign." She squeezed my hand.

"Here's some more good news. Isabelle and Luc bought a piece of land just outside Flagy. They're thinking about building another greenhouse, but they don't want to rush things, especially now."

Luc and Isabelle were both five years younger than my mother. For the last fifteen years, they had been living in Milou's parents' home, working together in the nursery business they had started.

"Why do they have to wait?"

"Béatrice, the young woman who works for them, is pregnant. Her first. She told them a month ago she doesn't plan to come back to work until the baby is old enough for nursery school."

"That means two or three, right?"

"*C'est ça, oui.* She could put the baby into a *crèche*—for day care—but she wants to take care of the little one herself."

"So Isabelle and Luc need someone to help them?"

Milou smiled at me, nodding. "It will be hard to find a temporary replacement, they think."

"Unless it's someone who isn't looking to stay."

"*Précisément.*"

"Milou!"

I laughed. When I finally caught on, her delight that her ploy had succeeded could not have been more obvious.

"*Pourquoi pas?* You love gardens. And Flagy. And you have time now to do what you want. Why not go to France for a while? I know Isabelle and Luc would be pleased if you did."

"You haven't written to them?"

"*Bien sûr que non!* I haven't said a word to anyone about this idea. Do you think I want to spoil it?"

We both heard the faint scratching noise at the same time. Only the chickadee's black cap was visible above the basket rim. I went to take a closer look.

"He's standing up, shaking his feathers."

"*Montre-moi!*" Milou held out her hand to take the basket.

As she reached over, I picked it up and set it on her lap. We both watched the little bird preen, stopping every so often to look around, examining us and the nest we had made for him with bright, inquisitive eyes.

"I always love watching the chickadees at the feeder in the winter. They are so greedy. And full of themselves."

I put the basket on one of the bookshelves next to the fireplace.

"He'll be happy to be out and about again."

The sky had begun to brighten; the wind had died. We could wait a day, we agreed, before releasing the chickadee. In the meantime, he would be able to eat his fill without fear of being chased away by the other birds.

THE NEXT morning, the storm-swept sky shimmered behind the dark, bare branches of the maple trees. The chickadee had spent the night in the laundry room. When I opened the door, he was standing in the middle of the floor. With a flutter of his wings, he hopped back into his basket and looked up at me.

Milou stuck her head in the door. "He's waiting for room service, of course." She scooped some sunflower seeds from the bag on the shelf over the washing machine and scattered them on the floor. With a small, satisfied "Cheep!" the bird hopped down to the floor and began to eat. "He looks right at home, doesn't he?"

As soon as I placed the basket on the ground, the chickadee hopped up onto the edge and looked around. Convinced that he was in his own garden, he shook himself and flew up to perch on the rain gutter.

In the kitchen at the sink, Milou turned when I came in.

"He seems happy to be back out there with the rest of the gang."

"So, what do you think of my idea, *chérie*?"

"If they want me . . . I want to do it."

Milou clapped, then hugged me. "I will call them today."

By the time I had gone to bed the night before, I had made up my mind. I had sat up for a while, thinking about what it meant to go away, perhaps for as long as two years. I was postponing the decision I knew I had to make about what I wanted to do with my life. But, having made a false start at Brookton, I wanted to avoid another one. This opportunity would give me time to think about my next step. Milou was right. The pleasure I took in plants and gardens was so much a part of me it had become as natural as breathing. Could it develop into more than that?

Besides, I loved Isabelle and Luc. Childless themselves, they had always treated me like a daughter. And then there was the village of Flagy. I had missed spending the summer there more than I had realized.

"This will be good for you, and for Isabelle and Luc. As for me, it's a dream come true."

"How do you mean?"

"I've always wanted you to go to Flagy to live, if only for a short time. The visits when you were little were one thing. This won't be the same. Now you're grown up. That changes everything." Before Milou could explain what she meant, the telephone rang. "I'm sure that's my neighbor. If I don't answer, he'll come up here to check on me."

I caught bits and pieces of the conversation. The man seemed to be doing his best to convince her to let him do her shopping for her and was losing the battle.

When Milou came back to the kitchen, she was laughing. "He's the little old lady, not me. Really! Too conscientious by half. But our arrangement works for us. He keeps the car running fine. And I like him, which is the main thing."

"What did you mean about its being a dream, my going to live in Flagy?"

"If we had never left Flagy in the first place, if there had been no war, if Henri hadn't disappeared, I would have stayed in Flagy. I'm certain of that." She took my hand in both of hers.

"Did I tell you that Henri came back? We lost touch for more than thirty years. Imagine! Then, one summer, when we all were back there—you were just a little girl—I found out he was married, living in Cluny. He's still there in his family's house, restoring antiques. He keeps the shop open three days a week." She seemed far away. "Henri, Jeanne, Suzette, and I—we're the only ones left. They have stories to tell about before the war. And after, of course. You'll meet the others, talk to them. And you'll write to me about them, won't you? It's as if my life were starting over, with something old and something new. There's the past, meeting the present, in that place I love so much." She looked at me. "That's what I'm talking about."

We spent the rest of the day looking through photo albums, including one I had never seen. In it, Milou had organized snapshots of her brothers and her friends from the village, from 1912 until 1914. "That's Henri. He was fourteen." She ran her finger along the edge of the photo of the grinning boy, hands in his pockets, standing with several others outside the old school. Although it was hard to make out his features, he seemed older than the others and not at all self-conscious about having his picture taken.

"Who's that?" I pointed to the dark-haired boy at the edge of the group. Standing there, his eyes fixed on the distance beyond the photographer, he seemed impatient, restless, maybe bored.

"That's Théo, Théodore Girard, Jeanne's eldest. A painter, a very talented one, but so angry, always so angry. He ran away. And he never came back." Milou had the faraway look in her eyes again. "Jeanne never forgave herself for letting him go. He and Henri were best friends." She turned the page and said in a low voice, "Ted is his namesake."

Had I ever known this? I couldn't remember. I wondered what it must have been like for Ted to be named after an uncle he never knew, who left home, never to return. I wondered, too, how Ted's father, Bruno Girard, felt, left alone at home with his aging parents, abandoned by his older brother.

Would I learn the answers to these questions, now that I would be living there on my own? One thing was certain. Together before the Great War, these children had dispersed into a much wider world, to become adults, parents, professionals. Bruno and Milou had emigrated; Henri and Suzette came back again and settled. Théo's disappearance, the mystery of it, lurked behind their story, a somber reminder of the uncertainty of life in France during those years, even in the small villages like Flagy.

"Suzette and me at Easter in 1912. We were so proud of those hats!" In this photo, their shoulder-length hair in braids, the two girls looked enough alike to be sisters. Wearing pinafores, carrying baskets filled with spring flowers, they held their heads high. The photographer had caught them just as a passing breeze lifted the ends of the ribbons tied around their hat brims, the fabric floating over their shoulders.

Milou closed the album, running her hand over its leather cover, as if reassuring herself these mementos and the memories they evoked remained unchanged. She pulled a small wooden box from the drawer of the side table and handed it to me. The shape and size of a deck of cards, the box had a mother-of-pearl honeysuckle blossom set into its lid. When I opened it, I found a handmade envelope, its edges yellow with age. It contained a dried honeysuckle flower.

"Henri made this and brought it to me the day he left Flagy to join up. He promised me he would find me when the war ended." Milou shrugged. "Then he disappeared. Like Théo. Except that he came back, long after I had left Flagy for good, after your grandfather and I were married." She stopped and leaned back, gazing out the window into the garden. "It wasn't until years later that Jeanne wrote to tell me."

For a while, we sat without talking. Milou ran her hand over the arm of the chair, as if clearing her mind. "So much time, so many memories." She smiled. "Would you do something for me?"

I reached for her hand. "Anything."

"I want to know everything, see everything through your eyes."

"I'll write to you as much as I can, as often as I can. *Promis, juré!*"

"And we'll have a real visit soon."

"Soon?"

"At the party for Jeanne."

"You'll be there?"

"I wouldn't miss it, not for anything."

PART 2

FLAGY, SAÔNE-ET-LOIRE

1971–1975

Henri and Théo

The market was just ahead in the square near the abbey. "When I finish, I'll wait for you here, *d'accord?*" Isabelle squeezed into a space on the *rue du Merle*.

Her look of concern prompted a rush of adrenaline, as though I were facing an exam, unprepared.

"*Ça va?*"

I had a cramp in my right calf, and when I tried to swallow, my tongue stuck to the roof of my mouth. "I still think my just showing up at the shop will be too much of a shock."

Isabelle pursed her lips and shook her head. "You'll see. When you meet him, you'll understand."

Earlier, when we planned this visit, Isabelle had convinced me that this was the right approach. "Meeting you will be a surprise, yes. A phone call? That would be a shock."

Now she nodded and smiled. "You'll be fine."

"But will he?"

She brushed her hand through the air. "Of course."

I had promised Milou I would remember all the details, be her eyes and ears, take in Henri's tone of voice, his expression, anything that might reveal his feelings. That responsibility caused as much anxiety as my concern about Henri's reaction to learning who I was.

Like old photographs, some parts of Milou's story had faded. Others remained as familiar to me as events in my own life. But now, seeing places Milou had known as a young girl, I could imagine her sorrow after the move from Flagy to Lyon and, later, her sense of abandonment when Henri disappeared. I wondered what it had been like to leave her family, her daily life, her language—everything that had made her who she was. Did she think then that marrying my grandfather and moving to the States was the only way forward, the only way to free herself from heartbreak?

All along the *rue du Merle*, clusters of shoppers, string bags or baskets in hand, their children trailing them, headed toward Cluny's *Place du Marché*. I turned away from them onto the *Impasse des Quatre Vents*. Restricted to pedestrians, the cobblestoned street smelled of old stone, and moss, and centuries of small-town life, quietly lived.

My footsteps echoed; pigeons cooed and fluttered from eave to eave above me. Dust motes gleamed in the sunbeams, falling into the shadows below. I could imagine the clatter of horse-drawn carts and carriages, the cry of street vendors plying their wares from house to house. The murmur of water dripping from a downspout onto the stones somewhere just ahead grew louder as I walked toward the end of the passage, toward Henri's shop.

Balcony windows opened to the beamed ceilings of apartments and studios and glimpses of wall hangings, paintings, and photographs. Geraniums and nasturtiums crowded the window boxes, unfurling their lavish blooms over narrow ledges and iron balustrades.

The first-floor galleries and shops had window displays, the artisans' names lettered on the windows or on small placards affixed to the window frames. One window showed colorful stoneware; another displayed a silversmith's work—brooches, pendants, and cuffs—gleaming with settings of mother-of-pearl and semiprecious stones. When I reached Henri's atelier, his display seemed austere by comparison.

Atelier Langlois flowed in gold script across the lower corner of the narrow plate-glass window. The glass looked new, but the dark-grained wood frame, with its oiled, hand-rubbed patina, had been patched in places to close the gaps between it and the surrounding stonework. Just inside, a mahogany tea table was perched on a dark red velvet cloth. According to the handwritten card on the table's inlaid top, the shop would open at eleven o'clock.

In fifteen minutes I would meet the man my grandmother had thought was lost to her forever. In fifteen minutes I would, I hoped, find a way to repair the broken link in their story so that it might continue. I shivered and straightened my jacket; my hands tingled.

I leaned close to the window, cupping my hands around my eyes to peer in at the tables and stacks of chairs crowding the middle of the room. Several armoires and breakfronts lined the walls. Finished pieces on display? Works in progress? I couldn't tell. No price tags or other markings indicated if these items were for sale.

At the far end of the counter, a jacket hung over a stool, its sleeves grazing the floor. Just beyond, shelves of tools and cans of wax or varnish filled the wall behind the workbench.

I heard the abbey clock strike eleven and opened the door. A buzzer sounded from the rear of the shop. It stopped when the door closed behind me.

"J'ARRIVE!"

I closed my eyes, savoring the sharp, clean smell of wood and varnish. The soft thuds of irregular footsteps approached from the back of the shop. A cane, perhaps? It wouldn't be surprising. He was seventy two.

Tanned and stocky, his right trouser leg folded and pinned up at the knee, Henri leaned on a crutch. A war wound? Surely

Isabelle knew. Just as surely, Milou didn't, or she would have told me.

What had happened to him? And when? During the Second World War? No, he would have been too old. The Great War, then. Henri smiled at me. Although it had been nearly sixty years since Milou's photograph of him was taken, the lively energy of his smile hadn't dimmed.

"*Bonjour, madame! Henri Langlois . . .*" His eyes went wide; the color drained from his face. He fumbled for the stool, reaching out to steady himself. "Excuse me, please." He pulled himself onto the stool and searched my face. "You look so much like someone else, an old friend, someone I haven't seen for years."

I started to tell him the story the way I had planned. But I realized it would be much simpler just to introduce myself. Whatever happened next, we'd take it from there.

"*Je m'appelle Malorie Ellsworth. Ma grand-mère, c'est Malorie Granger.*"

"*Malorie Granger? Ma Milou?*" He shook his head, baffled. "So my eyes don't deceive me. Your resemblance . . . You could be her." He pulled out a handkerchief and wiped his eyes. "Is she . . . ?"

"She's happy and well. At home." I stopped, uncertain how much he knew or had guessed about my grandmother. "At home in Vermont . . ."

"Of course, of course. This I know—at least this much. But the rest? There is so much I don't know. Where to begin? What to ask?" He took my hand and held it. "I'll make tea and we can talk. I have so many questions. You have shopping to do? Perhaps you would rather come back another day?"

I laughed. He looked confused.

"Yes, of course I want to come back. But I want to start now."

"*Allons-y alors . . .*" Henri smiled. "*Milou! Milou!* Incredible."

After locking the shop door and putting up the "closed" sign, Henri led me through the workshop into a narrow hallway. Rakes, hoes, and several different spades hung from hooks on the wall; a wheelbarrow and an assortment of flowerpots sat under the stairs. He opened the door to the garden and inclined his head. "*Je t'en prie*. After you, please."

I stopped there, at the threshold. Framed by the door, the terraced garden resembled a miniature from an illuminated manuscript. A low, tightly pruned boxwood hedge edged four parterres brimming with a rainbow of color: primroses, hyacinths, and daffodils.

"*Ça te plaît?* Do you like it?"

"Very much. *C'est ravissant.*" I stepped down to a stone patio and into the garden, inhaling the delicate fragrance that rose from the sun-warmed blooms. "It's so different from Milou's garden. I'll bring you photographs. You'll see."

He laughed. "Even as a girl, she loved lilies and roses—and color. I remember that. So I suppose her garden has masses of perennials. Yes?"

Of course he would know, without having seen Milou's garden, that this would be her preference.

"This garden, well, I planned it for my own convenience. The leg, that happened in the war, the first one." He gestured at a low cart that held a seat and box of gardening tools.

"I'm so sorry."

"It was a long time ago—almost sixty years. Memories fade; you get used to inconvenience." He looked out over the stone wall at the rooftops beyond.

"As you see, I can roll around on the paths while I prune the boxwood." He gestured back at the house. "My wife and I used to sit up there in the afternoon." He pointed to the second-story balcony with its French doors. "This is a garden you can enjoy from up there as well as from down here, but you enjoy it very differently depending on where you are." He smiled. "Please sit, Malorie. I'll go get the tea."

The parterres showed color, shapes, and textures to advantage. Although densely planted, the design had a simple system of knots and scrolls, one that displayed delight in pattern, echoing Henri's mastery of inlay as well as his love of plants. The stone wall that surrounded the garden on three sides supported the massive honeysuckle espaliered against it. The faint fragrance of the first open blossoms hinted at the glories to come.

At the sound of a pulley moving in the house behind me, I turned to see Henri remove a tea tray from the dumbwaiter that opened to the patio next to the shop's back door. I helped him arrange the tea things on the serving table and sat across from him.

"It is a cliché, I know, but I can't believe my eyes. You, here. Milou, your grandmother . . . Where to begin? I want to know everything about you both, but I want to savor the details. As you say, we can start today." He stopped. "You'll come back again, won't you?"

"*Promis, juré!*"

Talking to Henri was so much like talking to Milou; he had to ask me to slow down, or to explain something he didn't know, couldn't have known, because he wasn't Milou. As the shadows shifted under the sun, Henri and I pieced together her story and his.

He knew Milou had married an American botanist. He, too, had married. A schoolteacher. "*Elle est morte en 1969.*"

"*Et mon grand-père en 1966,*" I told him.

"It seems strange, doesn't it? We've had our lives, our separate lives. . ."

He didn't have to ask the question that hung in the air between us. I could see it in his eyes. *What will happen now?* His own son and daughter had left France to live abroad, one in England, the other in Canada. "But they, too, have separate lives. That's as it should be." He smiled and poured more tea.

For a time we sat watching the brilliant pinks, yellows, and purples pale as the sun moved higher. In the quiet of this garden, so similar to the quiet of Milou's, I could hear the occasional rustle of a bird in the honeysuckle and Henri's calm, steady breathing. "You speak like a native, really." He smiled, his eyes holding mine.

"Please tell Milou. She is a wonderful teacher! I've always spoken French with her."

He ran his finger around the handle of his teacup, then picked it up and drained it. "Why didn't she . . . ?" He looked at me, suddenly awkward, as if doubtful he had the right to ask.

"Why didn't she try to see you when we came over in the summer?" The relief I read in his eyes told me I had guessed right. "Being married to my grandfather made her wary, I think. Wary, that is, of unlocking the door to the past. She had a new life; Vermont was her home. She was determined not to change things."

Henri closed his eyes. When he opened them, he smiled. "I also had a good marriage." He leaned toward me, resting his hand on mine. "But I know I am certain of one thing." He squeezed my hand gently for emphasis. "Had things been otherwise, Milou and I would have married after the war. Still, I understand. It would have been awkward for her to visit. As long as your grandfather was alive." He patted his mouth with his napkin and cleared his throat. "She's coming for Jeanne's party?"

"She wouldn't miss it."

He beamed at me. "Then there's hope . . ."

He wanted to know more about the party, so I told him that planning for it had been well underway by the time I arrived in Flagy. In March, the newspaper had published the first of a series of articles about Jeanne's life.

Luc had showed me the first piece. "*Ça fait tout drôle.* I get goose bumps when I think that here, in this tiny corner of France, our simple lives go on and on. When I read about when Jeanne was young, about the events in our country, and in the world . . . We're here; life goes on as usual. Thanks to Jeanne, the past touches us right now, right here, in the present. It's bewildering, really."

Bit by bit, as we marshaled resources and made arrangements, the fact of Jeanne's age and the significance of her birthday gave way to our excitement about the celebration. Bruno Girard, Ted's father and Jeanne's elder son, had called Isabelle to let her know he had managed at last to clear his schedule. He, Ted, and my mother would arrive in Paris on the same flight.

As for Milou, all I knew for sure was that she planned to arrive at least two weeks ahead of time.

"Milou showed me the box you made for her."

His eyes drifted toward the stone wall and settled on the honeysuckle.

"And the honeysuckle blossom."

"I don't suppose you can still smell it?"

"The fragrance is very faint, but it's there."

He gave a little laugh and pushed his chair back. "I'd like you to see something. Can you stay a little longer?"

"Of course."

I heard him moving in the back of the shop and the sound of a cabinet door opening and closing. When he came out again, he held a small rectangular object wrapped in a paisley silk scarf, which he placed on the table in front of me.

"Please. Open it."

I removed the scarf and found the portrait of a smiling girl, her blond braids framing her face. Wearing a straw hat, she smiled at someone standing behind the painter. The interlaced initials, TG, and the date, June 1912, appeared in the lower right-hand corner.

"Beautiful, isn't she?" Henri lightly touched the girl's cheek, as if sensing her warmth.

The painter had captured an expression I knew well: Milou's eyes, their blue-green irises gemlike in their intensity, looked out at us with humor and affection. The straw hat's ribbons draped over the left side of the brim and fell to her shoulder in soft folds.

"Did she tell you about Théo Girard, Jeanne's older boy?" His eyes grave, Henri leaned his crutch against the chair and sat down.

"A little."

"We could have been brothers. We did everything together, always. He wanted to be a painter. I wanted to be an architect. We even talked about sharing a studio. Sometime I'll show you the building here in Cluny where we planned to put it." He shook his head, looking down into his hands folded on the table. "In the war; we don't know what happened. He just . . . vanished."

"And the painting?"

"I wanted a portrait of Milou. So Théo agreed to paint one. He had a sketch he made on the spot, the same day the photographer took the girls' Easter photograph. He had such a gift for conveying a person's expression, making it come alive on the canvas." He touched the portrait again, this time tracing Milou's upturned lips. "I used to have his sketch. . . ." He looked at me. "You've brought me something even more precious."

We sat awhile longer. Only the muffled noise of street traffic and the occasional footsteps of passersby disturbed the quiet. It was one o'clock when Henri wrapped the scarf around the painting and I cleared the table.

At the door, he took and held my hand. "You'll come back?"

"Soon."

"FÉLICITATIONS!" IN her excitement, Isabelle nearly missed the turnoff to Flagy, veering sharply left at the last minute. A loud blast of a car horn behind us startled us both. "Don't tell Luc . . ."

I laughed. "Of course not."

"Tell me again. Slower this time."

I repeated the details of my conversation with Henri. This time, she chimed in every once in a while. "Oui . . . C'est ça . . . Pourquoi pas?"

We'd just reached a stop sign, which gave her a chance to focus on me for a moment. "What's the matter?"

"We have to arrange for them to get together before the party."

"I'm sure Henri will invite her to lunch, probably without being asked. But I'll let him know her dates, once we hear from her."

I sighed and shrugged.

"Why is that a problem?"

"I want her to stay longer so they'll have more time after the party when things calm down. But I'd like her to think it's her idea." I couldn't control the outcome of Milou and Henri's reunion. Still, the party would be a distraction for both of them. They needed time together—alone.

"I'll write to her," Isabelle suggested. "I won't have much of a chance to talk to her ahead of time. I'll make that the excuse for her to stay longer." She made a face, one that managed to marry exasperation and forbearance. "Thankfully, if I live long enough, someone else will get to organize the party."

Although Jeanne's birthday was September 12, we had planned the celebration for Saturday, August 15. In August, during the *grandes vacances*, when almost everyone in France went on vacation, many relatives would visit family living in the village, especially over that long weekend, the Feast of the Assumption.

Isabelle showed me her letter to Milou the next day. "Tell me what you think about the last paragraph. That's the important one."

You won't have much time to visit with Jeanne, or anyone else, before the party because we'll all be so busy. Suzette keeps muttering that the only visitors we'll have time to talk to are the deliverymen. Wouldn't you like to stay a little longer?

"*Alors?*" Isabelle looked anxious.

"Perfect! It's relaxed, easy, as if you're planning one of her usual visits."

"Well, even if she reads between the lines—correctly—I very much doubt she'll let on. Anyway, as long as she says yes, we don't care, *pas vrai?*"

"That's right."

I gave Isabelle a pencil sketch I'd made of Henri to include with the letter. As soon as it was posted, I had second thoughts. "I hope we haven't gotten ahead of ourselves. Sure, they loved each other long ago. But they were only children, really."

Isabelle shrugged. "Even if we can't know how it will go with them, I am certain, absolutely certain, she will want to stay longer, just as I am certain she wants to see Henri as much as he wants to see her. Of course she wouldn't miss Jeanne's party. But we've given her a reason to stay longer, the best reason we can think of."

A week later, Milou's telegram arrived. *Arrive August 5. Depart September 15.*

Isabelle clapped. "Now the real fun begins."

"Real fun?"

"The matchmaking!"

August 5, 1971

"There she is!"

A porter held Milou's coat and handbag in one hand and supported her with the other as she got off the next-to-last car. Laughing at something he had said, she stopped on the second step and looked around. I waved; she waved back. She spoke to the porter, who turned and nodded, signaling with his cap that he had seen us, too. He placed her luggage on the baggage cart and offered her his arm.

As if by arrangement, by the time they reached us, the platform had emptied. Hugs and kisses, exclamations and laughter. And tears. Milou dried her eyes with her handkerchief. She gave the porter a tip; he handed her suitcase to Isabelle. "Shall we go?"

It had been a long trip for her: the drive to Boston from Alden; the flight to Paris; and the train to Lyon. She made an effort for our benefit, but her fatigue visibly slowed her down.

She reassured me. "Don't worry, *chérie*. I'm fine." She laughed a little. "I just can't believe I'm here. Ten years ago . . . I knew I would come back, but I never imagined it would take so long!"

I realized then it wasn't only fatigue that weighed on her. She was anxious—about how things had changed since her last visit and, surely, about seeing Henri again. As soon as we got to the car, she settled in the backseat with a sigh. She removed her jacket and placed it beside her on the leather seat. "*C'est à qui, la voiture?*"

"It's Suzette's car."

Isabelle glanced at me, then raised her eyes to look at Milou in the rearview mirror.

Suzette had insisted we take her Citroën. "How can she sleep if she's folded up like a can opener in your little truck? *Voyons, Isabelle, sois raisonnable!*" Isabelle knew better than to argue the point with Suzette. Secretly, I was elated. The truck had a tractor's suspension with a top speed of forty—on the flat.

"I couldn't possibly sleep now that I'm here." Milou leaned forward to pat my shoulder. "I'll have plenty of time to catch up later. But now, I want to hear the news. Tell me everything."

Once we were on the highway, Isabelle began with the stories: *fiançailles*, weddings, births and christenings, deaths and funerals. Milou interrupted occasionally to ask for details. I paid attention, trying to keep track of names and relationships.

"So many divorces! So many children!" Milou shook her head. "How many will come to the party?"

Isabelle looked rueful. We both laughed.

"What is it? What's so funny?"

"The number keeps changing," Isabelle sighed. "We asked people to let us know by last week." She shrugged. "We got three more calls yesterday. As of this morning, seventy-five are coming, a third of them have family still living in the village. *Je ne m'y attendais pas, vous savez.* Who could have imagined so many would come?"

"You know how much we love to *faire la fête*!" Isabelle glanced up and caught Milou's eye. "Jeanne's *centenaire* is more than a good enough reason to have a bash, don't you think?"

Milou leaned forward to pat Isabelle's shoulder. "I know it's been a lot of work for you. And I know you realize how much it means to Jeanne. It will be a wonderful party."

Milou and Isabelle had always gotten along, in part because Isabelle had a light touch and a ready laugh, just like her father, Milou's youngest—and favorite—brother, who had died in a car crash in 1960.

"Jeanne and Suzette and I have so much to talk about. We'll find a comfortable corner, out of the way, while the rest of you kick up your heels. I suppose Henri will be there?"

"Of course!" Isabelle said with a smile. She glanced in the rearview mirror.

Smiling at us both, Milou held up the sketch of Henri.

Once Isabelle turned off the highway, Milou sat back, gazing out the car window. From time to time, she clucked in dismay. As we passed through a hamlet, its Romanesque chapel now a chicken coop, she asked Isabelle to slow down.

"How can the commune let that happen?" She shook her head. "Of course it costs a lot to maintain these buildings, especially the ones damaged in the old days." She meant during and after the Revolution, when many old churches—even Cluny's great abbey—were vandalized. "But someone should figure out a way to do this, no? A small church like that, like Saint-Pierre . . ."

On the edge of the village of Brancion, itself a carefully preserved village, the *église* Saint-Pierre was among Burgundy's most beautiful examples of the Romanesque style.

I was happy to tell Milou that many in the commune agreed. "Henri and others are involved in restoration and preservation work now. He's the director of a small organization—all volunteers—that raises money to restore these old chapels."

"How do they do that?"

"They have performances and auctions, and they solicit from the big vintners, always. Now they have a plan to set up a special fund." Isabelle and Luc had taken part in these discussions.

"And Saint-Thibaut?" Over the years, several families in Flagy had spearheaded an independent effort to repair the stonework of Flagy's old church.

"You'll see!" Isabelle smiled back at her.

JEANNE HAD insisted Milou stay with her. "For once, my three spare bedrooms won't be empty. What good are all these rooms, all my *conforts*, if I don't put them to use? *C'est le grand luxe chez moi!*" She clasped her hands in pleasure, like a little girl. "Lucie and Milou each have a room; Bruno and Ted will share."

It had taken years to persuade Jeanne to install modern plumbing. She relented after Bruno threatened to stay in a hotel in Cluny when he came to visit. He arranged to have the work done as a gift on her ninetieth birthday. He had also installed an automatic watering mechanism for the goats.

"He makes such a fuss, my son." Jeanne loved to tease Bruno— and to joke about his modern ideas. "I will carry water to my girls until the day I die. I don't *need* this machine." Of course, she took every opportunity to show off the gadget to visitors. And to brag about her goats. "Being smart—they *are* goats, after all—they learned how to use it right away!"

When Isabelle pulled into Jeanne's driveway, Jeanne and Suzette came out to greet us. As soon as Milou got out of the car, they all began talking, each louder than the other, their exclamations and questions rising and falling like the swallows darting over the meadow across the road. Isabelle and I left them at Jeanne's kitchen table, drinking tea, absorbed in storytelling, and sifting through piles of photographs of grandchildren and great-grandchildren.

"I hope they'll let her take a nap."

Isabelle glanced back into Jeanne's kitchen. Leaning over the photos, the women's heads almost touched. "Too excited right now. But she'll sleep well for the next few days, I think."

At the house, Luc handed me a slip of paper. "Henri phoned awhile ago. He asked Milou to call him. He wants to make a lunch date."

Isabelle and I looked at each other and laughed. "First, we'll have to get her attention!"

WE ALL had dinner at Jeanne's that evening. Suzette and Jeanne had persuaded Milou to take a nap while they prepared the meal. Now she looked rested. And years younger. "All your favorite things, Milou. *Regarde les framboises!*" The raspberries in a bowl on the counter glowed in the late-afternoon sun.

As we ate, the women talked about the past, their children, and the changes in the world around their little village. "*Le village,* it hasn't changed. Only 137 *habitants*—almost the same as in 1871, when I was born!" Jeanne said this as if she had counted every head.

None of us mentioned the reason the village's population hadn't changed in a hundred years. Or that it was likely to get smaller still, once Jeanne and Milou's generations were gone. It was a fact of life that children who grew up on farms eventually left, reluctant to live the life of a small farmer, whose livelihood depended so much on the vagaries of nature and governments.

Luc caught my eye. He and Isabelle hoped their nursery would flourish, drawing a few more people to live and work in Flagy. Perhaps one day the commune would reopen the old school, closed now for nearly twenty years.

And then there were the summer and weekend people, the ones who bought the old farms, adding amenities, turning them into vacation homes or small hotels. This, too, would help Luc's business, but how would it change the character of the village and the valley?

After the meal, Suzette and Isabelle shooed everyone out of the kitchen while they cleaned up. Luc took his pipe and walked into the village. Milou and I sat on the verandah on Jeanne's settee.

"About Henri, Milou."

"*Oui, ma chérie?*"

"He phoned today to invite you to lunch."

"When?"

"He wants you to call him back."

She glanced at me. "You won't be joining us?"

The very idea made me laugh. "I'll drive you in. You can phone us when you're ready to come home."

Milou looked down at her hands, folded in her lap. "Talking earlier with Suzette and Jeanne about 1912, about our Easter hats, time disappeared—it is so strange to be so old and feel so young. I don't know quite what to think."

I took her hand. "There's something about this place. When I first arrived, it was like I was learning to walk again. Or as if I'd been ill for a long time and was just beginning to get well. I worked, slept, and ate. Even if I had wanted to do more, I couldn't have."

It had been for me the way Milou had described letting go of her grief that morning in Lyon, when she had heard her father's voice telling her it was over. "I woke up one morning in June, and the past was gone. Brookton, Jack, the miscarriage. And Dad. I had to repot five hundred seedlings that day. I could have repotted fifteen hundred. For the first time in months, I did some sketching. The pencil felt like a part of me again."

"As long as grief lasts, we feel like outsiders observing life, our own life, as if it were someone else's. Right after your grandfather died, I felt disconnected—from myself, from everyone."

"I remember."

For Milou, the worst part, the numbness, lasted only a few days. And then she found herself in a kind of limbo. It had seemed it would never end. "The small things, like weeding the garden, washing the kitchen floor, checking off each day on the calendar—that's what kept me going."

And then one day, she realized she was no longer frozen in time. "I looked out into the woods and noticed the first signs of fall." My grandfather had died in March, before the snow had melted, before the trees had begun to bud.

She turned to me. "This is something I never expected would come into my life again. I haven't forgotten the way Henri was then, the way I was then, so unafraid." She gave a little laugh. "So naïve. I know it sounds sentimental, but that memory—so vivid, as if we'd only parted a moment ago—gave me hope we would find each other again."

August 6, 1971

Hanging on the kitchen wall, Jeanne's copper pots reflected the morning sun into the corner behind the cast-iron stove. Squat and pot-bellied, it crouched there like a benevolent household spirit. Jeanne had been adamant: running water and new plumbing were all very well and good, but if Bruno wanted to install an electric stove, he would have to wait until after she was gone.

"You caught us!" Jeanne and Milou smiled up at me like a couple of six-year-olds. They appeared to have been up for hours. An empty coffee pot, a heel of crusty bread, and a cheese rind, remains of breakfast, had been pushed to the middle of the table.

"Gossiping." Milou rolled her eyes.

"That's the good thing about getting old. The only good thing!" Jeanne gave me a sidelong look. "There's so much more gossip. So many years, so many lives . . ." She laughed.

"Shall I come back in half an hour?"

"I'm almost ready. Come help me decide what to wear." Milou stood and folded her napkin.

On the bed she had laid out a mauve silk blouse and cream-colored linen trousers with a matching jacket next to a navy blue skirt and jacket. "No matter which outfit I choose, I'll wear white sandals. That part, at least, is easy." She frowned. "So?"

"The mauve, I think. It makes me think of spring. And, besides, it suits you. It makes your eyes sparkle." Milou wore her long hair in a braid wrapped and pinned around her head. Smooth waves framed her face, softening its lines and angles. Her blue-green eyes hadn't lost any of their intensity. I couldn't imagine a better choice than the mauve silk blouse. Something about the way she nodded and smiled at my selection made me think she had already made up her mind.

"Not too American?"

I could understand Milou's anxiety about what to wear. How much had her fifty years in America altered her? Although she had kept her French citizenship, she felt more American than French now. Even if she didn't dress like an American, would she seem American to Henri? Would it matter to him?

"You could wear a burlap bag and he wouldn't notice. Anyway, don't forget, Chanel made it chic for women to wear sportswear." I watched her eyes. "What are you thinking about?"

"I remember standing at the end of the road until Henri rounded the bend—out of sight, just like that. I didn't know if we'd ever see each other again. I'll never forget that moment."

AN HOUR later, I turned onto the *rue du Merle* toward the *Impasse des Quatre Vents*. "Nervous?"

"Like a schoolgirl." She patted her hair and straightened her collar.

"In a way, this is like a first date, isn't it? You and Henri never had a date, did you? You were so young. And he left before you had a chance to do anything so . . . well, formal." I could imagine their friendship and the early flush of their attachment. What I couldn't imagine was how much of that feeling would be there for them today. Or what their feelings for each other might be now. Curiosity, of course. Apprehension, too. And hope?

"*C'est ça!* And I don't want to disappoint him!"

I reached over to squeeze her hand. "Not a chance!"

I parked across from the *Impasse.* Milou got out and began to walk slowly, tentatively, as if carrying a fragile object. The bells began to strike noon just as we reached Henri's shop.

We stood together for a moment, looking into the window at the mahogany tea table. "Henri's work. I think I'd recognize it anywhere," Milou said. The door opened. Leaning on his crutch, his face luminous with welcome, Henri stepped toward her.

"Henri . . ." Milou took him in her arms.

"*Milou, chère amie . . .*"

"TELL ME everything!" Standing at the kitchen sink, Isabelle scrubbed and rinsed carrots, potatoes, and beans, tossing discards into a bucket for Jeanne's goats. I kicked off my sandals and leaned against the counter.

"I'll tell you as much as I know. You won't believe it."

"Try me."

"It's a fairy tale, *un vrai conte de fée.*"

Isabelle laughed and began to peel the vegetables. "Why am I not surprised?"

When I had arrived at Henri's to pick up Milou, I'd found the shop door unlocked, the buzzer off. The fragrance of honeysuckle drifted in and mingled with the smells of wax and wood. Out on the terrace, Henri and Milou sat side by side, their shoulders touching, in the manner of people who had known each other for a long time. Their posture, the angle of their heads, expressed their ease. Henri reached for Milou's hand and turned to her, intent, waiting. He spoke; she answered, leaning her head against his cheek. A dragonfly flashed blue-green over their heads and disappeared over the wall.

"And?" Isabelle looked at me.

"He asked her to stay."

Isabelle tossed a carrot in the air, caught it, and threw her arms around me. "I knew it!"

"Well, it's not a *fait accompli*, exactly. Not yet."

"What do you mean?"

"He wants her to take her time to decide. So, they'll spend time together—as much as they can while she's here—and she can make up her mind."

"I see." Isabelle nodded. Then she smiled, her eyes gleaming. "But I *know* she will agree."

"There's more."

"*More?*" Isabelle, eyes wide, stared at me.

I laughed. And then the tears began.

"*Qu'est-ce qu'il y a, chérie?* What happened?" Isabelle hugged me.

"She's going to sign over Prospect Hill. Sign it over to me, that is. Whether she stays in France or not. It's a long story." I told Isabelle about my father's will. "When Milou heard about the trust, about the restrictions, she made up her mind to give me the house as soon as she could figure out a way to do it—while she was still living there."

Isabelle nodded. "So she, too, thinks your father's will is . . . is *abérrant*. It's like a punishment. Why would he do such a thing to you, his only child? Of course, it's fine your children will inherit from the trust. But what about you?" She shook her head. "Well, I'm glad for you." She frowned and looked away. "Will this be a problem for Lucie? Doesn't she want the house?"

"No. Mom doesn't like it. Never has." I could have added that if Milou left Prospect Hill to my mother, she would have sold it.

Isabelle nodded. "So you think Lucie will accept this?"

"She might be upset. It's the principle of the thing, you know?" I shrugged. It was never a simple matter to predict how my mother would react to anything Milou might do or say.

"Surely Milou isn't leaving her out entirely?"

"Milou will give her Granddad's watercolors. She's always wanted them."

"So that's all right then."

"I hope so."

Milou had once told me she couldn't imagine leaving Prospect Hill. Of course, this was before my grandfather died. Since then, she had found herself daydreaming about returning to France, to Flagy. And my letters to her about my work with Luc and Isabelle, about living there, had helped nudge the fantasy closer to reality. Henri's invitation was both timely and fortuitous.

For the first time, I felt uneasy about what I was doing in Flagy. Learning something new every day, I hadn't thought—hadn't let myself think—about where the work I was doing might lead. I just wasn't ready to plan ahead.

AT DINNER that night, Milou's eyes glowed. She looked around the table, a half-smile signaling how much she was savoring her news, waiting for the right moment to tell us about her lunch with Henri. It didn't matter that Luc was the only one who hadn't heard about Henri's proposal. Hearing it together, as a family, would only make it more real.

At last, Milou cleared her throat. "Henri asked me to come back. To stay." She tapped the table. "To stay." This time, she shook her head as if she could not quite believe it yet. She looked around the table at each of us in turn. "He told me to take my time to decide. But I know how fast time goes. I don't need to think it over. I've made up my mind to accept." She paused and added, "We'll live in Cluny, in his house." She clasped her hand over her heart. "I've held so much hope, for so long. *Il était bien temps, mes enfants.* Here we are at last."

Isabelle jumped up from the table, laughing and crying, and came around to hug Milou. "Only this—only this could make me so happy."

"*Félicitations, tante.*" Luc raised his glass; we all toasted Milou and Henri.

After dinner, Milou and I walked into the village, to the crossroads. The old spring there filled a stone basin—a *lavoir*—where villagers had done their washing for centuries. Milou and I sat on the rim watching the sky dim into evening.

Every time I came by this spot, I thought about the spring that filled the basin with fresh water, day in and day out, linking generations through the force of life itself. Sitting there, I could imagine the women who came weekly to do their laundry and gossip, how this place tied families together as the seasons changed, and as the country itself changed.

Milou slipped her hand through my arm and began to tell me more about her conversation with Henri. "We had the same thought, almost at the same moment. Everything came into focus. After all these years—almost sixty years—we're like two streams that diverged long ago, only to come together again. *C'est extraordinaire.* Of course I want to stay with him. I want that more than anything."

"Did he talk at all about his leg? And where he went during the war?"

"He told me, yes. *C'était trop.* It's almost too much to take in."

I looked down into the water. In the half-light, her braided hair a gleaming crown, a young girl gazed back at me, her expression inscrutable.

Speaking slowly, weighing each word, Milou told me Henri's story.

"**LATE ONE** night in June 1914, Théo walked from Flagy to Henri's parents' home in Cluny. He threw pebbles at Henri's window to wake him. Théo had come to say goodbye. He made Henri promise not to tell anyone he was going to Switzerland. All he had with him was a rucksack. He pulled out the painting of me he had made for Henri. It was barely dry.

"Of course there was a huge uproar when his family realized he was gone. Jeanne cried for days. And prayed. Everyone was uneasy. There was so much bad feeling between the Germans and the French. Even in the countryside, there was talk of war. Jeanne worried about Théo. Henri worried, too, although he knew where Théo was headed.

"Weeks went by. The war began in August, when the German army invaded Belgium. Farmers were conscripted. There were food shortages. The fighting was terrible. In January 1915, Henri got a letter from Théo. He had found a place to stay outside Belfort, not far from the border between France and Switzerland. He was convinced he could live on his own, hide from the war. And paint. He urged Henri to join him.

"*Maman* was frightened of what might happen to us in the city, so she sent my brothers and me to stay in Flagy with family. In early March 1915, Henri left to search for Théo. That was the last time I saw him. I slept with the box he gave me under my pillow, imagining how he would look and what we would say when he came home—as if that might bring him back. I told myself that as long as I could still smell the fragrance of the honeysuckle, he was alive.

"In Belfort, Henri and Théo argued about what to do. Henri felt it was their duty to fight; Théo scoffed at the idea. Their battlefield, and their battle to create, not destroy, was a higher calling, the only one that counted. He had heard that many artists and pacifists had left France to go to Switzerland. In the end, he wore Henri down, convinced him to come with him.

"As they crossed the border into Switzerland in the middle of the night sometime in early May 1915, they surprised a Swiss militia on patrol. There was no moon; the Swiss heard, but couldn't see, them. When they began to shoot, it sounded like they all fired at once. Henri was wounded, his right tibia shattered, the artery severed. Théo refused to leave him. The militia took them both.

"Henri doesn't remember much of what happened to him over the next several weeks. Luckily, he was in a Swiss hospital. Even so, his leg wound became infected. They had to amputate below the knee.

"In the meantime, Théo disappeared. All anyone would tell Henri was that he had been taken away; no one could, or would, tell him where. As for Henri, the Swiss surgeon who operated on him knew what would happen if he went back to France. Although he could never serve, he might be sent to prison, even executed, as a deserter. So the doctor took him into his own home, where he spent the rest of the war.

"In 1918 he came home, back to Cluny. He told people only that he'd been in a camp. He let them believe he'd been wounded in action. He didn't want to betray Théo. You see, he believed Théo would return. To this day, I am the only person who knows about Théo. Now you know. But you must never tell anyone."

Even in the dark, I could see the urgency in Milou's face. "*Promis, juré!*"

I took her hand, felt the tension drain away. "Why didn't Henri write to you?"

"Ah, but he did!" Milou's voice cracked. She sobbed once. "He wrote to me every week, even though he received nothing from me. He continued to write until the end. Who knows what happened to those letters. When he got home, Jeanne told him I had married an American, even though Stephen and I were still only engaged."

"Did she know that?"

"Oh, yes. I'm sure she lied to Henri so that he wouldn't try to find me."

HENRI HADN'T revealed what he knew about Théo. Jeanne had lied about Milou's marriage. What good would it have done if Henri had told Jeanne of his and Théo's failed attempt to escape into Switzerland? It wouldn't have brought Théo back. As for the truth about Milou, and why Jeanne had kept it from Henri, I could only guess at her motivations. Jeanne was wise enough and loved Milou enough not to intervene in her engagement to my grandfather. Who could know what harm it might have caused to Milou herself, to Stephen Madden, and to Henri, if Milou had broken it off?

Milou and Henri had found one another again. In 1918, this was an outcome no one could have foreseen or even imagined.

Slow Waltz

August 13, 1971

Three days before Jeanne's party, the mower broke down. At noon, the baker in Cluny called Isabelle: Would it be all right if he substituted blueberries for raspberries on the fruit tarts? And, by the way, did Madame know that there were no local peaches this year? The swirl of last-minute preparations rushed around these *inconvénients* like a fast-running stream around stones. No one dared complain. That would spoil Jeanne's fun.

Luc repaired the mower's carburetor; Jeanne approved the blueberry substitution; and a neighbor donated just enough peaches to finish the fruit tarts. "When I was young, we didn't fuss about such things. You made your *tarte* with what you had. *C'est normale, ça!*" Jeanne's high spirits carried the day.

On Thursday, Isabelle confirmed orders and deliveries and verified names on the guest list. Luc organized a crew to set up the sound system, clean the church, and mow the verges. Out of respect for Jeanne, many local friends and family planned to attend Mass at Saint-Thibaut on Saturday. Afterward, they had only to cross the road to the courtyard of the old school for lunch, speeches, and dancing.

"*Une vraie fête!*" Jeanne had demanded we keep her informed of every detail. We complied. Her excitement had infected us all.

Isabelle had found a group to play dance music for us, members of La Bourguignonne—they performed traditional tunes on traditional instruments. "I finally broke down and agreed to have a stereo, too. Some of the kids plan to bring records. We'll have to come up with a system—otherwise, we'll have a battle of the bands—or worse!"

I stifled a laugh. Isabelle's dismay at the prospect was genuine. "The kids can play their music during the breaks, can't they?"

"That's what I've told them, yes. I hope they get it!"

Isabelle frowned at the RSVP list. "We still don't have final confirmations from everyone. I tried to phone a few people I think may have forgotten. The biggest problem is Bruno. It turns out he's got some kind of meeting, something last minute that might interfere. Or so he claims. You'd think he'd be able to re-schedule it for his mother's hundredth birthday! He's the head of the department, after all." She didn't have to add that we had picked the date based on Bruno's assurances he could and would clear his schedule.

Isabelle's misgivings were well-founded. Too often, Bruno made plans to visit Jeanne, only to cancel at the last minute. Jeanne never complained, as if she couldn't allow herself to reproach her only surviving son, simply because he was alive and well—and came to see her when he could.

"At least Lucie and Ted have confirmed." Isabelle glanced at me. "Have you heard from him?"

"From Ted?" I shook my head and turned away. "Not for ten years, since that summer when I fell off the fence. Why are you smiling?"

"How could I forget that day? I'm sure he hasn't either." She raised her eyebrows.

"What?"

"Ted restores antiques—furniture and houses."

"Like Henri."

"Just like."

In those days, apart from being the only two Americans sum-mering in Flagy, Ted and I hadn't had much in common. Ted hadn't paid me any more attention than he paid Louise. He had shown me how to work his telescope and to identify a few constellations. But he had shown others, as well. And he had taught me how to play chess. My idea, not his. I was just one of the group. Nothing special.

That, at least, was how it had seemed to me until the day in Mâcon, in the photo booth at the train station. But we hadn't even spoken again until he found me on the ground by the fence, after I fell. Had I missed something? Even if I had, it didn't matter. That was ten years ago. He was married with a child.

"I'm sorry if I've spoken out of turn."

"Don't feel bad. My crush—such as it was—never went anywhere. I was too young and shy. And I don't know how he felt. *If* he felt anything."

"How do you feel about him now?"

"Curious. To see what he's like." It should have been obvious to Isabelle, as it was to me, that Ted and I would meet again as old friends, nothing more.

"May I talk to you about something else?"

"Of course."

"Milou told me about your miscarriage and about the man you were involved with. . . ." She paused, giving me the opening—and the space—I needed to make my own way through the story of what had happened at Brookton.

"That seems far away, as if it happened in another lifetime, or maybe to someone else, even though it's been less than a year." Working long hours every day with Luc, I had been so tired at night that I sometimes fell asleep before I turned my light out. In the greenhouse, I occasionally replayed my conversations with Ardis about work—about the role of work in her life—which had helped me shift my focus to the work I wanted to do. I still wasn't sure what that would be. "I have to find out what I want to do before I fall in love."

Isabelle nodded at this and smiled. "Very reasonable. Too reasonable, perhaps? Don't forget that old saying about the heart's reasons . . ."

". . . that reason doesn't know."

"Yes. That one."

"Well, I'm going to do what I can to make sure I'm as reasonable as possible. For love to be part of my life, I need to find a way to keep my balance."

I HAD volunteered to make bouquets for the church altar and centerpieces for the tables. Once I decided on a mix of wild and garden flowers, I scouted the local fields and woods for ideas, choosing the plants I knew I could count on to bloom in time, like daisies, Queen Anne's lace, cornflowers, and lavender. Jeanne directed me to places she remembered, sure that I'd find the plants she knew and loved best.

She had told me about the party for all the children who finished elementary school—in 1883. "There were twelve of us and we were all twelve years old! We had our picnic in the courtyard—just like we're planning to do now." She leaned forward on the settee, eyes wide. "Imagine, Malorie! I'm the only one left. When I look around, it's almost as if they're still here, as if I can hear their voices, just around the corner. Why not? The houses are where they've always been." Then she smiled. "One hundred years old—just imagine!"

Jeanne hadn't said it, but she might as well have. Even with twentieth-century improvements like streetlights—there were two at the intersection in the center of the village—and the paved main road, Flagy's appearance hadn't changed since the nineteenth century. The original houses fronted the roads, their gardens arranged in neat plots behind them.

Jeanne could still recall everyone's name and who lived where.

Over the years, she had made scrapbooks documenting weddings, births, deaths, and special honors. She kept one dedicated to Bruno's accomplishments. Bruno, a renowned cardiologist, remained an enigmatic figure, cool, aloof—distant, I thought, in light of how much pleasure his mother took in his activities.

There had been 150 *habitants* in Flagy in 1871. As Jeanne had pointed out, there were 137 now. Most were farmers or vintners, whose families settled in the valley in the fourteenth century. Here in this corner of Burgundy, daily life had continued largely unchanged, even during wartime. Jeanne's husband, too old to fight in the First World War, held fast to the idea that even those who stayed behind, far from the battlefront, had a role to play. It was their duty to preserve the land—their patrimony—for those who would come back one day.

Even today, the villagers observed family and village traditions, making sure their children and grandchildren understood their ties to the *terroir* and their responsibility to manage and protect it, even from afar. Every year on Armistice Day, a few people gathered at the monument in the cemetery to honor the war dead. After her husband died, Jeanne had arranged to have Théo's name inscribed there, too.

The party menu, much of it provisioned and prepared in the village, included local wines, platters of summer vegetables, roasted goat, and chicken. "We have to have something for people who won't eat goat!" Isabelle had insisted. The meal would finish with cheese and the fruit tarts from the pâtisserie in Cluny. At the last minute, I had ordered a birthday cake and ice cream. Children, who knew the rules about birthdays, would expect nothing less.

August 15, 1971

Early in the morning, Isabelle and I sat on the porch steps going over the checklist one last time. We could see the field across the road from the school, the designated parking area, which had been mowed, cleared, and marked off with sawhorses so guests wouldn't drive into the drainage ditch running along its edge. The rented commercial refrigerator hummed behind the school, and three large charcoal grills stood at the far side of the school yard, like sentinels.

After a lively debate about the best time to start them—she said eleven, he said noon—Isabelle and Luc compromised: he would light the charcoal between eleven and eleven thirty to give them time to form an ample bed of coals.

I stood and stretched. "I'm off, but I'll be back by nine to set up the tables. Except for the bouquets at the altar, the church is finished. You'll help Jeanne get ready?"

"Oh, yes." Isabelle ran her hand through her hair and rubbed her eyes. "Milou and Suzette, too. Milou knows how to fix Jeanne's hair the way she likes it. Suzette will stand by with an iron, in case the dress needs a touch-up."

"Has she decided?" Jeanne had to choose between her own wedding dress and a dress she had inherited from her mother. It had been her mother's finest dress, worn only on special occasions.

"It's even older than I am," Jeanne had emphasized. But she fretted over the shoes, too fragile to wear. "So beautiful! Kidskin, you know. *Maman* had such tiny feet, like a bird."

I had bought a pair of ballet flats for her and held my breath when she removed them from the box. "Very nice. But will they fit over my stockings?" No one dared suggest she switch stockings. She wanted to wear the silk ones she'd had since before the Great War, as carefully preserved as the two dresses. Like Cinderella's, Jeanne's feet slid easily into the shoes.

"I think she's leaning toward the wedding dress. It's going to be a last-minute decision. I did take one precaution." Isabelle held up a glass and shook it. "I kept her teeth here overnight!"

Jeanne, who wore her false teeth as little as possible, often mislaid them. People who didn't know her found her speech incomprehensible without them. However, most of her neighbors understood her perfectly well. As did the goats, she took pleasure in pointing out. Still, she had told Isabelle she would be sure to wear her teeth for her birthday party, because she wanted to be able to enjoy the whole meal. Isabelle's decision to find and keep the dentures for her was the only way to ensure they weren't misplaced.

"Anything from Bruno?"

"He made it on time to the airport, so he's on the same flight as Ted and Lucie. That, at least, is a relief. They should be here in time for lunch." She looked at her watch. "They're probably boarding the train in Paris right now." It was seven twenty. "They'll pick up the car when they arrive in Lyon. It's tight, but they can do it. If their connections work. And Bruno drives." She held up both hands, fingers crossed.

I STOPPED by the goat pen to empty a pail of apple peelings and bread crusts into their feed trough. They butted and shoved one another as they scrambled to get at the treats. "*Soyez gentilles les grandes!* Let the little ones have something too!"

Across the valley, under the cloudless sky, the hillsides undulated, like a bolt of lavender velvet, slowly unfurling. Just past the school, the old road to Salornay, a dirt lane, turned up the hill through pastures and woods toward the Château de Sirot.

Stepping-stones of green and gold light dappled the road. The smells of damp earth, leaves, and moss reminded me of the path down through the woods to the lake below Prospect Hill—Milou's house, soon to be mine. Not even my worry about my mother's reaction to Milou's gift could dampen my happiness at the thought that I would live there one day. It didn't matter when; what mattered was that it would be there, always, keeper of my memories of my childhood with Milou and of Milou and my grandfather.

To me, the house *was* Milou: her voice, resonant with the particular tones and pitches of French vowels, the way she placed the furniture and objects on the furniture, the fragrance of the sandalwood soap she ordered from Paris every year. To live there would be like living forever within her embrace.

By eight thirty, I had collected enough wildflowers and branches for the table arrangements and the church. On my way back, I stopped at the clearing at the top of the hill near the château. I looked down at the school, the church, and the houses along the road.

Like the hub of a wheel, Saint-Thibaut sat in the middle of the village. To either side, single-story houses abutted one another along the two roads that intersected at the *lavoir*. With their red-tiled, peaked roofs, their blue shutters, and their window boxes heaped with petunias and geraniums, the houses presented a welcoming face to the world. Most had small stone outbuildings for chickens, geese, goats, and cows. All had vegetable gardens; some had small orchards of apple, pear, or peach trees.

Milou had told me about the day she arrived with my grandfather in Alden, Vermont. "He walked with me around the property, pointing out the village and lake below. As I looked down on the slate roofs glistening in the sun and the valley spreading out beyond the village, I had the feeling I had been there before, that I had come home again. Of course it wasn't Flagy. All the houses in Alden had white clapboards and dark green shutters. But the similarity! It was like seeing the face of someone who resembles a loved one across a room crowded with strangers—there was the church with its steeple; there were the houses along the two roads that came together in the center of town. I knew I would be happy there."

I had felt a similarly intense pleasure each time I stood in this spot. Flagy resembled a nest, I thought, a sheltering, welcoming place.

A movement at the edge of this tableau distracted me—a group of men carrying banners to the tent in the school's courtyard. By one o'clock, they would be aloft and fluttering in the afternoon breeze. A tractor moved slowly into view, drawing a wagonload of folding chairs. To get the tables ready in time, I'd have to hurry.

In the tent outside the school, I found pails filled with the summer flowers Luc had bought at the Mâcon flower market the day before. He had found everything on my list—snapdragons, dwarf nasturtiums, zinnias, campanulas, and greens.

I put on an apron and a pair of gloves and began to set the flowers into vases. The fragrance of sun-warmed lavender and newly mown hay floated into the tent. Already, a few bees had turned up to investigate the bouquets.

MY MOTHER stood with Ted and Bruno Girard at the foot of Saint-Thibaut's steps just as Jeanne emerged into the sunlight, holding Luc's arm, with Suzette and Milou right behind her. The *curé* took Jeanne's hand, made the sign of the cross over her bowed head, and kissed her on both cheeks. In her lavender blue wedding gown, Jeanne looked like a young girl.

Rosettes of moiré ribbon ringed the square neckline and trimmed the sleeves. The same ribbon fell in long tails from the wide embroidered belt. Erect and steady beside Luc, Jeanne smiled and waved when she spotted the travelers.

I finished the centerpieces just in time and hurried to get them onto the tables. The light filtering through the canopy transformed the vases into globes of Murano floating in a golden haze. I carried my basket of clippings—spent blooms and stems—out to the field behind the school. The goats pastured there had already lined up at the fence, curious about the commotion at the church. My arrival prompted bleating and foot stamping as they pushed one another aside to get at the clippings I dumped over the fence.

"So this is where you've been hiding out." He slid his sunglasses into his shirt pocket. The voice was deeper, its timbre unchanged. Squinting into the sun, I couldn't really see him. Was he taller? Heavier? Ten years ago, he had been a lanky, awkward seventeen-year-old.

Even before I could laugh at his joke, he had his arms around me, my head tucked under his chin—he *was* taller. His shirt buttons pressed against my cheek—sharp and warm, like shells on the beach. He smelled faintly of soap, toothpaste, and diesel fumes.

"How did you know?"

"Milou told me I'd find you here."

I looked at him looking at me, taking in my face as I took in his, his eyes questioning mine. He had a crescent-shaped scar, almost too faint to see, over his right eye.

"You've been here since March?"

"You just arrived?"

Laughter picked us up and moved us along to a place that felt as familiar as the sun on my face.

What else did he know about me, I wondered. Between the flight, and the train, and the drive down from Lyon, my mother had had plenty of time to fill in all the gaps.

"You first." Ted waited, hands in his pockets.

"Since March, yes. Milou's idea. It's supposed to be short-term. So far, I like it enough to stay as long as I can. Stoop labor suits me, I guess." I felt a rush of irritation. I was trying too hard.

He grinned. "I hope we'll have more time to talk, so you can tell me how you figured that out. Something to do with the nursery?"

There wasn't time to go into it with him now.

"Do you have a scar?"

"Not as bad as you might think." I turned around so he could see my right calf.

That summer day, ten years ago, I had taken a shortcut through the field behind the school. This very field, where the goats were finishing their snack. Instead of crossing to the gate, to save time I had climbed the fence, a haphazard wire-and-post construction. As I threw my left leg over the top, the fence collapsed under me. My right heel got caught in the wire so I couldn't jump clear. On the ground, as I tried to extricate myself, I had snagged my right calf on a nail.

Riding by on his bike, Ted had come to my rescue. Unfazed by the gore—there was blood everywhere, even in my hair—he wrapped his T-shirt around my leg, staunching the blood as best he could, and half-carried me home, where Isabelle hurried me into the car and on to the emergency room at the hospital in Cluny.

It didn't seem strange then that Ted came along. All the way to the hospital, he talked to me, distracting me with stories about school, about his interest in astronomy, about his plans for college—at that point, he thought he was going to be a surgeon.

It had taken twenty stitches to close the wound. The scar had faded to a thin line, white against my tan. "Not much to say about *that*."

He looked expectant. What had I missed? "Same shape as Cassiopeia."

I knew I was supposed to know this. "Cassiopeia?"

"The constellation shaped like a W?" He was offhand, as if he didn't care this had slipped my mind. But I did. "The throne of the queen who challenged Neptune . . ."

Sitting beside Ted, looking up at the stars through his telescope, my sense of time and space had been forever altered by the physical sensation of looking deep into the sky, seeing Cassiopeia for the first time. The memory jolted me so completely out of the present that my breath caught.

I wanted to get away from the crowd with him and talk about our lives since that last summer. To ask about the days, to let our conversation run on, to imagine our separate lives. *He's married.* When, exactly? What had I been doing that day? What was it like for him now?

"Malorie? Ted?" Isabelle stood at the door of the school, smiling at us.

"We'll talk later?"

"Sooner, if possible." He ran his fingers through his tangled curls, tried to smooth them, squashed them down with both hands.

I laughed.

He blushed.

"Would you like to borrow my comb?"

He grinned and gave his hair a final pat, as if soothing a small animal.

BY THE time the mayor began his speech, several parents had taken their squirming children down the road to the *lavoir*. Soon the dancing would begin. Sitting between Ted and Bruno, Jeanne leaned her head on Bruno's shoulder.

When the mayor finished, Bruno helped Jeanne stand to shake his hand. She smiled and nodded when the crowd cheered and applauded. As the applause died away, the musicians entered the tent, playing a dance tune that had the lively rhythm of a Virginia reel. Two couples in traditional costumes ran out to the center of the courtyard and began to dance.

A few at a time, others joined the dancers. It didn't matter that they didn't know the steps; they hooked arms, skipped around one another, and kicked up their heels. A few sang the words to the old song. Soon, everyone joined in the refrain.

Later, when the group played a waltz, Milou and Henri made their way to a quiet corner. Facing Henri, holding his hand, Milou smiled and nodded as she stepped around him in time to the music.

Ted came to find me. "Henri told me about your grandmother and him—about her coming back here to live. Imagine getting together again after all this time. He asked if I wanted to apprentice with him for a while."

"Do you?"

"I'm so tempted. It's almost the right time for me to learn some new techniques. Maybe I'll have a chance later to tell you more about what I'm doing. If you want to hear about it, that is."

"Yes, sure."

"Shall we dance?" Another waltz. Across the courtyard, Milou and Henri, arms linked, their heads together, looked at us, as if they were sending a signal. I glanced at Ted. Would Henri tell him Théo's story?

I took his hand. Unbidden, the memory of dancing with Jack in the dark that night in Brookton came to me. I had been happy that night, as if the ease I had felt dancing with Patrick—my emotional and physical selves in harmony—had brought about the desire I had felt for him for the first time. To feel that way again, now, with Ted, startled me, like a flicker of light on moving water.

As soon as they finished the song, the musicians took a break. Groups of dancers settled around the tables, laughing and chatting, fanning themselves with napkins and handkerchiefs. Most of the men had rolled up their sleeves and loosened their collars. It was close to four o'clock. They'd be leaving soon to begin evening chores. A few teenagers clustered around the stereo, negotiating.

"Your wife couldn't come?" Would he think I was prying? "And your mother?"

"Claire—my wife—would have liked to, but she's a librarian in a public school in Newport." He looked away, across through the tent opening, as if searching for something in the field where the cars were parked. "She had to be there for orientation. And we have a little girl, Annie. Claire thought it would be too exhausting for her to come for such a short time." He glanced at me. "My mother is recovering from knee surgery."

"You won't be staying long, then."

"Until the day after tomorrow." He had taken a small color snapshot out of his wallet. Annie leaned against Claire, who sat in a wicker chair, one leg curled under her. Caught in the middle of a laugh, they gazed directly into the camera, sharing the fun. "She just turned five."

His curls, his dark eyes, and his height. "She looks just like you."

"So they say. But she's much better coordinated, already a fine athlete." Ted looked into the photo, an expression of wonder on his face.

"What about Henri's invitation?"

Ted smiled and shook his head. "I hope I'll have another chance. Right now isn't the best time. For Annie. And that matters."

"AU SECOURS! Vite, quelqu'un! Help!"

We turned at the same time and ran out of the tent toward the field where the cars were parked. Suzette lay on the ground near her car, her eyes closed. Isabelle crouched next to her, fanning her face with a napkin. "We need Bruno!"

Ted and I split up. He hurried back among the parked cars, scanning the crowd. I went into the school. As soon as I stepped into the foyer, I heard Bruno's voice. He was somewhere on the second floor. I took the stairs two at a time and found him in the office on the phone, his back to the door. "Dr. Girard? Bruno?"

He turned around, irritated. But he stopped talking and covered the receiver. "There's an emergency at the hospital in New York."

"Here, too, Dad." I hadn't heard Ted on the stairs. How had he found us so quickly? "Suzette fainted."

Bruno spoke a few quiet words into the receiver and hung up.

When we reached them, Isabelle sat cross-legged, holding Suzette's hand. The crowd around them parted to make way for Bruno.

"*Et maman?*" Bruno looked at Ted.

"Lucie took Jeanne home earlier." Ted spoke quietly. Answering his father's unspoken question, he added, "She doesn't know about Suzette."

Bruno knelt and checked Suzette's pulse. "Suzette?" She stirred. "*C'est bien.* Don't try to talk. We'll take care of you." He stood. "Has anyone called an ambulance?"

"I'll do it." I ran back to use the school phone and got through to the emergency services right away.

"I'LL GO in the ambulance with Suzette, Ted. Follow me in our car," Bruno shouted.

As soon as they heard the siren, people cleared the entrance to the field. When the ambulance arrived moments later, Suzette had opened her eyes. Looking dazed, she managed a faint smile and mouthed her thanks to Isabelle, Ted, and me.

Isabelle held Suzette's hat and a bouquet of flowers. Her lips trembled.

Ted hugged her. "She's probably just overtired."

Isabelle smiled through her tears. "I hope you're right. Lucky for her, Bruno was here."

Ted came back with me to the tent to get my gardening tools and the buckets. I was happy to see that Jeanne's guests had taken so many of the centerpieces home with them.

Looking over the empty tables and chairs, the stacks of dishes, glasses, and cutlery, Ted turned to me. "I wonder if any of us will ever celebrate another birthday quite like this one." A cleanup crew of children and their parents cleared the tables and stacked chairs; they called out their hopes for Suzette as we left.

Only a few cars remained in the field. Clusters of discarded paper napkins and shreds of the crêpe paper streamers had drifted into piles in the hedgerow. Several children, each carrying a basket, picked up the bits and pieces.

"Here we are." Ted unlocked a gray Peugeot sedan and threw his jacket in the backseat. "Look, why don't you come with me to the hospital? We can talk on the way." He made an exasperated noise and slapped the top of the car. "You must think I'm an idiot. You haven't yet had a chance to talk to your mom, have you?"

"Not yet, no." I wanted to tell him it didn't matter, but it was too soon to talk to him about any of that. "I'd like to come along. We can stop at the house on the way and let them know."

"So they don't think you've been kidnapped?"

"Something like that."

As we drove out, we spotted Isabelle and Luc walking home along the road. I rolled down my window. When she heard the plan, Isabelle nodded, relieved. "Lucie and Milou will be glad. We all want to know what's happening. Call us from the hospital?"

"We shouldn't be late. So if they want to wait up . . ."

TED ADJUSTED the rearview mirror and shifted the car into gear. "Start at the beginning."

Somehow, I didn't think he said this just to be polite. Anyway, it was my story; I could choose how much or how little to tell him.

"What's it like to live here full-time?"

"Out there," I gestured ahead of us, beyond the valley, "everything moves so fast. Here . . ." I stopped. Was this the best I could do? "It's like being in a slow-moving river, just floating along. Things pop up, bob along, drift away. The river moves on. Out there, I always feel I'm struggling to make everything I do fit someone else's idea of who I am, to make myself fit in somehow, somewhere."

"You don't feel that way here?"

"No, I don't. If it's possible to inherit a feeling for a place, then maybe that's the best explanation for how I feel. Here, everything seems to work. Seamlessly."

"No pressure, no rush?"

"Not exactly. There is pressure. Lots, actually. There's so much that goes into Luc's business—planning, timing, managing the plants through the cycle. But the work itself, the connection to the soil, to the plants themselves—as tired as I am when I go to bed at night, I always feel a sense of closure, of completion. For now, I can't imagine doing anything else or living anywhere else."

We had never talked, really talked, before, even back then. So why did I feel so comfortable with him? Not like Jack. Rather than interpreting me to myself, or telling me what I should think, Ted had opened a space between us where I could let my guard down. So I told him about my parents' divorce, my father's death, Brookton—and Jack.

"Have you heard from him?"

"No." There didn't seem to be any point in telling Ted now, before we'd had a chance to talk more, that Jack had left Brookton after four months in Paris. He had told Matt he didn't want to spend his life being a footnote.

"How do you feel about Brookton and him?"

We had to take our time on the back road, stopping once for cows and once for goats crossing from the barn to the pasture. Ted leaned back in the seat, steering with his right hand, his left elbow resting on the open window.

"At first, I felt I'd blown it. I thought it was my fault I couldn't figure Brookton out, so many unspoken rules. But when I started there, I had no idea that what I wanted to do—to teach, mainly— had so little to do with being an academic."

"And now?"

"I just wasn't cut out for all the head games."

"What about Jack?" He took his eyes off the road to look at me.

Of course he wanted to hear more about Jack. Before I could think too much about it, I saw how to do it. "He knew how to get along, to work the system. He figured the department out. So the advice he gave me was good advice and might have helped me—if I had stayed." My throat felt tight. I hadn't answered his question, but he didn't push me for more. I looked out at the vineyards laddering the hillsides under the evening sky. "I couldn't. And I couldn't stay with someone who thought I should try." I couldn't talk about Danielle's plagiarism. Or the miscarriage.

On the main road to Cluny, Ted checked for signs to the hospital. I turned toward him. "What about you?"

"I got a degree in art history at Brown. My father was fine with that. But he wasn't happy I didn't go into medicine." Ted frowned. "You know about his brother?"

"I know he was a painter." I wondered again if Henri would ever tell Ted Théo's story.

"Well, as far as my father is concerned, art is why Théo was so wild, why he ran away. When I got my degree, all he said was, 'At least you're not a painter.'"

"That seems harsh."

"I've heard it all my life. He never stopped missing Théo. His disapproval is just a screwed-up expression of love."

Up ahead, I could see the lights on Cluny's outskirts, just beyond the turnoff to the hospital. "Why didn't you go on with art history?"

"I did—just not in the usual way. You know, get a doctorate, teach, write." What had begun as a hobby, woodworking, led him to courses in eighteenth- and nineteenth-century furniture, and to his involvement in the restoration of an eighteenth-century house in Newport.

After Brown, he'd apprenticed with several furniture restorers. Working on his own now, he focused almost exclusively on restoration work. "I'd forgotten about what Henri does. There's so much to learn. I hope I can take him up on his offer sometime. Maybe when Annie's a little older."

AT THE registration desk outside the emergency room, we learned that Suzette had been admitted to the hospital overnight for observation. Just then, Bruno Girard stepped out of the elevator and came down the corridor to meet us.

"How is she, Dad?"

"Awake and comfortable. Apparently she's had episodes like this before. Luckily, the doctor who's on duty tonight knows her. He called her cardiologist. We all agree a night's rest here would probably be a good idea. She's in good hands. Let's go home." Bruno took the car keys from Ted.

Ted seemed preoccupied, his eyes on Bruno walking ahead of us to the car.

I thought about the last time I'd been at the hospital, about my accident. "Just the smell of the place reminds me of that day. The admitting nurse was wearing real shoes." She had also worn a set of gold bangles on her right wrist. As she filled in the form, the bangles slid and jingled against the desk, setting my teeth on edge.

Ted chuckled. "Real shoes?"

"You know, not nurses' shoes. She kept calling me *ma petite* even though I was at least a head taller than her."

"You told everyone I was your brother and Isabelle went along with it, remember? And you didn't flinch when the guy sewed you up."

"Just trying to make a good impression."

"On the doctor?"

I laughed. It didn't seem at all strange or out of line that he was flirting with me.

Gradually, the darkened countryside swallowed the town's glare. In the backseat, I looked out the window into the sky, thinking about Ted's telescope. We had sat on Isabelle and Luc's porch while he showed me how to adjust it. When I first looked into the eyepiece, I felt dizzy; the stars I saw through it spun around me. I had leaned against Ted. He had put his arm around me, his cheek close to mine, sighting the telescope. That's when I saw Cassiopeia.

My scar, Ted's warmth, and Cassiopeia—one memory of that summer evening.

"MALORIE? WE'RE in here!" My mother's voice sounded hoarse, on edge. Anxiety about Suzette? Irritation that I hadn't phoned them from the hospital? I closed my eyes, imagined myself back in the car with Ted, driving through the night. To Lyon, to Paris. *Anywhere out of this world.*

"Does Bruno think she'll be okay?" My mother stared at me, her eyes wide and flat. In the dim light of the table lamp, she looked haggard. Sitting in the armchair across from her, Milou tried to smile.

"She'll be fine." I stood in the doorway, uncertain what to do.

"Jeanne asked us to wait for you and get the details." Milou's voice cracked. She cleared her throat. "She knows Bruno will tell her only what he wants her to hear."

"Where are Isabelle and Luc?" I was buying time, trying to gauge Milou's state of mind from her tone.

"At Jeanne's for the night. She's tired and anxious about Suzette." Milou reached behind her to adjust the chair cushion.

"I don't know much really, except that Bruno agreed with the other doctor that she should spend the night in the hospital." In the car, I had overheard Bruno say something about tests tomorrow. I knew better than to mention that now. "They think it was the excitement, then the letdown after the party. Bruno promised to visit her tomorrow. The other doctor seemed pleased to have him around."

My mother sniffed. "Why shouldn't he be? Bruno's a heart specialist, a famous one. Surely the doctor here has heard of him."

"You look tired, *chérie*." Milou's eyes moved from my face to my mother's and back. "We can postpone our talk until tomorrow, can't we, Lucie?"

"What talk?" I asked. Had Milou told my mother about Prospect Hill?

Milou clenched her hands. Her eyes slid away from mine, as if looking for a way out.

All at once, the circuits in the emotional force field between my mother and Milou reached a new, dangerous zone. My mother leaned forward. As if bracing for a blow, Milou pushed back farther into her chair, her hands gripping the arms, her eyes fixed on my mother's face.

"This won't take long." My mother patted the sofa beside her. When I didn't move to sit next to her, her mouth twisted. "Why are you looking at me like that?"

"Whenever you say that, I know better."

"That's not fair." She frowned and shrugged, sagging back against the cushion. "Never mind."

Milou looked at me. In her eyes, I saw that she was afraid. I brought a kitchen chair into the room and set it at the end of the coffee table so I could see their faces. "What's this about?"

"Milou told me about Prospect Hill." Her mouth turned down in distaste. "Of course it doesn't matter to me that she's given it to you. Even if I made all the changes I want, the house wouldn't suit me. It's old, yes, but not charming. Those upstairs bedrooms, so dark and dreary. I don't care about it." She shuddered. "This isn't about the house."

"Then what's the matter?" I felt no relief that the house wasn't the issue. I hadn't expected it to be, after all.

"We have to talk about things you don't know anything about." She looked at Milou. "All I ask is that you hear me out." She squared her shoulders and moved to the edge of the sofa, wary and resolute.

Milou's eyes were opaque; her expression looked frozen in dread. In her lap, her hands moved back and forth as if trying to escape, or to smooth the way forward.

"Milou?"

"Listen to your mother, Malorie. Just listen."

My mother pulled her robe tight around her and sat back again, staring across the room, her eyes unfocused. "I had an older sister." She closed her eyes. Each pulse of the ticking clock dropped into the silence. In the woods, I heard a bird cry out.

"What do you mean, an older sister?" Milou wouldn't meet my eyes.

"She died two years before I was born. Scarlet fever." My mother's voice caught. She opened her eyes, looking first at me, then at Milou. "Malorie. Her name was Malorie."

"What? No! *No!*" The roaring in my ears sounded like a gale. I swallowed, tried to clear my head, but the noise and the pressure seemed only to increase.

"I pretended she never existed," my mother said. "So did she." She glared at Milou, then closed her eyes again, shaking her head.

"Why, Milou? Why didn't you tell me?"

The mask crumpled. Milou's eyes glistened with tears. "I couldn't. I couldn't face the pain of remembering. I buried it, and the memory of it, when we buried her."

My mother opened her mouth. No sound came out. She tried again. "They say that children know when they are truly loved." Her mouth tightened, thin and accusatory. "You don't love me, you never have—not from the very beginning."

"No, Lucie. *Là, tu as très tort. Je t'en supplie!*" Clasping her hand over her heart, Milou shook her head.

"I am not wrong." My mother's face twisted. "What you just said, saying it in French, proves it. I am Lucie! I speak English!" She leaned forward, her jaw jutting out, her hands curled into fists in her lap. "You always talked to me in French. Tried to make me speak French. You dressed me up like a little French doll, *your* little French doll. All I ever wanted was for you to see me—me!—but you only saw *her*." Her sob sounded like a groan.

I gripped the seat of my chair, something to hold on to, something real. "So you never changed your name from Malorie to Lucie?"

"*She* was Malorie. *I* am Lucie." My mother clasped her arms around her knees and began to rock.

Milou's hoarse whisper broke the silence. "Malorie—Lucie's sister—had begun to say real words." She closed her eyes. "*Maman*, of course, and *papa*. Also, *Milou*. Sometimes she would repeat, '*maman, Milou, maman, Milou*'—over and over, like a little song. When she became ill—with scarlet fever—I stayed by her, day and night. At the end, she held my hand. She could barely breathe, but she spoke to me. I heard her last words: '*maman, Milou*.'"

"Do you have any idea what it was like for me?"

I watched Milou's face. She flinched at each word, her hands outstretched, as if to stem the flood.

My mother's voice grated. "I saw you take her picture out of the drawer. I watched you every time someone mentioned her name. When my Malorie was born, I thought at last you would see me. And love me. You loved *her*. And I wanted you to love her. But I wanted you to love me, too, because I gave her to you. I gave *my* Malorie to you."

When it was over, like a sudden storm, there were no more words, as if my mother's accusations and her revelation had drained them away. I tried to think beyond this, about what it meant to me and to us all. But the sound of Milou's voice repeating, '*maman, Milou, maman, Milou*,' drove all thought from my mind.

"If you don't believe me, Lucie, I must accept that." Milou's voice was clear and gentle. "When Malorie was born, I felt I had been reborn. For the first time since your sister's death, I could breathe freely, without fear or sorrow. Of course, I wanted her to speak French."

"You gave me no choice. Don't you understand? It was the only way."

I pushed myself forward and out of my chair and stood, trembling, in front of my mother. "How could you do this to Milou? How could you do this to *me*?"

From the dark hallway, at the foot of the stairs, I looked back into the living room. Milou had moved to sit beside my mother on the sofa, holding her, rocking her.

"*Pardonne-moi, maman. Je te demande pardon.*"

"*C'est fini, ma chérie, c'est fini maintenant. Calme-toi.*" Milou smiled at me over my mother's head.

My mother's apology, in French, using phrases the French reserve for the most grievous errors, shocked me as much as her outburst had. The glimpse of her resentment and her sorrow, the weight of Milou's grief, resonated through me in a deep current of pain. I couldn't think of what to say or do next.

I could only hope that Milou was right. That it was over.

The Way Back

September 15, 1974

Bleating, squealing, and the clang of Anisette's bell shattered the early-morning silence. Hadn't Jeanne heard the goats? Surely she was awake by now.

Maybe the dog had come back. It had appeared out of nowhere early one morning, hurling itself against the fence, growling and barking. Anisette had held her ground, her head lowered, shaking her horns; the others panicked, careening around the enclosure, scrambling to find safety in the middle of the herd.

On her porch, banging a pot, Jeanne had shouted until it fled up the road, its tail between its legs. It was several hours before the goats calmed down. Jeanne, in tears, had summoned the neighbors. No one knew where the dog had come from, or to whom it belonged.

Beneath the goats' urgent voices, I could hear the thud of their hooves as they ran around their enclosure. I dressed and grabbed my flashlight, hoping Isabelle and Luc, sleeping on the far side of the house, hadn't heard them.

Outside, wisps of ground mist swirled over the fields. A pale ribbon of early light outlined the hills beyond. I beamed my flashlight over the driveway and across the road. There was no sign of the dog, or an intruder. Or Jeanne.

"*Là, là!* What's the matter, girls? *Calmez-vous maintenant!*" The goats crowded around the gate, murmuring and nickering in relief at the sound of my voice.

I flipped the switch just inside the kitchen door. Under the harsh light, Jeanne was sprawled on the floor, her right arm outstretched, pills spilling from the bottle in her hand. Her shawl had fallen off her shoulder; her right leg was bent beneath her, as if she had been trying to get up when she collapsed there.

As soon as I heard Isabelle running down the driveway, I went out to the porch. Somehow I knew she needed to know, that I needed to tell her, not let her discover for herself, that Jeanne was dead. "*Elle n'est plus, Isabelle. Jeanne est morte.*"

We went in and crouched together, holding each other, holding Jeanne, murmuring over and over. "*La pauvre . . .*"

Only three days ago, on Jeanne's hundred-and-third birthday, we had joked with her about setting a new record. In 1955, Jean-Paul Roger, whom Jeanne had known since childhood, had died at the age of a hundred and two. Jeanne had vowed, "I'll set another record—*le bon Dieu* doesn't need me for a while. He knows I'm much more useful here." She had nodded, affirming her special arrangement with Him, as we lifted our glasses in our birthday toast.

She would have laughed to learn she had fulfilled her vow.

TED AND Bruno arrived in Flagy before the funeral, joining villagers from Flagy and from Cluny for the Mass. My mother appeared toward the end of the ceremony and stood with the ushers at the door. Afterward, everyone gathered at Isabelle and Luc's house for the reception. The warm September sun and the clear blue sky—a blue that reminded me of Jeanne's wedding dress—were Jeanne's parting gift to us all.

"I'm glad you found her." The sorrow in Ted's eyes belied his smile. He seemed to be looking through me. He didn't have to explain. Although the shock of discovery washed over me every time I thought of that morning, I, too, was glad I'd been there and that Isabelle and I had had those moments alone with Jeanne before the official business of her death separated her from us forever. There had been times when I'd startled myself, standing in the middle of the greenhouse with no idea how I'd got there or what I was doing. Ted's comment comforted me. It was as though he had been there, too.

"She was like Saint-Thibaut. Or the *lavoir*. You just assumed she'd always be here. Maybe because every day was so much the same for her, caring for her goats and her garden, visiting with her friends, watching over the village. You knew where she was and what she was doing, every minute." It was simple, really. Who Jeanne was, being there every day, gave us all a feeling of continuity, a sense of community, no matter where else we might be in the world.

For years, weather permitting, Jeanne had spent afternoons on her verandah, on her settee, reading or knitting. She greeted passersby, inviting them to join her, to tell her the latest news. To her, of course, the only news that counted was news from and about the village. Luc had once said she was the village's memory. She collected the bits and pieces, connected them into a story, and passed the story along to others. None of it had ever been written down; the scrapbooks she kept only featured the highlights.

When asked about this, Jeanne had scoffed, "*Mais nous ne sommes pas de grandes personnes, nous!*" Perhaps we weren't important people, newsworthy people. No matter. Jeanne kept track of us, advised us, scolded, and comforted us. Her interest and attention made us feel we mattered to her and to one another. That was enough.

Now that she was gone, would anyone keep track of the village's daily, intimate goings-on?

TED JOINED his father, greeting friends and family, smiling through the tears. Everywhere, people were saying the same thing. Yes, it did seem incredible that we had celebrated Jeanne's hundredth birthday in August, just three years ago. Isabelle and I made sure everyone had a place to sit and that the platters of food were passed and replenished. Luc and others grilled *merguez* sausage and chicken. Henri, Milou, and my mother sat with Suzette gazing out at the crowd, at all the generations gathered in one place, perhaps for the last time.

"Have you had anything to eat?"

I took the plate Ted offered me, but I didn't feel much like eating. Although I understood the importance of this gathering, a celebration of Jeanne and her life among us, I was adrift, an observer for the time being, not a participant. Around us, at the tables, people ate and chatted. Someone laughed. *Life goes on.*

Luc found us. "Have you heard the news?

Ted nodded at Luc, smiling, but his eyes were on me as he explained. "Dad asked me to stay for a while to help sort out *grand-mère*'s house and papers. I'm between projects; he has to go back to New York."

"So you'll be living in Jeanne's house?" What about Claire and Annie? Three years ago, Annie's age and Claire's job kept them at home in Newport. And now? If we had been alone, I might have asked him.

"Right. I think I can manage the legal part, but I'll need someone to give me a hand with the goats. Any ideas?"

I raised my hand.

Luc nodded. "I told Ted you'd been helping Jeanne."

"I'm no expert. But whatever I don't know, there's always someone in the village who does. We'll manage."

Later, I saw Ted sitting with Henri and Milou. Henri had a sheet of paper in front of him, explaining something to Ted, occasionally scribbling on it. Ted made a comment. Henri nodded, emphatic, and clapped Ted on the shoulder. He made several quick strokes and handed the piece of paper to Ted. Ted looked at it, removed a fresh sheet from a small pad, and began his own drawing under Henri's intent gaze.

They had found a way to communicate, seemingly without words. Their posture, the way they leaned toward one another, signified a closeness and an ease that required no explanation.

Henri had begun work on a restoration project, a group of unique pieces for an exhibition in Lyon in 1976. He needed help, preferably someone who had already mastered certain skills, so he had begun to search for an assistant four months ago. Several people had come to talk to him, none experienced enough to do what he needed. Time was critical.

"Ted's French is good, almost as good as yours," Milou told me. "And he has a good sense of humor. I'm not surprised he and Henri get along."

"Is Ted interested in the job? Three years ago, when they talked about something like this, Ted said it was bad timing."

Milou smiled. "He's had some good experience in Newport. Henri agreed to teach him more advanced techniques, if Ted will work for him for a while. He told Henri he's ready to start right away."

"He didn't mention Claire and Annie. Are they coming over, too?"

Milou's smile faded. She looked away, shaking her head.

"Why not? What happened?"

"They're getting a divorce."

"A divorce? Did Jeanne know?"

"It was Jeanne who told me. About a month ago. She didn't say why, only that Bruno is worried, especially about Annie."

"Not about Ted?"

Milou made an impatient sound and frowned. "He's disappointed in Ted. That's all I know. *Il est sévère, Bruno.*"

For weeks after Jeanne's birthday, I had followed the trail of all imaginable what-ifs. What if Ted and I had stayed in touch through high school and college? What if he weren't married? I always listened, of course, whenever Jeanne shared family news, but eventually I'd made myself stop wondering about what might have been. I was enough of a realist to know there was no "what might be."

As much as I wanted to hear what Ted had to say, I wanted him to tell me without prodding. For that to happen, he needed time. I could wait.

Early in the evening, Ted came into Jeanne's kitchen where Isabelle, my mother, and I were stacking dishes and drying glasses. "Milou said you did this drawing." He held up a charcoal portrait of Jeanne, careful not to smudge it. In it, Jeanne sat in three-quarter profile, eyes closed, her right cheek resting in the palm of her right hand. Her left hand lay in her lap on top of a newspaper. I had put the portrait on the table with the guest book and several photographs of Jeanne. I hadn't signed it.

"She was dozing on the porch when I came up from the greenhouse one day. I always have my sketchbook with me. I had to work fast. When she woke up, she scolded me, of course, for not letting her put in her teeth and fix her hair."

"She looks so young." He held the drawing out to me.

"Please. Keep it. I have others."

ONCE WE finished cleaning up, my mother and I sat on the steps looking out at the fields, red-gold now under the setting sun. During the day, whenever our eyes met, I'd felt as though we were feeling our way back to one another, one glance at a time. Her confrontation with Milou had blown the pain of the past away. What more was there to talk about, really?

The memory of my mother and Milou holding one another came to mind often. What would be the point of going back over it, picking it apart? None that I could see. Knowing how they had kept so much hidden from me explained everything and nothing.

It was enough. Just as my mother and Milou had moved beyond their painful history, so must I.

"Tell me what you've been doing. And your plans. Do you have any idea what you'll do when you finish here?" my mother asked.

Isabelle and Luc wanted me to stay and work for them for another two years. By then, they thought their business would have grown enough that they could hire a designer as well as someone to help Béatrice in the greenhouses, when she came back to work.

"I'm doing more design work, which I love. So I'll probably go to Alden, live in Prospect Hill, start my own business. I don't really know yet." I sounded as if I were anticipating an argument. Why must my mother get into this now? Why get into it at all?

"I see. But I want you to think about something. It's hard for a woman to make it in any kind of business. Men still seem to think it's their private bailiwick. You know the old cliché, 'It's a man's world.' In my business, I've had to do everything I can just to keep one step ahead of my competitors—mostly male interior designers working for or with male architects. You're living and working in a very isolated place. A lot is going on back home, changes that may make it easier—and harder, too—for you to have a career."

"You sound like a feminist." I was only joking, but I felt her tense.

"I suppose you could say that, yes. Aren't you?"

"Probably. But at least for now, I'm steering clear of rule books. I had enough of that at Brookton." I shuddered. I wanted to talk about Brookton even less than I wanted to talk about my future. "Anyway, you're doing fine, right? And you're happy?"

"Now, yes. But when I started in 1968, it was like someone was holding my head under water. There wasn't enough time in the day to follow up on leads, write proposals—and produce my designs, of course. I'm still working fifteen-hour days, but I'm managing my time better and I have some great projects."

"I'm glad for you, but what does this have to do with me?"

"Those classes I took, starting the year you were a senior at Alden . . ."

"What about them?"

"To be certified in interior design, I had to pass the exam. Now, when I pitch a proposal, I can show the client my portfolio—and my credential."

"So?"

"Think about going back to school for a while to be certified in something related to what you want to do. A master gardener's certification, for example."

"I've had so much hands-on experience here. I really don't see why that doesn't count."

"Of course you've had a lot of experience. The certificate is just a piece of paper, but it matters to people—you know the type, the ones who think it doesn't take any special talent to design a garden until they try to do it themselves."

"After what I went through at Brookton, the thought of taking classes, or passing exams, makes me want to run fast and far in the opposite direction, to just take my chances with my portfolio and my time here. It's been an apprenticeship. Which is another kind of certification, you know?" I yawned. "I'll think about it, all right?"

"Malorie?"

I shrugged away from her. "Please, Mom. Can we just drop this?"

"That's all I'm asking. That you think about it."

September 16, 1974

"Malorie!"

Two echoes came back to me across the valley, one fainter than the other.

Seven o'clock our time— one o'clock in the afternoon, his. Jet lag. No wonder Ted was up so early. I waved and leaned against a fencepost to wait for him.

Since June, I'd made the rounds several times a week before breakfast, checking on several gardens I managed for weekenders who wanted to enjoy them carefree. The contrast between working outdoors in the garden and working in the greenhouse surprised me at first. The basics were similar (plant, soil, water, fertilizer, pest control). But the particulars made all the difference. Like British English and American English. Or Québecois and French. Similar, but different.

In the beginning, Luc hadn't assumed anything about my knowledge of plants and gardens or my experience. He explained greenhouse conditions, the feeding programs, the ventilation system, and the watering schedule. "Most of all, you must pay attention, notice the smallest changes, be aware of how the air feels—how dry or damp—and smells. Sounds a little *excessif* perhaps, but it's the key. Even the smallest spot on a leaf can develop into a big problem. So, at first, you just get acquainted with everything, yes?"

He looked over the flats of begonia plants stretching from one end of the greenhouse to the other. When he turned back to me, he spoke quietly, emphatically. "If you see anything—*la moindre chose*—tell me. You must become a *malade imaginaire*. Even if you *think* it's nothing, tell me. That way, you'll learn what's important, what's not."

I laughed at the idea of becoming a hypochondriac. But I took his advice to heart and made sure that every minute I spent with the plants, I was working. No daydreaming.

Luc also showed me the value of fine-tuning. All the mechanical systems were on timers, of course; even so, he often adjusted them to accommodate external temperature changes or hours of daylight. Sometimes he tweaked them "just because." "I really don't trust them, even though I designed them myself. So I check and fiddle."

Eventually, I learned about the business side so that I could help Isabelle with bookkeeping. In the three years since I'd last seen Ted, I had learned enough to take over for Luc so he could travel and expand his list of contacts and customers.

PRETENDING TO struggle up the last rise, Ted doubled over, arms dangling. He made a show of wiping his face with the tail of his T-shirt and laughed. "I remember this hill. It's a lot more fun on the way down. For starters, there's that bump." He gestured at a spot about halfway down the lane in a clearing where sunlight streamed through an opening in the chestnut trees' thick canopies. "We used to take turns riding down as fast as we could to see who got the biggest bounce."

"Didn't one of you end up with a broken arm?"

"That was a bad day. Pierre's dad warned us he'd take our bikes away if we kept it up. So we stopped." Ted shrugged. "Luc told me you were out for a walk." He looked pleased with himself. "Where are you headed?"

"To the château. On the way, I'll check on a couple of gardens. The first is just around the bend."

Ted fell in step beside me, and we walked on for a while without talking. Early-morning sounds rose from the village along with the ground mist. A tractor rumbled to life; someone whistled for a dog. The smell of baking bread made my stomach growl.

We came to the stone wall that enclosed the first garden. Ted opened the gate and stopped to look at the hand-forged iron hinges, each in the shape of a tapered strap with a heart-shaped tip. "These are beautiful. I wonder if a local smithy made them."

"Probably. We unearthed some old tools here, too, ones that look to be about the same age. The hoe and pitchfork cleaned up so well that I've been using them."

Just through the gate, a narrow path ran down into the property through a small orchard of apple, peach, and pear trees, all staked to keep their branches from snapping under the weight of their ripening fruit. On the other side of the orchard, a cottage with a terra-cotta tile roof sat next to a small barn. In the low morning sunlight, the buff-colored masonry walls glowed.

"Don't they look like cats sunning themselves?" Although the two buildings were similar in size and structure to the houses and barns in the village, the way they were sited, nestled into the orchard up here on the hill, they seemed older.

"This place was abandoned, I remember. We used to come to the barn." He laughed.

"A couple from Mâcon bought and restored it about five years ago. They did most of the work themselves—he's a mason. They asked Luc to help them sort out the garden. That's how I got involved."

"You designed this?" His gesture encompassed the orchard and the kitchen garden.

"Not that, no. The orchard was here and there was a small, overgrown kitchen garden. I rescued what was left, applied some TLC—mainly loads of compost—and put in some new plants. I'm pretty sure the garden today is almost identical to the original one." Was I trying to show off my own restoration interests?

Ted didn't react. He had his eyes on the orchard.

We stopped by a pear tree. Already bees bobbed and dived, hunting for breakfast. I lifted my hair and fanned my neck. "This tree may be eighty years old. It was a mess when I started to work on it. Luc told me to do what I could, but said not to be too disappointed if it didn't survive." Luc had joked that I couldn't make matters any worse. "I had to read a book first. And talk to a few people." Ted grinned at that. I realized he knew as well as I that no book can provide all the answers. "Then I thinned it and shocked it into putting out new growth. That was two years ago."

"It looks like it could go another eighty years." Ted walked around the tree, running his hands over the branches, assessing it. "Did you know that pear wood has almost no grain? It makes beautiful small pieces—side tables, jewelry boxes, that sort of thing. Wonderful to work with, hard to come by." He rubbed his hands together, grinning.

I laughed. "Don't even think about it."

AFTER I watered the kitchen garden, we walked back out to the lane. On the way, I picked two pears that looked about ready to fall off the tree.

"The best thing about a tree-ripened fruit is that you can taste the tree, as if somehow it had absorbed the essence of the whole thing." With pear juice running down his chin, he looked more like a kid than a philosopher. "We're different. People are. Oh sure, we resemble our parents in lots of ways, but it's not so close a thing."

Was he trying to convince himself? Father and son, Bruno and Ted, could not have differed more in temperament. We threw our pear cores into the woods and went on, talking about Flagy, past and present.

Ted looked around, as if checking for familiar landmarks. "I still remember peoples' names, even faces, and all the shortcuts through the barnyards and fields. Most didn't mind if we jumped their fences to cut through, as long as we didn't leave gates open or annoy the animals. There was only one place we didn't go."

"With the dog?" One of the villagers had kept a guard dog on a chain outside the barn.

Ted nodded. "*Grand-mère* wrote to us when they finally left. *Ils n'étaient pas d'ici.* I've always wondered: If they weren't from here, how did they come to be here in the first place? She refused to talk about them."

"I used to have tea with her every afternoon when I first came back." Jeanne had always waited for me, putting the kettle on as soon as she saw me walking up from the greenhouse. "The first few weeks, I was on the outside looking in." Waking in the morning was like swimming up from the depths, struggling to find the surface.

"Makes sense. Everything you were doing was new, right?"

"That was part of it, yes. But in a way, it also had to do with a kind of block—there was everything that happened to me at Brookton and the shock of the Kennedys and King—and Vietnam—as if I needed to erase or shed all the bad news. The work helped. But having tea with your grandmother, that's what made the most difference."

A mix of sensations and particular memories helped me rediscover the village and my place in it. There was the light at certain times of the day, especially in the late afternoon, when it reached the top of Saint-Thibaut's tower, where it seemed to linger, warming the red tiles into a deep glow. There were familiar sounds of the village at work—in the early morning, the sound of tractors and trucks heading out to plow or to mow, the clang of cow and goat bells. And birdsong, always birdsong.

After the first cutting, in June, when the scent of newly mown hay wafted through the valley, as if I'd been working my way into a drawing, sharpening its point of view, I knew I had arrived. I knew that if I had parachuted into the village, blindfolded, I would have recognized it. Flagy hadn't changed, but I had. To find my way back, I had to blend then and now, to make them one. Flagy's sameness was the key.

"I opened my eyes one morning and knew I was exactly where I was supposed to be, doing what I was meant to do." It was as if I were filling in the blanks myself, fitting the old with the new.

WE STOPPED at the top of the hill. In the village below, wisps of steam rose straight up from the tile roofs. No sign of a breeze. It would be another warm day.

"You can almost see the Saône." Ted pointed across the valley where a narrow band of shimmering mist floated above the hills.

"I remember going to Mâcon with you, Louise, and Pierre." He made a scoffing sound. "We were so full of ourselves, Pierre and I. There was no way we were going to let you and Louise follow us."

"Where did you go?"

His eyes slid away. "I'd rather not . . ."

"The red-light district?"

He gave me a sheepish look. "A bordello, anyway." He grinned. "Pierre knocked on the door. The girl who opened it laughed in our faces. She couldn't have been more than eighteen, but she told us to come back when we were old enough to shave. Pierre was furious. I was relieved—but pretended to be furious, too, of course."

"Do you remember the photo booth?"

"Photo booth?"

"At the train station? While we waited?"

"The photo booth!" His hoot of laughter echoed across the valley. "We only had enough money for that one set of pictures, right? And what came out, those bits and pieces of us, were unrecognizable—except to us. Funny."

Before I could tell him I still had the photo, he was talking again.

"You sat on my lap. That's when . . ." He shook his head.

"What?"

"I realized you weren't my kid sister. But I didn't know what to say or do about it." His eyes searched mine. "And then it was too late."

I didn't say anything. The moment passed. We had reached the junction of two dirt roads. The one on the left continued up the valley. We took the one on the right, back to Flagy.

"DID YOU like Brown?" We had barely skimmed the surface the last time we'd seen each other; this was almost a fresh start.

"For the most part, yeah."

"But?"

"As I told you, Dad wanted me to go into medicine. Whenever I tried to talk to him about an art project or a paper that got me revved up, he found something else to do. After a while, I stopped trying. My mother encouraged me. That was good."

"What about Vietnam?"

"Another bone of contention with my father, of course. He wanted me to serve. The navy was his first choice. He had hoped at one time to be a pilot; he thought I'd do it instead. Then I collided with a hardball playing right field in '62, my freshman year at Brown. Ended up with a concussion and a detached retina in my right eye."

That explained the scar.

He shrugged and made a face. "So no navy for me. Dad was pretty good about it—although he analyzed the play dozens of times to prove I could have avoided that ball. Mom was beyond relieved."

"And you, too?"

"Yes. And no. I feel guilty, you know? I got off easy. A guy I knew, a conscientious objector, went to Canada. He wrote me about how angry he is—having to leave his family, his own country, just because he didn't want to fight in a war that wasn't a war, officially anyway. When Nixon resigned last month, I felt sick at heart. Of course, I'm glad he's gone. But what a waste. Too bad his resignation didn't come with a guarantee we'll never again do such a dumb thing."

"How did you end up in Newport?" If he knew I was fishing, he didn't seem to mind.

"The restoration projects I worked on—part of that course I took at Brown—put me in touch with some people there. More than three hundred eighteenth-century houses, most of them moldering away. So there's lots of work for someone like me."

I talked about the rhythm of my work with Luc, about learning something new every day. "I know I have to decide where to go with all of this. I'm not a horticulturalist like Luc. I'm interested in plants for what they can do in a garden or a landscape. Not in themselves. Some days when I'm rushing to finish potting another five hundred seedlings, I feel like the old woman who lived in a shoe. I'd like to do something that's a little less like playing scales."

"Such as?"

"Something that includes drawing and design."

He grinned. "I remember you used to sit for hours drawing horses—running, jumping, prancing. Annie seems to have entered a horse phase. Claire says this is normal. Apparently most nine-year-old girls go through it."

"Mine lasted until I was thirteen, so you have some time to get used to it." Before I could find out more about Annie, he asked about my drawing.

"I always have this with me." I pulled my sketch pad from my pocket. "I sketch all kinds of things—plants I don't recognize, gardens I visit with Luc when we do a delivery. It's just something to do, I suppose, but it helps me remember shapes and proportions."

"Maybe there's a drafting class you could take around here?"

"I thought of that, yes. At the technical school in Cluny, there's one starting up at the beginning of January. I need to see if I like that kind of drawing, you know?"

My mother had told me it didn't much matter if I liked to do it, that it wasn't *art*. But I knew better. For me, drawing would never simply be a means to an end. Would drafting satisfy me the same way, or would I learn to like it because it was part of the design process, which itself included so much more than drafting?

March 26, 1975

At five o'clock, I pinched back the last begonia. This process made me cringe, even though I knew it shocked the plants into filling out, rather than stretching up. It was miraculous, really, how quickly they recovered.

On my way out, I adjusted the ventilation system to its night settings, hearing it slow to a low hum as it drew the air through the greenhouse, carrying the fragrance of growing plants and soil. After I checked the irrigation timer, I took a last look at the flats. It would be several weeks before the plants' colorful blooms would differentiate them from one another.

With the feeding regimen Luc had developed, these begonias would easily double in size in plenty of time for shipment to flower markets all over Europe. He had recently developed a new hybrid, an unusual cross with a coral-edged double yellow bloom. He had named it "Madame Jeanne."

I heard Ted's motorcycle throttle down as he came around the bend at the top of the hill. Over the last seven months, his routine had become as familiar to me as my own. Today he was an hour early. What was up? Just as I got to the goat pen, he came around the back corner of the house. It still gave me a start to realize that he, not Jeanne, lived there now.

"I'll be there as soon as I can. Phone call . . ."

The goats had thrived over the winter. Several kids added their antics and mischief to the challenge of keeping the herd safe. Since they loved to climb and jump, Ted built them a kind of jungle gym. Even some of the does had tried it out.

Two years ago, standing among the goats, talking quietly to me about each of them, Jeanne had told me, "If you don't learn their names and their *trucs*—all their finicky little habits—they will make your life a misery." As if to emphasize the point, Anisette had butted me.

" '*C'est moi la* boss!' You see?" Jeanne had laughed, as much at Anisette as at her own command of English. "If you want to get along with them, never, ever push them. Take the collar and lead." She demonstrated with Anisette, who walked beside her, occasionally nuzzling her pocket. The others followed, anxious not to be left out—but respectful of their *boss*.

Luckily the goats had adjusted to Ted and he was a fast learner. Soon after he arrived, he had made a rubber gasket that he installed around the outside edge of the feed trough, making it difficult for Anisette to paw at it, something she did whenever she wanted to remind us it was time to eat.

According to Jeanne, Anisette was a born problem solver, a true leader. The others knew this and didn't challenge her. Once Ted finished the bumper, Anisette stopped pawing the trough, and the others had followed suit. Jeanne would have been amused, but not surprised.

As soon as I finished milking, I hung the pail on its hook and cleaned the sponges and grooming brushes. Still no sign of Ted. I latched the gate and headed across the driveway and up the hill to Isabelle and Luc's.

At the foot of the path to the house, I kicked off my clogs. Warmed by the sun, the broad, flat stones gave off enough heat to ease my aching ankles and calves. At either side, rosemary and lavender plants showed a hint of new growth at the tips of each branch. Across the road, beyond the meadow, the valley spread its spring patchwork of golds, greens, and blues into the hills. The last minutes of the sunset's amber light burnished the fields to the color of aged bronze as swallows spiraled effortlessly down over the woods to roost for the night.

AT THE kitchen counter, Isabelle sliced roasted beets, placing them on a platter next to a bowl of vinaigrette. A plate of tarragon chicken and a casserole heaped with steamed beet greens sat on the table beside a loaf of bread and a dish of baked garlic cloves. The table was set for four—the three of us and Ted, who came for dinner once or twice a week. Would he tell us about the phone call? I let Isabelle know he might be late. She nodded, but she looked as if she, too, wondered what was going on.

"*Ça va là-bas?*" Isabelle dried her hands and put the beets on the table with the bowl of vinaigrette.

"I'm betting this batch of begonias will be ready early."

"Don't tell Luc. He'll have the trucks here long before it's time." She looked up at the clock. "*On dine à 18h30.*"

It was six o'clock now. Half an hour to shower, if I hurried. Tonight, after dinner, I planned to finish some drawings, a garden design for a property belonging to a couple from Paris. They had completed the house restoration and had decided to update the gardens. After weeks of discussion—she wanted a formal garden, he didn't—they still hadn't settled matters between them. The last time I had visited to show them new drawings, the wife, looking strained, had met with me by herself.

"I know a formal design would fit the style of the house. And I love the balance and clarity of a formal garden," she had told me. "But my husband insists he won't pay to maintain it. For him, this is just a weekend place. It has to take care of itself." She had sighed, then frowned.

"It's asking a lot, I realize, but is it possible to design something that will satisfy us both?" She had looked down at the drawings, avoiding my eyes. "Could you ask Monsieur Labrosse to call my husband?"

I didn't mind that they wanted to talk to Luc. Perhaps he'd be able to suggest a solution.

After his conversation with the husband, Luc had come to find me. "They're happy with what you've done so far. That's not the problem. The problem is they thought I'd be doing the design, that you were my assistant."

"I can see their point. You know what you're doing. I'm just a beginner."

"Except that design isn't my forte. It *is* yours. You have a real talent for it. Really, they don't know how lucky they are that you're doing the work. For one thing, if they hired an experienced designer, they'd have to pay two or three times the fee they'll end up paying you."

"So what are we going to do?"

"*Ben, on continue, quoi.* You keep doing what you're doing. I'll sign the drawings. And the plant lists."

"But, isn't that . . ." I didn't know how to put it. I didn't want him to think I was accusing him of trying to get away with something. At the same time, I thought we needed to be on the up and up with these people.

"Cheating? *Pas du tout.* All the big design firms do this. The *patron* signs off on staff work. Always. To make my involvement official, I'll come with you to see them the day they sign the contract. *D'accord?*"

"I don't know."

"*Voyons,* Malorie. They both think your work is fine. It's just that they are anxious that you're young and inexperienced. We can't help that. However, if it reassures them that I'm in charge because they see my signature on your drawings, then that's how we'll do it."

TED REASSURED me that what Luc proposed was common business practice. "Someday you'll be signing off on someone else's work. No problem! It's a little like what I'm doing for Henri. I do the work, but he's the one who signs the bill. This whole thing is just a formality."

Formalities aside, I had struggled to find a way to blend the couple's different ideas into a harmonious whole. The set of drawings I had to finish that night was my last, best effort. I had mixed feelings about how well I'd managed to satisfy their criteria, but realized I was too close to the process to be objective.

The sequence of drawings began with the view from the wide stone terrace, just outside the living room. From there, you continued down four steps to a path that linked the terrace to the gardens. Closest to the house, a lawn bordered by two perennial beds ended in a low boxwood hedge. Beyond the hedge I had put a vegetable garden and a small orchard. At the far side of the orchard, I planned for a gazebo, the focal point. From it, you had a view of the fields and the woods below the house. Of course, you could also look back at the house itself. I thought the owners would like the idea of having an open structure there. If not, they could install a bench instead.

I took the drawings down to Luc's office off the kitchen. Luc and Isabelle came in to look at them. They had both seen the project at various stages; there wasn't much new for them to comment on. But it was the first time they'd seen the whole picture. I held my breath. Isabelle smiled at me.

Luc nodded. "*C'est géniale*, Malorie. I really like the way each space opens to the next one. You've done something very subtle. The overall design is classical, formal in the best sense. But thanks to the perennial borders, the lawn, and the orchard, it has a lovely, naturalistic feel."

"I hope they'll like it—that they both can agree on it." I was more apprehensive about the strain between the husband and wife than I was about presenting the design.

"You can't read their minds," Ted had told me. "So you can't know the hidden agenda."

"You mean, maybe they're not getting along about something else, and this is the way they work it out?"

"Something like that, yes."

"Ugh!"

Ted laughed. "At least they aren't yelling or throwing things."

Luc went through the drawings a second time and initialed each one. "What about the gazebo?"

I sighed, frustrated. "I haven't been able to finish that one." I had tried different ways of drawing the gazebo, but I couldn't seem to make it fit. The proportions and the perspective always came out wrong. I had to go ahead with the appointment without it. If the couple liked the idea of the gazebo, I would figure out what to do later.

Luc nodded, his lips pursed. "That should be all right. If they want to talk to me about it . . ."

Isabelle handed me a folder. "I've been updating the estimates along the way. Except for the one for the gazebo, everything is here."

The kitchen door opened behind us. Luc looked back into the kitchen. "I told Ted we were going to look at this tonight. Hope that's okay with you, Malorie." Before I could answer, Ted walked into the office.

He greeted us, glanced at me, then looked down at the table. "So you've got a gazebo idea?"

I had wanted to do the work myself, so of course I hadn't asked for help. Was it too late? I didn't yet have the drafting skills to do what was required. Ted did. I knew he would talk me through the process. It wouldn't be a matter of his verifying or correcting what I'd done.

"Beautiful house. Your drawings show its shape and size to advantage and make it very clear how the gardens work together. Lucky thing you don't have a day job."

We all laughed, Luc loudest of all.

"Now I understand why I see your light in the middle of the night." Ted's eyes met mine, signaling his embarrassment. "I sometimes get up and check the goats."

Before I could let him off the hook, the moment passed, and we were back to talking about my work. "I just hope the owners like this set. What I really mean is, I hope they can understand the effect I've worked out. It's the best I can do. But it may be hard for them to get the connection without a more finished drawing of the gazebo."

"*À table, tout le monde!*" Isabelle urged us back into the kitchen for dinner.

While we ate, Ted talked about his new project, the restoration of an ebony and walnut armoire. "Not much inlay, but there's some water damage, so Henri and I are trying to bring the wood back. Slow, but worth it. It's a beautiful piece."

Whenever Ted talked about his work, his eyes seemed to change color, deepening from brown to black. Even the most mundane details delighted him. I looked around the table. Like me, Luc and Isabelle hung on every word, as if mesmerized. I caught Isabelle's eye and we both laughed.

Ted grinned, sheepish. "Bet you can't tell I love what I do."

Luc got up to clear the table. Isabelle motioned to Ted and me not to help.

"Is everything okay?" Since he hadn't brought up the phone call, I took a shot in the dark. If he didn't feel like talking about it, we wouldn't. I left it up to him.

He sighed and shrugged his shoulders; bothered, yes, frustrated, yes, but dealing with it. "More or less. The call was about Annie's visit this summer. Claire thinks she's too young to be away from home for two months. So we compromised on six weeks. Mid-July until the end of August. I'm not worried."

"I bet she'll have a lot of fun here. You and I did."

Ted's mouth tightened. "Claire says she'll be homesick, that she'll miss her friends, and so forth. I'm pretty sure she'll make out okay. And I'm looking forward to seeing her every day. I miss her."

For a moment, I found myself sympathizing with Claire. It wasn't hard to read between the lines: She worried that Annie would love Flagy as much as Ted did. How could Newport and home begin to compete with wild raspberries, eggs straight from the nest, and, of course, goats large and small?

"You're laughing at me? What's so funny?" His puzzled look gave in to a smile.

"I'm just imagining how much fun Annie will have with the kids." By the time Annie arrived, the five kids would be nearly eight months old, their acrobatics a surefire cure for homesickness—if one was needed.

AFTER DESSERT, I went into Luc's office to put the drawings away.

"Shall we look at the gazebo?" Ted stood in the doorway.

"Tonight?"

"Why not? I'll have plenty of time to finish it before your meeting."

"May I watch?"

"That's the idea." He picked up the tissue sketch I'd done and placed it over the drawing of the orchard. "I like that it's not a traditional design."

"It's really more of an arbor than a gazebo. No roof." I'd made the eight-by-twelve wood structure a rectangle, open on all sides, with an overhead trellis to support a wisteria, or even a grapevine.

Ted took a pencil and straightedge. Working from the sketch, he quickly scaled and finished the design on a fresh tissue, making a couple of changes as he went along, explaining and checking with me to make sure I understood and agreed. At length, we sat side by side looking at the draft.

"If this seems fine to you, I'll take it with me and give you estimates and the finished drawing in the morning." Ted flipped back through the other tissues, checking them against his own sketch.

"Your drawing gives the gazebo the right proportions, and the view from it makes it possible to see how it fits in. It really ties everything together, gives the view from the house a focal point that's not too formal."

The gazebo, a small piece of the project, brought the whole design into focus. How could I have even considered going to my appointment with the owners without it?

"That's the idea—your idea. I'm excited about it. I bet they'll be pleased with the whole concept. But if they aren't sure, I can help you design other options."

"Seems like a lot of work."

"Don't worry. You'll do most of it. I'll show you how. Consider it payback for teaching me the ropes with the goats."

"Fair enough."

March 27, 1975

The next morning, I rolled up the drawings and put them into a cardboard tube. Drinking a cup of coffee at the kitchen window, I could see a red bandana tied to the goats' gate: a signal from Ted. He had gone in to Cluny early, but not before he'd done the morning chores. I checked Luc's office to see if Ted had left anything for me. No sign of the gazebo drawing. I tried not to feel disappointed. Or hurt that Ted had left early. At least he'd taken care of the goats.

Isabelle came into the kitchen carrying a leather artist's portfolio. "From Ted. The gazebo drawing's inside. He said to tell you, 'break a leg.' But I hope you do not."

After I explained what Ted meant, Isabelle looked amazed—and relieved. "He also said, 'Don't even think of not using the portfolio. It's just a loan.'"

"I'm glad to have it. It'll make it so much easier to show the drawings. I'm ready."

"Break your leg!" Isabelle called after me.

"SO?" TED caught my eyes, expectant.

Sitting on a cushion on the top step outside the kitchen, I lifted my cup of tea. "I broke a leg."

Ted laughed. "*Félicitations.*"

"They loved the gazebo. They saw right away how it works. Your drawing did the trick. He called it the *pièce de résistance.* She clapped. They want to get started right away. Wait till I tell Luc."

"Tell me what?" Luc rounded the corner of the house, drying his hands.

"Malorie's design. They're ready to sign the contract." Ted beamed. "*Bravissima!*"

"I'm taking her out to dinner to celebrate." The look on his face challenged me to contradict him.

I played along. "Since when?"

"Since right now."

"*Allez, allez!* Get going. I'll babysit." Luc made sweeping motions at us.

We looked at each other, then at Luc. "The goats?"

"*Faites-moi confiance, quand même.* I've had plenty of practice. I may be a little rusty, but I'll manage. Just be careful how you drive, Ted. We need this deal."

TED PARKED the motorcycle across from Le Vieux Carré, the bistro near the center of Cluny where he and Henri sometimes had lunch. The owner had turned his passion for cooking into a full-time job, transforming a corner café into a restaurant that specialized in regional dishes. He had kept the zinc bar top and a few café tables and added a dining room. The *Guide Michelin* had just awarded him one star, praising the *cassolette d'escargots* and the black currant tart. Tonight, as usual, locals stood at the bar, bantering with the barkeep, the owner's son.

Across the street was the Librairie Saône-et-Loire, a small bookshop sandwiched between a butcher and a green grocer. At this hour, there was no one browsing the shelves; the sales clerk sat on a stool at the cash register, reading. In a cage by the door, a large parrot called out to us, "*Bonjour, monsieur, 'dame! Entrez! Entrez!*"

Ted looked into the shop and turned to me. "I need to see if they have a book Henri has been trying to find, a guide to finials. It'll just take a few minutes."

"Did you say 'finials'?"

"I did."

"A piece of furniture?"

Ted nodded. "A piece of a piece of furniture. It's like an exclamation point—a finishing touch, a kind of ornament. On chairs of a certain era, you'll find them at the top of the chair back. Not a big deal. Most of the time it's just a little knob. You won't see them much anymore, since modern furniture is about getting rid of anything superfluous. If you're a restorer, you have to go to the experts and museums. Right now, we have to replace a set on eight chairs; none of the originals survived. Henri wants to make something that looks authentic, but is not a reproduction."

Barely fourteen feet wide, the bookshop had floor-to-ceiling shelves packed with illustrated travel and restaurant guides for the Saône-et-Loire area, regional cookbooks, and books about grape growing and wine making. There was even a set of illustrated pamphlets describing nearby Romanesque chapels and churches with a detailed self-guided tour map.

The clerk didn't recognize the title Ted wanted. "What you see is what we have. What you don't see—what's in storage—is on file in the owner's head. You just missed him. However, our reference books are shelved together." The clerk gestured toward the rear of the shop. "Take a look. If you don't find what you're after, stop by tomorrow afternoon after two. The owner will be here."

While Ted checked the dictionaries and encyclopedias, I leafed through a selection of nineteenth-century travel illustrations. Many showed hand-colored street scenes with individuals, couples, and families visibly enjoying an excursion.

"Look what I found!" I held up a view of the Pont Saint-Laurent from the quay opposite Mâcon. The horizontal print was about the size of an index card.

Ted took it from me, nodding. "I remember standing there, just across the river from that spot, in 1961. I haven't been there since. Have you?"

I hadn't. "It's as if the illustrator wanted us to be able to imagine ourselves there, with those people."

In the foreground under a cloudless sky, a couple stood on the quay opposite the town a short distance upstream from the Pont Saint-Laurent. Several barges and small boats bobbed at their moorings nearby. The man wore a top hat and a dark red three-quarter-length coat; the woman had on a blue empire-style gown, her hair upswept. A small dog balanced on its hind legs, one front paw on the man's knee, looking up into his face. Across the river, beyond the roofline, a layer of flat, gray clouds hung low in the sky.

"So, tell me the story."

"Maybe the artist knew this couple, or maybe they just appeared and caught his eye as he sketched the river and the boats. They don't seem to be posing. They've probably just had lunch and decided to take a walk. It really is an appealing scene, isn't it? The light and the boat reflections in the water . . ." I touched the man's right hand, lying relaxed and open on the woman's arm. "They seem to know each other well."

"Why do you suppose he's pointing to that barge?" Because the print was so small, only a little larger than a playing card, Ted leaned in, following the man's gesture to the barge, its deck crowded with barrels, coils of rope, and crates, as if waiting for a crew to offload its cargo.

"Maybe he's a local merchant and the barge belongs to him. They're courting; he's been trying to get her to say yes. Now he's reassuring her he can keep her in the style to which she is accustomed." I felt the light pressure of Ted's cheek against my hair.

"And those storm clouds?"

"This illustrator is a realist." Fast-moving rainstorms often blew through the river valley in the late summer and early fall.

"Or a moralist."

"What do you mean?"

"Well, life is like that, isn't it? Clear one day; stormy the next. Make hay while the sun shines?" Ted's pleasure in this idea showed in his teasing smile.

"Or maybe he—or she—wanted to show off: In such a small print, it's hard to show depth of field. The only way is to make the most of the sky." I looked at him and spotted a place under his chin that had escaped his razor. I slid the print back into the portfolio.

"Any luck?" Smiling, the clerk joined us. Evidently he had caught the tail end of the story.

"We'll have to come back. *Merci quand même!*"

"*Au revoir alors! Bonne soirée, monsieur, 'dame!*"

"*Au revoir.*"

The parrot stretched and flapped its wings, as if sweeping us out the door.

THE RESTAURANT'S owner greeted us at the door. He winked at Ted. "*Poursuis donc!*" Ted laughed.

After he settled us at a table near the terrace, he told us about the menu—four entrées, including *boeuf bourguignon*, and a limited number of side dishes. He made our decision for us when he explained that his version of *boeuf bourguignon* was adapted from his grandmother's handwritten recipe, handed down to her by her own mother—and so on and so forth.

As soon as he left us, I asked Ted what the owner had meant.

"About what?"

"When he said, '*Poursuis donc!*'"

Ted smiled and looked away. "He's been trying to fix me up. I keep telling him no thanks."

"So he thinks . . . ?"

"I'm so sorry." His look of chagrin made me regret I'd asked.

"What? Why?"

"I've played along with him a bit, but I'm not the presumptuous guy he thinks I am."

"I know that."

"Still, you should know you're the first woman I've brought here." So I *was* Ted's first date. If Ted didn't bring up his divorce tonight, I would. Wanting to know was shifting to needing to know. Did Ted understand that?

While the server set our plates in front of us, I looked around the room, taking in the beamed ceiling and the antique ironware implements next to the fireplace. With eight tables set for four, it was a comfortable, unpretentious setting. Only one other couple had been seated, but it was still early. Even here, in the provinces, people didn't usually have dinner until seven thirty or eight.

"They're having the same thing." Ted gestured at the other couple.

"Not hard to guess why."

When it was time to order dessert, Ted stood and spoke quietly to the server. I overheard just enough of their exchange to know that Ted had set something up, but what?

"A surprise?"

Ted shrugged and smiled.

"It's something you ordered in advance, something you know I like. How am I doing so far?" He nodded, enjoying the idea, with me and for me. "How did you know I'd get the deal? Or that I wouldn't turn you down?"

"I can read the stars, remember?"

The server arrived with a tray, took a kitchen torch from his pocket, and passed it quickly over the desserts.

"It's almost too beautiful to eat." The caramelized sugar of the crème brûlée yielded with a small, satisfying crackle. The perfect blend of cream, vanilla, sugar, and eggs was as much texture as it was flavor. "Isabelle had something to do with this, didn't she?"

"Let's just say she dropped a hint and leave it at that." He saluted me with his spoon. "To you, Malorie!"

When we finished our espressos, I looked around for the server. Ted reached across the table and took my hand. "You haven't asked. About the divorce . . ."

"I didn't know . . . I didn't want to . . . I wanted you to have time." I tried to breathe normally.

He leaned back and slid his spoon over onto the saucer under his coffee cup. "It's time."

My heart began to pound. Part of me wanted to stop him. Once he had told me, once he had answered my questions, everything would change. We had both been so careful not to step over the invisible line between us, just enjoying our friendship. I didn't want to let go of that. Once he told me about Claire and about the divorce, what would happen to us?

He leaned forward, turning a coin over and over on the table in front of him as he talked. He had met Claire at a party in 1964, their sophomore year. "My father was on my case about med school; I was flunking chemistry; I'd broken up with my high school girlfriend, a Catholic girl from home. Which gave Dad another reason to be angry." He looked down at the coin, pushed it aside. "It was spring. It was time for a change."

Just knowing Claire and her friends made it possible for him to stay in school. "She made me laugh. It was easy to get involved. Too easy, as it turns out. We got pregnant in November, senior year. Dad's devout, as you know. He didn't rant and rave. Not his way. He froze me out. Then, right before Christmas break, he called to tell me that he'd talked to our priest; they'd set a date for the wedding. Claire isn't Catholic. But her parents were no match for my father. We got married on Christmas Eve—only family and close friends. Annie was born on July 4, 1966."

They knew they weren't in love. But they liked each other "well enough." Since Bruno Girard's views on abortion and divorce were two sides of the same coin, they stuck it out as long as they could. By the time it was clear to everyone they weren't happy together, Ted was ready to stand up to his father.

"Last year we found a lawyer to get us a no-fault divorce. In the end, it was pretty painless. We decided to stay in Newport for the time being so we could both be with Annie as much as possible."

"And Bruno?"

Ted's jaw tightened. "Once he realized I wouldn't back down, he stopped speaking to me—until we came back for *grand-mère's* funeral."

Newport suited Ted. It was an ideal place to live and work. But Claire, who had grown up in Boston, found it cliquish and insular. Lately, she had talked about moving back to the city. This was no mystery: she wanted to marry again. And Ted didn't want to stand in the way. They would have to decide about Annie.

"You mean where she'll go to school and who she'll live with?"

"That's it. If I could figure out a way to persuade Claire to stay put, at least until Annie finishes high school . . ."

"But that's, what, eight years from now?"

"Yeah. A long time to put your life and your career on hold. That's what Claire keeps telling me, anyway. She wants to work in a big library at a university. Like Harvard." Ted sighed. He picked up the check and smiled at me. "I guess you could say that my life right now is all about unfinished business."

"I'm sorry, Ted."

"It'll work out."

STRADDLING THE motorcycle, my arms around Ted's waist, I thought about what it meant to like someone "well enough." It seemed plausible to me that two people could stay together, even marry, feeling that way. Especially under the circumstances. Once Bruno Girard had decided for them, had Ted and Claire had any choice?

Had Jack and I liked one another at all, let alone liked one another well enough? I shivered and buried my face in Ted's scarf, breathing in the smells of wood smoke, beeswax, and Ted. I turned my head to look at the sky. He reached back and around me, steadying me as we slowed to turn off the main road toward Flagy.

No, Jack and I hadn't had anything like the relationship Ted and Claire had at the beginning. For Ted and Claire, it might not have been love, but it was something solid, something to work with. Jack's self-assurance, his confidence in himself—the qualities I had told Milou attracted me to him—those qualities couldn't make up for what he lacked. Mistaking his detachment for calm, I had let myself believe I felt safe with him. What would have happened to us had I not miscarried?

I couldn't have married him.

Ted parked the bike and we stood beside Jeanne's dark house, listening to the motor tick as it cooled. The full moon flooded the sky with light. Beyond its range, the stars blazed and pulsed as if straining to touch one another.

"Did it ever make you feel dizzy?"

"Used to. Now, I try to look beyond the brightest stars into the background. It's like looking behind the scenes, or into very deep water. You've heard the expression 'the back of beyond'?" He didn't wait for my answer. "That's what I see out there. I used to imagine I could see the other side of the universe." He laughed. "But, of course, that's impossible."

"The back of beyond," I repeated. "Very far away."

Ted turned toward the house. "Very."

I could sense in him the same need to talk more, but I didn't know how to start. Thinking about Jack had revived my uncertainty and my malaise about Brookton and him. I shivered.

Ted opened the kitchen door for me and switched on the light. He had taken my hand at dinner, a casual, almost incidental gesture, the way you might touch a friend for reassurance. He didn't seem to expect or want anything more from me.

"Tisane?" He held up the teapot and two boxes of tea.

"Chamomile, please." While the teakettle heated, Ted sprinkled the herbs into the pot and rummaged around for cups. "My grandmother had more dishes than she could possibly use in several lifetimes, all chipped or cracked. She couldn't throw anything away. I started to sort them, you know, the ones that I could still use, the ones that I could get rid of. I ended up with one—unchipped, uncracked, with handles. So I gave up and kept them all. When I told Henri, he just laughed and showed me the box where he keeps his odds and ends. Bits and pieces, nothing you'd think worth saving. 'You never know what you might need or when,' he told me." Ted raised his eyebrows. "Broken bits and pieces of crockery? Really?"

"A way for her to remember the past?" We both laughed.

Sitting at the table, he seemed as far away as the other side of the universe. He was watching me, waiting.

"A penny?"

"Just thinking about the other side of the universe. To me, it's unimaginable."

"To me, too. But I like the sense of it. To have the capacity even to think about it, that's the thing. The mind . . ."

"I suppose."

"Malorie," he looked into my eyes, intent, "you can talk to me, you know. About anything . . . if you have questions about what I told you. And anything else." His voice was as warm as his eyes.

At a loss for words, I tried to smile. As I'd listened to him talk about the circumstances of his marriage, and the reasons for his divorce, I realized I *could* tell him anything. The question was when. *Now, now is the time.*

"You know, what you told me about getting pregnant, having to get married. It must have been so hard. But the divorce must have been even harder. For both of you." I sipped my tea.

"Yes." He gave me time.

"Jack and I got pregnant. In 1970, in the summer."

It was like telling him about a dream I'd had. The sharp-edged details came first—the crash of the tray on the floor, the custodian's sympathy and advice, the beginning and end of the pain. Like Jeanne's dishes, the original shape of the events had shattered into pieces.

Ted wrapped a shawl around my shoulders and held my hands until I stopped crying.

Annie

June 19, 1975

The hiss of the air brakes woke me as the train slowed to a stop just inside the Gare de Lyon. The train glided to a stop beside the platform. People stood and removed their bags from the overhead rack. A little girl, wakened from her nap, whimpered. Her mother soothed her. I smiled at them and motioned to the woman to go ahead of me. I'd told Ardis not to meet my train. I'd find her at the gallery. It had been three years since my last trip to Paris. I wanted some time on my own to take it in.

Working in New York, Ardis had made a name for herself, developing a style that had brought her into contact with the gallerist here in the Marais, where her work would be featured in a group show opening in September. I remembered one of the paintings she had shown me just before I left in 1971 to come to France. In it, translucent shapes overlapped one another in layers of green, water plants in a pond. Not until you looked closely—the narrow canvas measured four by eleven inches—did you see the fine network of inked lines stretched beneath the layers.

"I like the feeling of being in the water—you don't really *see* the leaves. What you see is blurred shapes draped over lines, the veins and leafstalks." To me, it always seemed remarkable that Ardis's description of her starting point always fit the experience of seeing where it had taken her.

I loved the painting because it captured so well a sense of being in contact with plants and their environment. Like the cables feeding power to the train, the leafstalk and veins held and channeled energy and power into the leaf blade.

In the gallery, Ardis stood beside a tall, dark-haired woman in front of a light table, her back to the door. Her hair hung loose down her back. She was wearing a blue tunic, black jeans, and boots. The woman—surely the gallery owner—leaned over, peering through a loupe at the slides laid out on the table. I could tell from their tone of voice that they were enjoying the conversation.

Skylights poured abundant natural light into the long, narrow room. Each had its own adjustable shade, just like the ones in the greenhouse. At the far end of the gallery, portable room dividers leaned against the wall, like attendants awaiting orders, and stacks of crated paintings stood by a loading dock, ready for shipment. Wondering what show had just come down, I thought again about the greenhouse, just emptied of the last flats of begonias now making their way out into the world to nurseries and gardens throughout France.

"Malorie!" Ardis hugged me, then held me at arm's length, shaking her head. "In my next life, I will be a blonde with skin like yours, so I can tan."

"If you like the Pop Art effect—the spots and stripes—then I hope you get your wish." Until I'd dressed that morning, I hadn't paid attention to my neck-up, wrist-down tan. Working with the crew at the garden site, digging, measuring, making adjustments, and so on, I had worn jeans and long-sleeved shirts, baring only my face, neck, wrists, and hands to the sun.

"See you later, Marcelle?"

The woman smiled and waved us out.

WHEN WE reached the landing outside Ardis's apartment, she opened the door with a flourish: "*Voilà!*"

There was just enough space in the tiny living room for a foldout couch and an armchair. In the bedroom, a double bed occupied almost the entire floor. Formerly a closet, the kitchen had a hot plate, a sink, and a miniature fridge below the counter.

A claw-foot tub, the bathroom's sole furnishing, was a mystery. "I don't know how they got it up there, but I'm sure they'll never get it out!"

She held out her hand. "Now for the best part. Close your eyes." Ardis turned me around and we stepped back into the living room. I heard the sound of drapes sliding open. "You can peek now."

"Oh my . . ."

An entire wall of floor-to-ceiling windows and French doors gave access to a narrow balcony. Tangled petunias and geraniums trailed in all directions up and over the wrought-iron railing. Not far away, above the rooftops of the Marais, gargoyles peered out over the Left Bank from Notre-Dame's towers—like the view my grandparents had taken in fifty-five years ago from the opposite side of the river.

Milou and my grandfather had lived in a one-room apartment in the fifth arrondissement from the time they were married until they left France. They had carried water from a well in the courtyard up the narrow stairs to the fourth floor where my grandmother cooked for them on a Bunsen burner. But the primitive, cramped quarters had mattered little. From one of the apartment's two windows, which faced the Seine, they could see Notre-Dame's towers, and it was only a short walk to the Jardin des Plantes, where my grandfather went every day to study and draw the plants.

"Is your grandmother happy to be back?"

"She is, yes. But, you know, I think she'd be happy anywhere, as long as she and Henri are together."

AS SOON as we found a table at the café on the corner, Ardis slid a folded paper across to me.

"I know we have the whole weekend. But it will go fast. So I made a list of things to talk about."

"Some list." In the middle of the page, Ardis had written "Ted." "Are you the same person who told me work makes the world go round?"

"That was before Matt. Now things are in much better balance, and so is my perspective."

"On life and love?"

"On love and life!"

Ted had been away several days a week during the month of May at a museum in Lyon, researching finials. My long days at the garden site left me little time to do anything except finalize plans for the new garden.

"So you haven't talked since you had dinner together in March?"

"Not about anything that matters. Not on the fly. It's not my way. You know that. And it's not his, either."

"But don't you want to know what he's thinking?"

"I get a sense of that when we're together."

"When? When *are* you together?"

"Mornings and evenings—when we take care of the goats."

"You're joking!"

"I'm not."

Ardis pursed her lips and leaned back. "It seems to me that you're really on the verge and you both know it. How can you not talk about it?" She picked up her knife and balanced it across the palm of her hand. "So, are you in love with him?"

It was so like Ardis just to push ahead, to jump in without hesitation. "Yes." I laughed, startled to hear my answer, so matter -of-fact, as if it always had been so.

"Well!" The knife clattered to the pavement. Ardis picked it up and slid the blade under her plate. "In that case, don't you want to know if he feels the same way?"

"Yes, of course. When he's ready, he'll tell me. I think—no, I *know*—he has to get past the divorce. The papers came in January and he hasn't been to Newport since. He needs to go back there, move out of the house and into his own place, you know?" I shrugged. "Anyway, it's just a feeling I have."

"And his daughter?"

"Annie's coming to Flagy in mid-July. I want to see how it goes. She's only nine. So far, Ted thinks she's doing okay. But I'm not sure she understands what it means yet. And she really misses him."

Ted had talked about Annie, about what she liked to do, about her energy. His eyes became darker, deeper, and regretful.

"The most important thing for Ted right now is Annie. I support that. I don't mind waiting."

Ardis looked down at the table, brushed a few bread crumbs into a pile on the tablecloth. "Don't sell yourself short, Malorie. If he loves you, he'll want to make a place for you in his life. For your sake, I hope it's as big as you need."

I felt less confident about Annie than I sounded. But I didn't want to talk about my misgivings now. I didn't want to turn them into predictions. Better to wait and see. Milou had reminded me about how certain plants transplant easily; others struggle, seeming to fight the gardener's best efforts to ease their transition.

June 22, 1975

In the car on the way back from the train station, I did most of the talking, telling Isabelle about Ardis, her paintings, and the Paris show.

"Did she want to know about you?"

I laughed. "Does it sound like she didn't? I write to her, you know."

Isabelle looked skeptical.

"She already knows about Ted and Annie. . . ." How far did I want to go with this conversation?

"And?"

"And that Ted and I haven't really talked."

"Maybe it's time to talk some more? Before Annie gets here?"

"You and Ardis must have ESP." That made us both laugh. "I don't know how to begin. I don't want to put him on the spot."

"You could give him an opening."

"Indirectly, you mean?"

"It all depends on what you want," Isabelle said. "And how much time you have—before he leaves. You could ask him about his plans. Maybe that way you'd at least find out when he's going back to Newport."

The legal arrangements for Jeanne's house had been settled in April. Ted's divorce was final. He had told Henri he would stay as long as it took to finish the work for the exhibition.

"I don't want to know."

"Of course not. But if you don't ask, you'll never know any of the rest of it. How he feels and so on. Anyway, maybe he doesn't want to put *you* on the spot."

In her matter-of-fact way, Isabelle had put her finger on my problem. Now, it was up to me.

The night Ted helped me with the gazebo, our collaboration in the process had been effortless. He had known what to do, but he had let me take the lead when I could, giving me a sense of working things through by give and take.

Was he waiting for me to begin the conversation about what was going on between us? How would I know unless I asked him?

THE TRIP down from Paris had given me time to think over my conversation with Ardis. After our lunch at the café, we had wandered the quiet streets of the Marais. She had told me about New York, the gallery, and Matt's enthusiasm, undiminished, for Leonard of Pisa and the Fibonacci system. And how their lives were about to change. Impatient to get away from Brookton, he had applied for teaching and research positions elsewhere.

I had just assumed he would find something in or near Manhattan, so Ardis could continue working in the loft. It was an ideal arrangement. But he'd had an offer from Berkeley, one they both recognized he couldn't turn down.

"What about you?"

"I don't know. We've been talking about this for a month, ever since he got the offer. The more we talk, the less we like our options. We have no choice, is what it comes down to. Not right now, anyway."

So Matt would leave for California at the end of August and they would try living apart for a year. When the show in Paris closed in November, Ardis would go to California for a while. "It will be hard for us both. I need him, more than I want to admit to myself or him. I'd like him to think I'm strong and independent—and I am, I know I am—but he helps me to stay that way. You know?"

She could have been describing how I felt about being with Ted. Except that I wasn't with Ted. Ardis had made her point. I had to talk to Ted, to sound him out, at least. When and how? If only it were as easy as talking about everything else in our lives—the goats, our work, the weather.

By the time we had settled on a bench at the Place des Vosges, it was nearly four thirty. The tops of the trees, green-gold in the sunlight, hovered over the twilit square, becalmed in the still air. A few pigeons fluttered from point to point, alighting to scratch and peck in the pale gravel, occasionally scuffling over a tidbit.

"What about Jack and Brookton?"

I took a deep breath. "You know how sometimes you can remember something that happened, in detail, including how you felt at the time?"

Ardis nodded.

"I hardly ever think about Jack or Brookton anymore, but when I do, I don't remember or feel much. At all. Nothing."

Ardis had brushed a piece of lint from her sleeve. "Matt hasn't stayed in touch with him, anyway. When Jack came back from Paris, he told Matt he'd leave Brookton as soon as he found a 'real job.' So he did." She made quotation marks in the air and glanced at me.

"What else?"

"He's getting married."

"Oh?"

"It was in the *Times*. She's finishing a PhD in art history at Columbia. Jack's working for some financial firm."

Fluttering overhead caused us both to look up as a pigeon landed on the statue in the middle of the square. A single gray feather drifted down, blown sideways by a sudden draft.

THE NEXT morning I woke early. I had a few hectic days ahead. Luc's comment on the list he had left told the whole story: "Be careful what you wish for!" Thanks to a combination of good stock, great conditions, and a new fertilizer, the plants had flourished. I'd be transplanting today, something I hadn't planned to do until the following week.

I made steady progress through the morning, so I could relax into the afternoon ahead, enjoying being on my own. At one, I heard Ted's motorcycle. Instead of going into the house, he headed down the hill, toward the potting shed.

"Is everything okay?"

"Absolutely fine, yes." He touched the end of my nose. "You've been transplanting."

I looked down at my T-shirt and jeans and gloves, covered in loose potting soil. "It amazes me any of it actually gets into the pots."

"Can you take a break? Have a picnic? There's something I'd like to show you." The gleam in his eyes reminded me of our dinner at Le Vieux Carré, when he had watched me watching the server as he flamed our desserts.

"Yes and yes." I'd have time to finish up later. At the house, I wrote a note for Isabelle and picked up the bucket of fruit and vegetable peels to give the goats on my way out.

Standing by the bike, Ted held out a helmet. "I just realized we haven't talked—really talked—for a couple of months. And it's a beautiful day."

"And the 'something to show me'?"

"You'll see."

We turned left down the hill into the village. A neighbor working in her vegetable garden waved at us, her shouted greeting barely audible over the motorcycle. As we passed the crossroads and the *lavoir*, I lifted my face to the sun. Paris had been exhilarating, yes, but exhausting, too. Visiting was one thing; I didn't think I could live there.

When the thought struck me, I laughed out loud. Did Isabelle have something to do with Ted's idea to have a picnic? Surely he could have come up with the idea on his own.

"What's so funny?"

I felt the bike slow as Ted downshifted up the road to the château. "Nothing important!"

We parked the bike at the top of the hill. Ted took a small picnic basket and a blanket out of the pannier. "This way."

Below the château, in the apple orchard, the branches tossed in the breeze, scattering petals around them. Gauzy clouds shouldered one another aside as they traveled in twos and threes over the valley. A tractor, a backhoe, and a pile of gravel filled most of the stable yard.

When I'd seen the château four years ago, shortly after I arrived in Flagy, it had seemed scarcely worth the restoration effort that was just getting underway at the time. Centuries of neglect and vandalism had taken their toll. Now, thanks to cleaning, patching, repairing, and replacing, the stone structure had been thoroughly renewed.

Sitting squarely in the middle of its small park, its entrance centered like a snub nose between windows topped by rounded arcades, the château looked like a pug—world weary and somewhat distracted. You could almost see a coach-and-four pulling up in front and a retinue of liveried servants lined up to greet the travelers.

"Here we are! Amazing, isn't it?"

Marked off by stone walls and hedgerows, fallow and plowed fields stretched out across the valley, their erratic shapes and sizes a holdover from feudal times. In the distance, we could just make out the top of Saint-Thibaut's tower and the glint of the main road on its climb out of the valley.

"WHAT'S THAT down there?" A small stone building, round with a conical roof, sat in the meadow's lower corner, partially hidden by several overgrown apple trees.

"That's it." Ted smiled. "That's what I wanted you to see."

Leaving the picnic and the blanket behind, we walked down the hill.

"It's a dovecote," Ted told me. "But it's not on any of Henri's lists of abandoned buildings, probably because it's so far from any of the main roads. It's not that easy to find." Ted gestured back up the hill to make his point.

"It's beautiful." I touched the sun-warmed stone. "Almost alive."

"And probably four hundred years old."

As we ate lunch, Ted explained that in the fifteenth century, only the landholder had the right to build a dovecote separate from the main house, that the local peasants always complained about the birds, especially in the spring, when they feasted on the freshly planted fields. Finally, in 1789, Parliament had banned separate dovecotes.

"Probably it was abandoned then. So here it is, saved by benign neglect. I love the history of this area and the architecture. But that's not the only reason I wanted to show you the dovecote." He poured me a cup of water from the thermos and took a folded paper from his pocket. "It's just a sketch. Take a look and tell me what you think."

I smoothed the sheet open on my lap. Ted had labeled the drawing "Finial: April 1975. Modeled after dovecote. Pear or pine w/walnut or ebony?" The sketch showed a round base with stone detailing and a conical tiled roof.

"For those eight chairs you told me about?"

He nodded. "There's nothing especially original about it. Round or rounded is fairly standard for these little things. After all the time I spent looking through the pattern books at the museum, I had a glimmer of an idea about what we could do. Then, one afternoon, I rode by this place and found the dovecote. I haven't shown the drawing to anyone else." He was smiling, but his eyes seemed anxious.

"What kind of wood will you use?"

"Something not too hard that will stand up to carving—all that stone detailing. And the tile roof . . . that will be a lot of work." He tapped the description he'd written.

"So each one will be the same?"

"Same size, shape, and features, yes, but they'll be hand-carved, so each one will be unique."

"It's so simple, so beautiful. I love it. And I think Henri will, too."

Cloud shadows played over the dovecote's roof. Ted's shoulders relaxed; he stretched out on the blanket, leaning on his elbow. "I want to show it to him today. But first I have to finish this." He sat up and pulled from his pocket a small object wrapped in paper. "It's okay. You can open it."

I removed the paper wrapping and found a model of the finial carved in pine. "It is perfect. How can Henri refuse?"

"I have to fiddle with it some more. One idea is to make the

thing in two parts, so that I can use two different types of wood."
He shrugged. "I think Henri may find that a bit over the top.
We'll see."

The scudding clouds had slowed and thickened into a dense
layer above us. As soon as we felt the first drops of rain, we lifted
the blanket over our heads and headed back to the bike. I gave
Ted the short version about Ardis and her show and the apartment
in the Marais. He had never been there.

"You'd like it." I was about to add, "Let's go sometime," when
the rain began in earnest.

Ted grabbed two slickers out of the pannier and shoved the
blanket and basket into it. I glanced back over my shoulder down
into the meadow through the apple orchard. In the half-light,
under the steady rain, the dovecote looked like a bird sheltering
there in the hollow, its head tucked under its wing.

July 17, 1975

Annie looked like Ted. Same coloring, same unruly curls, same
rangy build. They even had the same loping walk. She was tall
for a nine-year-old—boy or girl. At her age, I had towered over
everyone else. I had minded. A lot. Once, I'd overheard a friend
of my mother's ask her if I'd been held back a year or two. At last,
in my junior year in high school, the awkwardness faded away.
That was the year I stopped growing.

Before Annie arrived, Ted and I had agreed to speak French
with her and with each other. We weren't sure how this would
work. But as soon as Ted explained the rules—including the one
that let her take a daily break from French—Annie entered into
the arrangement without complaint.

A half-dozen children—boys and girls—spent their summer
vacation in the village with aunts and uncles or grandparents.
The morning after Annie arrived, a delegation came to invite her

to play soccer. Although she knew nothing about the game, she picked it up quickly, so quickly that both sides squabbled over whose team she would be on. Annie settled it: "Every other day, I switch. It's not confusing, because I'm the only one who does. *J'adore le foot!*"

Ted had described her as a natural athlete. He was right. Annie was focused, agile, strong. It was too bad most competitive team sports were closed to girls. Tennis wasn't one of them, which was lucky for her. But Title IX had just been passed. For girls like Annie, there would soon be more support and maybe—just maybe—a serious effort to develop sports for women. Maybe by the time Annie got to high school, girls' soccer would be the norm.

"*Ai*, Ted and Annie!" Luc stopped sweeping the porch and grinned down at Annie, who frowned.

"Luc! It's H-H-H-Hi!" Annie helped Luc practice his English pronunciation; he helped her with French. So far, the biggest hurdle for Luc was H. "He says it fine when we practice," Annie fumed.

"Could it be he's just teasing?" Ted's wide-eyed expression made Annie laugh.

She gave him a playful slap and ran up the steps, into the kitchen. "Guess what I found this morning!"

Isabelle looked around the kitchen. "My missing casserole?"

"No!" Annie giggled. "A cat and kittens! Four of them! In the goat pen! In the corner by the stalls. You know where I mean?"

"Ah!" Isabelle nodded and looked over at Ted, now standing just inside the door. He smiled and shrugged. It wasn't unusual for strays to show up. When the cute kitten brought home to a small city apartment became too much of a nuisance, the owners would drop it off in the country with the mistaken expectation it could survive on its own or that a farmer would adopt it. Not all such stories ended like this one.

"What did the goats do?" I began to clear the table, putting away the remains of breakfast.

"One of the kids came over to see what I was doing. She tried to eat my hair!" Annie made a face. "The others just stood around. Then Dad came out and told me not to bother them." She frowned and sighed.

"We settled them in a box in the woodshed. They seem healthy enough. Young mother. Probably her first litter. I'd say they're maybe six weeks old."

"And Mélusine? How's she taking it?"

"She doesn't pay attention to anything anymore. Except food, of course." Jeanne's old cat, now nearly blind, spent most of her time sleeping on the porch in the sun.

Annie rocked back and forth on the balls of her feet. "I want to take one home with me." She looked at Isabelle, then at Ted. "May I, Daddy?"

Ted rolled his eyes. "We'll have to check with your mom. But at least for now, you can take care of them—feed the mother, make sure those babies behave!"

Twirling a curl into a tight spiral, Annie smiled up at Ted.

"Annie?" Ted spoke softly, but his tone was unmistakable.

After the divorce, Annie had begun to fidget with her shoulder-length hair, winding it into knots. Claire's idea of a cure, to cut Annie's hair short, had worked, until her hair began to grow in again.

Annie put both hands in her pockets. "Like that?"

"Just like that."

ANNIE SNIFFED. "I smell something spicy. Sort of perfume-y, but minty, too."

"Lavender." Isabelle pointed to the hooks over the sink, where she had hung bunches to dry. "I cut it yesterday."

"Oh, no. Look!" Annie pointed up at the bees investigating the drying flowers.

Isabelle shooed them out the window and closed it. "They prefer blue flowers, especially lavender. Beekeepers say it keeps the bees and the hive healthy and, of course, it flavors the honey."

Annie made a face. "Honey that tastes like perfume or mint?"

"Honey that tastes like lavender. *Goûte!*" Isabelle dipped a teaspoon into the honey jar and handed it to her. "Tell me what you think."

Annie touched the tip of her tongue to the spoon. "Mmmmm. It doesn't taste like perfume, or mint. But it does taste a little bit the way the lavender smells." She licked the teaspoon clean.

Isabelle gave her another spoonful. "Have you thought of a name for the cat?"

Annie stopped licking the spoon, thoughtful. "She's striped. Like a tiger."

Isabelle nodded. "You could call her Tigrette."

Ted and Luc grinned at the expression on Annie's face.

"Tigrette . . ." Annie repeated the name a couple of times, trying it out. Finally she smiled. "Tigrette!" Then she glanced at Ted and back at me.

"What is it, Annie?" I had been feeling my way, giving her time to become as comfortable with me as she was with Isabelle and Luc.

"Daddy showed me the picture you made of *grand-mère*. He says you can help me with my drawing."

"I could do that. What do you like to draw?" When Ted and I had talked about this, drawing seemed a natural way for me to create a rapport with Annie. I knew I'd been right to wait for her to ask.

"Horses!" She threw a quick glance at Ted and ducked her head.

"Would you like to draw the kittens, too?"

"Don't they move around too much?" Her doubtful expression opened to a big smile. "I guess we could wait until they're taking a nap, couldn't we?"

Annie had yet to show any sign of giving up her horses. She filled her sketchbook with them—galloping, trotting, standing still—and read every horse book she could find.

"Can we start now? Please?"

"You're going with Malorie this morning, remember? Out to Buxy?" Ted glanced at me, letting me off the hook. I didn't want to refuse Annie's request. That would have started us off on the wrong foot.

I smiled at Annie. "We'll have time later, Annie. *Promis, juré!*"

Annie smiled at me. Her puzzled look was my cue. "That's what Milou used to tell me whenever she promised me something. It's like 'cross my heart and hope to die.' So you know I won't let you down."

WE GOT out of the car and stood for a moment, watching the work crew. After a month, they had nearly completed preparations for the borders and the stonework. The owners would arrive on Friday for the weekend. They'd be pleased, too. So far, the work was on time and on budget. Best of all, they'd finally be able to see what my drawings could only suggest.

The previous week, Annie had spent a day with me here. At first, she had sat on a crate near the car, reading. After lunch, she went to the field across the road, where she made an obstacle course of stones and branches, a crude set of jumps. For the rest of the afternoon, she circled the course, cantering, prancing, imitating a show jumper.

As soon as we got out of the car, she asked if she could go back to the field.

"*Oui, oui. Vas-y! Mais*, stay in the field, Annie." I hadn't yet told Ted that Annie and I both bent the French-only rules while we were on our own. She'd usually begin in French—she wanted to, I could see that—then switch to English when her thoughts ran too fast for her to catch them and pin a French word or phrase on them. I switched back and forth sometimes, myself. She relaxed and managed her own side of our conversations very well.

She lifted the gate latch and used both hands to open the gate wide enough to slip through. It swung closed behind her with a thud as she cantered up the hill to the first jump.

While I waited for Robert, the contractor, to finish with two workmen pushing wheelbarrows of stone into the back of the border, I thought about my conversation with Annie in the car.

"I love Flagy. . . ."

From her tone of voice, I thought she had something, some qualification, she wanted to add, but didn't know how. "*Mais . . . ?*"

"*Mais* I still don't like goat cheese." She made a face. "But I really like the goats, especially the kids. They are so funny, the way they jump around and climb on each other. Like puppies, sort of. I want to come back next year."

"Have you told your dad?"

"He says we have to ask Mommy." She fiddled with a scrap of foil, a gum wrapper or something, smoothing it on her lap and turning it over.

"You miss your mom."

"And my friends." Her voice dropped. "But not so much now. Since Amélie came." Amélie was Louise's daughter. Louise, who was my age, had married right after she finished school. My life had been so different, my experience with my own parents fraught at every level. Even before the miscarriage, I hadn't thought about what it would be like to have a child, let alone a nine-year-old daughter.

"Amélie is fun, even if I don't understand everything she says." Like a cloud, Annie's homesickness faded away. "Promise you won't tell Daddy?" She giggled. "You know Amélie's mom, Louise? She told Amélie she thinks Daddy is handsomer than Alain Delon." Annie managed to repeat most of this in French, sounding like Amélie sounding like Louise. "What do you think, Malorie?"

"I agree, of course!" I was sure Annie had no idea who Alain Delon was, but she got the idea. The comparison would amuse

Ted: he had none of the actor's pouty glamour, but maybe that's what Louise preferred. After all, that summer of the photo booth, Louise had had a crush on Ted, too.

THE PROPORTIONS of the area marked off as lawn and perennial borders looked fine, exactly like my drawings. But something seemed off. I walked around, looking at it from all angles. Under Robert's watchful eye, several of his men maneuvered wheelbarrows heaped with topsoil over the rough ground. He left them and came up to me, looking concerned.

"*Qu'est-ce qui vous trouble?*"

"Something seems out of place." Until I figured out what it was, I couldn't begin to place the plants.

"If I may?"

So he had noticed, too? Robert had been more helpful than I could have hoped, knowledgeable about plants as well as land-scaping. He had known Luc for years and gave me the full benefit of his experience—advice and encouragement. "Of course. Tell me what you think."

That's when I saw the problem. It couldn't have been more obvious. An ancient Lebanon cedar anchored the far corner of the space marked off for the terrace. The near corner had held a large decaying oak that we had removed the previous week. Without the oak, the cedar loomed, throwing the whole space off-kilter. We would have to find a replacement. But what?

I looked at Robert, shaking my head. "Dumb mistake."

Robert smiled. "*Pas de problème.* I have an idea." After giving his crew instructions, Robert beckoned to me to follow him. As we headed down into the meadow, I looked for Annie. Tossing her head, prancing in place, she prepared to circle her jump course.

Below the house, in a pasture across a narrow stream, six Charolais cows dozed under the broad canopies of several live oaks. Light and shadow camouflaged them, concealing them almost entirely from view. I got out my pad and made a quick sketch of the trees and the cattle. Beyond them, the hills and hedgerows composed a landscape of dips and curves. *No straight lines*, I thought. That's what held the eye; that's what made the landscape work as a whole.

At the bottom of the hill, Robert pointed to a young cedar about thirty feet away against the far bank of the stream. It formed a ten-foot cone, as though an expert had pruned and tended it regularly. Most likely, being in the lee of the bank protected it from the wind, shaping it evenly over the years.

"Will it survive being moved?"

"Leave that to us." He gestured toward the house. "Once we finish the stonework and the beds around the terrace, we'll dig the tree out and plant it up there. *Pas de problème!*" With attention and feeding, he assured me, the cedar would thrive, a sturdy replacement for the oak.

Up at the house, someone shouted. The cattle lifted their heads as one and turned toward us. Robert gave a whistle that started low and ended in a shrill, questioning tone. Two short whistles came back to us, emphatic, imperative.

"Someone's hurt."

I walked as fast as I could up the deeply rutted lane, nearly falling once when I stumbled on the rough ground. Robert grabbed my arm to steady me. It seemed we would never get there. My mind raced ahead: I knew we didn't have phone service up here. How fast could we get to the hospital? Did Robert have a first-aid kit What if someone needed CPR? I'd taken a CPR course years ago in high school. Would I be able to remember the steps?

ON THE terrace work site, several men from Robert's crew crouched next to Annie, who sat on a pile of stones, white-faced, her mouth closed tight. The men held their caps in their hands, uneasy. Annie clasped her right hand in her left hand, like a small wounded animal.

As soon as I knelt next to her, she began to sob. "The gate latch slammed on my hand. I don't know how . . ." The men moved away from us, talking softly among themselves. One of them came over with a cooler.

"I have ice and lemonade. *La petite* would like some?"

Annie pulled away from me when I reached for her hand. "I just want to go home. Please?"

"Soon. Can you do this?" I wiggled my fingers. Wincing, she moved hers.

"That's great. Can you show me the other side?"

The tips of her third and fourth fingers were red and beginning to swell, the nails dark and bruised. Her wrist had escaped harm. I took off my bandana. "I'd like to put some ice on your hand. That will make it feel better." I was pretty sure Annie had had bumps and bruises before, certainly falls and sprained ankles. But this was a different situation for her. The accident had happened in a strange place, among strangers. No doubt her tears had as much to do with her embarrassment as with her pain.

I scooped some ice out of the cooler into the bandana and knotted the ends to make an ice pack. "We're going straight home. Would you like some lemonade first?" She shook her head.

Once she was in the car, cradling her right hand in the left one, I set the ice pack down slowly and gently over her pinched fingers. She looked so anxious. I said the first thing that came to mind, that I would drive slowly so she wouldn't feel the bumps in the dirt road. "You'll be fine. *Promis, juré!*"

Robert came to the driver's side as I started the car. "So, I should go ahead and plan to move that cedar?"

"Thanks, yes. I'll be back tomorrow."

"*Ne vous en faites pas.* She'll be fine, Malorie, don't worry."

Ted stood on the porch as we pulled into the driveway. When Annie didn't get out of the car right away, he came down and opened the door for her.

"What happened?"

She struggled to tell him through sniffles and hiccups. Sitting on the ground now, his arm around her, Ted listened and made soothing noises. Once she finished, he stood and turned to me. "These things happen. Don't blame yourself." He looked as if he wanted to say more, but Annie interrupted.

"Daddy?"

He picked her up and carried her into the house. In the rocking chair by the stove, she curled up in his lap, holding her injured hand and the sodden bandana in her lap. The ice had long since melted.

"I feel like such a baby. I tried not to cry. But it hurt too much."

"I know. That kind of hurt really hurts. Two banged-up fingers. Do you think you'll live?"

She smiled up at him. "'Course."

"The bad news is, those fingers will be very sore for a while and the nails might fall off."

"Gross!"

"Very. In the meantime, I'll make a splint and bandage them. You'll have a fine finger puppet." She hiccupped and drank some juice from the glass I handed her.

"So I can't play soccer?"

"At least for a few days, maybe a week. No writing or drawing, either. That's the bad news. The good news is, you might finish *The Black Stallion*."

I heard a noise behind me and turned around. Béatrice leaned against the living room door, listening. I had forgotten Ted was helping her with a drafting assignment. "I could take you out to the *manège* to see some horses, if you'd like that, Annie," she said. The French National Show Jumping Team trained at the equestrian center in Cluny. "I have a friend who works there now. She could show us around."

"Can I, Daddy?" Annie jumped out of Ted's lap, bumping her hand on the arm of the chair.

"Ouch."

"First, let's splint those fingers. That should help. And, yes, of course you can go with Béatrice. Tomorrow or the next day. Let's wait and see how you feel." At the kitchen table, Ted pulled a chair out and began to splint Annie's fingers. Béatrice came and sat beside her.

Sitting together at the table, they seemed engrossed in each other. It was time to go. "I'll see you all later." I touched Annie's shoulder on my way out. "I hope you feel better soon, Annie." In the doorway, I glanced back. Leaning against Béatrice, Annie had opened her sketchbook.

TELLING ISABELLE about Annie's accident later that afternoon, I mentioned Béatrice's invitation.

"Béatrice is a lot like Claire, I think." Isabelle pursed her lips.

"What do you mean?"

"She's very friendly, very social. I think Annie misses Claire a lot more than she's letting on. She doesn't want to say or do anything that would hurt Ted's feelings."

"So Béatrice is a surrogate mom?" It was difficult for me to say this, to admit it to myself.

"Or a surrogate for everyone she misses. Also, little girls get crushes, you know."

"I'm sure you're right. You should have seen Annie's expression when Béatrice offered to take her to the *manège*. Compared to coming along with me to Buxy? No contest."

Isabelle crossed her arms and looked at me. "This isn't just about Annie, is it?"

"Not exactly."

She laughed.

"What's so funny?"

"Would it help to know that Béatrice and Gilles are getting married?"

This was the first I'd heard of Gilles. The father of Béatrice's little boy was someone local. That was all I knew. "He's the one?"

"*Ben, oui!* I wish you could see your expression!"

It was my turn to laugh. "So it's up to me, then. Now that I know about Gilles and Béatrice, that takes care of the competition for Ted's attention."

"But?"

"Annie's remains an open question."

The Pont Saint-Laurent

July 31, 1975

"Malorie? Are you ready? Malorie!" Holding on with her left hand, Annie straddled the porch railing. So far, she had managed her left-handed life very well. I could hear Ted whistling a jazzy version of "Oh! Susanna" somewhere in the house. In the open kitchen windows, the curtains fluttered, dancing to a tune of their own.

I opened the kitchen door and waved. "Ten minutes!" While I made notes on the day's to-do list, I ate the last bit of toast on my plate and finished my tea. Isabelle and Luc had left early to spend the morning preparing an order. Although Annie's hand was almost healed, it was too soon for her to rejoin the soccer players, so we decided she would keep me company in the greenhouse.

Absorbed in *The Black Stallion*, propped open beside her on the table, Annie ate yogurt and cereal with her left hand without spilling a drop. She smiled at me, unaware of her yogurt mustache.

"All set?"

She sighed. "I don't want it to end."

"I felt the same way."

"You've read *The Black Stallion?*"

"And *National Velvet* and *Black Beauty*. And I spent hours drawing horses when I was nine. I even entered a contest, Name This Horse. First prize was a thoroughbred. I didn't win, and I was so disappointed that I made my mother call the company to make sure. I also watched *My Friend Flicka* every Saturday morning."

"*My Friend Flicka*?"

"A TV show about a horse named Flicka." Ted stood in the door to the kitchen. He looked at Annie and pointed at me. "Told you so. She's horse crazy too."

"Used to be."

Ted grinned. Annie clapped and winced. "I keep forgetting."

I would have liked nothing better than to spend the rest of the day in the kitchen, just the three of us, chatting—about horses, about nothing, about everything. It was my birthday. Although no one seemed to have remembered, I didn't care. I felt warm and drowsy, as content as Mélusine, who was curled up in a patch of sunlight, her front paws folded under her.

"What's the plan, you two?" Stacking the breakfast dishes in the sink, Ted checked the time.

I slumped over on the table and sighed. "The usual—thinning, thinning, and more thinning. So much thinning, so little time."

When he finished rinsing the dishes, Ted leaned down so Annie could kiss his cheek. "Let Malorie get some work done, okay?"

The thing about Annie, something I had learned right away, was that she had no problem at all being on her own. If she wasn't reading, she was drawing or sitting quietly, daydreaming.

I'd given her a few drawing pointers—Ardis would have been amused at my lesson on negative space, featuring several squirming kittens. Now, her drawings included kittens mixed in with horses. She missed being with the other kids—missed the physical activity of their soccer games—but she had accepted being cooped up until her hand healed.

In the greenhouse, I set up a stool and cleared a space at the potting bench. Sitting there with the sun streaming in over her head, Annie became engrossed once again in her book.

Horse crazy. What was it about horses, anyway? There was their beauty and strength and the intelligence in their eyes. Beyond that, the stories I had preferred were the ones where a human and a horse forged a bond of trust. At nine, I had needed to believe such a bond was possible. I was beginning to think Annie felt the same way.

"LUNCHTIME!" I took off my gloves, rinsed my hands, and stretched my aching shoulders and neck.

Annie yawned. "Doesn't it seem like we only just got here? Time is so strange. Sometimes, whatever I'm doing seems to take forever. But not when I'm reading. Then it always goes fast. Too fast."

Between mouthfuls of sandwich, she talked nonstop, mostly about horses. She had ideas and opinions about all the breeds. "I like Morgan horses best."

"Tell me about that."

"Well, first of all, there's the true story of Justin Morgan, the first Morgan horse. In the beginning, no one wanted him." She stopped and looked at me, as if wondering if I already knew the story.

I nodded. "Yes, he needed to find someone who could see through his appearance."

"People thought he was too small to be good for anything. But he showed them. He could run faster than a thoroughbred and pull as good as a workhorse. And he had a great personality." Her face fell. She put her sandwich down.

"What?"

"I really want a horse, you know? Mommy says no. Daddy says maybe. Now they're not married anymore; they'll have separate houses and Mommy says we won't have enough money for extras. Except for flute lessons." Her chin trembled.

"I guess a horse is a pretty big extra."

Annie brightened. "I thought maybe I could take riding lessons instead of flute lessons." The uncertain look returned. "But I don't think Mommy will like that idea. What do you think, Malorie?"

"At least you don't have to groom it and muck out the stall." I watched her expression. Did she realize I was evading her question? I knew that Ted and Claire differed about what Annie could and couldn't do. I also knew better than to offer an opinion. Annie wouldn't let me get away with "I don't know," and whatever else I might say, I'd be taking sides with Ted or with Claire.

"Maybe my friend would help me." Her eyes lit up. "She likes horses, too. We could share."

When I told him about this conversation later, Ted laughed.

"To Annie, nothing is impossible. She simply cannot believe that she can't have whatever she wants. Thanks for telling me about this new horse idea. It gives me some time to figure out another way to say no!"

"She said something about riding lessons."

"I like that idea fine. But Claire will never agree. She thinks Annie is involved in enough sports at school. And she's adamant about the flute."

I wanted to talk more about Annie's idea, but something in Ted's expression warned me off.

IN THE kitchen, Annie sat cross-legged on the floor, playing with the kittens while Luc and Ted set the table.

"*La voilà!*" They all turned and stared at me. Annie giggled.

"*Me voilà, oui! Et alors?* What's going on?"

"It's somebody's birthday and somebody thinks we don't know!" Ted put on a stern look and shook his finger at me.

"I thought . . ."

"We forgot?" Isabelle grinned.

"How could we?" Luc looked at me, his eyes playing up the joke. "Milou calls every day to remind us!" Luc poured a glass of wine for Isabelle, Ted, and himself and handed me a glass of black currant juice.

"May all your dreams come true." Isabelle lifted her glass.

"*Santé!*" Luc leaned toward me and clinked.

After dinner, I helped Isabelle clear the dishes, while Annie told Luc the story of Justin Morgan—in French. He listened closely, helping her when she didn't know a word. Ted looked on, his expression intent, pleased with Annie's progress.

Isabelle hugged me, urging me back to the table. "*Et maintenant, ma belle, ferme les yeux!*" She gave me a little push.

At the table, eyes closed as requested, I heard her opening cupboards, drawers, and the refrigerator. Someone struck a match. Annie's giggles and Ted's shushes made me smile. At last, a plate settled on the table.

"Open!"

On a crystal cake plate, a vacherin heaped with whipped cream and raspberries sat next to a Hostess CupCake holding one lighted candle.

I hugged Isabelle and pointed at the cupcake. "And the sidekick? Where did that come from?"

"Not the pâtisserie. But you probably guessed that much." Ted had asked a friend in Newport to send it, had worried it would arrive too late. His idea was: blow out the candle and throw the cupcake away. But I knew Annie had other plans.

It wasn't possible to undo the past. Some memories wouldn't fade, no matter how hard I tried to put them out of my mind. Gradually, I was learning to accept this. What I wanted—my only wish for this birthday—was to remember times like this one, to hold them the way Annie held Tigrette, never to forget. Around me, the dark red tile walls of the kitchen reflected the last rays of the sunset into the room. I squeezed my eyes shut and blew out the candle. Annie clapped.

After a whispered consultation with Ted, Annie requested and devoured a second helping of the vacherin and then the cupcake. "Did that girl, that friend of yours, really not eat the vacherin?"

"Really and truly. She expected a birthday cake—you know, chocolate frosting and sprinkles?" At my eighth birthday party, at the sight of the serving of meringue, berries, and cream, she had burst into tears.

"She wouldn't at least try it?" Annie's disbelief made everyone smile.

"Not even a taste. But there was a happy ending."

"What?"

"Guess."

"You got to eat her share?"

"I did."

Ted pushed away from the table and reached under his chair. He came around to stand next to me, his hands behind his back.

"Which hand?" He couldn't keep a straight face.

"Right one." Behind him, Annie shook her head at me.

I pointed to the left. He held it out, empty.

"No fair, Daddy!" Annie pulled on his arm.

"One more chance," he said.

"Both, then." I winked at Annie. She giggled.

He held out a box wrapped in gold foil paper and tied with a blue ribbon. I shook it gently. "Not a goldfish." I held it to my ear. "Or an alarm clock."

Luc and Isabelle laughed. Annie started to twirl her hair. Then she looked at Ted—who wasn't paying attention—and stopped of her own accord. Inside the wrapping paper, there was a layer of tissue paper taped at both ends and along the seams.

Ted's eyes caught and held mine. Annie, Luc, and Isabelle stared at the package.

"Could you maybe go a little faster?" Annie came around the table to stand next to me. She had meringue and cupcake crumbs at the corners of her mouth; her breath smelled of raspberries and chocolate. I slit the tissue paper with my table knife and let it drop to the floor.

Cassiopeia appeared in an inlay of mother-of-pearl on the lid of a small mahogany box. On each of its four sides, in a light wood—pear, perhaps?—Ted had inlaid familiar local sites: Saint-Thibaut, the *lavoir*, the château, and the dovecote. The seams were nearly invisible on the smooth, waxed surface.

"Aren't you going to open it?"

"Annie . . ." Ted's smile belied his tone.

I released the latch. The inside of the lid had another mother-of-pearl inlay, this one of a crescent moon and Venus. The box itself was lined in blue velvet.

"Ted . . ." I couldn't speak past the lump in my throat. I looked up into his eyes, dark as the night sky, gleaming in the candlelight. He understood.

"I told Henri what I wanted to do. He trimmed my sails a bit, then helped me."

I stood to hug him, felt his fingers clasped behind me, drawing me to him. I closed my eyes, turning into his shoulder, leaning into his heartbeat against my throat.

I WOKE in the middle of the night, listening for the goats, as I so often had since Jeanne died. A wind had come up, worrying a loose shutter and the leaves of the quince outside my bedroom window. When I couldn't go back to sleep, I got up, pulled a shirt on over my nightgown, and tiptoed downstairs.

Jeanne's house stood dark and quiet under the starlit sky. Across the valley, up the hill, a security light at the château flickered intermittently through the wind-tossed trees.

The stars seemed to swirl in clusters above me, like the swarms of fireflies in the field behind the house in Long Meadow. Like the van Gogh painting. Try as I might, I couldn't pick out Cassiopeia.

Not for the first time, I wondered how it was possible to count the stars, let alone discern and name the constellations, even with the help of a telescope.

I closed my eyes. When I opened them, I spotted Cassiopeia right away. Like a dancer making her entrance, she leapt to the foreground. The glittering array within her range now appeared dim and insignificant. But I knew this was an illusion. Cassiopeia only seemed brighter because I had at last located and recognized her.

I walked down the driveway past the goat pen and around to the front of Jeanne's house. Anisette's bell sounded, then quieted. None of the other goats stirred, calm and quiet under her guard. Slick with dew, the grass and gravel in Jeanne's front yard made it too uncomfortable to go any farther barefoot. The kitchen door opened behind me.

"Can't sleep?" He sounded wide awake.

"Not really."

"It's such a beautiful night."

I went up to the porch to the settee and pulled a cushion behind me.

"You're shivering." He eased his arm around me, drawing me close.

"I've been thinking about what you said the night we had dinner in Cluny, about how you and Claire liked each other well enough to try to make a go of it. It made me think about how it was with Jack, how I felt alone with him, even when we were together."

"Go on."

"That's not what it's like with you."

I turned toward him. I could see the starlight reflected in his eyes. "I had such a crush on you."

"Had?"

All I could see now was his smile. Did he see mine?

"When Jack and I split up, I decided I'd be better off, that I liked myself better, alone. Then you showed up at Jeanne's birthday party and I realized how lonely I was." His arm tightened around me. I could feel his warmth through my shirt and nightgown. "After we talked on the way to the hospital, I didn't want you to leave—even though I knew we couldn't be together."

"I felt that." We held hands now in the quiet night, gazing out over the dark fields and woods. "And now?"

"I hope so."

"Me too." He shifted his weight and drew me closer. "You reminded me about that day in Mâcon. I looked for my copy of that picture."

I could feel his eyes searching my face in the dark.

"I found it."

"Here?"

"Upstairs, in a drawer in my room. Where I put it, I guess." My laugh startled us both. "Jeanne must have known you'd look for it someday."

"She'd be pleased."

"That she was right?"

"About you and me, together here now, yes. It's what she wanted. I can hear her, can't you? *Enfin, les enfants! Il était temps!*"

Yes, it was time.

Leaning against him, my head on his shoulder, I fell asleep, waking only when his weight shifted. In twos and threes, early swallows darted over the village. "What time is it?"

"Barely five."

I yawned and stretched. "Are you getting up?"

He reached for me, pulling me up to him. "Listen, I want you to know that I am sorry Claire and I couldn't make it work, sorry especially about the divorce. You know, it's confusing for Annie, harder than we thought. But for our sake—yours and mine—I'm glad."

"Me too."

One of the kids bleated. Anisette's bell clanged, as if summoning us. A kitten pounced on my foot. The others clambered up the settee, tackling each other, playing hide-and-seek behind the cushions.

"Daddy?" Wrapped in her blanket, Annie stood in the door. She looked from me to Ted and back again. "Did Malorie spend the night?"

Ted hugged me and reached out to pull Annie in. "Not all of it."

Annie tilted her head back, craning her neck to see my face. "Will you stay for breakfast?"

I looked at Ted, who nodded at me. "That would be fun, Annie."

"Can we have pancakes?"

"Give me fifteen minutes, okay?"

September 4, 1975

Ted's flight from Boston arrived in Paris in time for him to meet my train at noon. We planned to meet Ardis for a drink before the opening at six thirty. During the afternoon, I had promised Ted a tour of the Marais. The walk I'd planned was one I could easily adapt, depending on his fatigue. And interest.

As soon as we dropped off my bag at the hotel, we picked up cheese, bread, and fruit on the *rue Saint-Antoine* and walked over the bridge to the garden at Notre-Dame. Children played there under the watchful eye of their mothers; a few people sat on the benches, eating lunch or reading. The sounds of the water lapping against the stone abutments and the breeze in the trees provided a refuge from the traffic flowing along both banks of the river. Even the occasional siren couldn't dispel the quiet.

Had it been only a month since we had last seen one another?

I told Ted about the goats, about the broken water pipe in the greenhouse, about a project that had fallen through. He spoke of catching up with friends, his mother's health, and sailing with Annie, who had decided she wanted to practice with him so that she could race with her friends next summer.

Afterward, we walked through the Marais and back to the hotel. Aside from pointing out architectural details I thought Ted might enjoy, we didn't talk. He seemed distracted, as if he were holding something back. Or maybe he was just tired. It had been a long day. What needed saying, we couldn't say in passing.

In the hotel room, we undressed as though we had known all along this was how it would be with us: no words, only our bodies moving together, close, so close, listening to the sounds rising up through our open window from the street, watching the late-afternoon light flicker and dim on the ceiling. Time slowed, like the river nearby, flowing to the sea.

OF COURSE Ted and Ardis hit it off. We met for a drink before the opening, talking in shorthand, finishing each other's sentences. As soon as we got to the gallery, Ardis went to do her part, introducing herself, welcoming the other guests. Ted and I steered clear of the crowd to look at the paintings.

"You described them so well. I feel I know them already, that I'm here for a second look, or something, so I can pay attention, find those highlights you talked about. She's spent a lot of time looking at clouds and fog—looking through them, I should say." He pointed out three paintings grouped together in the middle of one wall. "See what I'm talking about?"

In these mixed-media works, blue, gray, and green watercolor shapes drifted across the surface over gold filaments that streamed and swirled in dynamic tension with them. Ardis had shown me several pencil and charcoal cloud studies, her efforts to find ways to suggest depth and movement behind the surface. "She had the idea about the gold filaments after she saw some stone and gold mesh sculptures."

Ted nodded. "It's like trompe l'oeil, but much more subtle. You get the same sense of three dimensions when you stand across the room from Monet's *Water Lilies*. As soon as you look closer, you see the small patches and swirls of color that help create the effect. Amazing." He gazed longingly at the paintings. "I can't do anything close with inlay. No way."

WE LEFT the opening and went to have dinner at Le Trumilou on the Quai de l'Hôtel-de-Ville. Only the brightest stars pierced the city's glow. In the early evening, the *Bateaux Mouches* motored along the river toward the Pont de l'Alma with their cargo of diners and jazz combos. A light mist rising from the Seine gave the air the texture of watered silk.

The sounds of quiet conversation, the clatter of cutlery, and the cheerful banter of the servers pushed the traffic and boat noises into the background. For the second time that day, we were on an island in a slow-moving stream.

When we finished eating, Ted folded his napkin on the table and leaned back. "There's a lot to talk about. I'll start with Annie, I guess."

I pulled my sweater over my shoulders. A current of cool air circled around me, bringing the river's scent with it. "How is she?"

"She didn't want to go back to school, had tantrums every day for the first week. She hasn't done that in five years."

"But she loves school. At least, that's what she told me."

"She does. The problem is Claire has finally made up her mind to move back to Boston, to find another job or maybe get a master's degree at Simmons. That's what set Annie off. She doesn't want to go. She's angry and blames us both."

Annie was upset for another reason: Ted had spent much of his month in Newport packing and moving his belongings into storage. "That shocked her. She didn't really understand what the divorce meant to her, to her life, until she watched me pack and carry all those boxes away."

"I understand how she feels, I guess."

"It gets more complicated." He sighed. "Annie told Claire as soon as she walked in the door that I have a girlfriend." He fidgeted with a piece of paper, folding it smaller and smaller. "That would be you, of course."

"Claire's jealous?"

"I think that's part of it."

Until now, I hadn't considered at all how Claire might react if Ted met someone else. What Annie had told her made it sound as if what was going on between Ted and me was a *fait accompli*. It wasn't, quite. Not yet.

"Well, Claire wanted to go back to Boston anyway, right?"

"She's been toying with the idea, but the girlfriend comment gave her a push."

"Does this mean Annie's mad at me, too?" I didn't know what to make of these repercussions, but I needed to pay attention to them. That I knew.

"I don't know. Maybe. I hope not." He slid the folded paper into his shirt pocket.

"Is there something else about this? You look so miserable."

He nodded, his mouth tight. "I have to go back to Newport sooner than I planned, at the beginning of January at the latest. I talked Claire into postponing her move until next summer. Her condition is that I come back for the second half of the school year. Who knows if that will make a difference in how Annie feels. I sure don't. But I want to make things easier for her."

"What about your work with Henri?"

"I'll have to finish my part of it by Christmas." Henri had been so pleased with Ted's idea for the dovecote finial that he had given Ted the detail work to do on other pieces. "I know he'd like me to be here for the show next year—that was our deal."

"Well, that's the answer then. The good news is, now you can get going on your plan to find a larger workspace in Newport."

I heard the effort in my voice. I felt queasy, as if the floor were shifting under me. I drank some water.

"Your turn."

I had questions, but now wasn't the time. I needed to absorb Ted's news—what it meant to him, what it meant to us.

Ted smiled at someone behind me and stood up. Ardis stood in the entryway, her hair hanging loose, gleaming in the candlelight. She spoke briefly to the server and crossed the room to our table.

"I can't tell you how relieved I am you're still here." She leaned down to kiss me. "I sold three paintings!" She high-fived me, then Ted. "When I called Matt to tell him, he'd been awake most of the night—too excited to sleep. Drinks are on him."

When the server brought us the champagne and three glasses, Ted spoke to him in a low voice. He left and came back with some Perrier for me. Our glasses filled, we clinked and toasted.

Ardis glanced at me, then at Ted. "Have you solved the world's problems?"

Ted smiled. "We started with Annie. And got stuck."

"Oh, my." Her eyes met mine, waiting to hear my part.

"Claire has decided to move. Annie's angry about that. So Ted has to make some changes." Hearing myself tell Ardis, seeing in her eyes an instant understanding, released the knot of tension in my throat.

"I know the feeling." Ardis had made up her mind to sublet the New York loft and was already talking about the views of the East Bay and San Francisco from Tilden Park. So much for the year apart that she and Matt had planned. "*Et madame?* Will she be making some changes too?"

Trying to match her tone, I said, "*Madame's* crystal ball remains cloudy, at present. She hopes it will clear up soon."

"The thing about crystal balls, in my experience, at least: sometimes you have to give them a good shake." Ardis and Ted looked at one another, as if sharing a secret.

"Whatever the crystal ball says, whatever I decide, you'll be the first to know. *Promis, juré!*"

RETURNING TO Lyon the next day, Ted and I talked on the train about his plans for the house in Flagy. He had started work on it, replacing floorboards and joists, installing a new roof, and repairing water-damaged plaster. He had to decide how much he could finish over the next three months and how much could be postponed.

"I'll be able to finish the roof, I think. But I'll have to leave the plastering and painting—and a few other things—to someone else."

"Like who?" There were local craftsmen who could take on this kind of project. But Ted was uneasy about handing the work over to a stranger.

"Henri knows someone, a carpenter, who needs a place to live. He might be willing to stay in the house and do the work in lieu of rent. I'll have to decide soon. I'm going to have to talk to my father, and I'd rather have a plan before I do that. If I'm going to make any progress on the big stuff, I'll need to make time for it, starting now."

"How?"

"Weekends, I guess." He made a face. "But if there's no other way . . ."

"Does Henri's carpenter know anything about goats?"

"Good question. Anyway, I'm planning to talk to people in the village. Maybe one of the neighbors will agree to adopt them." He looked at me. He knew I'd be willing to continue caring for the goats, with help. I couldn't take over by myself, not with my other work.

Talking with Ted, helping him plan, it was as if we already had a life together. Annie hadn't grasped how the divorce would change her life until she watched him box and carry his life with her out of the house, the only home she had ever known. Worrying about the goats, about what would become of them after Ted left, made me aware just how much his departure would change things—everything about my daily life would be different. I'd become so accustomed to sharing chores with him, talking to him about his work and mine. Easy, familiar times. And now?

"Malorie, don't cry!"

I pulled a crumpled tissue out of a pocket and blew my nose. "Probably the goats won't care. It's not like they're being taken far away, right? And no one's going to eat them." That thought just made me cry harder.

Ted hugged me. "I can't believe you're crying about the goats. What about me?"

I looked at him.

"Oh."

ONCE A week I met Milou for lunch at the tearoom near Henri's shop. It was the one day I always took a break. I enjoyed walking around Cluny, mingling with the noon crowd, and window-shopping.

As I was leaving, Luc handed me a list of errands. "If you don't get out of the greenhouse once in a while, you'll turn into a begonia." I didn't mind the teasing or the errands. Having to do some shopping gave me a good reason to explore the town. I knew its narrow streets and cul-de-sacs now almost as well as I knew Alden's.

On the corner across from the tearoom, I waited for the light. Milou had already found a window table. Chatting with the proprietor, an English woman, she laughed. The other woman shook her head and shrugged. You could see it was a casual, easy conversation, the kind you'd have with someone you saw regularly, an acquaintance, not necessarily a close friend.

Milou had changed since her return. No longer solitary, as she had been after my grandfather died, she often walked around her own neighborhood in Cluny, visiting with the artists and shopkeepers, becoming a member of their community. And when Milou and Henri were together, they basked in each other's presence; their shared energy and joy made itself felt even when Milou was with me.

I leaned down to kiss her cheek. *"Bonjour, Milou."*

"Bonjour, chérie." She smiled and waited until I had settled in my chair across from her. "Would you like to talk now or after we eat?"

"This is going to take a while. . . ."

"Just tell me. Don't worry about how long it takes."

She already knew that something had come up, something to do with Ted's plans. I cleared my throat, searching for the best way to start.

I plunged in. "Ted plans to go back to Newport. At the beginning of January. I haven't said anything to Isabelle and Luc. I don't know if he's talked to Henri."

Milou nodded. "This must be what they talked about yesterday after work. Henri didn't say anything to me, but he seemed preoccupied."

I explained what Annie had told Claire about me, about Ted's worries about her, and Claire's decision to leave Newport.

Milou sighed. "I'm sorry, but I'm not surprised. As much as I want Ted to stay here, to be able to finish his work for Henri and go to the show, Annie needs him more than Henri does." She sighed again and shook her head. "I know how you feel about your parents, that you wish they had divorced when you were young. But divorce is hard on a child in so many unpredictable ways."

"I think I understand that. But there's something else. It's as though Claire doesn't want another woman competing with Annie for Ted's love." Or maybe Claire didn't want another woman competing with her for Annie's affection. I couldn't say this. Not yet. "I think Claire is using her unhappiness and the threat of moving away to put a stop to Ted and me."

"Have you and Ted talked about this?"

"Not really. And that's part of the problem. I don't want to make things any more difficult than they are." My voice caught.

"What exactly is it that bothers you?"

"That Annie jumped to this conclusion about how things were—are—between Ted and me, and that that is making trouble for Ted. I don't want to be part of that."

"I see."

I laughed. It seemed absurd. I *felt* how Ted felt. We both knew what we knew.

"Why are you laughing?"

"Ardis asked me."

"Asked you what?"

"How I felt about Ted."

"And?"

"I told her. It just slipped out."

"Well then. Aren't you assuming the worst and making things more complicated? For Annie, Ted, and yourself?"

"Milou . . ."

She waved her hand, cutting me off. "You know how I feel about you and Ted. I'm speaking for Jeanne, as well. Nothing would please me—us!—more than if the two of you could find a way to be together. I've watched you, you know. I see how Ted is with you and how you are with him. You suit each other. Two peas in a pod!" She crossed her middle finger over her index finger and laughed.

"He'll be gone soon. That won't advance the cause."

Milou scoffed. "It's only September! Plenty of time left."

I wondered if Milou understood that the words "I love you" seemed like poison pills to me. I trusted my feelings, but putting them into words felt like a kind of death, as if the feeling the words described would wither if I said them aloud. I wanted my feelings for Ted never to stop evolving, to be with him, to make a life with him, without losing that.

"It's not very romantic, I guess, but do you know what I want to tell Ted?"

"What?"

"That I had hoped we could make this . . . thing . . . between us—affection, companionship, friendship, whatever you want to call it—who we are together, who we'll be together, always."

"Marriage? Children?"

"That too." Even I recognized it wasn't Milou who needed to hear this. It was Ted. "You know . . ."

"What, *chérie*?"

"This is like getting halfway through a wonderful book only to find someone's torn out the last fifty pages."

Milou gave a little laugh and reached for my hand. "We'll see about that."

December 22, 1975

I showed Ted my Christmas present for Annie: the sketchbook I had filled with drawings of Tigrette and her kittens wrestling, cleaning themselves, curled up, or sprawled, belly up, in the sun.

He stopped at a page midway through the book and smiled at me.

"What?"

"Annie will enjoy them all—this one, especially." In the foreground, two kittens tussled, one of them biting the ear of the other. Standing nearby, Anisette, a quizzical look on her face, observed their mock battle.

"I hope so."

During her month and a half with us, Annie had discovered the pleasure of sketching the goats, the kittens, and Tigrette from life. She had sent a few of these drawings to Claire, thinking they might persuade her to change her mind about adopting Tigrette. No such luck.

Until the last minute before she left in August, Annie sat with the kittens and Tigrette, sobbing. I knew my gift would please her. I also knew it wasn't the same at all as having Tigrette with her in Newport.

After an afternoon Christmas shopping in Cluny, we sat at the kitchen table, warmed by the woodstove. Watching Ted go through the sketchbook, I felt his absence looming ahead, a hole in the wall of my life.

"What is it? You look like you're about to cry." He touched my cheek.

Why make matters worse for us both by talking about it?

Ted smiled. "Look, I believe the Rumpelstiltskin theory."

"And that would be?"

"Name the thing that scares you and it will go away."

"If only . . ."

"You'll never know unless you try."

"I'm sitting here with you—with you!—and imagining you not being here. Here, then not here. It's awful." I tried to smile. "You're as much a part of my day as the goats."

"Now there's a compliment."

"You know what I mean, right? No matter how busy we are. It's like breathing. Or your heartbeat."

He pulled me close.

"Even if you manage to come back next summer, that's six months away, one hundred and eighty days, lots of breaths and heartbeats." A part of me wished he were already gone.

He pulled an envelope out of a folder on his worktable. "I got a letter from Sandor yesterday." Sandor, a landscape architect in Newport, had worked with Ted on several restoration projects. "There's a package of photos on the way. They show a few of the garden sites he's planning." He took out a typed page and handed it to me. "Read it. Then we'll talk."

I skimmed the letter, then went back over it, slowly. I felt Ted's eyes on me, as if he were reading each word with me. "It seems as though he wrote this proposal for me, that he's pitching the idea to me. Does he know that I work for Luc and Isabelle? Here?"

Ted leaned forward, intent. "Sure. He knows all of that."

"Ted . . ."

He kept going. "I'd like you to come back with me to Newport."

"How can I do that?"

He touched my lips. "Just hear me out. I've thought about this so much since I got back in September." He turned the envelope over, ran his finger over the address. "Every plan I imagine includes you. I feel like this is supposed to happen, as if our grandmothers somehow made sure that it would. I couldn't wait to get back to tell you. But I held off. I wanted to have something concrete. Also, I wasn't sure what you'd think, you know? I knew you might want to stay here, stick it out with Luc. Will you at least think about it?" He took my hand, turned it over, and lightly touched my palm.

I remembered my conversation with my mother, the day after Jeanne's funeral, when she talked to me about my plans. I had thought about her idea of getting a credential off and on, but kept postponing a decision about going back to the States. Ted's proposal—Sandor's proposal, really—wouldn't be as easy to defer. For one thing, my feelings about Ted's departure gave a sense of urgency to the whole idea. I had a choice: I could spend the next six months missing Ted, uncertain if he'd return to Flagy; or, I could spend them looking forward to joining him in Newport and taking on a new job.

"I'd like to think about it. I don't . . ."

"What?"

"I don't want to mess things up."

"Talk to me about that."

"You're not Jack. And Newport isn't Brookton. Still, the idea of being together, trying to do our work, with everything that's going on with Annie, with Claire. I just don't know how . . ."

"I understand. But, as you say yourself, I'm not Jack, Newport isn't Brookton, and you, Malorie, are a different person now than you were five years ago. To begin with, you like what you're doing and you're good at it. And you're going in a direction that will allow you to do design work, exactly as you told me you wanted." He stopped, leaned toward me, and took both my hands in his.

"There's not a minute we're apart that I'm not imagining being together. I want to tell you everything I know and feel. I want you to do the same." He looked into my eyes, as if trying to pour his feelings and thoughts into me. "And, above all, I want you to be able to do the work you want to do."

"You're talking about living together, right?"

"Or not. The house I've found to rent is small, but there's room enough for you and me, and Annie when she visits."

"How would it work, exactly? I've told you I'd like to take courses, maybe get some type of certification, but if we're going to live together, I need to work, too, because I want to pay my own way."

"That's what Sandor's proposal is about. Work for you. Once we finish each restoration and the general plan for the garden, he always hires someone to take over the planting. Now he'd like to have someone working with him who can plan and plant, so he can take on work he'd otherwise have to turn down."

Could I do this on my own? How would I manage without Luc and Isabelle? I had learned a lot, yes, but I always had the benefit of their advice when I had questions. And what about Sandor? Would we be able to work together?

Ted leaned toward me. "Malorie, listen. The lots are in the old part of Newport. Small. Compact. So we're really talking about cottage gardens. And these houses all will be rentals. So far, all we've thought of is some flagstone work, some perennials, nothing fancy or fussy. In fact, the less fussy the better. The design plays a big part in making their upkeep manageable. But you know that." He looked puzzled. "There's something else bothering you."

"I'm wondering how it will be to work for Sandor, that's all."

"For one thing, he's not a micromanager. Once I'd explained to him about what you've done here, how much you've been on your own, he was relieved—and excited. He wants to give these projects to someone who doesn't need a lot of hand-holding. Another way to look at it is that you'll get to know the place and people will get to know you. You want to start your own business? Starting this way with Sandor will give you an entrée."

Ted's enthusiasm and reassurance buoyed my spirits. What if I did this? Wasn't it a plausible next step? And living with Ted? I needed time to think things over and to discuss the idea—and my departure—with Luc and Isabelle.

FACING EACH other across the flats of plants, Luc and I culled the seedlings, each barely an inch high. At the end of the row, he took off his gloves and wiped his face with a handkerchief. "What's up, Malorie? You've been here but not here all morning. I can tell you have something on your mind."

I had to get this part over with. I knew Luc well enough now to be sure that a direct approach was best. Still, I'd held back because I knew how much I'd miss him, miss mornings like this, working with him in the quiet, miss our conversations about everything he knew that I needed to know in order to do what I'd been doing for the last four years. I couldn't have had a better teacher.

He leaned back, hands in his pockets, eyes on mine.

"I'm thinking about going back in April or May."

He nodded and shifted his weight, waiting for me to go on.

"Ted has a friend in Newport, a landscape architect who'd like me to work for him. He sent me a proposal about some projects he has planned for the spring and summer. I'm thinking it would be a good step for me now, a chance to figure out if I can do it by myself." I explained about the restoration work and the small gardens Sandor had in mind.

"Do you know Newport?"

"Only that it's on an island and there are a lot of old houses. That's one advantage of working for someone who's already established there."

Luc smiled. "Of course, plant selection, climate, all that stuff." He thought for a moment. "Don't you have a sketchbook of garden drawings you did last year?"

Milou and I had taken several long walks around Cluny, looking at kitchen and cottage gardens. Most made a virtue of their small scale by combining a plot of vegetables and herbs with a cutting garden. "I've got a very basic understanding about how to design a manageable small garden, yes. There are only a few principles, really—how to balance plant variety with strong growth, for instance. And in design: simplicity, simplicity, simplicity. It's the difference in climate and weather that concerns me most, I think."

"How does Milou feel about all of this?"

"She has mixed feelings, as we do." It was my turn to wait.

He sighed. "I don't know how we'll get along without you. This friend of Ted's, he's very lucky. I know you. You'll keep learning; you'll get some more training in plant materials—no matter where you go next, you'll need that and, besides, it's a lifelong process. You're going to be fine, Malorie." He patted my shoulder. "Béatrice wants to come back to work now. But it won't be the same. Not at all."

When I told Isabelle, she hugged me, told me how happy she was for me. But the tears in her eyes sent another message. "At least we have some time to get used to the idea."

The question was, would I?

ON CHRISTMAS Eve, after dinner in Cluny with Henri, Milou, Luc, and Isabelle, Ted and I sat in his kitchen by the woodstove, sipping a tisane. We had bought beeswax candles to place on the shelves and countertops, using Jeanne's chipped and cracked saucers and cups as candleholders.

When Ted took our empty cups to the sink, I got up and leaned my head between his shoulders. Just then, the bells of Saint-Thibaut began to ring. Midnight. He went to the sideboard and opened the top drawer. "*Joyeux Noël*, Malorie."

The small, irregular package felt weightless. I pressed it gently, recognizing the object by its shape through the red and gold wrapping paper. The day we had taken our picnic to the field below the château, when Ted had shown me the dovecote, came back to me. I took the finial from its wrapping and turned it around, running my finger over the roof, with its finely carved tiles.

"It got a bit tired, being handled and worked on, but it cleaned up nicely, I think. Now it even has a layer of beeswax to protect it. That day, when I realized I'd found the right design for the finial, I hoped so much we'd end up where we are right now." His kiss felt like a promise.

"My turn." I took his gift from my bag.

He shook it gently. "Not a goldfish." He held it to his ear. "Or an alarm clock . . ." He put the wrapping paper on the table. As we looked at the print together, I felt his breath, warm against my cheek. The boats with their cargo moored on the river; the Pont Saint-Laurent with the town in the background; the couple on the quay. The little dog.

"I see what brings this scene alive."

"What's that?"

"Look at the dog. It's standing on its hind legs, but only one of its front paws touches the man's knee. The other doesn't because the dog's leg is bent, as if it were about to put it down again. It's ready to move on; they are, too."

Ted nodded. Of course he understood what I meant. We were about to make a change, to move into a new current, to leave Flagy behind.

In his room, we undressed in the dark. He drew the duvet up around my shoulders and sat on the bed beside me.

"It's only five months."

"The problem with that sentence is 'only.'"

He slipped his arm under the duvet, around my waist; I closed my eyes and tucked my head into his shoulder. When I turned my face up to his and kissed him, he drew me down into the bed and pulled the duvet over us.

The waning moon sat low in the sky. A few stars flickered behind slow-moving clouds.

PART 3

NEWPORT

1980–1992

Beech Street

August 18, 1980

In the harbor a half-block away, a solitary sailor guided a small boat to its mooring. Nearby, Goat Island's green light blinked at us through the fog. Up and down Beech Street, water dripped from trees and eaves onto the sidewalk in a syncopated riff around the foghorn's drone.

Steve Barker, our realtor, was late.

Ted and I wanted to live on the waterfront in this neighborhood of gaslights and narrow streets, where he had helped restore several eighteenth-century houses. The workshop he shared with a boat builder occupied an old garage on an alley just around the corner between Third Street and America's Cup Avenue. After four years in Newport, we'd outgrown our rental house and were tired of battling our landlord over maintenance and repairs.

When we decided to look for a house to buy, it made sense to begin our search here on the Point, where Quaker settlers had built modest frame homes on neat, narrow parcels. All the streets bore the names of trees because the Quakers didn't believe in naming streets after people. Many of them became wealthy, but only their Meeting House and the properties of Quaker ship owners spoke to the community's prosperity. A half-dozen of these substantial homes lined the waterfront, with plenty of room along their seawalls for docks.

Ted first noticed the for-sale sign just after the house on Beech Street came on the market. When he drove by the next day, the gate was open. "The house looks empty, so I took a look around. Wait till you see the garden, Malorie. It's a disaster!"

I knew he wasn't exaggerating. After spending the last four years planning and planting gardens on long-neglected lots around Newport, I knew what to expect: poor soil, rampant weeds, and at least one trash pit.

"There's one good thing about it." Ted's tone and expression telegraphed his delight.

"I'm holding my breath."

"A wonderful big tree—a huge tree—at the top of the lot."

"The north end?"

"Yep. And the lot runs north to south. Pretty good light in the summer, I think, at least at the south end."

"I like it already."

I peeked through a gap in the gate at the helter-skelter tangle of grasses, wildflowers, a forsaken forsythia, and what looked like a lilac draped in wild cucumber. I had to stand in the middle of the street and crane my neck to assess the tree.

"Huge" didn't begin to do it justice. From what I could see, the foliage identified it as a maple. But the bark crawled up the massive trunk in shaggy slabs, gray on top, pink underneath. The canopy looked like a vast topsail, fanned out to catch the wind, swaying from side to side. If it was a maple, it wasn't a common variety. I hoped it was healthy. I decided to find out about it, even if we didn't buy the house. Maybe Sandor would know.

"Great fireplace," Ted exclaimed. He was standing on the sidewalk, looking in one of the front windows, his hands cupped against the glass. "Must be the living room."

I grabbed onto the windowsill and pulled myself up on tiptoe. No good. "Give me a boost, would you?" With his help, I managed to get my elbows on the sill, my nose just above it. "What a lovely room!" I could see crown moldings and a chair rail, and the brick fireplace. I had an instant impression of light and warmth.

Behind us, a car door closed. Ted helped me down.

"I see you got a head start!" Steve grinned at us. It was hard to tell if he knew he was making a pun.

"At least we know passersby have to have a stepladder or be as tall as Ted to look in the windows." In the rental house, I'd had to get used to the idea of living right on the street. At first, I worried it would be noisy. But because it was a one-way street, and our bedroom was in the back, we seldom heard any street noise.

"It was standard back then to build at the edge of the lot, so you didn't have to walk through the mud or slops to get in the house." Steve wrinkled his nose. "Anyway, in those days, most men weren't six foot three, and everyone went to bed early. Nothing to see, even if you were tall enough to look in!"

He opened the gate and motioned us through. Perhaps it was the gambrel roof, shaped like a cupped hand. Or maybe the embrace of the towering tree. I felt the house reach out in welcome and closed my eyes, listening to the foghorn and the traffic on the Newport Bridge a few blocks away.

Steve knew most of the information about the house by heart. Built in 1719, its original brick chimney and four fireplaces—two up, two down—were intact. The current owners had redesigned the kitchen and put in a fireplace there, as well. Excluding the kitchen, there were five rooms, all with wood floors and plaster walls.

At the top of the front steps, he unlocked and opened the front door for me. I heard a thump and a gasp. Behind me, Ted was rubbing the top of his head. "The door is lower than I thought. Like a boat." He grinned and shrugged.

Steve laughed. "They think a ship's carpenter built this house. I'd say you just confirmed it."

The owners of the house had already moved to San Francisco. This explained why there were no personal belongings or furniture to filter our first impressions—no family photographs, no bric-a-brac, no distracting art on the walls, no lingering odors of cooking or aftershave. Still, the house didn't smell empty. It held a mix of fragrances—wood smoke, plaster, and something indefinable—perhaps the accumulation of years of living, ghostly traces of the generations that had come and gone, leaving only this faint hint of their time here.

In the living room, Ted ran his hand over a plaster wall, dimpled and uneven in places. "That's because there's no drywall under it," he said, as if talking to himself. "Horsehair plaster. It almost feels alive."

I went into a small back hallway, where I found a closet door that opened into a brick-lined storage space, wide at the bottom and narrow at the top, like a beehive. I was beginning to believe the ship's carpenter idea: only a ship's carpenter would have known how to make use of every inch of space.

In the next room, the original kitchen, I crouched down beside a brass handle set into one of the floorboards. "What's this?"

"Give it a tug," Steve said.

When I yanked on the handle, the floorboard began to move. With Ted's help, we lifted the board out, exposing what appeared to be another storage area. Steve handed us a flashlight.

Ted laughed. "It's a cistern, with about a foot of water in it. I knew there were springs in this neighborhood. Maybe this is one of them. Imagine having water right here, under the kitchen, in 1719."

My skin prickled. It was as if the spring at Flagy's crossroads had followed us here.

"I wonder why they didn't fill it in when they restored the house." I looked at Ted and Steve.

"This is a careful restoration," Steve told me.

"What do you mean?"

Ted's turn. "Rather than replace everything, they left as much of the original house as possible, which makes the cistern a rare, historical feature, at least as old as the house." An expression of delight played over Ted's face.

"He looked bewitched," I wrote to Milou later. "If he could have, I think he would've written a check on the spot."

AFTER STEVE left, Ted and I walked down Beech Street to the harbor. At low tide, the sea grass lay at our feet in dark mats studded with periwinkles and mussels. The fog appeared to be lifting; it wouldn't last into the evening.

"This is it, Malorie." Ted tripped and caught himself with a laugh as we walked back to the car. "The house has everything we want—character, location, condition. The main restoration work is done. Sure, the lot's a wasteland, but what an opportunity for you. You can do what you want for a change—clear, organize, and plant whatever and wherever you like. Just think!"

I had already begun to consider the challenges that lay ahead—for anyone who bought the house. For one thing, the big tree's huge canopy would narrow plant choices to ones that would flourish in the shade, at least at the upper end of the lot. I smiled and nodded. "It will be fun to plan a garden for us, instead of for someone else."

"But?"

"The upstairs ceilings are so low you can't stand up straight. There isn't a single door you don't have to duck through. Your chiropractor bills will be as much as the mortgage." I shook my head. "And the *stairs*!"

"You don't think I can get used to crawling up and sliding down?"

I laughed. So he, too, recognized these drawbacks. Still, I couldn't stifle the flickers of excitement I felt when I thought about the tree and making a garden there. My own garden. Solving my own problems. Learning about a new microclimate and finding plants that would suit it. I took a deep breath.

"There's one other thing."

"What?"

"Is it big enough for all of us?"

"You, me, and Annie?"

"You, me, Annie. And our baby. When we have one."

It had never been a question of *if.* We knew we wanted children. The only question was when. Moving to a larger house, a house we would own, had been a condition we had both agreed on.

"We can put the baby upstairs in the second bedroom." He was matter-of-fact, reassuring. "When she's with us, Annie can stay downstairs in the room next to the living room. The den, or whatever we're going to call it." He waited a moment. "Besides, she'll be going to college in four years."

There was a fluttering sound behind us. We both turned around. A panicked cluster of menhaden swerved and leaped out of the water, trying to elude a school of bluefish not far from shore.

"Another thing. Where will you do your design work? I thought we decided you need a home office." The shop space he shared didn't include a suitable place for drawing and designing.

"As long as you're working for Sandor, I can make do with the den. I'll put some shelves in so I can store my stuff when we have Annie."

I was splitting my time between coursework toward the master gardener's certificate and working for Sandor, using his studio, an arrangement that suited us both. Within the next year, when I got my certification, I could start my design business at last. Sandor had offered to let me continue to use his studio, combining work for him with projects of my own. So Ted's idea of using the den made sense. As long as Annie wasn't staying with us. As long as we didn't have a baby in residence in the second bedroom upstairs.

I could see in Ted's face how much he wanted me to agree with him. For a moment, I let myself feel my own version of Ted's elation: designing and planting a garden at the Beech Street house would be a perfect inaugural project. But his need for a studio gnawed at me.

"Will the den give you enough room? For your books and your drawing table and things?"

"We can make it work, Malorie. I know we can."

He had made up his mind. And nothing short of an outright refusal on my part would change it.

"I want to say yes."

He nodded. "But you'd like to look around some more before we commit?"

"Could we?"

"Of course. And we'll keep talking about Beech Street?"

"Of course!"

September 9, 1980

On Saturday morning three weeks later, Ted answered the phone. "Hi, Steve."

Across the room, listening in, I understood enough of Ted's end of the conversation to know that our lives were about to change.

"Really?" Ted pumped his free arm and made a thumbs-up sign at me. "That is fantastic. Yeah. She's here. We'll talk and call you right back." He dropped the phone into its cradle, crossed the room to me, and swung me around.

"What happened? What's going on?"

"The owners lowered their price."

"And?"

"Guess how much."

"Just tell me!"

He took out a piece of paper and picked up a pencil, hiding the paper from me as he wrote. He folded the note and gave it to me.

"They've dropped the price fifty thousand dollars? Why? What's wrong with the house?"

"Nothing. Steve said they don't want to leave it empty. If they can't sell it before mid-October, they'll have to find a renter. They don't want to do that. Not all renters are like us." Ted had seen the effects of renters' neglect—and abuse—in many of the houses he had worked on.

"Okay. I get that. So?"

"You realize what this means, right?" Ted grinned.

So far, we hadn't found a property we liked nearly as much. We had agreed that if we couldn't find another place, we would offer the asking price, which we could afford—just. The lower price meant a smaller mortgage. A smaller mortgage meant that both of us could continue to build our own businesses. I could cut back on the garden maintenance work I did to keep a steady income coming in, and Ted could focus on designing his own line of furniture.

"It's like it was meant to be!"

Sooner than either of us could have imagined, we moved in, and began to live with—and love—the house's idiosyncrasies. Ted became adept at managing the doors, the ceilings, and the stairs, thanks in part to the sign Annie put up on the fridge: "Daddy! Think shorter!" The sign included an illustration of a cross-eyed stick figure sporting a huge bump on his head.

As for me, I began to plan and design the garden.

October 10, 1980

Across the street, Ardis and Matt unpacked their car. We hadn't seen them since our wedding in 1978. Matt had landed a teaching job at Columbia and they had moved back into their loft. It was a huge space—twenty-five hundred square feet, room enough for a studio for Ardis and living quarters. They'd been renovating it in their spare time.

"We figure by the time we're ready to retire, the elevator will work, the rats will be gone, and we'll have heat when we want, not just when it decides to work." Standing inside the gate, Ardis looked around. "Just the opposite of here."

"What do you mean?"

"My studio is the finished part. Our living space is the work in progress." Her teasing smile was enough. I got the point: my studio—the garden—had a long way to go.

Matt eyed the house. "It's almost three times as long as it is wide—a nearly perfect ratio. Your ship's carpenter knew something about proportions, I guess."

Ted nodded, happy that someone else got this. To Matt, it was a simple matter of geometry. To Ted, it was a question of aesthetics. "I should show you some of the other gambrel-style houses around here."

"You could easily fit this house into our loft, no problem—except for the chimney, that is. That might have to go."

"Small house, big stories." Ted's eyes flicked from one end of the house to the other, as he decided where and how to begin. "First, you have to understand the difference between a 'restoration' and a 'renovation.'"

I caught his eye. "The short version?"

Once he got started, the storytelling became an end in itself. I knew Matt would listen and ask questions. He would want to know all the details. There would be time for that later.

"The people who sold it to us didn't change the original floor plan. They preserved the old materials wherever they could—the chimney, for instance. The bricks are two hundred and forty years old. Of course they updated the electrical and plumbing systems and modernized the kitchen—new gas range, butcher-block counters. But it's an antique. They respected that."

"Do you know anything about who built the house? Or the original land owner?"

Ted and I laughed.

"What's so funny?"

"If this house were right on the harbor, we'd probably have lots of information. Those houses belonged to merchants and ship owners, who left business records. But a lot of information about houses like this one has gone missing. We're not even really sure about the date it was built."

"You mean 1719 is just idle speculation?"

"Not entirely. Let's just say that people at the Historical Society, who've done the research, have put two and 1.99 together and came up with four."

Matt nodded, smiling. "Sounds like higher math to me."

"We know more beginning in 1785, when Louis Duchesne bought this house from John Crawford, who was most likely the original deed holder's last surviving family member."

"Duchesne? Isn't that French? Do you know where he came from?"

"Not so far." It was my turn. "But that hasn't kept us from claiming him as a distant relative, from Burgundy, of course." Some of the soldiers who accompanied Rochambeau and Lafayette to Newport stayed on after the War of Independence. It was at least plausible that Duchesne was one of them. We had made him our French connection.

After dinner, Ted took Matt to the shop to see some of the designs he had been working on.

"Tell me about the garden."

"You mean the one in my head, of course."

"It's not exactly like having a blank page, I realize. I want to know what you're going to do and how you figured it out. Especially since all I can see of it is that huge tree and heaps of dirt. And that pile of lumber."

The day before the closing, we had stopped at the house for the final walk-through. Ted had gone in with Steve. I had stayed outside to look again at the lot. I stood in the center of the dusty expanse of weeds and brush and did a slow 360-degree turn. Only a bird feeder, on a lopsided post, the struggling forsythia, and the cucumber-draped lilac showed that someone, once upon a time, had had a garden here.

Ted was right. I would have to start from scratch. All of my previous projects had had features I could work with and around, like signposts pointing me in the right direction. Here I had only the tree—some signpost.

I had walked around to the far side of the house. A rusted oil drum, converted into a barbecue grill, leaned against a heap of empty champagne and wine bottles. I toed it gingerly, causing several bottles to roll off with a clatter. No question about it. A general cleanup was the first order of business.

Sandor had helped me identify the tree, acer pseudoplatanus, a pseudo-plane, also called a sycamore maple. He was blunt. "Take it out, Malorie. It will suck everything out of the soil, for one thing. For another, when you combine its canopy with the ones along the border, you'll have very little light. Which means you'll be restricted—severely—as to what you can put in your garden. Seriously, take a deep breath, call the arborist, and cut it down."

Ardis looked at me, shocked. "Sandor said that? I thought he was a save-anything-at-all-costs guy?"

"Usually is, at least when you're talking about specimen trees." Sandor favored the European beeches, imported in the nineteenth century, now magnificent examples of the spare-no-expense thinking of the Astors and the Vanderbilts. "This isn't one of those. Anyway, I told him I'd think about it. But I'd already made up my mind. I found out that this tree is the same type as the Darnley plane, in Scotland outside of Glasgow. That one's about four hundred years old. I've seen photos. Ours looks just like it—much smaller, of course, and a youngster—probably only seventy-five."

"So, the tree stays?"

"The tree stays. Even Sandor agreed, once I told him about the Darnley plane. We'll prune it up, give it a good feeding. Maybe it, too, will live to see its four hundredth birthday."

We were standing at the street end of the lot, looking toward the tree. Except for a few stakes driven in as markers, only the dozen or so piles of topsoil and mulch hinted at what was to come.

"I hope you're taking pictures as you go along. You might get a prize for the one that shows this landscape. In some ways, it looks intentional, like an earth sculpture or something." Ardis threw me a questioning look.

"Something like that. But all those heaps of soil and mulch, like your tubes of paint, are just waiting to do their job. At last, I have a glimmer of an idea about what that is."

THE CLEANUP had turned out to be a reclamation process. We had found three trash pits along the east boundary. Based on a broken tile we had found in one of them, a local historian told me he thought it dated back to the mid-eighteenth century.

"He told you not to bring in a backhoe? Was he planning to do the stoop labor himself?"

"What he meant was that it would be better to clear the trash pits by hand, then bring in the machines."

Two high school boys had helped with the digging, sifting, and clearing, under orders to throw nothing away. Each day they unearthed pieces of the past: clay tobacco pipes, glass marbles, more broken tiles and pottery, a doll's porcelain arm, a cow's molar, even arrowheads and a perfectly preserved child's teacup. They also found hand-forged nails, some long enough to hold a rafter, others likely used for framing. These I had sorted and stored in boxes, imagining the stories behind each one.

"So now you can put in the soil?"

"Right. And that will go fast."

My design made a virtue of necessity, with a lawn running up the center of the lot and a twelve-foot border around it. The simplicity pleased me enough that I didn't mind I hadn't had much of a choice in how to organize the space. It wasn't an eighteenth-century design, but it fit the house: modest, quiet, and inviting.

"I want visitors to look up at the big tree when they first come in. That fan-shaped canopy and the symmetrical trunk draw your eye back down again into the lawn and border. My hunch is that you won't much notice the neighboring houses, thanks to the trees and plants in the border."

"Will you put a fence in?"

"A cedar fence, yes. No stain or paint. After a while, it will blend in so well, you won't see it."

STAYING AT a B&B a short walk away, Ardis and Matt arrived for breakfast early the next morning.

"Door's open!" Ted and I were in the kitchen making coffee.

Ardis put pastries and fruit on the table. Matt handed me a package. "Housewarming."

"Now or later?"

Ardis smiled at me. "Now, of course."

I opened the package and found one of the Brookton paintings Ardis had shown me in 1970, the night she arrived to spend the summer. "I thought you sold these."

"Three of them, yes. But this one has always had your name on it."

I didn't have to say it. I knew she understood. The view from the basement window up and out into the hydrangeas' foliage, the beginning of our friendship, our shared delight in the balance of light and dark, symmetry and asymmetry—the painting was all these things, and more.

"This is a wonderful gift." Ted hugged Ardis.

I could only nod. Ardis hugged me.

"I'll put it between the two windows in the dining room. It will be out of the direct light, but it will get plenty of reflected light from the opposite wall. What do you think, Malorie?" Ted held the painting at arm's length, as if imagining it in place. In the dining room, we watched him position the painting on the wall.

"Perfect." Ardis stepped back. "It belongs there, you know?"

After breakfast, Ardis looked at me, expectant. "Will you show me your garden plans?"

"As long as you understand you'll be seeing the latest version, which is far from final."

WHEN I arrived in Newport in the summer of 1976, I had known about plants that thrived in Burgundy's mild climate. It had taken awhile to learn some new rules—about plants and about climate. Although Newport winters were generally mild, they could be severe, and sudden thaws and April cold snaps could wreak havoc on perennials. In the summer, it might be foggy and humid, or dry and hot, for weeks at a time.

It was a challenge to find perennials that tolerated both extremes. The gardens Sandor wanted me to help with had to be both practical and pretty. I hoped I could achieve this without resorting to the easy—and expensive—way out: annuals, the weekend gardener's boon, the perennial lover's bane. Learning what worked became a process of trial and error and the topic of long conversations with experienced gardeners. Sandor had dozens of contacts; I consulted most of them.

Before I began taking classes for the master gardener's certificate, I read books and catalogs and visited local nurseries and gardens. Recently, someone had asked if I planned to recreate a colonial cottage garden at the Beech Street house. "That garden likely was a vegetable garden," I told her. "There was more light then, not so many trees." From the preliminary research I'd done, I knew there were many shade-loving plants that would survive and thrive in the microclimate down here by the harbor.

"So, the more you know, the more you need to know." Ardis shook her head.

"That's just it. I'm glad I'll have the winter to pare down my plant lists. I can at least get started with bulbs and shrubs before December."

Ardis looked up at the big tree. "It's like a great green-gold dome. Not like the tulip trees in Desmond."

"You're right. Those look as though they're inviting you to dance—something with minimal footwork."

"Tango?"

"If that's what you call minimal footwork, I suppose so." I imagined the tulip trees standing almost still, while Ardis and I stepped toward and away from them.

"Well, anyway, this one doesn't have that formality; it's more sheltering, I guess you could say. No tango for this one. More likely a waltz. It must be wonderful to watch in a big breeze!"

I put out my sketches on the kitchen table. Most people had difficulty reading landscape design work. Not Ardis. She saw right away that the curved border created depth and variety in the narrow lot.

"It's the best solution. I don't want to cut the space up into rooms. Besides, there is no way to hide that tree."

"You want to let it be who and what it is. I approve."

"It's not like I have much of a choice!"

I didn't mind the constraint. I had realized that this wasn't really my garden, after all, at least not in the way Ted had meant when he had described the space as my own first garden. It would be the tree's garden, one that sat at its feet within its canopy. I was the designer, yes, but I was also a collaborator. That responsibility had become a kind of mission. But I knew I would find a way.

"What is it?"

"We might as well be talking about Annie."

"How is she?"

I made a so-so motion. "I'm trying to stand back, for now. It's been rough."

At first, Annie had been happy that Ted and I were together. After Claire moved to Boston at the beginning of the summer of 1976, Ted drove up Fridays to bring Annie down to spend weekends with us. Now fourteen, she took the bus. Usually, as soon as she stopped by the house to drop off her books and her clothes, she was out the door, off to visit her friends. This familiar routine made it seem as if she were still living nearby with Claire.

It hadn't been easy for Annie or me. I guess I should say it was less easy for Annie and me than it was for Annie and Ted. From talking to other parents with kids about Annie's age, Ted and I understood that this wasn't unique to us. For a while, when she was ten, Annie had refused to eat certain things. Sometimes it was the color that put her off—there was the month of no red foods, including her favorite spaghetti sauce. The summer she was eleven, she insisted on sleeping with her light on and wore the same clothes for weeks in a row. Still, even during these times, there had been moments when she reverted to the sunny, outgoing child I had gotten to know in Flagy.

Lately, she seemed to be elsewhere, refusing to look at me when I spoke to her, answering in monosyllables.

THE FIRST sign of real trouble came when I drove her to an appointment with the orthodontist. She had sat slumped against the door, silent, until I parked and got out of the car.

"Don't!"

I got back in the car. Annie's face was red, her eyes hot with tears. She clutched her wadded-up sweatshirt to her chest as though it were a life preserver.

"What's up?"

"I don't want you to come in with me."

"But I always come in."

"Well, I don't want you to. Not anymore."

"Okay. I'll wait out here. I've got a magazine." Had I sounded as flustered as I felt? "Could you tell me why?"

She shook her head.

"Is it something I've done?" Annie stared back at me, bright and hard. "I'd really like to know what's going on." I reached out to touch her shoulder.

Annie had shrugged away and wrenched her door open.

"You're not my mother! Get it? You. Are. Not. My. Mother." She ran up the steps, two at a time, dragging her sweatshirt behind her. I let her go.

Up to this point in the story, Ardis had listened without comment. She sighed and leaned toward me. "What did Ted say?"

"At the time, he wasn't too concerned. He said it was just a phase—like the food phase and the clothes phase."

Ardis nodded. "Teenagers. Hard work, I guess."

"Recently, she just withdraws. As soon as she arrives, she goes to her room and closes the door. She used to like to go to the shop with Ted, or to be with me, reading or drawing, when I'm working. Not anymore. So Ted came up with a plan. The other day, he asked her if she'd like to help him build a tree house."

"She needs more of a space of her own?"

"Something like that." I sat on the front steps, motioning to Ardis to sit, too. "During the week, Ted did a design and figured out the materials he needed. He and Annie went last weekend, when she was here, to get everything." I gestured at the pile of lumber under the tree. "On the way, she started to talk, out of the clear blue sky, about how unhappy she is in Boston. It isn't just that she misses Newport. Turns out Claire has a boyfriend. Annie feels excluded. She really doesn't like the guy, although she couldn't tell Ted why."

"Poor Annie. I can't say I blame her."

"There's more." I turned toward Ardis. "She told Ted she doesn't really like boys. She likes girls."

"Like as in *like*?"

"Yes. And Claire, whom she also told, told Annie she doesn't know what she's talking about."

"Oh, my. What did Ted say?"

"I haven't talked to Annie, of course. We're not there yet. But Ted told her he believes she knows what she's talking about and that he loves her and wants her to be happy, to have happy, fulfilling relationships with girls *or* boys. She should concentrate on that." The dark intensity of Ted's eyes as he had told me this expressed just how much he wanted me to understand his love for Annie.

"Then what?"

"He called Claire right away, told her about his conversation with Annie, asked her to keep an open mind, to support Annie. He also explained Annie's discomfort with the new boyfriend."

"That must have been some phone conversation."

"I was out at the time. When I got back, Ted was lying down, exhausted. But glad to have cleared the air."

"And the tree house?"

"Ted understands Annie so well—intuitively, I guess I should say. They are very much alike is what it comes down to. She can't wait to get started on it. Doesn't want to go to Boston. Wants to come back here, to live here, with us . . . et cetera."

"Wow. Talk about a change of heart. What are you going to do about that?"

I looked down at my hands, folded in my lap. "It's not going to happen. Claire . . . let's just say that Claire won't agree. Anyway, Annie's so excited about the tree house, she's thinking about that most of all."

The Dying of the Light

July 15, 1983

Growing into the Beech Street house, we observed and listened, attending to it as if it were a fragile, occasionally cranky family member. In every season, it responded with subtle and not-so-subtle changes to the weather. Each fall, as soon as we turned on the heat, certain floorboards and stairs creaked or snapped underfoot, sometimes on their own, as the house settled and contracted.

We grew so accustomed to the hairline cracks that appeared in the plaster walls in January and February that we ignored them until spring. As soon as we shut off the furnace, Ted got out his repair kit and the paint. In no time, the cracks—and the repairs—were invisible.

In June and July, fog seeped in, slicking a damp coat onto floors, walls, and doors, encouraging blooms of mildew. These I tackled with bleach and a sponge.

After a morning spent washing the living room ceiling and walls, I took a break on the front steps. It was nearly one o'clock. I would finish by the end of the afternoon and hoped that the effect of the bleach solution would last a week or two. A hummingbird flashed by me, heading into the neighbor's garden. The kitchen phone rang.

Ted opened the door behind me. "It's Dr. Hoffman. Do you want me on the other line?"

I swallowed hard. "Let me talk to her first."

WE HAD been trying to get pregnant for two years. Early tests showed that my hormone levels were adequate, as was Ted's sperm count. No one seemed to think my age—thirty-six—or Ted's—thirty-nine—had anything to do with what we had resolved to call our "situation." We were determined not to name names until we knew, beyond a doubt, we were infertile.

Three weeks earlier, at the end of June, the night before an appointment with Dr. Hoffman, I'd dreamed of the house, filled with a warm, glowing light that dimmed and brightened as I moved from room to room, as if I were its source. I discovered a small room I had never seen before. White-washed from floor to ceiling, it had two narrow windows, both open wide. Sheer curtains, so long they draped and pooled on the floor, swirled into the room in the breeze. I called out to Ted. No answer.

I woke from the dream, my face and my pillow damp with tears.

In Dr. Hoffman's office that morning, I had sat beside Ted on the couch, listening to her explain why she was recommending I have a laparoscopy. She spoke matter-of-factly, her calm tone reassuring. "Since all the other tests show everything's fine, the laparoscopy will tell us if the parts are working the way they're supposed to."

"What does that mean?" Ted put his arm around me.

I closed my eyes. I heard my own voice, my own question that day, in September 1970, sitting in Dr. Stein's office after my miscarriage. His warning, forgotten until now, ambushed me. It was his voice I heard, like the voice of a prompter, behind Dr. Hoffman's answer.

"We'll find out if there's an obstruction somewhere. Even if only one of the fallopian tubes is blocked, conception is sometimes difficult."

"Or impossible?" Ted asked.

They both looked at me. Dr. Hoffman's eyes held mine when she answered, "Let's wait and see."

Ted had followed me out of the office. As soon as we got in the car, he turned to me. "Can you tell me what's going on?"

I couldn't meet his eyes. "Let's talk when we get home." I leaned back against the headrest and closed my eyes. Since the miscarriage, since Ted and I had been together, I had never doubted that I could have a child. I hadn't once thought about Dr. Stein's warning. It hadn't meant anything then. I *had* gotten pregnant then, hadn't I?

And then, the dream. What was it about, exactly? What was it in me that had produced the room, the feeling of joy, of excitement, even? I wanted to believe—needed to believe—that the laparoscopy would prove I was all right, that we must be patient. I knew that. What if I was wrong?

We sat in the living room, facing each other. I felt miles and years away. Ted had put a box of Kleenex on the coffee table. I took one and smoothed it over my lap. Searching his face, I saw his concern and confusion. He waited, his eyes focused on me.

"Whatever it is, tell me. We can get through it."

"There's more to the story of the miscarriage, about what Dr. Stein told me then."

Ted nodded. "What did he say?"

"That's the part that's about you and me." I closed my eyes. "He told me I might have trouble getting pregnant—later on—because I'd had an ectopic pregnancy."

"I know what that is."

"So you know it can cause scarring or blockage?"

"Well, that's what we're going to find out. That's why you're going to have the laparoscopy."

"What if I can't . . .? What then?"

I knew how I'd managed to forget Dr. Stein's warning. Since I hadn't wanted to be pregnant at the time, I hadn't considered—at all—that I might eventually change my mind. I had focused instead on putting the recent past—Brookton, Jack, the miscarriage, Danielle's plagiarism—behind me and getting on with my life. It was like removing the weeds growing among seedlings. As long as they were in the ground, growing stronger every day, they used up nutrients and water, sapped the seedlings of their strength, and crowded them out. Of course, removing weeds meant more than pulling them up. You had to destroy them.

Maybe I *had* to pull up the weeds. I had to face the possibility that the pregnancy and miscarriage had caused irreparable damage.

"Once we know, we'll decide what to do." Ted smiled.

ON THE phone with Dr. Hoffman, I made notes as she explained the test results, watching her words shape our future. At the end, I wrote: "No go."

"Malorie, are you still there?"

"Yes, sorry. What did you say?"

"I asked if you and Ted want to come in tomorrow."

"Can I call you back?"

"Whenever you're ready."

ON THE floor in the den, Ted sorted invoices and filed them into folders. I sat down beside him and put my head on his shoulder. He swiveled around and took me in his arms.

"It's what she thought." I could feel Ted's pulse under my ear, breathed in the familiar smells of wood, wax, and varnish, and him. I had imagined feeling our child moving inside me, that it would be like hearing Ted's heart in me, the throb of his pulse beating with mine.

He waited.

"She said that both of the tubes are blocked." I slid around to face him. "She says it's related to the miscarriage, at least in one of them. So Dr. Stein was right."

His eyes darted away.

I kept going. "It just doesn't look good for us." I took his hand. "We can go talk to her, if you want."

"Later. How are you doing?" He stroked my hair.

"I really thought I was okay, you know?"

"I know how much you wanted this. I did too. But maybe there's another way."

"Another way?"

"We could adopt a baby."

I pulled away and looked down at my hands cradled in his. I thought about how much we both worked with our hands and wondered if that had something to do with the closeness I felt with him. It was always possible to misunderstand a word or a tone of voice. Not touch. His hands were warm and relaxed, reassuring.

"There are so many children who need parents. We'd be good ones." His voice trailed off. He was looking at my hands.

"I don't know if I can. Even with your help."

"Does this have something to do with Annie?"

"It does, yes. Our adopting a baby could make it harder for Annie and me. We've made some progress, but we've got a long way to go. Another thing . . ." Did I dare go on?

"What's that?"

"To me, Annie is like an adopted child. It's like I'm in the backseat and you and Claire are driving. It's just a feeling I have. But I have to trust it. As Annie gets older, the longer we're together, I hope that will change."

Ted leaned back against the wall, his eyes on the floor.

"I agree." He pulled me close.

August 5, 1983

Tan and taller, her hair almost as short as Ted's, Annie strode through Logan Airport's international arrivals gate as if she owned it.

"She looks French!" Ted caught her eye and waved.

She looks like you, you mean. In fact, she looks more like you all the time.

At seventeen, five feet ten, long-legged and narrow-hipped, wearing low-slung jeans, a tank top, and espadrilles, Annie could have been a model. She had recently discovered fencing and long-distance running, claiming she preferred sports that let her compete one on one. Already considering college, she had narrowed her list to a few that supported these sports for women.

As soon as she saw us, she waved and darted through the crowd, rushing to Ted, throwing her arms around him, greeting him in a cascade of French and English. "*Salut*, Daddy! I can't wait to tell you everything. I had such a great time!" She broke away from him and reached into her carry-on.

"*Pour toi*, Malorie."

"*Cassis* from Isabelle!" I could smell the ripening fruit and feel the sun on my face as Isabelle and I stripped the black currants from the bushes in her garden, a labor-intensive, late-summer ritual we had both enjoyed. Just holding the jar felt like a hug.

"Earth to Malorie." Ted touched my shoulder.

"Thinking about Flagy, is all." I smiled at him and Annie. "And thinking about where to hide this jam . . ."

Ted laughed and put his arm around Annie, who tilted her face up to kiss his cheek.

"Did you park close, Dad?"

"Close enough. I'll bring the car around and meet you where the limos stop outside the baggage claim."

Annie shrugged and smiled. Ted gave her a squeeze and left us.

As we walked through the terminal, weaving our way around passengers with small children, elderly people in wheelchairs, and couples clinging to one another, Annie talked about her month in Flagy. Mostly in English. I didn't interrupt. Amélie came up in conversation almost as often as someone called "Jackie." Evidently it was the latest French fad—teenagers giving each other American nicknames. I couldn't place Jackie. Was he one of the village boys or a relative of someone living there? There were kids I hadn't met; maybe Ted knew who he was.

Standing on the curb, waiting for Ted, Annie stopped talking for a moment, as if she'd lost her train of thought. "I'm . . . well, I'm not supposed to tell you."

"You're not supposed to tell me what?"

"Promise you won't tell Isabelle?"

"I can't promise you that, Annie. I have no idea what this is about."

Annie sighed. "Two weeks ago, Milou had to go to the doctor."

"Had to?"

"She fainted. Something like that. So Henri took her in for a checkup."

"And?"

"I don't know exactly. I overheard Isabelle and Luc talking. It's about her heart. Do you know anything about that?"

In a letter, a year ago, Milou had mentioned heart medication. When Ted asked Bruno, all he'd been able to find out was that it was something for hypertension, for high blood pressure. Bruno had dismissed it. "This happens to people our age."

I looked at Annie, her eyes wide with worry. "I know about her heart medicine. But that's about it. Thank you for telling me. I'll try to find out what's going on."

"And Isabelle? You won't tell her I told you?"

"I won't have to tell her. It's okay. Don't worry."

"DADDY?"

"What, sweetie?"

"I invited Amélie to come visit."

"Good idea." Ted passed a car that had stopped in our lane, someone having trouble finding the exit from Logan in rush-hour traffic.

"I thought you'd say that. She's coming on August twentieth, because that's when Louise thinks she can get a ticket. But she has to go back on September third."

In the backseat, I waited to hear Ted's response. He was straddling two lanes, moving toward the exit ramp. Had he even heard Annie? When he didn't say anything, I leaned forward. "Annie, this really isn't a good time for us. Could we do it next summer?"

"But I promised her. I told her about the beach, about all the things we can do, about sailing. I even told Paulette. Amélie really wants to come!" She turned around to look at me. "Besides, Louise already got the ticket."

Paulette had been Annie's closest friend in Newport since she started school. Telling Paulette about Amélie's visit was tantamount to signed, sealed, and delivered. I had a good idea how this conversation would end.

"Wait." Ted caught my eye in the rearview mirror. "I thought you said Louise *thinks* she can get a ticket."

"I meant to say she already got one." Annie had turned away from Ted, her voice low and flat.

I sat back. When Ted made eye contact with me again, I shrugged and smiled. We would work it out.

Ted didn't mind last-minute changes. I did. I always needed to prepare, to adjust, to manage disruptions. At times like these, I tried to keep in mind Milou's admonition, "*Ne cherche pas midi à quatorze heures, chérie,*" the French rendition of "Don't go looking for trouble." Was that my problem? That I always anticipated the worst? I knew well enough that bad things happen, life goes out of control. But I always prepared for the worst. This wasn't the same as asking for trouble. Not by a long shot. For me, it was a way to avoid it.

All the way home, Annie regaled Ted with stories about her friends in Flagy: who got along, who didn't, and how much she loved being with Isabelle and Luc. I let my mind drift, thinking about what it meant not to be Annie's mother. To Annie, it seemed to mean she didn't have to ask me if she could invite a friend to stay for two weeks. That she hadn't asked Ted, either, had to do with his own, very relaxed, attitude about parenting. Claire kept a close watch on Annie—too close, Ted thought, especially as she continued to reject Annie's sexuality.

Since Ted and I had decided not to adopt a child, I'd thought more about my relationship with Annie. It was exhausting always to be thinking about how to manage the push-me-pull-me currents that flowed between us. I had wanted to cancel out the terror and the estrangement of my own childhood, to make a gift of love and support to a child of our own.

Since that was not to be, would I be able to shift my emotional and psychological energy from the child I had hoped for to Annie? If I could do that, might she and I someday have a "good enough" relationship, one that would be different, yes, but as strong as the one I had longed to have with my own child? For Annie's sake, and for Ted's, and for my own, I hoped so.

We dropped Annie off at Paulette's, where several girls waited on the front steps. They ran to greet her, squealing, just like Jeanne's goats jostling each other in anticipation of treats.

At home, Ted made tea. "I can't think of any way to cancel Amélie, can you?"

I put the cups on the table and looked up at him. "Louise needs a lesson on parenting."

He looked horrified. "I decline."

I saw then that he needed me to reassure him that I could manage this change of plans, so that Annie's thoughtlessness wouldn't build into an issue between us. "At some point, we have to sit down with Annie—together—and explain again about limits. This time, she's way out of bounds, but I don't want to lower the boom. This is really Louise's responsibility, after all. Since she didn't know any better, we can't really blame Annie."

"How do you think Louise would react if we called and told her Amélie can't come?"

"She'd be huffy. Then she would be elaborately apologetic to make us feel guilty."

Ted laughed. My shoulders relaxed.

IN MILOU'S next letter, she told me that Louise's mother had apologized to her for Louise's behavior with the Amélie trip. She also identified "Jackie." She didn't mention her recent visit to the doctor. I decided to call Isabelle as soon as I could. First, I showed Milou's letter to Ted.

"So, Jackie is a girl? I don't remember all the cousins, but the nickname doesn't surprise me. Wasn't there a Claude in your group who preferred to be called Claudette?"

"Yes, but that's not really the same, is it? In French, Claude is a girl's name as well as a boy's. Anyway, that's not the point."

"And that would be?"

"The way Annie talks about Jackie? Sounds like a crush to me."

"You know that doesn't matter to me, right?"

"Nor to me. I'm just paying attention. I think we should." Who knew how Jackie felt about Annie. Or if Annie's feelings ran deeper than an infatuation. And then, there was Claire. What new ideas would she come up with to *help* Annie? Would she blame us for giving Annie yet another opportunity to be different?

"Ted. About Milou. I'm going to call Isabelle."

Ted put his arms around me. "Just like the last time, get as much information as you can. I'll check with Dad. This time, if we're not reassured, we can talk to someone else, too."

"Like who?"

"The local heart guy. There, local. The guy Dad knows."

"Before we do that, I want to speak to Milou, too."

August 27, 1983

Amélie spoke Franglais—fluently—which made her just exotic enough to be an end-of-summer distraction. Bored with vacation and their part-time jobs, looking forward to school, Annie's friends took her to their favorite haunts and spent hours talking about life, love, and rock stars. No one had heard of any of the French singers Amélie mentioned. That didn't matter. She knew all the American and British groups and held her own in the sling fests. (Annie described one of these as a standoff between Amélie and everyone else: She had been to a Paul McCartney concert, after he left the Beatles. To her that was enough. He was it, and that was that.)

Loud knocking at the front door woke us at six o'clock Saturday morning, a week after Amélie arrived.

"I'll get this." Ted rolled out of bed and pulled on his shorts.

I only caught part of the conversation. I didn't recognize the man's voice, but there was no mistaking his tone, urgent and emphatic. "On the beach . . . around five . . ."

The front door closed. I shrugged into my bathrobe and went downstairs.

Ted was at the kitchen sink, rinsing off Annie's beach bag and towel, both dripping and streaked with mud and sand. Her waterlogged wallet lay on the counter.

"Where's Annie?"

"That's what I'm about to find out." He dried his hands and went to the phone.

Annie and Amélie had been invited to spend the night at Paulette's house, which was near the harbor and a small beach hangout for college kids. I listened to Ted's end of the phone call while I made us coffee.

"Paulette? Yes, this is Ted. Sorry to call so early, but I'm trying to find Annie and Amélie. They aren't? When did you last see them? By themselves? Great. I'll write it down."

Ted hung up, his mouth set in a hard thin line.

"Annie and Amélie didn't spend the night at Paulette's. They left her house around ten and went off with a girl named Joan Elliot to a party at the beach. I've got the Elliot girl's number."

Neither Ted nor I knew the Elliots. Ted paced as he talked, managing his tone, keeping it calm, even. To me, he sounded detached, as if he were calling to inquire about nothing more important than the time. "They did? There's no need to apologize. Thanks."

Ted hung up and turned to me. "Annie and Amélie spent the night there. They're on their way home. Mrs. Elliot thought we knew where they were." I watched his face relax in relief.

"We don't have much time to talk."

"About?"

"About what to do."

"I know. But let's not make too much of it." He shrugged. "I want to hear what she has to say."

"What *can* she say? We've told her not to go to that beach." I heard the tone in my voice, the tone that made it sound as though I blamed Ted.

He flinched. "Right. Well, I'm going to let her talk. Then, I guess I can just reemphasize that point and make it clear that the reason we don't want her going there is because we worry something like this, or worse, could happen." He looked at me. "Agreed?"

He had a point. All we knew is that this man, a stranger, had found the beach bag and towel in the driftway near the beach. We really didn't know what that meant. Of course Annie wasn't supposed to go to that beach. All by itself, that point wasn't really *the point*. Ted was right. It was the consequences of her behavior that *were* the point.

"All right. But then what?"

Ted had been doodling on the phone pad. His eyes fixed on mine. "Then what? I don't know, Malorie. I guess I hope she'll get it and this won't happen again." Like a door slamming shut, his face closed.

"DAD? DADDY?"

"I'm out here, babe." His face brightened.

We're out here. I wanted to say something, anything, that would remind him that I was part of the equation, the one that gave Annie two parents, as long as she was with us, but there wasn't time. The two girls came into the kitchen, their muddy legs and arms dotted with mosquito bites. They looked like shipwreck survivors. Amélie was missing a shoe. She, at least, still had her beach bag.

"Who found my stuff?" Annie's eyes darted back and forth between the sink and Ted, who leaned against the counter, hands in his pockets, watchful. She didn't look at me. When he didn't answer right away, she frowned. "If you're going to yell at me, I'll leave." Her mouth was set in a pout.

"Why don't you go take a shower and change, Amélie? I'm about to make breakfast." I smiled at Amélie's look of relief. Off the hook.

As soon as Amélie left the room, Annie slumped to the floor, sniffling. Ted sat down cross-legged next to her, his back against the cupboards.

"Tell me what happened."

The details of the story came out more or less as I had imagined them: Annie and Amélie had spent the early part of the evening at Paulette's with several other kids. Paulette's parents were out with friends. At nine thirty, Joan Elliot had stopped by on her way to the beach party. Everyone except Paulette left with her. Annie had dropped her bag and towel "somewhere" on the beach. She didn't realize the tide was coming in. By the time she and Amélie left to go home with Joan, it was so dark, the tide so high, she couldn't find the place again.

"Did you invite Paulette to go with you?" Ted's tone was neutral.

"Yes, but she couldn't because her parents were supposed to come home around ten thirty."

"You mean, if she hadn't expected her parents back soon, she would have gone along?"

"Well, yeah. Maybe. Or she could have spent an hour with us at the party and gotten home before they did."

"Do you think that would have been an okay thing to do?"

Annie sniffed, exasperated. "I know what you want me to say, Dad. So, I'll say it: no, it would not have been okay."

My back to them, I put fruit, cereal, and juice out for the two girls, wondering how this conversation would end.

"So, do you also agree that what you and Amélie did was wrong?"

"I just wanted Amélie to have some fun, to meet some older kids and hang out with them. She doesn't get to do that at home."

"I see. But here's the thing. A man came here early this morning, a stranger. He had your bag and towel. Luckily, our address was in your wallet—which was still in your bag. I was—we were—very, very frightened. We expected the worst." He stopped to let this sink in. "Well?"

Annie whimpered. "I'm sorry." She picked at her flaking nail polish, her voice barely audible. "I'm sorry for making you worry."

Ted hugged her. "I know you are. This isn't going to happen again. Clear?"

"*Promis, juré.*" Annie smiled through her tears at Ted and looked up at me.

She didn't have to say another word. Her glance alone gave me the scene: Milou and Annie talking; Annie listening to Milou's stories about teaching me French, about this expression in particular. I smiled at her.

Ted pulled her around to face him. "Another thing?"

"What?"

"Can you tell me how your talks with Dr. Bennett are going?"

Annie shrugged. Her eyes seemed to turn inward, away from us, her expression flattened into a protective mask.

"I haven't seen him since June, since before I went to Flagy. Plus he took August off."

"I know. Do you want to talk about before that?"

Annie's face crumpled. She began to sob. "Oh, Daddy . . ."

Amélie came into the kitchen, running a comb through her wet hair. I put my arm around her and took her into the living room.

"This is my fault." Her eyes filled. "If I hadn't been there . . . I'm so sorry, Malorie."

It touched me that Amélie stood up for Annie. "Ted and Annie have talked it over. She understands about how worried we were. He understands that she wanted you to enjoy the party. It won't happen again." Amélie nodded, smiling. "Right now they're talking about something else. We'll have breakfast in a little while."

Amélie dried her eyes.

As soon as we heard Annie on her way up to take a shower, we went out to join Ted in the kitchen. At the sink, rinsing out Annie's towel, he didn't turn around right away. When he did, I could see that he was struggling for control. I got out a cereal bowl for Amélie.

"Why don't you go ahead with breakfast, Amélie? Annie will come down as soon as she's showered and changed. I'll rinse out your towel."

Ted came outside with me. Running the hose into a pail, I listened. He spoke in short, clipped phrases, as if cutting them out of the air. "The guy is trying something called 'conversion therapy.' He's told her all kids experiment. It's not unusual for girls to have crushes on other girls. But he insists she's heterosexual, that her lack of interest in boys, like her passion for sports, are just a phase."

"What nonsense. But I thought she liked him." I was chagrined to think we had used the same explanation for Annie's behavior.

But we had also tried to get beyond this oversimplification to understand her better. How could a psychiatrist, especially a specialist in child psychology, offer the same tired non-explanation for something as complicated as sexuality?

"At first, she did. At first, he just let her talk about herself, encouraged her to describe her feelings for the girls she likes, and for sports. Obviously this was just a pretext to gain her trust, so he could guide her into treatment of what he calls her 'condition.'"

"What are you going to do?"

"Talk to Claire. That's the first thing. Having joint custody gives me a little leverage. I have to persuade Claire to stop the therapy right away." He said the word as if it left a bad taste in his mouth.

"What if Claire refuses?"

"I'll remind her that our marriage resulted from an arbitrary decision. Surely she doesn't want to inflict one on her own daughter."

WHEN I phoned, Isabelle wasn't able to tell me much about Milou's condition. What she reported—all that Henri had told her—made us both uneasy. The doctor had decided to keep Milou in the hospital for several days, for observation, and then he had released her, telling Henri only that she would be more comfortable at home.

Isabelle began to cry. "I'll call you if there's any change."

When she called two weeks later, I had already packed.

September 13, 1983

The balcony doors opened to the evening sky, where the waning moon floated in a sea of lavender clouds. Milou lay on her back, her profile silhouetted against the fading light. Henri sat beside her, a book open in his lap, his crutch leaning against the wall. He lifted his face to me, his eyes shining pools of still water. The months of uncertainty and weight loss had left him drawn and pale, his skin worn to the color and texture of parchment.

I crossed the room to close the balcony doors. It had been a fine, warm September day in Paris when my mother and I arrived at the Gare de Lyon. Here, in Cluny, it was clear but chilly. Henri had prepared the room looking out over the garden. When Milou felt well enough, he sat with her on the balcony. He had also arranged for nursing care. Regardless, except at night, he never left her side.

I sat in the chair next to the bed, watching the blue silk duvet rise and fall. At times, the movement seemed to stop. I held my breath until I heard a slight stuttering sigh. I pushed the duvet back, uncovering Milou's hand, her skin dry and fine as silk. Isabelle had warned me. To no avail.

"*Chérie?* Malorie?"

I knelt down beside the bed at her eye level. "*C'est moi.* I'm here. Don't be afraid."

" . . . not to call you."

"I know."

She squeezed my hand. "Glad . . . I've wanted you here. You have no idea how much. Just to see you . . ." Her voice faded; she closed her eyes. When she opened them, they were clear and focused. "Every day, edges seem softer, blurry. Sometimes there's a mist around things and people, like a halo, as if everything were dissolving. Except for the light shining through. I didn't know that everything, everyone, had its own light. Yours, *ma chérie . . . most beautiful. Like an opal. You must have always had it." She swallowed and moved her hands, restlessly smoothing the duvet. Her eyes closed again.

I sat in the chair, drifting, half-asleep. I heard Milou calling, "*Viens voir,* Malorie! Come and see what I've found."

We were together in the garden at Prospect Hill. A light mist swirled through it and around us. Every leaf and blossom, every blade of grass, shimmered, each droplet of water a source of light.

Milou beckoned to me from below the house, at the far end of the stone wall. "*Regarde, chérie, regarde le lys!*" She cradled a day lily in her arms, its bloom resting on her heart.

As I came closer, I recognized the pink day lily, Yasmin, that I had given her years ago. A single drop of water at the lip of each petal reflected the flower's deep golden heart. It seemed to reach for me, each petal unfurling to caress my face.

"*Je t'aime ma petite fille, chérie. Malorie . . .*" Milou whispered.

KNEELING BESIDE the bed, I pressed my face against Milou's. Henri stood next to me, stroking my hair. I had heard her say my name, heard her last words, the way her voice slipped away from us. At the moment she stopped breathing, I lost all sense of time. There was only emptiness, an immeasurable gap.

"*Elle n'est plus.* She's gone, Ted."

"I am so sorry. Please tell Henri?"

"Yes."

"How is he?"

"Very calm, very quiet. But he looks right through me. As though he sees something . . . something beyond."

"And Lucie?"

"Haunted. They never really talked, you know, after that time. Maybe they didn't need to. Lucie was gentle with her. That's all anyone could ask, really."

"What about you?"

I told him what Milou had said about the light. And about my dream. "I woke up feeling a sense of peace. So different from the shock of your grandmother's death. But, really, it's the same. Gone now; both gone," I sobbed. "When I get back . . ."

"Shall we go up to Alden, to Prospect Hill?"

Of course he guessed right away. "Just for a few days."

"We'll stay as long as you want. Take as much time as you need there. We can go as soon as you get back."

"There's one other thing. I finally told my mother about what we found out from Dr. Hoffman. She said I should write to the lawyers. About the money my father left me. You know the terms." I hadn't thought about the trust for a while. That the lawyers might be able to find a way to release the money to me sooner than my fortieth birthday hadn't occurred to me. "I told her I'd talk to you before I do."

"Whatever you say. Don't worry about this. There's plenty of time. . . . *Je t'aime*, Malorie."

"*Moi aussi, je t'aime.*"

I had the row to myself on the flight to Boston. Too enervated to sleep, I opened the novel I'd bought at the airport, but I couldn't concentrate. I closed it and shut my eyes, listening to the engines' drone and the sounds around me. I felt isolated, drifting as if drugged.

I DOZED off and on until we got to the exit off the Mass Pike on our way to Vermont. I felt Ted's eyes, glances that told me he was there, waiting, giving me time. Like leaves stirred up and lifted in a gusty breeze, random, daily memories of Flagy and Cluny came and went: Ted sprawled on the ground, laughing, the day Anisette kicked over the milk bucket; Jeanne on her settee, observing the village at her feet; Milou cutting branches from the honeysuckle while Henri pruned the boxwood; Isabelle and Luc going over the accounts. Accidental and arbitrary, the humdrum, vital connections of life in the moment tugged me back.

"Feel better?"

"Slowly, yes."

As we continued across southern Vermont on Route 9, the late-afternoon glow drained into the deep blue Connecticut River Valley. We were making good time. We would be in Alden by eight o'clock at the latest.

"Can you talk?"

Ted checked the rearview mirror and nodded. "As soon as I get over this bit." The two-lane road narrowed into a series of winding curves toward the top of the mountain. Traffic streamed steadily in both directions.

Once we got over the pass, I told Ted about leaving my mother in Paris.

Although we had separate flights, we had waited together at one of the airport cafés. When I left her at the gate, she promised to phone later in the week.

"We'll be at Prospect Hill. Call us there."

Her eyes had widened, as if she realized only then that Milou was gone. From Prospect Hill, from her life. She reached for my arm, as if making sure she had my full attention. "At least you have Annie."

"What do you think she meant by that?" Ted glanced at me, surprised.

"I think she was trying to comfort me. Not being able to get pregnant . . . you know." When I had told my mother, she hadn't asked if Ted and I planned to try to adopt a child. For the first time—ever—I felt she understood me. That had bearing on her comment about Annie. It didn't occur to me until then that maybe I'd felt it was my responsibility to have a child—for her.

"About adopting, have you given it any more thought?" He reached across the car to take my hand.

"Somehow—maybe it's instinct—I know that adopting a child would change our marriage, and change us, in many unpredictable ways. Probably we'd be fine. But Annie has to come first." I looked over at him. "I think we both want to make sure of that."

Ted pulled the car over onto the shoulder and came around to my side. He opened the door and crouched down, taking both my hands in his. "What you said about Annie, that's what I want too. I can't undo the divorce, but without your support, helping Annie accept it would have been so much harder. Especially now."

"You talked to Claire?"

"Dr. Bennett and Claire."

"Oh, my."

"I got through to Claire. That is, she agreed, reluctantly, to allow Annie to stop seeing Bennett."

"That's a huge relief."

"Yes. Especially after I talked to Bennett."

"What do you mean?"

"That he's most emphatically not the shrink I want my daughter, or anyone else I love, to see."

"Tell me."

Ted had met Bennett at his office, which was cluttered, dirty, and smelled strongly of Bennett himself. Someone else might have said he was too involved helping his patients to care about housekeeping or personal hygiene, but Ted didn't credit that explanation. "He's just a slob. Then there's his attitude: patronizing and arrogant. He kept interrupting me: 'Now, Ted . . . ,' sort of a 'There, there, dear,' approach. By the end of my first five minutes with him, I wanted to squish him, like a bug—which is what he reminded me of most."

I laughed. And I wondered if Dr. Bennett had any sense at all of how off-putting his environment and demeanor were to outsiders. Probably, most especially, to his patients, too.

"Then he explained his 'position.' Just hearing him say the words 'adolescent sexuality' made my skin crawl. I couldn't imagine Annie spending an hour a week with the guy. I found out later that Claire met him only once—not at his office, at a meeting over at Harvard. A friend told her he's an expert. That's all she knew when she made the appointment."

"That's grotesque."

"You mean irresponsible."

"That too."

"Well, it's over now. I made it clear to him that Claire and I had decided Annie wasn't getting anything out of her sessions with him."

"How did he react?"

"Oh, you know, of course it was our 'right' as 'the girl's parents' to make this decision, but he urged us to reconsider. Based on his years of experience, Annie needs help—now, not later. I did a fairly good imitation of my father putting his foot down and left."

"Patrick told me once about his experience with a shrink. Same idea. His parents were so alarmed that he was gay—that he even thought he was—that they sent him to a psychiatrist when he was a junior in high school. He realized there was no way out of it. So he pretended, called it his first starring role. He acted straight—went out with a girl who knew he wasn't but didn't care and went along with the scam because she loved his car—until he graduated from high school and left home." Patrick's story had surprised me because I'd thought stage people were more open-minded, I guess. When I told him this, he scoffed and said that his parents made even Emily Post look like a radical.

"I don't want Annie to have to pretend to be someone she's not. I want her to be herself."

"Me too."

WHEN WE got to Alden at eight o'clock, the house looked bereft, as if it, too, were in mourning. At the beginning of the summer, we had decided not to rent it again, in the hope we would find the time to use it ourselves. This was only our second visit in five months.

Ted pulled the car into the driveway, close to the garage. I got out and stood listening to the crickets, taking in the crispness in the air, the faint smell of the lake rising through the woods.

Ted unpacked the car. He had shopped for essentials in Newport so we wouldn't have to go to the store for a day or two. As soon as I walked in the front door, smelled the familiar fragrance of sandalwood and beeswax, and stepped onto the familiar dip in the entry-hall floorboard, I sank down on my heels. Milou was nearby, present still, welcoming me home.

Then, everything went dark.

"Malorie!"

Ted held me close, peering at me anxiously in the dim light.

"Why am I on the floor? What happened?"

Ted helped me stand up. "I came into the kitchen through the garage. I thought maybe you were upstairs. I called you. When you didn't answer, I came out to the hall and found you. Your eyes were open, but you didn't seem to hear me. I was just about to call 911 when you came out of it. Let's go up, shall we? You can lie down; I'll organize something for dinner. Get the house going for us. What do you say?"

"I want to help."

"Later. For now, it's bed for you. You're tired, sweetheart, exhausted by the last ten days. The best thing for you is sleep."

As I fell asleep, I heard Milou's voice again, calling to me to come out into the garden. The rush of air as the furnace turned on, the warmth of the duvet, and the sound of Ted walking around downstairs soothed me.

I woke to find him in bed beside me, watching me. Sunlight streamed through the bedroom window and door. He moved close, cupping my face in his hand. I thought of the day lily in my dream.

"It's called Yasmin."

He kissed me, "What is?"

"That day lily. The one in the dream I had. Did I tell you the bloom is pink and gold, like the sunrise? There may be one left."

"We'll take a look. Later."

After we made love, Ted told me I had slept nearly forty-eight hours. A selection of my grandfather's watercolors, a larkspur and a trillium, still hung on the walls where Milou had placed them long ago. The door of the walnut armoire in the corner gaped open, as it always had.

Before I could stop myself, I looked for the photo, the one taken of my grandparents the day they left Le Havre. It was on the wall beside the armoire. I knew it so well, I could close my eyes and see them standing next to the boat train. My grandfather smiled down at Milou, who smiled at the photographer. There was nothing posed or formal about it. Something about the way they were standing, as if they were about to step away from the viewer—toward the future—told you they were ready for whatever came next, confident in themselves and in each other.

"Why are you smiling?"

I hugged him close. "Does that answer your question?"

"Somehow, I think there's more to it."

"I'm thinking about Milou and Granddad." I gestured at the picture. "They were happy in this house and with each other. Milou wanted me to have a happy marriage, a fulfilled life. I miss her terribly, but I'll have her here always. More to the point, I have you. And we both know how much she—and Jeanne—wanted that."

New Directions

May 8, 1987

Tucked away on a back road in western Rhode Island near the Connecticut border, Hope Valley Nursery specialized in hostas, the shade-loving plants I had learned about at the end of one of my master gardener courses. Throughout the summer and fall, the nursery's six acres displayed more than a thousand varieties, a kind of living Persian carpet. I took my time there, walking the rows, taking photographs and notes, sketching the foliage shapes, sizes, and patterns.

Our second spring in the Beech Street house, I had planted several types of miniature hostas. With roots fine as baby hair, they felt almost weightless in the palm of my hand. The ruffled lime green leaves, no more than two inches tall, were soft as rose petals. Using only my fingertips, I patted the soil around each one so I wouldn't break or tear them. I could already imagine how they would emphasize and light up the border behind them, once they'd settled in.

Early the next morning, I took my tea out with me and walked around the border. There were gaps, of course, because each new plant needed time to fill out. It was a truism: Every garden needs sun, water, and nourishment. Every gardener needs patience.

When I reached the section of the border where I'd planted the miniature hostas, all that remained of them were their ragged stumps, some still oozing sap. Around and in between, a network of silvery trails identified the vandals—slugs or snails. Both lurked in the leaf mold. Of course, I knew about slugs, but this attack was over the top, beyond anything I'd seen before in this garden or elsewhere. I went back in the house to phone the nursery.

The owner took my call. "Not much you can do. You can pick them off by hand at night. Best to wear gloves. Or you can poison them. Or you can put in plants they don't like so much. Or . . ."

"Or?"

"Why don't you drive over? I'll give you samples of some varieties we're breeding. We call them 'slug-a-lators'!"

The grin in his voice made me laugh.

"That's 'slug-resistant' in English. Doesn't mean slugs won't gnaw holes in the lower leaves. But they won't chew them right down to the ground."

So it wasn't a guarantee. None of the tricks and tips I'd learned came with one. But it was a pretty good deal. Free plants. Fewer slugs. So I had become one of the early adopters of Hope Valley's slug-resistant hostas, ones that had proved to be a good bet at Beech Street.

At the Newport Bridge tollbooth, I glanced at the flat of hostas on the backseat. This year, I had picked out several new midsized varieties. Three years after they'd launched their experiment, Hope Valley's slug-a-lators were no longer a novelty.

I pulled over into the right lane as I made my way up to the crest of the bridge. From this point, Rose Island and Goat Island in the water below looked like stepping-stones between Jamestown and Newport. In the distance, Fort Adams's ramparts turned their dark, blank face toward the harbor and the bay, warding off intruders. Several small sailboats followed a J boat, heeled over on a close reach to the southeast. With its islands, outcroppings and flowing shoreline, the passage reminded me of a Japanese rock garden.

As soon as I opened the front door, Ted called out to me. "In the kitchen!" He was at the table with his calculator, making lists.

"Something tells me . . ."

He jumped up and hugged me. "They want eight!" He waved eight fingers at me, grinning. "And . . ."

"And?"

"A table in the same style." He shook his head in disbelief.

Last year, more or less on a whim, he had designed and submitted a chair to the annual fine furniture show in Providence, with no expectation it would lead anywhere. At that point, just being invited to participate was enough. Small wonder he was in shock.

"This calls for a celebration."

"Done! I made the reservation. La Petite Auberge at seven."

This tradition had begun with our dinner at the Le Vieux Carré in Cluny, after I got my first design contract. Since then we marked our milestones with a dinner out, a simple ritual that defined and connected our individual successes, one to the other, a way of confirming how much we shared. It wasn't as if we had ever decided to do this; it had just happened.

AT DINNER, Ted told me the whole story. "They asked if I could finish the set by Christmas. I said the chairs would be ready, but not the table."

It was only May. Surely he could do it. If he ordered the materials right away, he could get started at the beginning of June.

"I had to give myself some breathing space, just in case. But I will give it my best, try to get everything done by then. I know they really want the table—some kind of big family Christmas they're planning."

"What did they say?"

"They were cool about it. Of course, they added that if I finished sooner, that would be fine. I'm going to write up the proposal and a contract. And figure out what to order and where to get what I need."

"Can you fit this in with everything else you're doing?"

"Provided I get some help with the sanding and waxing."

"So they don't want varnish?"

"When I explained what waxing involves and how beautiful the finish will be, and hold up, they declined varnish. That's what I used on the chair they fell in love with, anyway."

Listening to Ted talk about what he had to do, thinking out loud, my attention drifted. Since March, I'd been feeling restless, on edge, out of focus. Sandor and I had a busy winter and spring, without a break. Maybe I needed a vacation. If I decided to take time off, Ted wouldn't be joining me. I thought about the flat of hostas. My excitement had faded, replaced by resignation.

"Sweetheart? Malorie?"

"Sorry. What were you saying?"

"You seem distracted. Disappointed, maybe? Preoccupied, anyway. As if you had seen something you want and can't have." His eyes shifted away. "Want to tell me what you found today?"

Was he right? Was I disappointed? I didn't have anything in particular to be disappointed about. I had plenty of work; I enjoyed working with Sandor. Still, it was as though a dense fog were moving in around me and I couldn't see through or beyond it. "Oh, you know. More hostas." I tried to laugh.

"That's good, right?"

"Yes. Good." I put my fork down. "It's just that I seem to spend more time stargazing than working. It's too much of an effort to concentrate. I can do my work, but I can't seem to generate any enthusiasm about anything I've got going on." I looked at him. "I hate to put it like this, but maybe I'm envious that you've found a new direction. Please don't misunderstand. I am really happy for you."

"But?"

"I guess I'm in a rut and I'd like to find a way out, that's all."

"Burnout?" He spoke quietly, consolingly.

"Could be." Once, I might have felt defensive. As though it were my own fault I no longer felt the same excitement about what I was doing. Now, I let the idea sink in. Felt the tension in my shoulders release. "Why do you think that?"

"It's been awhile since you've talked to me about your projects. I've been wondering why."

Usually I brought home stories to share with him: new plants I'd discovered, solutions to installation problems Sandor and I had tackled, issues that had come up with clients, usually based on their inflated expectations of how fast plants could and did grow in this climate.

"It could be burnout, and I haven't wanted to admit it. The work has felt stale, anyway. Something like that. Although each garden is different, they all begin to look too much alike—they're square or rectangular; we use the same plants. They fit the same general idea of things. A bit like staying within the lines. It's scary to think I might be losing interest."

"Maybe you should ask Sandor. Maybe he can point you in a new direction."

How would Sandor react? I hoped he wouldn't think I wanted out. To say I just needed a change of pace, rather than a complete break, made a lot of sense.

"I'll think about that." I couldn't help laughing.

"What?"

"What if he suggests I take over the computer? Then what?"

THE OFFICE Sandor and I shared was on Long Wharf, on the harbor downtown, a tourist attraction every summer. At first I thought it might be too noisy, especially during Newport's high season, with the windows open to the street. Unexpectedly, the changing light, the boats moving around each other, to and from their moorings, refreshed me and satisfied my need to break away from my lists and grids. Another advantage: I could walk five blocks to have lunch at home and stop by Ted's shop on my way back to work. The office's only drawback was its size: if the business grew enough for Sandor to hire another person, we would have to find a larger space.

When I arrived in 1976, Sandor had been thinking about giving the office up entirely to work from home. We still laughed about his change of heart. It turned out the office wasn't the problem. He just needed someone to talk to. "You came just in time," he told me.

At his desk the next morning, Sandor had the manual for a new software program lying open in front of him.

"Software?" What little I knew about computers, I'd learned from Matt. The ones he talked about seemed as unfathomable as the origins of the universe. Matt was convinced a computer would soon be able to help answer that question and others like it. A computer? Not a human being? He had laughed and shrugged his shoulders.

"Hardware is the machine. Software is the program you need to use it."

I knew better than to joke about this. Still, I had yet to be convinced we needed the computer or the software. Sandor himself seemed to have doubts. Try as he might, he hadn't been able to explain to me exactly how it would help us. All I knew at the moment was that the software included drawing tools that might simplify our preliminary design work—the drudgery of multiple hand-drawn tissues.

There was another way the computer would help. Saving, storing, and retrieving each drawing had become a time-consuming task now that we often had multiple projects in various stages of development. When Sandor explained to me how the drawing and storage tools worked, he kept patting the machine, as if convincing himself that what he was saying was, in fact, possible.

"So?"

"Almost there." He grinned. "I know. That's what I said yesterday. Today, it might actually be true. One thing I'm learning is that reading the manual doesn't help much. Trial and error seems to work better."

"Is our appointment with Ellen Bates still on?"

"Yup." Sandor checked his watch. "I told her we'd meet her at nine. Let's leave in ten minutes."

I HAD continued my practice of analyzing existing gardens, identifying and drawing ways to bring out hidden features. Sometimes I experimented with the plantings, reorganizing them to open up new sight lines. Sometimes I took a more radical approach.

I had shown one of these to Ted. The "before" view had an extensive terraced perennial garden sloping away from the house to a driveway. In my drawing, I removed the terraces and laid out a mix of native plants and grasses. In my notes, I described the contouring and drainage required to offer year-round visual interest and easy upkeep. Unlike a labor-intensive perennial garden, the new design required only seasonal mowing to thrive, and offered a beneficial environment for birds, butterflies, and other wildlife.

"In other words, if you take out the perennials, which have a limited blooming season, and put in native plants, like the wild roses and bittersweet, you'll have color, even in the winter." Ted looked at my drawing, comparing it to the perennial garden.

"The ferns and grasses will have an effect, too, although they're there for texture as much as for color. The idea is to bring out the site's contours, so that the plants, the light, even the snowfall, will give you something to look at." I jotted a note in the margin: *stones?*

"It's almost like sculpture. You're using the plants the way I sometimes use binding—those strips of wood in between the pieces of the pattern—in an inlay. You're shaping the site so that the shadows become an important feature of the whole look."

"I just have to figure out a way to talk to Sandor about why this makes sense. And then find a client who might let us try it out." I meant let *me* try it out. Sandor, with a degree in landscape architecture, handled design and installation; with my master gardener's certification, I researched and selected the plants. Would he agree to give me primary design responsibility on a large project?

"What are you going to call it?"

Until Ted asked, I hadn't thought about naming it. Most gardens had some sort of descriptive name: "cottage garden," "herbaceous border," "cutting garden." This meadow was similar to a park, but not a park. "Maybe 'planned meadow'? That at least says what it is." It struck me then how radical the idea was. Planned or not, it enlarged the idea of what a garden was, allowing it to include aspects of landscape design.

On the way to our appointment, Sandor told me that Ellen wanted to "rejuvenate" the house, not restore it.

"What does that mean?"

"She'll brighten the rooms—they're dark and dreary, lots of mahogany—and she'll rewire, put in new plumbing and radiant heat. That kind of thing." Sandor wasn't a purist and wouldn't work for anyone who was—because, he said, he had better things to do than to fight the Battle of the Bulge every day.

"Sounds practical."

"Yes, but she's also a collector, and her tastes run to modern art—large-scale abstract paintings and sculpture is what I've heard—so I expect she'll be hanging big pieces on white walls and won't be putting in a lot of period furniture and bibelots." He laughed. "I'm not sure what the Preservation Society will think about all of this."

"Well, she can't change the exterior, but since it's a private home, they really can't dictate what she does to the interior, can they?" I knew how difficult it could be for a new owner of a home in a historic district to deal with the preservationists. The Preservation Society managed the Gilded Age homes of the Astors and the Vanderbilts as museums. There were stringent regulations about the types of changes private homeowners could make in proximity to these properties. "What about the garden?"

"The Preservation Society will be pleased to hear there will be no changes in front—big trees, nothing complicated under them, on account of the shade, if nothing else. Sounds simple, but the trees need a lot of work. All of them are nearly seventy-five years old and haven't had any regular maintenance for ages. The one problem—at least as far as permission to make changes is concerned—is that some of them may not be salvageable."

"And the back? Big lawn and a perennial border along the seawall, right?"

"Right. Here's the thing. She'd like us to propose some options. She's open to restoring the lawn and the perennial border, of course. But she'd like to know what else we could do. She has dogs—standard poodles, I believe—and she wants them to have the run of the place and not have to worry about the garden."

"The lawn area is fenced?"

"And hedged. She has a lot of privacy, considering that the Cliff Walk runs along the foot of the property. The hedge down there is an eight-foot monster!"

"Wild roses . . ."

"Yup, rosa rugosa." Sandor's eyes lit up. "The rabbits get through it, no problem. Anything larger goes somewhere else."

ELLEN BATES had recently bought her house. The site represented an important opportunity for us—and a huge commitment, encompassing nearly two acres on Bellevue Avenue, a neighborhood of historic properties, many of them museums. The house, a private home, was designed in the gabled, shingled style of oceanfront homes in other New England resort towns, unlike the grand "cottages" built by the Astors and the Vanderbilts just down the street.

She waited for us at the end of the driveway. Wearing jeans, sandals, and a French sailor's jersey, she had a clipboard under her arm and two dog leashes draped around her neck. She was about my age, but with her dark hair pulled off her face into a ponytail, she looked younger. She waved us into a parking place beside her station wagon, a beat-up Ford. As soon as we got out of the car, two white standard poodles ran down the front steps toward us.

"Jasmine, Lulu, sit!"

Instantly, the dogs stopped, sat, and looked at her, their mouths open, tongues out, ears pricked. They looked like they were smiling. When they turned their attention back to us, their tails thumped the ground and they pranced in place.

"I've never seen a dog do that!" It seemed as if they were both trying to speak.

"They've figured it out. As long as their rear ends are on the ground, they can do whatever they please to show how happy they are to see you. Jasmine, Lulu, down!"

The dogs lay at Ellen's feet, looking back and forth at her and the two of us, scrutinizing every facial expression and gesture.

"They understand so much, these two. They're sisters and they've never been apart. Sometimes I get the feeling they share a brain." Ellen grinned and reached out to shake Sandor's hand, then mine.

Accompanied by Jasmine and Lulu, as if we were official members of their pack, we walked around the front of the property, looking at the trees. Ellen paid close attention, taking notes as Sandor showed her which trees could be pruned and salvaged.

"Have you thought about what else you'd like to do with this space?"

Ellen took out some photographs of several sculptures. "These pieces—they're in lockup down in New York—they need a home. This is it." She gestured in the general direction of the trees. "It's just a question of placing them." There were five sculptures in all, all abstract forms. "It's hard to tell from these pictures, but they're a mix of materials. Three are stone; two are bronze."

"Once we know more about the trees, we can do some drawings that will help. Possibly we can put these sculptures in place of the trees we remove."

Ellen was enthusiastic. "Like memorials or something. I like that idea very much."

By the time we finished in front and went around the house to look at the back garden, the morning fog had lifted enough that we could see the tower of the private school at the top of the hill on the opposite shore.

"At ease, you two."

The two dogs had flown down the hill after a rabbit that darted off in the direction of the hedge, where it disappeared. Thin and patchy, the lawn sloped from the house's back terrace toward the perennial border along the lower fence and the hedge. Even from this distance, I could see that brambles and wild vines had taken over the border.

I pulled out my sketch pad and drew the lawn's shape and general features, marking the position of several boulders crouched within it like sleeping mammoths. I added the border, the fence, and the sea beyond, with a few quick strokes.

"Wouldn't you like to take some pictures?" Ellen seemed taken aback.

"I'll be doing that, too, yes. And measuring, of course. Drawing the space gives me a good way to feel its shape and contours. The photos will show me how it looks, so I can decide about plants."

Her face relaxed. "I guess Sandor told you I want Jas and Lu to have the run of this area. Of course I'd like to enjoy looking at it, too, but a formal garden isn't part of that picture. My grandmother had a place on the coast of Maine, lots of rocky outcroppings and meadows with native plants. Twenty acres." She looked at me, as if embarrassed by what she was suggesting. "This isn't that, at least in terms of size. But maybe we can have something like it, just on a smaller scale?"

I held my breath and looked away, feeling the smile on my face, hearing Milou's voice in my ear. "There is no such thing as coincidence, *ma chérie*." It was as if Ellen had already seen my idea for the planned meadow, as if she had read my mind.

"Are you sure? Not even a cutting garden? You've got plenty of room." Sandor's skepticism made Ellen smile.

"I know. It's out of keeping with the other properties around here, especially the ones the Preservation Society owns. But I am certain it's what I want." She turned away, looking for the dogs. They were at the bottom of the hill, digging vigorously. She laughed. "As you can see, they know this is their place. I'm not going to discourage that idea, or try to win the battle over where or when they're allowed to dig. As far as I'm concerned, they can dig wherever they like."

BY THE time I got home after the appointment with Ellen, Ted had made us sandwiches, set the table, and put out two steno pads. Often, when I talked to him about a new project, he listened without interrupting as I laid it out, jotting his thoughts as I went along. He knew how important it was at the beginning just to talk, to let the ideas flow.

This time, I told him, so many pieces fit together. Ellen's response to Sandor's proposal to place the sculptures among the trees and her description of her grandmother's Maine property were just the beginning. "It was as though she'd read my mind. She opened the door, Ted."

"What?"

"I don't want to get too far ahead of myself."

"It is definitely a plus that she had an open mind about what would work best for her. The drawing you showed me? Your planned-meadow trial balloon? Is it as close to what she wants as I think it is?"

"Close, yes. I'll have to make some adjustments, but, in general, it's the right idea. It'll be an amazing environment for her dogs. They'll love it."

Ted laughed.

"What?"

"A garden designed for two standard poodles? Well, it's actually not so strange, really. They're smart dogs."

"We can't start on the back part until they finish the work on the house—which is fine, since we're busy with summer work. But the first stage—protecting the trees from further damage, taking out the ones that are dying—that we can take care of right away."

I was relieved we would have the rest of the summer, and the fall and winter months, to plan, schedule, and organize what we needed and when. Even so, once we began, it could take a year or more to finish. To accomplish my goal, I'd need to do a lot of research to find the plants I expected to use. I couldn't go around digging up wild ones. In the first place, that was probably illegal; in the second, I couldn't afford to spend all my time driving around to find the ones that would work best from a design point of view.

"If we take this on, that will be it for new projects for a while."

Ted looked at me, expectant. "You keep saying 'we.'"

"I showed Sandor the trial-balloon drawing."

"And?"

"At first, he didn't say much. Then he asked to see the sketches I'd done of Ellen's place. The ones I did while we were there. I let him look, take his time. Rough as they were, I knew he'd see the connection. But I decided to let him figure out what to do about it."

After a few minutes of moving the sketches around on the drawing table, Sandor had turned to me. "I like this. Ellen obviously wants something similar. Why don't you get together with her and talk it over? If she thinks it will do, the design work is yours."

"Yahoo!" Ted punched the air.

"I know. This is a real break."

"Dad? Malorie? Anybody home?"

WHEN THE spring term ended, Annie had told us only that she hadn't planned anything before the start of her summer job. Ted had hoped she'd come to Newport for a few days at least. But he hadn't pressed her about it. He knew how much she needed to make her own decisions.

During her spring break, she announced that she had found a way to major in French, history, biology, and art history, thanks to a new multi-disciplinary program at the University of Vermont, where she was a junior. Even Claire hadn't objected. At long last, she had learned to let Annie be Annie.

As for Ted, from the beginning he had refused to subject her to the same pressure to achieve and produce that he'd felt at Brown. "I don't care what she majors in. She's smart enough to do anything she wants. Let's give her some time to figure out what."

Annie came out to find us and paused in the kitchen doorway. Bowing low and flourishing an imaginary hat, she gestured behind her. "*Mesdames et messieurs, je vous présente*—Josie!"

Nearly as tall as Annie, Josie shook hands with me first. With her blond hair in a single braid, wearing white jeans and a jersey, she could have been a crew member on any one of the big boats moored at the yachting center. When she handed Ted a bottle of wine, I noticed that she, like Annie, wore a single silver bangle on her left wrist. Ted caught my eye and gave me a slight nod.

While Ted and I made dinner, Annie and Josie took turns telling us about the apartment they had rented in Manchester. They both had summer jobs at the bookshop there; Josie's aunt owned it. "We moved our stuff down from Burlington last week. Work starts July first. Lucky for me, my birthday is on Saturday."

"And the bad news is . . . we have to work on Saturday."

"You're kidding!" Annie looked horrified, then laughed at herself.

"Nope!" Josie patted her shoulder. "We'll have a short first day, though. I made sure of that. So we can plan a hike. I'll show you the best place to see the fireworks on the Fourth. Deal?"

"Deal!" They clinked bangles.

No further explanation of the bangles was required.

After dinner, I set up the slide projector in the living room and took down a painting so we could use the wall as our screen. Annie and Josie sat together on the floor. Taken six years ago, when Ted and I had gone back for a visit, the slides showed views of many of the gardens I had worked on in and around Flagy and Cluny. I paused at one that bordered a stone terrace, looking out over pastures dotted with Charolais cattle.

"I really like how this one has come along. Do you recognize it, Annie?"

"It's the one across the road from that field, the field I ran around in, pretending I was a horse. Every time I tossed my head, I could feel the wind in my hair." Annie gave a soft laugh. "Did you know you can see all the way across the valley from the top of that hill?"

I caught Ted's eye as Annie turned to Josie.

"The gate slammed on my hand one day when I was there with Malorie. I was afraid to look at it, it hurt so much!" She held out her right hand.

Josie held it while she examined it front and back. "Not even a tiny scar."

"That's because Malorie put ice on it right away. Dad told me I'd probably lose the fingernails." She made a face. "But I didn't." She smiled at me. "You were awesome. The workmen were so nice. They tried to help me, but I was afraid if I said a word I'd start to cry. I was so relieved when you came. *Then* I bawled like a baby."

"I just remember how brave you were. All by yourself, in shock, until I got there."

Josie, who hadn't let go of Annie's hand, hugged her.

Annie looked up at us. "I reread *The Black Stallion* a month ago. Amazing. So much of that summer came back to me. The way Isabelle's kitchen smelled, the kittens playing with each other, climbing all over everything, the vacherin for Malorie's birthday. Happy days. I showed Josie the sketchbook you gave me." She smiled at me and slung her left arm around Josie's shoulders.

August 5, 1987

The day the registered letter arrived, Ted signed for it and called me at the office. "It's from your father's law firm. Do you want me to bring it over, or open it and read it to you? It's more than a letter."

"More than a letter?"

"It's fat, you know, as if there are forms to fill out or something."

"The trust. That's the only thing it could be."

No one had called me, but I had been expecting something like this. The trust was the only reason the firm would send me registered mail. Four years ago, I had brushed off my mother's suggestion that I contact the lawyers. Why bother to tell them I couldn't have children, since the funds would revert to me as soon as I turned forty? Besides, it wasn't something I felt comfortable discussing with them over the phone. Or at all.

I knew what my father would say. I could hear his voice, still, haranguing me about not being practical. I tried to block him out, imagined hanging up on him. It didn't work. Not today. Today I felt the adrenaline spike as soon as I put the phone down. My heart pounded. My hands were shaking.

"Bad news?" Sandor's worry made me more anxious.

"A family thing," was all I could manage.

"Best to go take care of whatever it is, I think." He urged me out the door and waved goodbye to me from his window.

On my way home, I tried to prepare. Ted and I lived on our income, which paid the bills, the mortgage, and our taxes. Jeanne's house in Flagy we had rented to Béatrice and Gilles. Prospect Hill, too, was rented. I knew approximately how much money was in the trust, but I never thought about it, except when I got the annual statement from the firm. Every year I did the same thing: I opened it, glanced at it, and threw it away.

Ted came to the door with a cup of tea and a hug. "Kitchen or living room?"

"Kitchen."

The letter, from one of the partners, reiterated the terms of the trust and encouraged me to call if I had questions about the signature form, which had to be notarized. There was another form, an affidavit to certify that Ted and I had no natural children. Ted sat across from me, motionless and silent. What was he thinking?

"It's four hundred thousand dollars invested in stocks and bonds. No restrictions, apparently. I can cash out all or part of it, or have it annuitized. Or leave it alone." I smiled. "Of course, the lawyer suggests I talk to an accountant about taxes before I make a decision." I leaned toward him, handing him the papers. "I hope you understand how I feel about this. It's a joint decision, regardless."

He shook his head. "It's your money, Malorie—yours to do with what you want."

"What if we want the same thing?"

He started to contradict me.

I shook my head. "What about this? Let's each make a list. Then we'll see."

After dinner, we sat in the living room and talked about what we might do. The more we discussed our options, the more we realized how complex our situation was.

"Land rich, cash poor—at least until now." Beech Street, Prospect Hill, and Jeanne's house in Flagy all required regular maintenance and repair. Both of us self-employed, both of us earning just enough to get by—the one thing we agreed about was that the money from the trust would be an enormous help. "We're such good penny pinchers. Maybe we can learn to be spendthrifts?"

Ted grinned. "I'm not sure Jeanne would approve."

"The money can't cancel out how I feel about my father— and why I feel that way—but what we do with it might." We postponed our discussion of our lists until we'd had some more time to digest the news.

The dream woke me early and gave me the idea. I knew what I wanted to do with the money, how to turn it into a gift we could share.

Ted stretched and yawned. He rolled over and looked at me. "You're awake early. Restless night?"

"I dreamed about the house and the secret room. That's the answer to our question about what to do with the trust fund."

"Tell me more." He put his arm around me, his head against mine.

"We'll give ourselves time, three years, let's say, to see how things develop: your furniture, my new design work. Suppose we make a go of it. We'll both need more space, studio space—and a workshop for you."

"We could always rent."

"We could. But then we'd have to fit ourselves and all our stuff into someone else's place."

"We'd have to make do, you mean."

"What if we could design and build exactly what we want?"

"That's a lovely idea. But we can't build anything here on Beech Street—too small and too many restrictions, I'm sure."

"And we can't pick everything up and go back to France, to Jeanne's house, as much as we might like to."

"I can tell you've solved this. Why don't you tell me how?"

"Prospect Hill!"

Prospect Hill's house, garage, and garden occupied less than a third of an acre of land, leaving plenty of room to build a studio space for us both. I sat up in bed and took a piece of paper and a pencil from the nightstand. I sketched the house and garage at the top of the hill and added a small building at the bottom of the hill near the road.

"What's that?" Ted pointed to the vertical line that intersected the bottom of the new building.

"You need a shop—with double doors for deliveries—so we'd use the space downstairs for that."

"There's something else, isn't there."

"We will have amazing views of the woods and the lake from the second story!" I was imagining the lake through the trees, the Congregational church steeple to the left, and the hillside just across the valley. *A fine prospect*, I thought. "So, what do you think? A good start, yes?"

"A good start, yes."

"Somehow, you don't sound convinced."

"I'd like to keep this between us. Until we're sure that our new ventures are well and truly on their way. You know my father."

At eighty-two, as sharp and acerbic as ever, Bruno likely would find something to fault in the idea. Pie in the sky, castles in Spain. I could imagine his misgivings and his tone.

"I get that. We'll let my mother and your parents know about the trust decision. And if they ask what we're going to do with the money, we'll just say we're saving it for retirement."

Ted relaxed enough to laugh. "I can imagine their reaction!"

"My mother will disapprove because she thinks we should travel more, 'enjoy life.'"

"My father at least will take it as a sign that I've finally developed some common sense."

"Well then, we'd better make a convincing case for our white lie."

"There's one other person we might want to talk to about this."

"Who's that?"

"Ethan."

"You don't want to do the design?"

"I'd love to. But I don't know enough. I could probably do the drafting work for someone else—as I did for you for that gazebo. We need Ethan. He's an architect, so he knows all the local regulations and codes. He also has the design experience and the eye."

"And he's local."

Whistling in the Dark

September 9, 1991

The lawn had given up, dormant after weeks of dry heat. Even the heat-loving coneflowers and daisies drooped and faded, like corseted Victorian ladies cinched too tight to breathe. It had rained occasionally throughout August, flooding the streets and gutters with runoff and leaf litter. But these coastal storms blew through too quickly to do more than leave dust puddles wherever they touched down.

I had decided to look into in-ground irrigation systems, thinking we might try something like that before I recommended it to clients. The catalogs covered the table. Who knew there were so many possible solutions, most of them intended for gardens many times larger than mine.

I set my glass of iced tea on the table to answer the phone, grateful for the interruption.

"Malorie . . ." I heard Ted's voice, weak and raspy, the thud of a door closing in the background, someone speaking over a loudspeaker.

"Where are you?"

"The ER. I'll explain later."

I drove to the hospital in a daze. The light hurt my eyes; everything seemed sharp-edged; my skin prickled.

Ted lay on a gurney, his left hand wrapped in gauze, his eyes closed. There was blood everywhere—on his collar and shirt sleeves, spattered on his shoes, on his jeans and arms. *Why haven't they cleaned him up?* When I touched his shoulder, he opened his eyes. I leaned over to kiss him.

"What happened to you?"

"I don't really know. The gouge slipped. There was so much blood. It's okay, Malorie. I'll be okay."

"The gouge slipped?" He was careful using the hand tools—the skew and the gouges, especially—and he drilled the apprentices in the importance of slow work. At first, he didn't let them cut for more than short periods so they would learn to pace themselves. He had a sixth sense, he'd told me. He always recognized when someone's attention began to drift—the danger zone. That's when he would take over, send the person on an errand, or give him something else to do for a while. So how did this accident happen?

He was talking again, explaining. "It's my index and third finger on my right hand. The surgeon on duty called the plastic surgeon. She can save it, he thinks."

Before I could ask him what he meant, a doctor entered the cubicle. "Mr. Girard?" Anonymous in scrubs, the plastic surgeon's voice sounded young. Or did I just think this because she was a woman? "We're ready for you."

A nurse and an attendant stood behind her.

"Mrs. Girard?"

"Would someone explain to me what happened, what Ted meant about saving his finger?"

She put her hand on my arm. "I'm not sure how long it will take to reattach the fingertip. It could be several hours. Would you like to wait?"

My knees buckled. The nurse reached out to support me. Reattach the fingertip? Had Ted told me that? How could I have missed it?

"Take a deep breath. That's good. Better?"

I straightened up and went to Ted. He smelled of antiseptic and, faintly, lavender soap.

"Don't worry." He tried to smile.

WHEN THE incisions healed, Ted started physical therapy. The numbness in his fingers subsided gradually. He joked about the cure being worse than the disease. After several weeks, he mentioned the pain.

"From the surgery?"

"Different. I noticed it before the accident. I've had it off and on for a few months." He looked away, defensive. "I didn't tell you about it because it went away. It's back. I thought it might be from the PT, but I've got it in both hands." He still wouldn't meet my eyes. "And other places."

"What about aspirin?"

Ted gingerly pressed the joints at the base of his fingers, one by one. "It helps a little."

"Milou always kept Epsom salts around, for soaking. It was the only thing that helped my grandfather's arthritis. I'll get some today."

"I'm forty-six, not seventy-six!"

His irritation startled me. What wasn't he telling me? "It's just a suggestion, Ted."

His face went slack; his eyes slid away. Somehow, growing up as the son of a surgeon, Ted had learned not to talk about pain, and to bottle up his problems. This wasn't the first time he had tried to spare me. He also downplayed annoyances like project delays and client disagreements. This was different. Was he afraid? Why?

I tried another tack. "At least you won't have to drink it."

He chuckled. "It's just—I've been so crazy busy. You know that. Over the last few months, I've been cutting a lot. Too much. No wonder my hands hurt."

Was this whistling in the dark an effort to reassure himself, or me, or both of us? "Is there anything else bothering you?"

"Not really. I'm a little stiff in the morning."

I knew he hadn't been sleeping well, getting up sometimes as early as three thirty or four to look over drawings and schedules.

With several projects at various stages of completion, he had to keep track of the details and the apprentices. He was working on a catalog for the 1992 furniture show in Providence. To do what he wanted to do involved more than the hours he spent perfecting his designs on paper. Was he driving himself too hard? Maybe he had reached his limit. Maybe the accident was a warning.

What was clear was that he was trying to convince me that he had to keep going. "I don't have a choice, especially after the accident. Two months off! I can't afford to slow down. But I'm almost there, you know? Soon I should be able to hand off more of the cutting and finishing to my guys."

Another week went by. Each day Ted looked more haggard, more preoccupied. I called our doctor and made an appointment. Anticipating an argument, I worked out a plan. It was simple, really. I would ask Ted to do it as a favor—to me. When he agreed without discussion, I knew his problem, whatever it was, was worse than he had let on.

LISTENING TO his answers to the doctor's questions, I learned that the pains had started at the end of April. At first, the discomfort was intermittent. Now, it was constant, and getting worse. He had been taking the maximum dose of aspirin daily since before the accident.

He took my hand, his eyes pleading with me to understand. "I didn't want to scare you. Since the symptoms went away once, I just assumed they'd go away again. Last week, when I weighed myself, I'd dropped ten pounds. I thought it had something to do with these killer workdays. I didn't want you to tell me to take a break or slow down."

As Ted explained and described the last few months, the doctor took notes, occasionally asking follow-up questions. "To rule out the most obvious culprits first, we'll do some blood tests. The panel includes a test for rheumatoid arthritis." He pulled a pamphlet from the shelf behind his desk and handed it to Ted.

"Men are less likely to develop this disease than women, but it doesn't hurt to find out if that's what's bothering you. It could be something else. It could even be overwork. Still, this is an obvious place to begin. In the meantime, you can take an anti-inflammatory with ibuprofen, instead of aspirin, to control the symptoms. Once we know what's going on, we'll decide about treatment."

By the time the test results came back, clear of any signs of rheumatoid arthritis, Ted felt almost well. Reassured, he stopped taking the medication. As time went on, with no recurrence, we grew confident that muscle strain had caused his right hand to give out the day the gouge slipped, and that the mysterious pain he felt was only that—mysterious. And, now, gone.

I took him out to dinner to celebrate.

TOWARD THE end of November, awake in the middle of the night, I felt him move, restless beside me. "Can you tell me what's going on?"

"I'm worried. It's not the pain in my hands—not just the pain in my hands, I should say. I'm so tired that I can barely move when I'm up and I can't seem to sleep at night. The pain has moved into my elbows and shoulders."

"And?"

"And my knees."

I moved closer to him, hugged him to me. "We'll go back to the doctor. Tell him about the new symptoms. We need to test for anything else—everything else—to find out what's wrong."

"My father always says, 'Medicine is an art, not a science. It's not how much you know—tests results are just data—it's how you interpret what you observe.'"

I steeled myself for his reaction to what I had to say next. "I think we may need a second opinion. I think you should call Bruno."

He pulled away from me to lie on his back, his arms crossed over his chest. "I'd rather not."

"I understand. But, you know, he's so smart about this kind of thing. Besides, you know how much he hates being retired. He stays in touch with people. He may know someone, some kind of specialist, or suggest a direction we haven't considered."

"I'll call him. After we do a second round with our guy."

After more tests—also clear, no sign of any identifiable infections—I could see that Ted was frightened, too. He had lost more weight. He had episodes of fever and his sleeplessness had gotten worse. The persistent fatigue prevented him from cutting altogether, for fear of having another accident. Several projects had fallen seriously behind.

Ted called Bruno, who was infuriated that Ted hadn't phoned earlier and alarmed we had so few answers to his questions. This time, at least, his irritation didn't faze either of us. Ted listened without interrupting, waving his free hand around, as if to speed him up. Listening in on the other phone, I smiled and blew him a kiss across the room.

"How long did you say this has been going on? Six months? At least? And the guy you've talked to can't figure out what's wrong? I want you to come to New York. I'll get you in to see a specialist—a friend of mine—who'll sort you out in a hurry."

"I can't do that, Dad. I have a lot of catching up here; I have to work."

Bruno made an impatient noise. "You need to see this guy. He specializes in weird diseases; he's the best in the world."

"We've got good people here, too, you know." Ted spoke in a low, flat tone.

"In Rhode Island? You must be joking. At least let me call my colleague. You should talk to a clinician, someone who's on top of current research with a direct line to a clinical database."

"I understand that. But I want to find someone here."

I waved at Ted, urging him to calm down.

"Dad, please. Let's not argue about this."

Why make matters worse by arguing about what to do next? At last Bruno promised to talk to his colleague, to try to find someone nearer to us.

After the call, Ted looked grim. "He makes Rhode Island sound like a third-world country. And, of course, as usual, he knows best."

Bruno's disappointment over Ted's choice of profession seemed an insurmountable emotional barrier between them. Bruno Girard could not understand how Ted had decided to spend his life doing something that, in his view, required nothing more than an aptitude and manual dexterity. The residue of his anger and sorrow over Théo's flight and disappearance fed his impatience with Ted, making it almost impossible for Ted to have a conversation with him about anything important to him. Not even Bruno's age had moderated his views.

"We have to be grateful he is still in contact with so many people. Maybe the person he wants you to see down there will have a contact up here." I didn't spend any time wondering why Bruno hadn't considered Boston's abundant supply of medical professionals. There was no point.

"We'll see." Ted held his arms out to me. "Can you help me up?"

I knelt down, looking up into his face. Dark shadows circled his eyes; his skin was dried out, rough-looking. "Why don't you stay here? I'll go make us a tisane, shall I?"

He leaned his head back and closed his eyes. "If this is what it feels like to be old, I'm going to take another bus." He kissed my forehead.

Two days later, Bruno called us before breakfast. "Alan Jacobson at Tufts. He's the one you want to see. And before you ask, I did explain to my friend that you live in Newport. He assured me there is no one closer who can help you. Jacobson's expecting you to call. Let me know right away how it goes."

December 3, 1991

In the waiting room at the Tufts Department of Epidemiology, a few people, like Ted, filled out forms; others read magazines or books. At least half of the group appeared to be about our age. Here we were, most of us waiting to see a specialist who would diagnose our symptoms, determine the cause, and prescribe a treatment. It was a peculiar rite of passage. We were aging. We were ill. This was life. Seeking a specialist's expert opinion was no more mysterious than going to the orthodontist for braces.

Ted caught my smile and nodded.

A dozen large-format color photographs hung on the walls around us. They were similar enough to have been taken by the same photographer; however, they weren't labeled. Each featured apparently random patterns projected against different backgrounds, washes of muted color. The views reminded me of Manet's portraits, where the subject stands alone in an indefinite, undefined space.

The photograph closest to us featured orange filaments floating over yellow islands in a sage green sea. Some of the filaments looked like tiny eels, coiling and uncoiling, some like deformed letters or mathematical symbols.

"Ted Girard? Bruno Girard's son? You can call me Al. Please."

Of course he knew we'd catch the reference to Paul Simon's hit; we were all about the same age. It was an obvious—and effective—icebreaker offered by someone who wanted us to understand that he didn't stand on ceremony. I could imagine Bruno's reaction. Ted smiled. I was pretty sure we'd had the same idea.

Short and round, like a cherub in tortoise-shell glasses, Al Jacobson had a fringe of wispy gray-blond hair and none of the somber authority I'd expected. I was glad. I didn't want a father figure looming over us with age and honors. Ted needed a diagnostician. I needed that, too. We also needed someone who would encourage and comfort us, a coach and team leader, someone who wouldn't give up until he figured out what was wrong. Someone just like Alan Jacobson.

"I've read over the notes and tests your physician faxed me. He did a lot of the preliminary work to eliminate the obvious culprits. That will save us time." He made a little hum of satisfaction and smiled. "Based on what I see here, I'm pretty sure you've come to the right place. Infectious disease guys are like prospectors. We keep drilling until we find oil." He leaned back, beaming at us as if we'd won the lottery.

"More tests?" I had a vision of Ted strapped down like Gulliver with thousands of lab-coated technicians sticking needles in him. I shuddered.

"It's not bad, really. We can run lots of tests on one blood sample. That's one good thing. We won't keep you here very long." He made the satisfied sound again. "That's another good thing, yes? But before we get to that part, I'd like you to tell me as much as you can remember about where you were and what you did during the two months before you felt the first symptoms. So, let's see," he looked down at the folder, "that would be starting in April, right?" He sat back, flipped open a steno pad, and looked at Ted, a rapt expression on his face, like a pointer, its prey in sight.

Ted closed his eyes. When he opened them, he looked baffled. "That's correct, but I don't recall going anywhere in particular."

"Don't worry. I'll get you started. You'll be amazed how much you remember." Al Jacobson's eyes sparkled. "Did you travel outside the country in January or February?"

"No. As much as I might have liked to." Ted made a rueful face.

"Did you spend time in any big cities?"

"Big like Newport?"

Jacobson laughed. "Big like Boston or New York."

"Nope. Dr. Jacobson . . ."

"Al, please."

"Al, the thing is, I have my own business. I've got so much work that coming to Boston today is the first time I've been off the island in a year."

"What about the time you and Sandor went over to Westport in February, around Valentine's Day?" I remembered this only because I had spent that day in the office, grateful to have it to myself.

Al folded his hands over his stomach and leaned back. "Tell me more about that day. Everything you can remember."

Sandor had had an appointment at a nursery in Westport. On the spur of the moment, he called Ted, who had learned that a delivery he expected that day had been delayed. So he gave himself the day off. After Sandor's appointment, they had bought a picnic lunch to take over to Horseneck Beach.

"It was a warm day, so we had lunch on the beach. There were even a few surfers."

"A sandy beach, right?"

Ted looked mystified. "Of course. But there are sea plums and grass on the dunes there. Why?"

"Did you walk through the grass?"

"We had to park on the road—the parking lot was closed off for some reason—and took a trail over the dunes to the beach. So we weren't exactly walking through the grass. At least as far as I recall."

Al straightened up in his chair, unfolded his hands, and made some notes on the steno pad. "We know you don't have rheumatoid arthritis, although you do have arthritis-like symptoms. We know you probably don't have some kind of flu. What may be your problem is something I've been looking at closely since the early eighties. Have you heard of or read about Lyme disease?"

Neither of us had.

As he described LD, Al explained the cause, the symptoms, the diagnosis, and the treatment. "We've learned that ticks carry the disease and that, when one bites you, the saliva releases bacteria into your system. Often this causes a rash in the form of a ring, with a clear area and a red center. Like a bull's-eye."

Ted made a face. "I'd sure remember it if I'd had something like that."

"What about any other type of rash?"

"No, nothing like that. Just the achy joints, fatigue, and the fever, off and on."

"Don't forget the weight loss." I put my hand on Ted's arm.

"More than the ten pounds you reported at your last appointment in Newport?" Al looked over the chart from Ted's doctor.

"Fifteen pounds or so." He glanced at me. "I've had to add two notches to my belt, for example."

Al chuckled. "I'd be happy to lend you some of my extra ballast. But I'd rather you got your own back." He took out a medical order form, scribbled instructions on it, and handed it to Ted. "Since you live so far away, we're going to squeeze as much blood out today as we can. Normally, I'd send you to the lab. You'd probably have to schedule something on another day. But I can accommodate you here, in the office. My nurse will do what's required. You can go home. As soon as we have the results, probably by mid-afternoon on Monday, I'll call you and tell you what we're going to do. Sound good?"

We'd be back from Vermont by then. Could we put all of this out of our minds until then? As I turned to say goodbye, I remembered the photographs.

"I like them all, especially the one with the yellow filaments against the green background."

"I'll tell my colleague. He's an epidemiologist and a photographer. They're his work." Al looked at me, as if we had just shared a secret. "The one that caught your eye happens to be Borrelia burgdorferi, the bacterium that causes LD."

"You mean . . ."

"That's right. Each photograph shows a different organism caught in the act of multiplying. As deadly as they are, my friend happens to think they're beautiful."

When the nurse finished with the blood draw, she put on a reassuring smile. "Don't worry. There's plenty left."

Back in the waiting room, the receptionist handed us a packet of information. "Usually we have the test results back in three days. Because it's Thursday, I'm sure they'll come in on Monday."

We arranged with her to leave us a message at home. We could dial in to our answering machine and pick up messages, in case we stayed in Vermont longer than we planned.

IN THE front seat, Ted adjusted the seat back and stretched out, his eyes closed. I tuned in Boston's classical music station and began to relax into the drive, mentally reviewing our route.

"What are we going to tell Annie?"

Annie would worry, no matter what we told her. "Why don't we just tell her what we know?"

"What we don't know, you mean."

"We can talk about Lyme disease without saying you have it. We don't know yet if you do."

"As much as I'd like to go through the whole business—the uncertainties—I'd rather wait on that until we hear the results of the tests and we have a better idea about the prognosis."

As soon as he said this, a dark curtain fell across the future. For the first time, fears of what might happen to Ted crowded my thoughts.

"Do you want to talk about something else? Or not talk at all?"

"It's not that." How to tell him what I was thinking? That I was afraid to face the reality of the unknowns that loomed ahead of us.

"It's hard to know how to talk to her when we don't know for certain what's wrong with me and we don't have confidence in the treatment—if it turns out I have Lyme disease."

Ted and I had tried so hard to help Annie tell her own truth, to be true to herself, I realized we had to tell her as much as we knew—and didn't know—about what was wrong with Ted.

A bin of remainders sat on the sidewalk in front of the bookshop. It was nearly four thirty. I parked the car in front. Just then, Annie came out the door. "You made great time!" She leaned in Ted's window to give him a kiss and got in the backseat.

"Josie's closing up. She'll meet us at home." She slid to the middle of the backseat, put her head next to Ted's, and hugged him. "I'm so glad you're here."

"Me, too, sweetie."

Like Prospect Hill, the house Annie and Josie had found was a classic Cape. It had a garden of roses and delphiniums in the back and an old sugar maple abutting the stone wall in front. Annie had wanted to build a tree house in it; the owner, claiming liability issues, turned her down, then offered to put up a swing. The one he'd installed was the old-fashioned kind, a plank hanging from ropes. I couldn't understand why, but it finished the house, somehow, as if it had filled a gap.

Ted and Annie carried packages from the car—jam, cheese, bread, and pasta. I followed them with some dishtowels and potholders. The ones Annie and Josie had, all castoffs, were threadbare. Although they had lived together for two years, this was their first house. Annie had told Ted that apartment living was too temporary—to both of them. The house, although only a rental, felt like a commitment.

I stopped just inside the door. To the left, the living room held the glow of the streetlight, where shadows of the sugar maple's branches played against the walls. To the right, empty except for scattered boxes of books, the parlor looked bereft. With its crown moldings and narrow brick fireplace, the room called up visions of afternoon tea served to visitors whose only purpose in stopping by was to be able to say they had. In the kitchen at the end of the hall, silhouetted against the windows behind them, Ted and Annie put away the food.

Standing there, hearing Annie's exclamations, I had the sensation of stepping into a dark place, uncertain if I would find my footing—or fall. Annie and Josie were happy together and settled in their life here. Until Ted's accident, and the discovery that he was ill, his business had developed to the point that he could work exclusively on his own designs. I was almost there, spending more time these days writing proposals and drafting designs than on maintenance work.

As we had hoped. Now what? Of course we couldn't know what lay ahead. I brushed away my tears and my apprehensions and went out to the kitchen.

Ted was telling Annie her favorite joke, a family tradition. They gave the punch line, in unison, and collapsed in each other's arms, giggling. Ted nuzzled the top of Annie's head and smiled at me. "Happy?"

"Happy." Just seeing Annie and Ted together, relaxed with each other, gave me confidence.

"Yeah," Annie murmured. She pulled me into their hug.

AT DINNER, Annie and Josie told stories about the bookstore and life in Manchester. Once a sleepy summer resort town, it had developed into a thriving community of artists and artisans, people who had come up to live there year round, many of them with small children.

"What does this mean for the bookstore?" Ted leaned forward, his arms folded on the table.

"We're looking into that." Josie glanced at Annie.

"You know, mostly we stock best sellers, cookbooks, craft manuals. We're thinking we need to expand a bit. The problem is, we have so little shelf space. So Josie and I cooked up a survey, a handout to give to customers, just to see if we can figure out what people would like more of." Annie took Josie's hand.

"Or less of. So far we've collected about seventy-five, but we haven't compiled them." Josie shrugged. "At least we know our customers are interested enough to give us feedback."

After dinner, Annie leaned across the table. "Can you tell us what you found out?"

Ted laid out the short version.

"Lyme disease? Isn't that something you get from deer ticks?" Annie seemed concerned, but not alarmed. Josie said nothing.

"Everywhere you have deer, you also have deer ticks. Even in the sea grass on the dunes at Horseneck Beach. Anyway, we'll know more on Monday."

I tried to catch Annie's eye.

"It's curable, right? Isn't that what this doctor does?"

"Of course it is."

When Annie looked at me for confirmation, I nodded and smiled. I, too, wanted to believe that Al held the key to the cure.

After helping clear the table and clean up, Ted and I drove to the inn where we'd made reservations.

Ted lay on the bed while I unpacked for us both. "Tired?"

"A little. I'll be fine tomorrow." He closed his eyes.

Below the inn, at the foot of the hill, the village spread out, its Christmas lights glimmering through the trees. A lightning bolt flashed—a warm front, unusual for this time of year, passing through. I counted the seconds, *one one-thousand, two one-thousand, three one-thousand*, waiting. On six, thunder rolled over the valley. I ran my hands over my arms, smoothing away the static.

Thinking he was asleep, I slid into bed, trying not to wake him.

He rolled over to kiss me. "Try to get some sleep. I'm going to beat this thing. I promise."

DRIVING BACK to Newport on Monday morning, we talked about the customer feedback idea for the bookstore. It was clear Annie had been more in favor of it than Josie. But they were in it together. Josie had made that clear.

"They've figured out how to manage their differences and they're only twenty-four. Some couples never figure it out."

"Maybe because they're women, it's easier."

"You mean because they've both been molded that way?"

"Not Annie." Ted laughed.

"That's true. Once she makes up her mind, she holds the course."

"Well, somehow they've figured out how to get to a consensus. If they're going to stay together, that will help. A lot."

When we stopped at a service station on the Mass Pike just after two, Ted used the public phone to check our answering machine.

"It is Lyme disease." He sounded resigned. "Al wants me to start on an antibiotic right away."

Neither of us talked for a while. Knowing the diagnosis wasn't enough. We needed reassurance that the antibiotic would work. And that was the problem. There was widespread uncertainty about the effectiveness of the treatment simply because LD was largely a mystery.

Ted shuddered. "Just knowing there's this microorganism in me, dividing, multiplying, looking for places to hide, makes me itch all over."

"Another symptom?"

"I hope Dad won't insist I get a second opinion."

"What will you tell him?" I did not want this diagnosis to cause dissension between Ted and Bruno. Ted would need to devote his energy to getting well. Stress of any kind would make that harder.

"Just that we'll wait and see how it goes." He looked at me. "One part of Al's message was for you." He blew out a little puff of breath, more like a sigh than a laugh.

"Oh?"

"He has a signed copy of that photograph for you. The Borrelia burgdorferi one."

April 3, 1992

Absorbed in his drawing, Ted reached for a pencil without lifting his eyes from the page.

"How do you do that—find the one you want without looking?"

He swiveled his chair around. "Habit, or something?" He gave me a crooked smile. "How does Isabelle decide how much garlic to put in the aïoli?"

"You have to have a nose for it." When she prepared aïoli, Isabelle peeled whole heads of garlic until she had a bowlful of cloves. But the final touch, judged by fragrance alone always, was more garlic.

"Same thing. It's like a sixth sense." Ted tapped the pencil against his forehead. "Still. I don't take any chances. I always put them back in the same order."

We'd been living day by day since Ted's diagnosis and treatment, feeling our way, questioning each twinge. Was it overwork or a recurrence? You do the best you can, taking your chances, making your decisions based on guesswork, clinging to small habits of daily life for reassurance. We made a tacit commitment to keep everything as much the same as possible. One thing we had learned: there was simply no knowing the future. You could take a stab at it, hold tight to your hopes, but you had, always, to remember how tenuous that hold was.

We realized the first round of antibiotics hadn't worked when Ted's fatigue and pain returned, forcing him to limit himself to designing and drafting. When he could—when he was feeling rested enough, strong enough—he spent time in the shop, answering questions, checking the work in progress. He couldn't have managed without Andrew, who had been with him since 1982.

Ted continued to oversee routine business details—invoices, orders, and so forth—even though this part of the work drained him almost as much as the physical part once had. He didn't have to tell me. I knew how much he missed making the designs he drafted. It was like creating the recipe for a dish he'd never taste. "Imagining what the finished piece will look like isn't good enough, not by a long shot."

For the first time in several years, I dreamed of the secret room. At first, I welcomed the curtains billowing and parting in front of me as I walked through the house toward the light. But the light dimmed, the curtains closed in on me, trapping me in a narrow corridor. My struggle to get free woke me. Beside me, Ted breathed easily, deeply. Careful not to wake him, I got up and tiptoed down the stairs, avoiding the creaky places.

In the kitchen, I heated milk and stirred in some honey. Anxious and helpless. The dream said it all. I hadn't talked to anyone—certainly not Ted—about my fear that Ted would—we would—have to learn to live with and manage his condition.

Al Jacobson called it "recurrent Lyme disease." Others called it "chronic Lyme disease." Whatever name we used, we learned it might be incurable. The symptoms appeared without warning, becoming more severe over time. Often, Ted seemed to be looking over his shoulder, as if stalked by his own apprehensions. I knew he was trying to shield me and I understood his thinking. Maybe by not talking about the disease, it would disappear. But this was reality, not a fairy tale.

Al wanted to try a new intravenous treatment, this one specifically for recurrent Lyme disease. They had recently learned the oral antibiotics worked only at the beginning, within a month or two of infection, he told us. I knew better than to ask how confident he was that the IV would be their silver bullet. *Guesswork again.*

In the morning, I got up late with burning eyes and a pounding headache. I made coffee and sipped orange juice, thinking over what I planned to say to Ted.

I heard him on the stairs, moving slowly. "Coffee?" I forced myself to smile.

He nodded. "Bad dream?"

"The house dream. Only this time, the curtains grabbed me. As if they were alive somehow."

He took the mug I handed him, put it down on the counter, and hugged me. "Would you like to go away for a while?"

I tilted my head so I could look him in the eye. "Could you?"

"What I had in mind is, you could take a trip by yourself—go visit Ardis, or your mother, or Annie and Josie."

"You mean run away from home?"

"Why not?"

I stepped back from him. "I've got another idea. Come in the living room with me. I'll tell you."

IN JANUARY, Ethan had sent preliminary plans for the building that would house our studios at Prospect Hill. We had agreed on one structure with a workshop on the first floor and two studios on the second. After we finalized the drawings, we worked out a schedule, with a start date of early April. Then Ted had such a severe recurrence that he had spent the month of March in bed. We postponed the groundbreaking until May.

When he was too tired to get up, he worked in bed using the collapsible drawing board I had given him. I had come home every day for lunch.

"I hate that you have to check on me." In bed, holding the drawing board across his lap, surrounded by piles of crumpled paper, he was pale, unshaven, his eyes red-rimmed.

"Don't flatter yourself. You're just my excuse to get out of the office. I need a break from Sandor once in a while, especially when things are so crazy."

His smile twisted into a grimace. "Pain is just a four-letter word, but it comes in a hundred varieties." I took his hand, then held him close. He shuddered. "I'm so tired, tired of being tired." The strain had made him hoarse.

"Al says—they all say—the intravenous treatment takes effect fast, much faster than the pills."

"Well, that's great." His laugh came out like a groan. "The question is, will it work better than the pills—which didn't work, not that that's particularly important, since the IV 'works faster.'" He sounded like his father. The older he got, the more Bruno resorted to sarcasm, as sharp as his scalpel, as if he could eviscerate time itself.

"I can't remember what being well feels like." His voice dropped to a whisper. "I'm scared, really scared. What if the IV doesn't work?"

"It will. Believe me." I folded him into my arms, rocking him against me, hoping he didn't hear the effort in my voice.

"Let's call Ethan and tell him we're ready to start." Before Ted could protest, I picked up the phone. A week later, at the end of the first week in May, Ethan let us know that he and his crew had spent their first day at Prospect Hill. For the first time in months, Ted's smile held nothing back.

Since the groundbreaking, Ethan had called us several times a week to bring us up to date. The one piece of the plan—to sell the Beech Street house so we could move to Prospect Hill—remained up in the air. Although there was no rush, no urgency, Ted wanted to be settled in Alden by the late fall, to have everything he needed in place so he could make the prototypes for the designs he was working on.

TED PROPPED himself against the sofa cushions so he could look at me. "What's your idea about all of this?"

"Let's put the house on the market right away so we can move as soon as we can. By September, if possible."

His eyes widened; he started to sit up.

"Just listen, okay? You'll have the first IV treatment next Friday; you'll be finished on June nineteenth—that's three weeks. That means you could go up to Alden a week later. You won't need to take anything with you except drawing materials. You'll be able to work, uninterrupted, as much or as little as you like. Spend time at the lake. Walk in the woods. Relax and recover." I read—and had anticipated—the question in his eyes. "I know we don't know how you'll react to the IV. But if you're feeling well enough, wouldn't you like to do that?"

He sat up and rubbed his hand over his face. "There's just one problem with your idea."

"And that is?"

"You'll be here by yourself. You'll have to manage the house through the sale—and do your own job. Seems like a lot, to me."

"I don't mind. Besides, I like the upside."

"What's that?"

"We'll be able to do three things at once, don't you see? First, you won't have to interrupt your design work because you can do it up there. Second, if questions come up about the studios, you're on site. No more phone tag with Ethan."

"And the third?"

"We'll sell the house sooner." Even though I knew my logic leaked like a sieve, I was determined. If I sounded confident enough, Ted would go along with me. There was a practical side to this, one I didn't need to explain.

Ted, thoughtful, nodded at me. "Let's talk some more."

So we made lists and penciled in dates on our calendars, beginning with the dates of Ted's treatment days at the local hospital. He leaned his head back and closed his eyes.

"What's worrying you?"

"I'm not sure Ethan will want me up there hanging around. It's one thing for one of us to talk to him on the phone. It's another for me to live there full time. I know just enough to be a nuisance, if I decide to get involved."

"That's up to you, isn't it? You'll be busy enough with your own work not to interfere with Ethan. Besides, he can take care of himself. He'll listen to what you have to say, maybe even take notes. Then he'll tell you to buzz off." I pressed on. "Deal?"

"Deal."

Our shared laughter and our relief dispersed the cloud of apprehension. I knew, and believed Ted did, as well, that making this decision wouldn't affect the outcome of the treatment. Still, it helped us both shift into a renewed sense of hope.

ARDIS LAUGHED when she heard how I'd persuaded Ted to go to Vermont for the summer.

"It *is* funny, I agree. It was almost as if he'd had the same idea, but didn't want to make the first move. Maybe because he's afraid of the outcome with the IV. The other thing is—maybe this is what convinced him—they think that stress triggers these recurrences. So why not give his system the best chance for recovery, get him away from the shop and the guys?"

"Sounds like one of those umbrella insurance policies, the IV plus a stress-free summer."

"Whatever it takes." If only it were as simple as that. Would Ted ever recover fully? Had the LD bacterium already found its way into his brain or his heart, where it could cause fatal damage? If so, if it had crossed the blood–brain barrier, the IV was our only hope.

"There's a plus side to this, about the house. If it sells quickly, you could be up there with him by the end of the summer."

"Or maybe the end of September. All of a sudden, that seems like tomorrow, not four months away. At least I'll have time to finish the projects I'm doing here while the house is on the market. That part feels strange."

"Why?"

"For the first time in sixteen years, I won't be taking on any new work." I pushed away the question of what I'd be doing in Vermont. I felt ready to make the change, to go out on my own. I would have plenty of time to figure out the specifics over the winter.

"Who's your broker?"

"Steve Barker. The realtor we used when we bought the house." It was obvious why handing the house sale over to Steve made sense. Steve knew the Beech Street house. He'd find the right buyer.

WE HAD our first open house the last weekend in June, right after Ted left. At the end of the day, I called him. "Forty-three people stopped by. Several even knew something about eighteenth-century houses. Steve's laying odds we'll have an offer by mid-August."

"You sound dubious."

"Better to wait until the chicks hatch, I think."

"Speaking of hatching. Ethan's backhoe guy told me today he's never seen so many big stones around here—fourteen of them so far, and those are just the really big ones. It's as if the glacier that came through made itself a nest, laid its eggs, and left them behind when it got going again."

"So that's slowing things down?"

"They're about three weeks behind. I've mailed you some pictures."

"Of the stones?" I imagined them lined up like Jeanne's goats, waiting to be fed. I'd been thinking about Flagy a lot as I began to plan the move from Newport. How much simpler the move from Flagy to Newport had been. We'd had a few pieces of Ted's furniture, a few cartons of books I'd had in storage, and high hopes. Laughing with Ted about the stones and the goats reassured me. We could manage. The move was a good idea and the timing was right.

"You'll see. They are truly massive. I'm thinking we should install them somehow, somewhere, paint faces on them."

"*All* of them?"

"I'm only half-serious. Ethan knows someone who might want them."

"We could put an ad in the paper. With a photo. 'I'm Dolly. Adopt me! I weigh five tons and I'm very quiet.'"

BY THE second week in July, Ethan's crew had begun framing the building. Ted had sent me a picture of the two of them standing where the workshop would be. I had put it on the refrigerator with the ones I had of the stones. Others I taped to my computer. As for Beech Street, several prospective buyers had returned for a second or third look without making an offer.

"They like the idea of owning an antique house, until they understand what's involved," I told Ardis when she called.

"Isn't that a little like saying you love abstract expressionism, but it's the colors you can't stand?"

"A bit, yes. I don't blame someone who wants the antique part along with the 'mod cons.' Really, when you think about it, you have to be a little bit crazy to buy a house that comes with its own retinue of specialists—in anticipation of all the things that might go wrong. What's strange is that most of these people haven't a clue about what they're looking at. You'd think they'd be curious, at least, and do some research."

Ardis laughed. "You lucked out, I guess, marrying someone who knows what horsehair plaster is and thinks repairing it is fun."

THE NEXT time I talked to Ted, I tried to explain my frustration. "I think it's a waste of time to show this house to people who expect an old house to behave just like a new one."

"Don't take these comments or criticisms too much to heart. Steve doesn't."

"Of course he doesn't. It's not his house!"

Behind Ted's silence on the other end of the line, I could hear a power tool, probably a drill. Ethan's crew was taking advantage of the longer days to work late, making up for the time they'd had to spend moving the boulders around.

"Ted?"

"Is this too much for you?"

"Some days it's a drag to get the house ready. Cleaning, putting things away. But the main thing is, it's like having a child the other kids pick on—because she's knock-kneed or wears braces." I decided not to tell him how much easier it had been to maintain an uncluttered house; his books, drawings, and other design paraphernalia had gone to Vermont with him. And he didn't need to hear how impatient I was to see for myself the progress on the studios.

"I know. Just don't take it out on Steve. He's not responsible for other people's dumb ideas."

"I know. We can hardly expect him to make people fill out an application or a qualifying questionnaire. Still, I want to be *there*."

Ted laughed. "This may be over sooner than you think."

PART 4

A LDEN

1992–1993

Gifts of Love

August 8, 1992

Steve waved and came toward me, patting his face with a bandana. He was supposed to have a showing that afternoon. Had the people canceled? Looking down at the spent leaves and stalks piled on the lawn beside me, he shook his head. "The slugs are really something this year, aren't they?"

"Slugs and the heat. The plants don't stand a chance." I got up and stretched. There was only one way to do this job: on the ground, on all fours, one plant at a time. It was a necessary, tedious garden task. Setting the world right was impossible; cleaning out wilting or rotting foliage was both possible and intensely satisfying.

"I tried to call earlier."

I wiped my face on a shirttail. "Sorry. I've been out here for a while."

"Just to let you know, I'm meeting this couple at the office at one o'clock. I'll bring them by at one fifteen or so. Okay with you?"

It was quarter past twelve now. "That's fine. I'll make myself scarce."

He looked around the garden. "Sure looks nice, Malorie." He tilted his head back, craning his neck. "I'll bet it's ten degrees cooler under this tree." He laughed.

"What?"

"I'm just thinking how much I'd like to climb up there into Annie's tree house with a good book right about now. Who knows? This might be my last chance."

Later, I'd remember the feeling that came over me then, as though Steve's anticipation of this showing had pulled something in me out of alignment, leaving me breathless and light-headed with dread.

He looked at me, nodding, as if appraising the value of the deal he hoped to close. "These people have been looking for a year, plus they're crazy about eighteenth-century houses. They *know* about old houses."

"What about gardens?" This wasn't the first time I realized that leaving the house meant leaving the garden. Still, I felt sandbagged.

Steve's mouth tightened. "Not sure."

It wasn't fair to expect him to value the garden in the way I did. Ted had reminded me recently that no one could know how different it was now from the way it had been when we bought the house. How could they, before they saw the photographs that recorded the transformation year by year? So I did what I could to smooth Steve's ruffled feathers. "At least they'll get the house."

He smiled. I'd been forgiven.

I had half an hour to rake and clear the lawn and get out of the way. I wondered about this couple. As much as they might know about old houses, how would they react to the simplicity and modesty of this one? A block away, a similar house—same roof style, same central chimney—sat right on the harbor. It was twice as large as ours. Built by a wealthy Quaker merchant, it had one of the best pedigrees in town.

Twenty minutes later, Steve returned, his clients in tow. Wearing a Panama and a blazer, the man fanned himself with a folded newspaper. In a pink sleeveless shift, the woman held a straw tote in one hand, a sweater in the other. She pushed her dark hair back and took off her sunglasses. Under the tree, with the glare of the sun in my eyes, I couldn't see their faces.

Steve left them at the front steps and joined me under the tree. "They were early, so I decided to come over. Better than sitting in my office—this heat . . ."

"The AC's on. It'll be cool in the house."

Just then, the condenser added its hum to the rumble of bridge traffic and the roar of a nearby lawn mower.

Steve gave me a thumbs-up. I laughed.

"I'll stay out here until you're done." I nodded toward the woman, who was checking her watch. "If they want to see the garden, I can go for a walk."

"It could be an hour, maybe more?"

"I'll be fine." I slipped off my hat, sipped some water from my thermos, and waved him away.

The woman had folded her sweater into her tote. Her sunglasses sat perched on top of her head. The man held his blazer over his right shoulder; his shirt cuffs were folded just so, as if starched. Through the heat waves rising from the flagstones at the foot of the steps, his forearms, wrists, and hands wavered, not quite attached to him, somehow.

Hot as it was, I shivered.

STIFLING HUNGER pangs, I stretched out in the grass. The lawn mower had stopped. All I could hear was the traffic on the bridge and the pulse of the foghorn. Above Annie's tree house, near the top of the tree, I spotted a bird's nest tucked into the Y of a branch. Was it my imagination, or was a breeze beginning to move up there? I felt the grass and the prickle of sweat against the back of my neck, imagined lying on the beach at the lake in Alden.

As much as I wanted to be there, I knew Ted and I had made the right decision. From all reports—his and Annie's—he was feeling well enough to work several hours a day and was taking time out to swim or walk. He told me he had gained six pounds. As for his fear of interfering—despite himself—with the construction crew, that had proved to be a nonissue. When Ethan needed Ted's input, he made an appointment. Otherwise, they got together once a week for updates.

Barring interruptions, the work would be finished by mid-September or early October. All that remained was to sell this house. *And the move.* Although I dreaded the very idea, I'd begun to make lists of what to take and what to donate. Milou had left all her furniture at Prospect Hill, so Ted and I had agreed to take only a few pieces from Newport, giving what we didn't need or want to Annie and Josie who, lacking everything, needed anything we could pass along to them.

I heard the front door open and close. I checked my watch. It was already two thirty. An hour and a half had passed. I must have dozed off. Steve showed the couple out the gate, closed it partway, and turned in my direction, striking Rocky's victory pose. Then he mimed holding a phone to his ear and waved at me.

At four thirty I finished. I raked and gathered up the debris in the wheelbarrow and dumped it onto the compost pile. As I was hosing off, I heard the phone. Ted, perhaps, or maybe Steve? There was no need to rush. There would be a message.

On the back step outside the kitchen, I took off my shoes, the grass cool against my bare feet. In the lavender dusk, a single white lily glowed at the far end of the border. The breeze, steady now, carried the growl of a thunderstorm making its way down the bay toward Newport.

Like will-o'-the-wisps, the turned-up cuffs floated above the garden in the half-light.

The answering machine flashed: one message. I rewound the tape.

"It's me, Malorie."

Jack?

I saw the cuffs again. Jack had ironed his own shirts, the cuffs starched to stay put when he turned them up. *Just so.* I closed my eyes, saw his wrists and forearms, an afterimage, like the Cheshire cat materializing out of thin air.

"We want to buy your house. Steve is writing up the offer. Said he'd bring it to you later today or tomorrow." He cleared his throat.

If I had met him face-to-face, I would have recognized him. Of that I was certain. Still, it had been twenty-two years, after all. Twenty-two years. The incongruity began to sink in. Never, not once since I had left Brookton, had I considered it even remotely possible we would ever meet again. Apart from Jack's friendship with Matt, which had faltered long ago, we had no other connection.

"Liz, my wife, doesn't know about us. *I* didn't know you owned the house until I saw Ardis's painting on your dining room wall." He laughed. And sighed. "At first, I couldn't believe it. Even now, hearing your voice on the machine . . ." He paused, cleared his throat again. "This is harder than I thought it would be. What happened to you, anyway?

"Steve told us your husband has been sick. I'm sorry. I hope he'll be okay." A deep breath.

"Was that you in the garden? It's so shady under that big tree, I couldn't tell."

"Call me. Call me back, Malorie."

When the phone rang, I hesitated. *Jack trying again?* I let the machine do its job.

"You've got . . ."

I picked up the phone. "Steve?"

"Malorie? You've got an offer. Can I bring it over?" His excitement blurred his words into an uninflected sound stream.

There was no plausible reason to say no. At the bottom of the hole I'd fallen into, the one that was closing over my head, I sat as still and mute as my own shadow.

Steve rushed on, filling the silence. "She couldn't stop talking about the chair rails, the wonderful restoration work, how unspoiled it is, and so on and so forth. You'd have thought she was the seller." He laughed. "Love at first sight. That's what this is. So can I come by?"

I swallowed. Found my balance and my voice. "Yes, fine. I'm here."

"Is everything all right? Something happen to Ted?"

"No, nothing. Ted's fine." *Ted. What would Ted say about this?* "Come by now, Steve. It's a bit of a shock that this is finally happening." I had that sense of dread again. But now I could pin it on something. On someone.

"Sure. Well, I'll be there shortly."

As soon as we hung up, the machine blinked at me. Someone had tried to call while Steve was on the line.

Businesslike this time, Jack's message was brief. "It's me again. You can call my cell." Something about the way he said the number, repeating it twice, made clear that he expected me to call him back. That tone, that self-assurance, hadn't changed.

STEVE PUT a legal-sized folder on the kitchen table and sat across from me. "This couldn't be more straightforward." He beamed. "The Nelsons, that's Liz and John, are offering asking price."

John, I've got to remember to call him John. "That's a surprise . . ."

Steve frowned.

"I'm relieved, actually."

He smiled and nodded, his expression open and relaxed. He flipped through the folder he'd brought and removed the top several pages. I understood he wanted to go over the details. I didn't want to hear them. "Steve, I'm glad about this. Ted will be too. I'd like to call him as soon as possible. So, can we cut to the chase?"

"Of course, I understand."

If he was disappointed, he hid it well. "There are a couple of things they'd like us to do. Such as they are, they're pretty trivial."

Knowing Jack—*John*—whatever extras they wanted had probably been his idea. "What do they have in mind?"

Steve leaned toward me, reassuring me with a smile. "For starters, a new water heater. I think we can replace it, don't you? And they'd like to close by September twenty-fifth. They're going to Europe for a while." He sat back, tapping his pen on the paper in front of him.

"Is that it?"

"They'd like that big tree pruned. They're worried there might be a hurricane while they're away."

That big tree. One day soon, I'd walk out the gate, never to return. Most likely, I wouldn't see the tree again, except in my photographs, or in my mind's eye. Might as well get used to the idea.

"We had it done in April. The receipt is in with the others I gave you." If this was all Jack—*John*—wanted fixed, it was manageable. The closing date was fine, too. I would have time to organize and pack, and finish my local projects. For a moment, I wished they'd been unreasonable—asked for a new roof, say. I wished I could just say no. Punish Jack? For coming back into my life?

"That's it, then." Steve nodded at me, smiling. "We've got two days to sign or counter. You'll talk to Ted this evening? He'll be pleased, don't you think?"

"Yes, probably he will be."

Steve raised his eyebrows in surprise.

"Yes, of course. He'll be very relieved, Steve." I pushed the papers toward him. "Is it all right with you if I call you in the morning?"

He reached across the table and took my hand. "Ted will beat this thing, Malorie. When you call him, tell him there's no reason for either of you to be here for the closing. Just give your lawyer power of attorney. Do you want me to talk to him?"

"Thanks, Steve. Ted or I will take care of that." I hadn't thought that far ahead. I was thankful that Steve had. I wouldn't have to see Jack.

I walked out with Steve into the dark, cool garden. Tattered clouds, remnants of the thunderstorm, trailed across the waning moon. Under my bare feet, the wet grass felt ice cold. A few remaining hosta blooms bobbed in the border. Clumps of alyssum cast their own faint glow along the border's edge. Overhead, leaves rustling, the neighboring maples spread their dense, sheltering canopies. I opened the gate for Steve, inhaling the tarry smell rising from the sidewalk and pavement.

Steve patted me awkwardly. "I miss Ted. He's been a good friend. Hell, I miss you both. Annie, too. It makes me feel a little better getting you this deal." His eyes were deeply shadowed. "Well, let's get it over with, shall we?"

He crossed the street to his car, feeling his pockets for his keys.

"JACK *NELSON*?" Ardis's voice slid up to a shriek of disbelief.

I had to hold the phone away from my ear.

"Like a bad penny, isn't he? What are you going to do?"

"For starters, I'm not going to call him back." I had made up my mind even before I listened to his second message.

"I see."

"It's obvious he didn't tell Steve he knows me. Steve would have said something." He *knew* me? Not now, not then.

"But he might?"

"I *think* he won't, not if I don't call him."

"True. If you do, you'll give him a reason to talk about the house, about the coincidence, but that's just the beginning. He'll have questions, won't he?"

That was the problem. *What happened to you?* Even his tone of voice reminded me of the way he spoke to me back then, at Brookton, always assuming—*presuming*—I owed him an answer.

"Have you thought about what to tell Ted?"

"Yes. Short answer: I don't know. I just keep going in circles."

"Some advice?"

"Of course."

"Wait. Ted is relaxing, recovering, resting. You know he's getting better. Maybe he could laugh this off. Maybe not. It's better not to take any chances."

"You mean, if it were just that Jack and his wife want to buy the house, that's a coincidence. But his phone call, his asking me to call him back, makes it weird. A coincidence bearing ulterior motives."

Ardis had told me what I wanted to hear. Better to wait to decide whether to reveal that Jack and his wife were the buyers. It crossed my mind then that I might not have to tell Ted at all. I hoped that Jack would get my message: surely not returning his call would make him understand I didn't want to talk to him. What could we possibly have to say to one another, anyway? The coincidence of the house would only get us so far. What then? What was left? The past? The miscarriage? That was a subject I wanted to avoid at all costs.

"HELLO?"

"Did I wake you?"

Ted yawned. "I dozed off in Milou's chair. For sure I'll have a stiff neck." He laughed in the middle of another yawn. "What happened today?"

"Good news."

It didn't take us long to agree to the Nelsons' offer.

"I didn't think we'd get a deal so fast. Did Steve tell you anything about the buyers?"

"She's an art historian; he's in business. She's the one who knew what she was looking at." I'd said enough. "Anyway, Steve was right—about getting a deal before the end of the summer."

"Well, it's definitely a plus we won't have to go to the closing. Now you get to do the fun part."

I decided to play along. "And that would be?"

"Pack." He gave a short laugh.

"Just what I've been looking forward to."

He laughed with me.

"Ted?"

"Yes?"

"All I'm really looking forward to is getting up there—as soon as I can."

"That's the carrot, all right."

"WHO ARE they?"Annie sounded tentative. As if she didn't really want to know.

"Just some people, a couple from Brookline. I think this is probably going to be a second home for them."

"Do you know anything else about them?"

Holding the phone against my shoulder, I looked up at the old map on the wall over Ted's desk. An elaborately inked sea monster thrashed around in the Pacific Ocean, its snout flourishing a toothy grin. *Here there be monsters.* As long as I kept looking straight ahead and stuck to my story, I'd be fine. "They loved the house and they want an early closing."

"I suppose they want you to take the tree house down." Annie's voice trembled.

"I don't think so. Anyway, they didn't say anything about the tree house."

"I used to climb up there every day, remember? My hangout. I loved listening to the tree sounds. I pretended it was speaking a language only I could understand." She sniffled and blew her nose.

"You know what? I bet they have grandchildren, or might have some someday. Wouldn't they have fun in it?"

"I guess. Thanks. That makes me feel a little better."

Now the sea monster appeared to be leering, its smile a sinister reminder of all life's uncomfortable surprises. I shuddered. It was grotesque that Jack and his wife had bought the house, that they would live in it, occupy the space where Ted and I had shared our most intimate moments.

"About the maps," I began.

"The maps?" Of course she was confused. "Oh, right, Dad's old maps! What about them?"

"I'm making lists—moving lists—and I know you two talked about his giving them to you. Wouldn't now be a good time for the hand-off?"

"I'll check with Josie. We're still trying to figure out the parlor. If we hang them in there, maybe we'll buy some furniture. At long last . . ."

Annie had been eleven or twelve at the time. Sitting on the floor beside her, Ted had told her about the map spread out in front of them, about what the world was like, what was known of it, when it had originally been made. She wanted to know if sea monsters were real.

"I've never seen one, sweetheart, but that doesn't mean they don't exist."

As soon as Annie moved up to Burlington for college, she had heard about Champy, Lake Champlain's monster. Ted had promised to take her and Josie out on the lake to look for it.

Maybe next summer we'd all go. Annie, Josie, Ted, and me. *If Ted is well enough.* In my mind's eye, I saw the LD bacillus leering at me, twitching its tail.

THE CRAWL space under the roof, our only storage space, looked a bit like a coffin, with its curved ceiling and low sides. Twenty feet long, six feet wide, and four feet high—between the crossbeams—it gave me just enough headroom to crouch or kneel. I tucked my ponytail into my collar, rolled up my jeans, and surveyed the contents.

Piles of skates, tennis rackets, and mismatched running shoes told the tale of Annie's interests over the years. Here and there, a few broken lamps and several typewriters mingled with a dozen or so stacks of boxes. I put the dead flies and spiders out of my mind.

I gathered the disused skates and tennis rackets, which I had originally planned to donate. Until I told Ted. He insisted I keep everything. Reusable or beyond repair, it didn't matter. Every item reminded him of Annie, growing up and learning to accept her height, her strength, and her ability.

Once I got past the gear—deposited and wrapped in a canvas drop cloth—I carried the lamps one at a time down the trapdoor ladder and out to the trash. Next, I eyed the row of cardboard boxes slumped under an eave. My heart sank. Some were so dilapidated I doubted they'd survive the move. Still, I knew better than to discard anything. Ted again. It had become a family joke. He kept everything—all his books, all his projects, even papers and notebooks from high school.

I remembered the shelves of mismatched cracked and chipped crockery in Jeanne's kitchen, how Ted had laughed at her habit of preserving every teacup and saucer, no matter how badly damaged. Waste not, want not. Born in hard times, she had survived two world wars, thanks to this principle. And her faith. It wasn't a matter of "God will provide"; it was a matter of "God helps those who help themselves." Since one could never know what the future might bring, it was best to prepare for the worst.

Ted's practice leaned more toward the metaphysical. He preserved his past, weaving it into the present, in the same way he combined different woods in the complex inlays he created. To him, to truly understand your own life, you had to fold in the strands, keeping track of each day, every experience, in a constant development of context and texture. "How can you learn anything about yourself if you don't remember who you were yesterday, or the day before, or last year?"

I tackled the box of Christmas ornaments first. That box, at least, seemed sturdy and undamaged. After I carried it downstairs, I started on the rest, sliding them over to the trapdoor and carrying them one at a time down to the landing. The last carton, its commercial label barely visible, began to fall apart as soon as I gave it a tug. I stopped to adjust my grip. But before I could gather it up, the whole thing collapsed with a sigh.

In the dim light, I got my first glimpse of the contents. Instantly, I was standing at the end of a corridor lined with doors, one of them ajar. A narrow beam of light crossed the floor in front of me. I knew what I'd find on the other side.

On top of the pile, I found the syllabus for my seminar with Hal Rose, the one about the novel, with a note penciled in the top right corner: "Wed., 2 p.m., office." At that meeting, the week before I gave my paper, he talked; I pretended to listen. Now the scene replayed like a silent movie. Hal tilted his chair back, snugged his belt, and smiled at me. I tried to ignore the prickling at the back of my neck and looked up at the ceiling rose, its curved petals and leaves shaped by someone who obviously had never observed a real one. Wasn't this what Hal Rose had tried to do to *Le Grand Meaulnes*? Shape it to fit his theory? Until I came up with a better idea, and he helped Danielle to steal it.

Of course I had been naïve to think I would find my way at Brookton, in the belief that as long as I remained true to my own ideas, I would manage, get through, and do what I wanted with my degree. The admonition in Hal's smile had been unmistakable. "Play by our rules, or you don't stand a chance." But, just like Jack, he had misread me. I wasn't willing to capitulate. Hadn't capitulated.

In a folder under the syllabus, I found my paper about *Le Grand Meaulnes* and the offprint of Danielle's article. The offprint was heavily underscored in red: passages Danielle had copied verbatim from my paper cross-referenced to the original.

Had I done the right thing not to report her plagiarism?

I considered the strikes against me: first, the department itself, hierarchical, arbitrary, and hypocritical. Superior power and influence might have given you an edge; but it was how you manipulated others that determined the outcome. There was no question that Danielle had been better at that than I.

The second strike against me: my fear of confrontation prevented me from learning—and using—the rules of engagement. I had given up, surrendered without a fight.

Last, I had lacked an advocate, someone I trusted who understood me—and the system—who could have helped me to step out of myself, master the rules, and defend myself. If I had to deal with the same situation today, could I be my own advocate and take my case against Danielle to the department and to the dean?

Yes. But I would not. I would do today exactly as I had done then—by choice. It had surely been a fight worth fighting. But only at great cost. And for what purpose, in the end? Even without the miscarriage, even without Danielle's plagiarism, I would have left Brookton, because I couldn't change the system. And I wouldn't change myself.

Then, I hadn't known that I would find a career that would satisfy my need to do my own work, work that would combine activities I enjoyed and was good at—drawing and gardening.

I put the paper and the offprint back in the box and taped it shut. On it, I wrote: *Recycle*.

September 18, 1992

Annie had parked her VW behind Ted's truck, leaving space in the garage for me. I looked up at the house, remembering how Milou had always come out to the front steps to greet me. Had she known all along I would come back to live here, that Prospect Hill would become my home?

The house made no claim to be anything but what it was: a plain, square, story-and-a-half Cape. Clad in white clapboards, its broad granite steps ended at a classic raised-panel door. There were four green shuttered windows on the first floor, two on each side of the door. When I was eight, my grandfather set up a stepstool for me and showed me how to pull the shutters closed to keep out the winter drafts. Over the front door, four narrow panes, their glass as old as the house, transformed the sunlight into flickering, swirling patterns on the floor of the narrow entry hall.

Annie came out the front door. In jeans and a T-shirt, her hair pulled back in a loose ponytail, she looked fit. And happy. I waved. Just then, the sun slipped beneath the tops of the maples, their foliage flashing gold and orange against the lavender sky over the new studios.

Although I had seen photographs of it as it progressed, the building startled me. Not that it was obtrusive. Far from it. Ethan had promised he would make it fit the site, and he had largely succeeded. The landscaping I had planned would finish the job. What surprised me was its size. It was larger than I'd expected. I waved at Ted at the bottom of the hill. He held up both arms, opening and closing his hands twice.

Beside me, Annie laughed. "What's he doing?"

"Two times ten fingers? Looks like he'll join us in twenty minutes."

"So we'd better talk about Dad first. And fast."

In the living room, Annie sat on the couch; I relaxed into Milou's wing chair, its familiar contours folding around me like a hug.

"He seems more tired now than he did a month ago. But maybe I'm expecting too much? I met someone the other day; her sister had Lyme disease. They thought she was okay after the treatment, but then it came back. Isn't that what the IV treatment will prevent?"

A month ago, Ted had assured me he was feeling much better. To be sure they had cured him, Al Jacobson asked him to come down to Boston for a checkup. Ted had finally made an appointment when I convinced him that *I* needed to know what was going on, even if he didn't.

"We'll find out at the end of October. By then, it'll have been four months." I watched Annie's face, forcing myself to breathe slowly, shifting my gaze beyond the living room to the garden. I didn't want to talk about my own concerns, at least not until after I'd spoken to Ted.

Annie sighed. "It's so hard not to know, isn't it?"

I tried to smile.

Annie smiled back. "He seems happy, anyway. About the studio, the workshop, the new designs he's been working on."

Behind us, in the kitchen, the screen door slammed. "And over the moon . . . You're here, at last!"

Like Annie, Ted was tan. Maybe it was the light, but to me he looked thinner—at least thinner than I'd expected. Under the tan, his face seemed hollowed out, drained of energy. Annie stood to give him a hug, turning to me, her eyes anxious again.

"Gotta run. My turn to cook!" She blew us a kiss on her way out.

TED HAD made a salad. While he dressed it, I lit candles and set the table. The conversation that drifted between us strung together bits and pieces of small talk, about Newport and Alden friends and neighbors, the weather, and the garden. Like dancers, we moved toward each other, stepping back into our life together.

"How did it feel to leave?"

"Like I was abandoning them."

"Them?"

"The garden and the tree."

"And the house?"

I had lain awake the night before thinking about Jack and his wife, imagining them moving around, sitting, talking, cooking, all the daily acts of a life in common. Theirs. It had been as if they were already there. I had taken a sleeping bag and spent the rest of the night in the tree house.

"Not the same. Maybe because I'm so glad to be here. Home. This really is home, you know?"

After dinner, we walked down the hill to look at the studios. There'd been another setback, a problem with the windows, Ted told me. He explained how they had had to send back the first batch. The new ones—the right ones, this time—had arrived. So they'd begin installing them sometime in the next few days.

Ted found us each a director's chair and we sat together looking down through the woods to the lake. "We'll have to decide soon who gets which one." His grin carried with it a clear message: it didn't matter to him how we worked out this decision.

"Because?"

"Because we have to figure out which shelves and cabinets to put where. My needs are different from yours, I think."

"Agreed. But we don't have to do that tonight, do we?"

"The end of the week will be soon enough. So this can be ready in time for the housewarming."

He took my hand and we watched the night sky settle over the hills beyond the lake, with only the sound of the crickets in the background. "We have so much catching up to do. All the details about the sale and the movers. I know it's just boring, routine stuff but I still want to hear all about it."

For the last few weeks, I had imagined this moment, imagined telling Ted that John Nelson was Jack. *And isn't that an incredible coincidence?* I wouldn't have to tell him about the phone call. I hadn't called Jack back, after all. But somehow, I knew that telling Ted anything meant telling him everything.

Now.

I'd finally understood that I wasn't afraid to tell Ted about Jack. I was afraid of what Jack wanted. But telling Ted about the phone call meant letting Jack back into my life. Ardis had been right about that: Jack had started a conversation, one I didn't want to continue. That was one outcome I could control. The intrusion of this painful episode from my past into the present must go no further, especially not now. Ted's illness, supporting him through the next stage of diagnosis and, possibly, another treatment—only that mattered now.

No, Ted did not need to know that John Nelson was Jack.

"There isn't much to tell, really. I never met them, as you know. The closing is all set. We'll get the papers as soon as the legal work is done and the check is deposited." I managed the half-truth without wavering.

"Is that really it? As simple as that?"

"You mean, how do I really feel about selling the house?"

"I know it's a done deal. But somehow I get a sense that there's still unfinished business. Or maybe I'm just feeling that way because I wasn't there at the end to help you organize the move and deal with the movers."

There was so little light now that I couldn't see Ted's face. "You're right about the unfinished business part. But I'm a little embarrassed to talk about it."

"What do you mean?"

"He'll—*they'll*—be living there. In our house." I would feel the same way about anyone who bought the house.

"Malorie . . ."

"I know. I *know* it's not ours anymore. But I still feel as if they're intruding—especially in the garden. And in our life."

Ted gave a short laugh. "You sound like Annie. She told you, didn't she? When I first told her we were selling the house, she wanted us to take down the tree house so no one else would have it." He squeezed my hand. "Would you feel differently if they were strangers?"

"If they were strangers? What do you mean?" Could he hear the panic in my voice?

"Well, if you hadn't been there the day they came to see the house. There you were, out in the garden, imagining them walking through the house, talking about it to each other and to Steve. That must have been hard."

"You could be right. But when I got here this afternoon, as soon as I walked in—the familiar smells, the light in the living room—it was as if Milou herself were alive still to welcome me. But Beech Street will always be our first home. It may not have felt like *home* to me the way Prospect Hill does. Still, we made it ours."

"Tomorrow morning, you'll see. Starting with the garden. It's desperate for some TLC. And you have another garden to work on, the one around the studios. For Milou and for us." Ted put his arm around me.

I leaned my head on his shoulder. "I just need time now to settle in." I felt his nod. "And you? Are you settled in?"

He pulled back from me to answer. "I really am. Details to follow."

October 1, 1992

I took Steve's call the weekend before the housewarming. He'd be driving up to Alden for the party with Sandor. If we hadn't yet received the papers for the Beech Street deal, he could bring them with him.

I stood looking out the window with its view of the stone wall and the woods beyond. A movement toward the bottom of the hill distracted me. Barely visible in the shade at the bottom of the hill, a fox stood, its front paws resting on the stone wall. It flicked its ears and turned to look toward the house. Its eyes, shining out of the shadow, seemed to focus on the window, watching me watching it.

"Malorie? Are you still there?"

"Yes. Sorry. We did get the papers. Last week, in fact. So, just bring yourself."

"There's one more thing."

Had I left something in the house? I had checked thoroughly after the movers left. Still, I could have overlooked books or files tucked into a corner somewhere. I glanced down the hill. The fox stood there still, its head now turned away from the house. Listening? Waiting?

"It's not a big deal." Perhaps sensing my apprehension, he put a smile in his voice.

"John Nelson asked me to give him your phone number up there. He didn't say why."

So Steve didn't know about me and Jack. I felt a rush of relief at first, then irritation.

I forced myself to keep my answer neutral and short. "No" would do it. But that, surely, would make Steve curious. It would be better for this to be one of those things he could let go of, even forget.

"Why don't you just tell him to call you or the lawyer? You're both there, after all. And we're up here. Anything about the house, anything that might come up, that would be the best thing to do. Everything he needs to know is in the binder I left. He can always check that."

"Binder? What binder?"

"The one with the lists of repair people and explanations about the garden."

"Oh. Right. I gave it to them at the closing. So I'll find out what's on his mind and pass along your message."

I swallowed. "Anyway, for now, our number is unlisted. We're still working on getting the business side of things squared away. We'll both have listed numbers later."

"Of course. I understand." He cleared his throat. "How is Ted, Malorie? How is he really, is what I'm asking. And how are you?" He sounded tentative, apologetic, as if worried he might be prying.

"Still gaining weight and sleeping fine. Ted, that is." We both laughed. "Nearly normal, I'd say. We'll know more after his next checkup. Meanwhile, the house is in good order. Everything's unpacked and put away. Best of all, the studios are almost finished and we're negotiating now. So far, I seem to be winning."

"Negotiating? Winning?"

"I've got the best views. But Ted has access to the workshop. Which is, after all, his space." I smiled to hear Steve yawn, relaxing at last. "You'll see next week."

A movement in the underbrush beyond the stone wall alerted me. The fox disappeared into the woods.

October 10, 1992

Friday night before the housewarming party, we had a dusting of frost, just enough to transform everything it touched. Early the next morning, piles of maple and oak leaves sprawled over the glistening grasses and underbrush in red and gold banners, honoring the season.

Ted and I put out three folding tables on the front lawn, and a smaller table, for the coffee urn, wine, and apple cider, along the edge. A neighbor's teenaged son and his girlfriend set out plates, glasses, and tableware. By one thirty, when Annie and Josie arrived, Ardis, my mother, and I had finished in the kitchen. We sat on the front steps, awaiting early arrivals.

"No one objected that you closed at noon?"

"One customer arrived just as we locked up." Annie cast a sidelong glance at Josie, stifling a smile.

"Annie actually told her to read the sign." Josie's can-you-believe-it tone underscored how unlike Annie this was. Normally, she was the one who stayed late at the shop to accommodate someone who "just had to have" a particular book right away.

"She wanted to know how 'Gone partying' was a good reason to close early, even on a Saturday." Annie shrugged and turned toward the tables, their checked tablecloths weighted down with stones. "Looks like you're all set."

"For now, yes. Never fear. You're on the cleanup crew."

At two o'clock, guests began to arrive in twos and threes. Some brought casseroles that required warming up. We arranged everything else on the serving tables. When Ted finished helping Sandor park, he glanced up at me. I thought I saw someone else in the car. Before I could take a closer look, Annie came to ask for help with the oven. I sent her out to help Sandor unload his car while I fitted a piece of foil over a baking dish of scalloped potatoes.

"Malorie?"

"Ellen? What a nice surprise. I thought you had other plans?"

"Me too. They canceled. I caught Sandor just in time. Lucky for me!"

"Lucky for us!" I hugged her and slid the potatoes into the oven. I took a quick look around the kitchen, at the platters of vegetables, the casseroles, and desserts, remembering Jeanne's funeral reception, almost exactly eighteen years ago. It had been a day like this, clear and bright. Too much food. Everyone sharing memories and tears. No tears today. I could hear Milou scolding me gently: *Ne cherche pas midi à quatorze heures, chérie.* I pushed away my apprehension about Ted's upcoming appointment. *No, Milou, I won't go looking for trouble.*

"Is everything okay?"

"Do you think we have enough food?"

Ellen made a show of looking around at the tables and counters laden with food. "We could always call out for Chinese."

Annie and Josie came to the kitchen door.

"Annie? Josie? Ellen's here. Come say hi!"

They walked in, side by side, holding each other close, both struggling to keep a straight face. As soon as they cleared the door, a white standard poodle puppy pushed by them, ears and tail aloft.

"Chloe!"

The puppy stopped and sat, looking up at Ellen, ears pricked, tail thumping the floor.

"What a good girl. You must be one of Jasmine's babies." When I crouched down to her, Chloe nuzzled my cheek and leaned against me, panting.

"She's the only one left, five months old this week. Doesn't she look like Jaz?" Ellen's eyes gleamed with approval.

"And Lulu! Are you going to keep her?" I stroked Chloe's curly topknot.

Ted, Sandor, and Steve had crowded into the kitchen, along with Ardis and my mother, all avoiding eye contact with each other and with me.

"What did I miss? Could someone please clue me in?" I hugged Chloe, who had squirmed into my lap and put her head on my shoulder. She licked my ear. We all laughed.

"Dad?"

"Annie?"

The two of them began to talk at the same time. Everyone else clapped and hooted. Like a conductor rapping his baton for attention, Chloe barked twice. Order returned. Ted cleared his throat and looked down at me, sitting cross-legged on the floor with Chloe half in, half out of my lap.

"Ellen called me a couple of weeks ago to tell me her plans had changed, so she could come up for the party. She wanted to know what she could bring." He paused and looked around the room. "I'm sure she expected me to say wine or cheese."

Ellen grinned.

"I knew she had one of Jasmine's puppies left. Even without seeing her or meeting her, I decided Chloe would be a perfect addition to our family—and our new place. It's a bit late in coming, I know. But I wanted to give you a special birthday present." He leaned over and kissed the top of my head. *"Joyeux anniversaire, ma belle!"*

I scrambled to my feet to hug him. Chloe pawed at me, pushing her head against us both. "I love her already." My voice caught. I'd said enough.

Ellen went to get the dog crate from Steve's car, and Ted and I walked Chloe around the garden. While she sniffed every leaf and blossom, looking up at us occasionally, wagging her tail, we admired her. Her undercoat had a faint apricot tinge; her dense topcoat was cream-colored. I kept patting her topknot; I couldn't stop smiling.

Meanwhile, Annie, Josie, Ardis, and my mother carried platters and casseroles from the kitchen out to tables on the front lawn. Several children entertained themselves doing logrolls and somersaults down the hill while their parents made the rounds, catching up with one another.

At four, Ted banged once on Milou's garden gong. "Ladies and gentlemen, as your designated guide, I invite you to join me now for a tour of the latest addition to the Prospect Hill campus, the Annex."

Several called out, "Go, Ted! Pass the hat!" Someone whistled. "First come, first served!"

As I watched the first group head down the hill after Ted, I overheard someone comment that if you didn't know the building was there, you wouldn't notice it. Ethan would be pleased. He had tucked it into the hill and had given it a green roof. "It's probably the first one in Vermont," he told us. "There will be others. Count on it."

THE GREEN roof blended completely into the meadow, just another natural feature of the landscape.

"So smart." Ellen's enthusiasm didn't surprise me. In many ways, she and Ethan had the same outlook. She pulled out a photo album to show me. "He took a look at these latest snaps of your meadow at my place. He had no idea you did this kind of work."

"You make it sound like I've done dozens." The effects of texture and contour, the mingling of grasses and shrubs, had worked out even better than I'd hoped. I was happy, too, to see the boulders settling into their new context. At first, they'd seemed obtrusive— naked and monumental. After two years, with the waves of grass lapping around them, they looked like the islands I'd envisioned in my plan.

"Maybe not, but that's one of the things I want to talk to you about. A couple, friends of mine, just bought an old potato farm on Long Island. They need an architect and a landscape architect, preferably people who can collaborate from the start." Her eyes lit up. "You and Ethan would be a dream team." She leaned toward me, intent. "What do you think?"

"Sounds like a great project. But I have work to do here—soon, before it gets cold—and there's Ted. He's a lot better, but not well yet. There's the appointment in Boston. Can your friends wait until the spring?"

Ellen's gaze shifted from me. She was looking over my shoulder. I turned around.

Ethan had joined us. He stood behind me, listening in. "I told Ellen pretty much the same thing. We have some loose ends here, just for starters."

"Also, I'm not a landscape architect, you know. Sandor—he's the landscape architect—had as much to do with the design I did for Ellen as I did." In fact, I had probably learned as much about landscape architecture from Sandor as I would have in a formal course. But my lack of a degree might matter to Ellen's friends.

Ellen shook her head, smiling. "I know Sandor weighed in from time to time. But the idea was yours, after all, and, besides, you have the eye, and the hands-on experience, to take this on. There's a work-around in here somewhere." She snapped her fingers. "Here's an idea: I'll ask them to send you some photos, a site plan, and a map, so you can see what you think, if it's something you're even interested in. Up or down. You could have a conference call with them. Would that work?"

Ethan laughed.

I patted Ellen's shoulder. "Now you see why no one ever says no to her!" I smiled at Ethan. I knew it wouldn't take us long to figure out if the project was interesting and doable. That, we could manage. We shook on it.

The sunset was fading behind the last tour group, their silhouettes merging into their elongated shadows; the first stars blinked through a light wash of low-lying clouds. Laughter and teasing went on behind the clatter of folding chairs as the clean-up crew put things away. Ethan and Ellen walked down the hill, toward the studios, continuing their conversation. I helped carry dishes and cutlery into the house. Soon, all that remained of the party were flattened tracks in the grass, traces of the logroll.

"MALORIE?"

"Are you off now?"

Annie held a canvas picnic bag in one hand, a container of food in the other.

"Soon. Josie's helping Lucie with the dishes. We were wondering if we could talk—you, Dad, and us."

"Is everything all right?" Were she and Josie breaking up? Was one of them sick? Had they decided to give up the bookshop?

Annie's face fell. She struggled to smile. "Everything is fine. We have an idea and we'd like to hear what you think. That's it. Really."

"I'll find Ted. Shall we meet down at the 'Annex'?" Her laughter silenced my apprehension and lifted my spirits.

I went into the house to get Chloe and walked out through the kitchen, where Josie and my mother were drying the dishes; Ardis was putting everything away. "We're going for a quick walk. Back soon." I caught Josie's eye. "See you down the hill?"

"On my way."

"Be careful!" my mother called over her shoulder to me.

Talking to Chloe, feeling how to manage her on the leash, I wondered at my mother's warning. What had she meant, anyway? Small flickers of apprehension told me I wasn't yet in the clear.

In his studio, Ted had begun to shelve books next to the worktable. He greeted me with a sheepish look. "I couldn't wait to get started on this." He leaned over to pat Chloe. "So, how do you like your new digs, Chloe?"

Chloe lifted her head, grinning up at him. She pawed his knee.

"I'll take it that means 'very much.'" Ted laughed softly and stroked her head.

In one smooth motion, the puppy gathered herself on her haunches and stood up on her hind legs to put her front paws on Ted's chest. He hugged her. "I suppose we shouldn't encourage this, but she's certainly careful about how she does it."

"Malorie? Dad?"

"Come join us." Ted pulled out a couple of stools.

As soon as they settled, Annie took Josie's hand. "Here goes. We . . ." She shook her head, started over. "Everything's fine."

She looked down at the floor, then out the window, everywhere but at us. "It's . . ."

". . . bigger than a breadbox?"

Laughter broke the tension, filling the studio like a warm breeze. Lying between Ted and me on the floor, Chloe looked from face to face, as if trying to reach a decision. At last she stood and walked over to Annie, leaning against her, panting slightly.

"You could say that, yes." Annie curled her fingers into Chloe's topknot, looked at Josie, and took a deep breath. "Josie and I want to have a baby."

I opened my mouth to say—what? What could I say? What should I say?

Annie and Josie held one another, trying not to cry. Chloe had pushed her way between them, nuzzling them.

Ted stood and opened his arms to them. "We couldn't ask for a better housewarming gift."

They looked at me. Surprise, wonder, fear, and, yes, envy, coursed through me. I had to say something. I started toward them, to hug them. Once again, I heard my mother. *Be careful.* Whatever I said had to come from my heart.

"Nothing, *nothing*, could please me more, Annie and Josie. I am happy for you, for our whole family. Tell us everything."

Annie smiled. "There are lots of details."

"Tell us."

Chloe, who had been following every word, lay down by Josie and began to chew one of her shoelaces.

"We thought about adopting, but then we found out about a way to have our own baby. There's a clinic in Burlington and we chose a donor and . . ."

"And?"

"We—*I*, I should say—had one false start. But we'll keep trying. It could take some time." Annie stopped and looked at Josie, then at Ted and me. "It sounds weird when I say it like that. The point is that I'm going to go first. But I don't want Josie to miss out on her own chance."

Josie cleared her throat. "What Annie isn't saying is that I'm so disorganized, we think it's a good idea for her to do the dress rehearsal, to help us figure out how to manage the whole thing."

"You are *somewhat* disorganized. But you'll have a chance and I'll help you. That's what I'm saying. We'll do it together." She hugged Josie.

"Have you told anyone else?"

"Josie's mom. She's already knitting booties. I'm going to wait until we know for sure to tell Mom." Annie stood up. "Lucie. I told her, too." She looked down at the floor, then at me. "Guess what she said?"

Ted and I waited.

"She said it was 'glorious news'!"

"She's absolutely right about that." I replayed my mother's warning. This time, I heard the smile in her voice.

"We'd better go say good night to her. And Ardis. Maybe we'll see you next weekend?" They hugged us. Chloe got up to go with them.

"Chloe, stay!" Chloe turned around several times and sank down with a contented sigh.

WHEN WE could no longer hear Annie and Josie, I pulled the director's chairs closer together. "You first." I leaned back. "What do you think?"

"I admire and support them."

"But you're afraid for them? Or anxious, at least?"

"Yeah. Anxious."

"They've got good friends up there, all of them living somewhat unconventional lives. They, at least, will rally around them, and it will be okay."

"For now, anyway."

"One thing." I stopped. An owl hooted somewhere down by the lake. "Annie was right. It could take awhile. We'll need to prepare for that, to help them." After all Ted and I had been through, this, at least, was something we knew about.

"And then there's Claire." Ted's tone told me how much he dreaded Claire's reaction. "She tolerates their relationship, but that's all. If—when—they have a baby . . ."

"Two babies!" I couldn't help laughing.

"I'm not sure how she'll react."

"And your father?"

"I won't tell him until the baby arrives. We'll see." Ted sighed. "One thing we can be sure of, your mother will be standing by."

We sat for a while longer, looking down into the dark woods. Chloe snored lightly. A breeze had come up.

Once, I'd watched an ice floe break apart out on the lake. I had that feeling now, as if my own energy, pent up through the summer of selling the house, my apprehension about Jack, packing to move, holding back on decisions and plans, had begun to carry me along to the next bend in the river. I let the idea of the potato farm project float for a while, enjoying the first flickers of excitement and hope.

On the Tuesday after the party, I spent the morning mulching the border along the stone wall. Around eleven, Chloe began to bark. A squirrel? A passing cat? Someone at the door? After less than a week with us, did she already understand what to bark at or when? I had no idea. I started up the hill. As soon as I rounded the corner of the house, the DHL messenger saw me and came down the front steps with a package from Isabelle. In the living room, I sat in Milou's chair and opened it. Delighted to have me to herself, Chloe darted into the kitchen and came back with her ball.

"Soon, I promise."

She cocked her head, as if analyzing the meaning of "soon," and lay down at my feet.

Ted came in just as I pulled off the wrapping paper. "You look stunned."

"You're just in time. There's a letter, too. We can read it together."

He looked down over my shoulder at Théo's oil portrait of Milou, the one he had given to Henri before he ran away.

"I'll read what Isabelle says, shall I?"

Ted sat down beside Chloe.

Isabelle knew that Henri had promised the painting to me. She had kept it after he died, planning to give it to me the next time Ted and I visited. As soon as I wrote to her about the move to Prospect Hill, she had decided to send the portrait. "Consider it Henri and Milou's gift to you both—a housewarming gift."

Ted got up. "It makes me happy that my grandmother, Milou, and Henri all had something to do with its reappearance in our lives." He walked around the living room, eyeing the walls.

"What do you say we hang it right here?" He held it against the wall next to me, close to the wing chair.

The narrow wall between the fireplace and the bookshelves had room only for something the size of the small painting. Before his eyesight failed him, Henri had made a frame for it, with a scroll inlay of light and dark wood. Henri's frame and the wall itself made a perfect setting.

I looked into Milou's eyes, felt the warmth of her smile and her gaze. "Doesn't it feel to you as though we've brought them all home?"

"All?"

"Jeanne, Milou, and Henri."

"And Théo. They were together in Flagy when Théo painted Milou's portrait. It's as though they've found one another again."

So he knew? "How long have you known about Théo?"

He put his arms around me. "Henri told me after Jeanne died."

Henri had asked Ted not to tell Bruno. So he hadn't. "My father has grieved enough."

We both looked at the portrait. Although neither of us spoke of it then, I believe we both sought and found Milou's agreement in her smile.

Unintended Consequences

March 12, 1993

"How's it going down there?"

"It's a zoo. Almost twice as many exhibitors as there were two years ago. New people, a few new ideas. Lots of younger people now." He laughed. "It's great to be back in circulation."

Last year, Ted had been too sick to attend the Providence fine furniture show, so Andrew had gone instead. Andrew was there again this year, taking turns with Ted at the booth. "I've been catching up on the gossip. Everyone says the rare wood market is only going to get tighter, especially since the sustainable forests idea is taking hold. Supply and demand, the old story."

Over the background noise of the convention center, I heard someone call out to Ted. "Should I try you again later?"

"I'm not sure later will make any difference. Before I forget, have you heard about the storm?"

"Down there?"

"We just found out there's a doozy of a nor'easter moving north; big snow, big wind. It started snowing here a couple of hours ago. Not a big deal yet, but I called Ethan, just in case. There's plenty of wood in the garage, if the power goes out."

"Don't worry about us. We've got plenty to eat and lots of candles." The woodstove in the kitchen and the living room fireplace would keep the first floor of the house warm enough.

Chloe and I would be fine. *As long as the pipes don't freeze.* I kept this to myself. No need to give Ted something else to worry about. "I haven't had a snow day for a long time. Chloe will be happy to keep me company." There was no backup heating system for the studios. Maybe this storm would give us reason to regret putting that off until next year.

"What about you? Are you feeling okay?"

In October, all the tests came up negative—there was no evidence of damage in Ted's brain or central nervous system and no sign of the bacterium anywhere. Even so, off and on, he had had spells of fatigue and pain. Thanks to CompuServe, he could manage the business paperwork. But he had to pace himself. Now that he had the workshop in Alden, having to take it easy frustrated him.

"Andrew's making sure I behave." From the way he said this, I knew Andrew was listening in. "There isn't much for me to do, thanks to him. He's got everything at his fingertips. Wish I could say the same. Any calls?"

"I heard your phone a couple of times. The machine will give you a full report." We had an agreement not to answer one another's business calls. "I spent the morning making lists and putting material together to discuss with Ethan on Monday." Ethan and I had had two phone conversations with Ellen's friends about the farm on Long Island. "We're going to look at the photographs, the plat map, and the new surveys they sent. We both have questions. We'll see."

"Think you'll be able to make a decision?"

"Maybe. Until we have some idea about how to handle the whole thing, I'll be up in the air. You know me."

Ted chuckled. "You could say that. Any other news?"

"Annie left a short message. On the house phone."

"How did she sound?"

"Excited. And anxious. I think she forgot you're away." After a second false start on their pregnancy, Annie and Josie had been waiting to hear the results of their third try. I guessed this was Annie's reason for calling.

I shut off my computer and turned the studio thermostat down to fifty-five. There was no point in leaving it set at sixty-five if there was a power outage. And if there wasn't, the thermostat's timer would go on as usual in the morning.

On my way up to the house, I stopped at the mailbox at the foot of the driveway. Chloe ran around me, snapping and barking at the clumps of snow that tumbled from the branches above us. It was just warm enough for the ice on the eaves to melt, dripping into the drains below. Out of nowhere, a squall blew up, darkening the sky, dumping fresh snow on us. In the flurry, for a moment I could see only Chloe's eyes, onyx chips gleaming through the frothy snow. She spun around, then hopped stiff-legged toward the house, shaking it off.

I moved the teakettle from the top of the woodstove to a stove burner. The pile of mail I'd set on the table included the usual assortment of plant and seed catalogs. The grays and browns of mid-March made a mockery of their lavish display of high summer's colors. It was too soon even to fantasize about how the border along the stone wall would look in July.

As I dropped the catalogs into the trash barrel in the garage, a flash of white caught my eye. I pushed the catalogs aside and retrieved the envelope addressed to me. Forwarded by the post office in Newport, it bore no return address, but I recognized Jack's handwriting. He had written to me twice before. Those letters I'd burned unread.

I made a cup of tea, taking my time, my mind blank. Chloe snuffled and stretched, settling into a nap under the table.

The only thing worse than knowing the worst is not knowing it. Wouldn't it be better to read Jack's letter, even though I might, this time, have to do something about it—about him? If I didn't read the letter, I'd be stuck like a fly on flypaper in my dread of receiving another letter, paralyzed by my own indecision. The cloud of not knowing would remain, hanging over my head, weighing me down.

There was another consideration, as well: I still hadn't told Ted about Jack. The letters made it harder not to. Each one felt like a nudge to just get it over with. The longer I waited, the more Ted would wonder why I hadn't told him in the beginning.

Chloe whimpered in her sleep. When I sat down at the table, she opened her eyes and lifted her head.

"In a little while, Chloe. Go back to sleep." I slit open the envelope with a table knife and read.

Dear Malorie,

It's so strange to send my letters to you at the Beech Street address, but I know the post office is still forwarding your mail. I'm writing to you from the kitchen. I imagine you in this house, going about your daily life, and try to see it as you did. It must have reminded you of your mother's place. It even smells the same—to me, anyway. Wood smoke, old wood, plaster.

Jack and I had spent a spring weekend at the house in Long Meadow. I had been studying for my orals; Jack had had papers to grade. It surprised me that the Long Meadow house had made such a strong impression on him. Except when he was taking pictures, he never seemed to pay much attention to his surroundings.

Sometimes when I'm alone here, I close my eyes to listen—just now in the kitchen, say. I'll hear a floorboard creak, or the sound of the wind in the big chimney. It's as if someone else is here. Then I open my eyes. To tell you the truth, I'm always a bit surprised not to find you here.

The other day, on Thames Street near the post office, I spotted a woman about your height who looked so much like you that I ran after her. I startled her, but she was nice about it. We had a good laugh.

Brookton seems so far away, such a long time ago. I'm not the person I was then. I can hardly remember who that was. And yet, I see you so clearly still, as you were, I should say. But you must have changed, too. I wonder how?

I want to see you.

Jack

PS: I kept all the photos from our first Desmond visit. I don't think you knew then how beautiful you were. I imagine you still are.

AS SOON as she heard why I was calling, Ardis cut me off. "Don't summarize it. Read me the whole thing."

There was something about the letter that struck me when I read it aloud. In it, Jack said nothing about the first two. Why not? Didn't he at least wonder why I hadn't replied? There was no rancor, no recrimination.

"It's not surprising he wants to see you, is it? Still, his persistence is a bit weird."

"Pushy. But that's just the way he is."

"Yes, and creepy—to me, anyway, all that talk about imagining you in the house. About keeping the pictures from the afternoon at the park. Something like this happened to a friend. After the guy sent her several letters—she didn't answer them—she found him parked across the street one morning. She went to the police. At least keep the letters just in case?"

"Too late. I burned the first two; didn't read them. I hoped he'd leave me alone when I didn't write back."

"You could write to him now. Tell him to stop."

"If only I were sure that would work. The problem for me is that the more I think about this, the more annoyed I get. And the more stuck I feel. I can't help remembering how often I felt like this when we were together."

"What did you do about it back then?"

"Nothing. I'd had plenty of practice just pushing my feelings down, stifling them, you could say. That's how I dealt with my father."

"I see. Well, now you don't have to put up with it. And you have to decide what to do about Ted. Isn't that more important?"

"I know I have to tell him. But how? And when?"

"You're giving that talk for the Newport Garden Club in April, right?"

"That's in May."

"What if Jack finds out and comes to hear you?"

"You mean, I should talk to Ted before then?"

"I would. He might not want you to go down there alone."

"That's the best reason *not* to tell Ted."

"What do you mean?"

"*If* Jack shows up at my talk, I don't want Ted there. I'd feel as though I were hiding behind him or something." I sighed. "I don't know. Really, truly. I just don't."

Ardis mentioned the storm. I looked out the window at the overcast sky and the snowflakes drifting by. They were huge, some as large as a half dollar. Maybe we were on the fringe of the system; maybe we'd be spared the wind, at least.

I REREAD Jack's letter. I couldn't ignore the feeling that he was lurking nearby. Ardis was right. It was like being stalked.

Jack, Brookton, the miscarriage, Danielle's plagiarism—all that had faded from my memory. It was understandable that Jack's return revived them. But I had another life now. Why, after twenty-three years, was I having such a hard time with this? I didn't owe him an explanation. Sure, I'd been wrong about Brookton—it hadn't been the right choice for me, no more than Jack, himself, had been. But I'd started over. I'd found what I wanted to do. So why couldn't I put the past behind me? Why couldn't I leave whatever was unfinished alone? Or, at least, accept that it *was* unfinished and that nothing I could say or do would change that?

I hadn't been in love with Jack. Had he been in love with me? Is that why he couldn't let me go, as if loving me then gave him a reason to pursue me now? I couldn't know his motives. I wondered if he did. I needed to give very careful thought to what to do about the letter, and about the possibility—no matter how tenuous—that Jack would show up at my talk for the Garden Club in May.

Twenty-three years ago, that last, explosive phone conversation with him had been the catalyst. A new path had opened, the one leading to Flagy. Had I told Jack about the miscarriage, he would have expected me to explain why I hadn't told him about the pregnancy. Would an explanation have made any difference? Would it have led us to a new, more open and honest relationship? I would never know. Anyway, what did it matter now?

As hurt and angry as I had been that day when Jack hung up on me, I had also felt relieved—and released. Somehow, I had to get back to that place.

Chloe stood and stretched, her dark eyes focused on me. She went to the back door and nuzzled the leash draped over the handle. Time for her afternoon walk. Maybe by the time we got back, I'd have figured out what to do about Jack's letter—and Jack.

OUTSIDE, THE thin wintery light belied the smell of thawing soil and the rush of snowmelt heading down our driveway. Chloe strained at the leash, pulling me past the studios toward the road. She knew the routine as well as I: our regular afternoon walk took us down Prospect Street into the village, to the Congregational church, past the post office, around the cemetery, then home. When the roads were dry and clear, the two-mile circuit took an hour, at most. Depending on the weather, it could take us longer today.

The sky grew darker, heavier, pressing down on us. Across the lake, a snow squall draped a ragged curtain over the hillside; a light snow began to fall and the wind picked up. By the time we reached the church, our halfway point, fine, needle-sharp flakes swirled around us.

"Home, Chloe!"

Slippery under its coating of fresh snow, the road was difficult to see through the thickly falling flakes and the late-afternoon gloom. A flock of Canada geese flew above us, near enough to hear their wing beats, but hidden from sight in the churning snow. They were headed to shelter from the storm.

Struggling to keep my footing, I leaned into the wind, now pummeling us from all directions. On both sides of us, tall fir trees whipped from side to side, their boughs swooping up and down. Chloe paused repeatedly to shake off the snow as it accumulated on her head and back. I pulled my hat down and my collar up, leaving an opening just wide enough to see through. I had a snow mask, but I hadn't expected I'd need it.

At the foot of the last rise, Chloe balked. I knelt beside her, brushing off the snow, checking her all over for an injury. We hadn't been out long enough for her to have frostbite. What else could it be?

As soon as I lifted her right front foot, I found the problem: tiny balls of ice—snow that had melted, then frozen—had formed in the hair between her toes. I took off my glove and removed as much of it as I could. She pranced in place, then leapt ahead, dragging me behind her the rest of the way. Just as we reached the driveway, a wind squall hit us, pushing me against the mailbox and into the snowdrift beside it. Chloe cowered next to me, whining. A groan, then a shriek followed by a muffled crash, came from somewhere close by. A tree had gone down. But where?

In the moment of calm that followed the squall, I saw the dark shape of a sugar maple, lying across the street. It had fallen over the spot where Chloe and I had stopped. We'd had a narrow escape.

AS SOON as I opened the door, I heard the phone. The ringing stopped before the answering machine clicked on. Annie? Ted?

I turned the thermostat to seventy, pulled out all the beach towels, and stripped off my wet clothes. Chloe lay on the floor, panting. Her dense, curly coat had accumulated a thick cover of snow and ice. Once I'd cleared most of it off, I blotted her with towels and used the blow-dryer to finish the job. She lifted her head to lick my hand. Soon the kitchen smelled of drying dog.

The phone rang again. This time the answering machine took over. "All's well. Call me back when you can. The blizzard is likely to hit you tonight. Well, it's March. What can you expect? I can't remember if you have plans. Call me, please." At the sound of Ted's voice, Chloe thumped her tail.

I called Ted back. It took only minutes to tell him about our walk and the downed maple. It was four fifteen. We'd been gone for a little over an hour. "What's it like there?"

"It's a serious storm, all right. I'll have to stay here until Monday, at least." Power outages, strong winds, and drifts had made driving hazardous throughout New England. All the airports had shut down, and a travel advisory had been posted warning people not to drive, except in cases of medical emergency.

ANNIE PICKED up on the first ring. I gave her a quick report about the tree blocking the road.

"You'll stay home, right?"

"Of course." I shuddered, thinking about our narrow escape.

Just then, a gust of wind shook the house hard enough to rattle the pots on their hooks and the dishes in the cupboard. The lights flickered. I wondered if the house had ever been through another storm like this. I certainly hadn't.

"I tried to call you earlier, around four fifteen. Josie and I got some great news today."

Josie, on their other line, chimed in, "Really great news!"

Annie had had the same exultant tone the morning she found and rescued Tigrette and her kittens. I laughed. Josie sounded just like her.

"Do you want to wait until Ted gets home?"

"We can't wait another minute. You can tell him when you talk to him again." She took a deep breath. "Josie and I are twelve weeks pregnant—officially pregnant, that is—and I am officially just fine." Strong at the beginning, her voice trembled at the edge of tears toward the end.

Ted and I had shared Annie and Josie's anxiety and disappointment through three attempts, each one a test of their hopes and their confidence. That Annie hadn't waited to tell Ted first was an immeasurable gift to me. How far we had come, she and I. To share this gift with Ted made it our gift, Annie's and mine. I sat in Milou's chair, savoring my joy and anticipation, long after I'd hung up.

I stoked the woodstove and put a slice of bread in the toaster. That and tea would do for dinner. I got out candles, matches, and flashlights. Just in case. Wrapped in a quilt in her bed in the kitchen, Chloe twitched and sighed, dreaming. The lights flickered again. Gust-driven snow lashed the windows.

Seven thirty felt like midnight.

I collapsed on the sofa in the living room, pulled the coverlet over me, and fell asleep. When I woke in the night, the wind had dropped; scudding clouds filmed the sky, luminous with moonlight. The storm had moved on. I pressed the switch on the floor lamp. Nothing happened. I picked up the flashlight and peered over the top of the sofa. Training the flashlight beam on Chloe, I could see only the top of her head above her quilt.

I pulled on socks, wrapped my robe around me, and went out to the front hall. The thermostat at the foot of the stairs read forty-five degrees. At least the pipes wouldn't freeze. Back in the kitchen, I lit a candle on the counter and added a log to the woodstove. A plume of steam drifted from the spout of the teakettle. I opened a can of chicken broth, poured it into a saucepan, and left it on the woodstove to warm. Chloe lifted her head; her tail moved back and forth under the quilt. I knelt next to her, stroking her head. "Soup's on. But it'll wait. Go back to sleep."

March 13, 1993

The current of warm air flowing around the living room smelled of maple sap and summer breezes. It would soon be light. It was only now, half-asleep on the sofa, that I thought again about Jack's letter. I heard his voice, the way he said my name. He gave it its French pronunciation—equal stress on all three syllables—but it always sounded off. He wasn't French, so the miss wasn't his fault. He tried too hard. That wasn't his fault, either. It was just the way he was.

I followed the trail of smells and sounds he had described from the dining room to the kitchen of the Beech Street house. It wasn't Jack I found there, writing by the light of the table lamp; it was Ted.

Once I began to write to him, the words took shape effortlessly on the blank page. This task carried no greater weight than the pressure of my hand through the pen onto the paper.

Don't try to contact me again, Jack.

No explanation; there was no point. He wouldn't accept my reasons anyway. *He* wanted to see *me.* As if this were enough of a reason for me to go to him, as if the year we had been together obligated me somehow.

Through the snow-spattered windows, I could just make out the windswept terrace and the four-foot drifts, mounded and curved like giant meringues over the top of the stone wall. A breeze blew the snow from the trees, tossing it into the air, where the early light transformed it into sparkling rainbows.

AT SEVEN thirty, the sound of chainsaws coming from down the hill told me the road crew had begun to remove the tree. I let Chloe out through the garage, enjoying her leaps and bounds through the snow.

At nine o'clock, Ethan arrived to plow our driveway, something he did for neighbors and friends. As he put it, "I've got the truck and the plow. Why not?"

"Do you need anything?" Judging by the clumps of snow above his knee-high boots, we'd had nearly two feet of snow overnight.

"Nope. Anyway, I don't want you to have to make another trip."

"Not a bother. As a matter of fact, I'm thinking we could do our planning session later today, instead of tomorrow. I could be back here by lunchtime."

This made sense to me. We were supposed to call the Long Island clients on Wednesday. The extra planning day would take some of the pressure off. "I've pulled everything together. I'm ready to talk."

"Deal."

"So, in that case, could you pick up a couple cans of chicken broth for us? And mail this letter for me?" Now that I'd written it, I couldn't wait for the mailman to collect it from our mailbox. The sooner Jack got the letter, the better.

"Of course."

When Ethan knocked on the back door at noon, Chloe wagged at him and smiled, but didn't move out of her bed. He put the shopping bag on the table. "Ted caught me at home, just as I was leaving. He told me about the tree. You didn't have to wait for the road crew to do the job. I'd have been glad to come up here yesterday to get it out of the way."

"The phone went out around five o'clock. Besides, I didn't mind being snowbound, given the weather. We were fine here. The woodstove and fireplace saw to that."

Ethan nodded; his face relaxed.

"I MADE two sets of photos of the site: one for you, one for me," Ethan told me. "I discovered one thing about the property that we need to add to our list of challenges."

The potato farm on Long Island had several advantages: there were no structures on it and no historical or archeological impediments, such as Native American burial sites. So far, our biggest challenge was to determine how much of the acreage was buildable. To figure that out, the owners would have to get a new survey and secure all the permits. They had told us to go ahead with our design work as if they had secured all the permits. Their plan was to pursue the permitting at the same time.

"That makes sense," Ethan explained to me. "As long as they understand how much additional work might be required to adjust to any permitting constraints they run into."

"So tell me what you found."

"It's right here." He pointed to an area he had circled in pencil on the plat map. It was about the size and shape of a fifty-cent piece.

"It looks like a depression."

"Right. Some kind of depression. Maybe an old pond? It's marshy enough in certain areas out there. There may even be an underground spring." He looked at me.

"Sounds like this is a bit more than a hunch."

"Let's just say I'm 99.9 percent certain." In all likelihood, the pond had been used to irrigate the potato fields. As long as the land was actively farmed, the owners had kept the pond clear. But once the farm fell into disuse, it had silted in. "Since it likely was spring fed, we should be able to figure out a way to open it up again."

"So we should let them know, right? And we should think about how to make this pond a part of our plan?"

"Definitely. Make that *most* definitely. This will give us both a special feature to work with. It's a great mid-view focal point."

"You mean, between the house and the ocean?"

"Exactly. It's an amazing gift, one we can't say no to."

We had been working with three potential plans, with the house sited differently vis-à-vis the ocean in each one. Ethan's discovery of the old pond made our choice for us: one of the plans included a water feature. Now that we had the pond to work with, we could take the plan to the next level of detail. We laid out the site plan on my worktable and dug in.

For the next several hours, we went through the photographs, making notes and drawing different views from the house to the pond and the ocean beyond it. One decision, the most critical one for Ethan, involved fitting the house to the site. The owners had already agreed to a one-story structure with a green roof of native meadow plants.

The form Ethan had settled on sloped up, away from the drive and the road. Along the drive and the front of the house, the roof would sit on alternating wood and tinted-glass panels to preserve the owners' privacy. The green roof, visible from the road, was a visual sleight of hand: passersby would see the meadow, not the house.

Acer pseudoplatanus

March 15, 1993

On Monday morning, Ethan and I picked up where we left off. By noon, piles of slides, maps, surveys, and drawings crowded the table.

He had found a project management program we used to organize and track all the moving parts on our schedule. We even had a flowchart that allowed us automatically to update the whole schedule. We joked about being just a keystroke away from finishing our plans.

It was a simple matter to make these changes. Then we had to confirm them with all our suppliers and subcontractors. We couldn't afford to pay people to stand idle, waiting for a delayed shipment.

"Same time, same place tomorrow?" Ethan eyed the clutter.

"By then, I'll have sorted these piles." I waited to hear his reaction. Although he had a sharp eye for detail on plat maps and blueprints, sorting and organizing weren't among his strengths. At the rate we were going, we could send the plans and schedule to the owners at the end of the week. They hoped to have the new survey ready by the beginning of April.

I looked at the calendar. A red X marked the date of my talk for the Newport Garden Club, May 5, two months away. *No more excuses.*

"How's your talk going?" The last time Ethan had asked about it, I'd told him only that I hadn't yet decided on a topic. Since then, I'd been preoccupied with our potato farm plans and planning my own garden.

"I've got too many ideas. I need to find a theme. Then I can start pruning and shaping."

"I understand."

"If only they had told me what to talk about!"

He gave me an amused look.

"Sounds like seventh grade, right?" I joked.

"What exactly *did* they say?"

"They left it up to me. They were sure I'd come up with something everyone would enjoy." I scoffed. "That's ridiculous."

"You could take them at their word."

"And watch half of them fall asleep?"

He shook his head, grinning at me. "Not exactly, no. You could talk about the new work you're doing. It seems to me you are coming up with a whole new approach to design, one that blends the garden into the landscape. And you have an advantage down there in Newport."

"And that would be?"

"The planned meadow you did for Ellen. Of course, not everyone has the space she has, or the space we have at the farm. Still, it's the thought that counts, right?"

"I don't know. Most speakers at this event talk about practical, hands-on things. A few give slide lectures about special gardens. I'd been thinking I'd stick to the tried and the true, you know, helpful hints for the coastal gardener."

"That would be useful for the group, I'm sure. But it seems to me they might like to hear some new design ideas. And yours are good ones. Maybe you can set up a tour of Ellen's meadow. Or at least do a slide show. I've seen your before-and-after shots. That would be a way to introduce it."

"That would put the whole emphasis on me and my work."

"Well, what's wrong with that idea? I enjoy behind-the-scenes talks. I bet they will, too."

Put like that, I could see Ethan's point. Why not at least think about it?

He put his notebooks and slide carousel into his backpack and picked up his briefcase. "I'll be glad when we wrap up this phase."

"Me too."

Ethan was right about one thing. I was no longer designing traditional gardens. For instance, Ellen's planned meadow, where it all began, was a hybrid that combined landscaping with garden design. Because I liked the idea of blending these two areas, and because I had learned so much from working with Ethan on the potato farm, it would certainly be more fun for me, an opportunity to gather my ideas into a more coherent form than I had thus far.

WHEN TED got home later that afternoon, I was going through slides in my slide viewer; islands of open books dotted the floor.

"Whatever needle you're looking for, I hope you find it soon!"

I laughed and told him about Ethan's idea. "At first, I thought it might not appeal to the group. You know, it's so much about me and about special sites and circumstances. But I've decided to suit myself. Besides, a few people in the club have seen Ellen's meadow and told me how much they like it. So, I'm going to follow that lead. What's interesting," I waved at the piles, "is that everything I've done since I first went to Flagy is related. For the first time, I see that, and I'm trying to figure out how to talk about it."

Ted looked thoughtful. "So it's a talk about where you've been and where you're going."

"It's not like I had a plan. You know that. And for a long time, I just accepted that I didn't have the right degrees or the right training to move beyond the ground floor. Which was fine. I didn't mind. But as soon as I started work on Ellen's place, I knew there was more I wanted to do."

"And *could* do."

"I believe that now. I'm going to build the talk around my portfolio so the group can see the traditional and nontraditional designs and how they are linked. That's a good thing. Ethan didn't quite say that. But I know it's true. That's why I need to talk about it."

"Yes. You do. I am glad you see it that way."

"There's something else I want to talk to you about."

He looked around at the piles of books. "Shall we go to my place?"

I cleared one of the director's chairs, made a show of brushing it off. "Have a seat."

AS I told Ted about Jack, Beech Street, and the letters, I heard my own voice, easy, natural, no strain, and felt my breathing, steady and strong. I looked into his eyes and saw his strength, freely offered, unstinting in his love and confidence.

"So you wrote to him." His voice was quiet, barely audible above the sound of the birds squabbling around the bird feeder outside the window.

Ted took my hand. "Would you like to tell me why you've kept all this to yourself?"

"At first it was because I thought it might upset you. I wanted you to heal. I thought not talking about it was the right thing to do, to save your energy and strength for getting well."

"And now?"

"You mean, why am I telling you now?"

"Yes."

"I don't know what he wants, but I know now I can take care of myself. I want to handle it, whatever happens." I watched Ted's eyes, shadowed with concern. "Because it's possible Jack will ignore my letter and come to my talk."

"I'm sorry you've been carrying this for so long on your own. It might be nothing. It really *is* only a coincidence that he and his wife bought the house. But it's annoying that he hasn't let up. I don't like it either." He looked out the window, then at me. "It could be he just wants to find out for himself who you are now, maybe to convince himself one way or another that your breakup didn't really ruin his life." Ted smiled. "Or that you were wrong for each other. Or, maybe he just wants to have the last word."

"You mean, I jilted him, so now he wants to jilt me back?" Knowing Jack—at least the Jack I remembered—this sounded plausible. "Either way, it's just a power trip, isn't it?"

For weeks, Ted had been studying and practicing origami. Dozens of cranes and other animals lined the shelves and windowsills in his studio. He pulled a small piece of paper from his pocket and began to fold it, unfold it, and fold it again, each turn a precise and calculated movement. I watched a crane take shape in his hands.

"Did you ever think about what might have been? If you had stayed together? Or wonder how he might have changed, what his life was like, or what you would talk about if you met him again?" He looked up at me.

"He's on my Brookton list—right up there with Hal and Danielle. But I've never wondered about him, not in the way you mean. And now this. It's as if I still don't believe he bought our house, that he lives—*they* live—in Newport."

"The question is, what are you going to do if he shows up?"

"I can imagine seeing him from a distance. That's not much different from remembering him. But talking to him?"

"At least you could find out what he wants."

"And finish this, once and for all."

Ted handed me the crane. "For good luck."

I held it gently, making a nest for it in my palm. "Now for some good news." I'd waited long enough.

"Annie?"

"She called on Saturday. It's official. She's three months pregnant. You can imagine . . ."

With a *whoop!* of delight, Ted hugged me, picked up my phone, and called Annie and Josie. He pulled me close so I could listen to their conversation of questions and answers liberally sprinkled with enthusiastic "yeses" and "rights."

Annie, Josie, Ted, and I were a family, confirming the best possible news and sharing hopes for the safe passage and arrival of our newest member.

ARDIS CALLED at the end of April. She was putting a new show together and couldn't make it up to Newport for my talk.

"I'll send you my outline and fill in the blanks later."

There was a long silence.

"What's on your mind, Ardis?"

"Have you decided what you'll do?"

"If Jack turns up?"

"Yes."

"Ever since I told Ted the whole story, I haven't given it another thought. I've really been too busy. One thing I do know: If he shows up, he won't be able to speak to me alone. It's a public place and I'll be with Sandor and Ellen." I sounded more confident than I felt.

"Call me right away. One way or the other."

"You know I will."

May 4, 1993

Ted had taken Chloe up to Manchester to visit Annie and Josie. Five months pregnant, Annie had an ultrasound the next day.

She and Josie were more excited than anxious. After weeks of discussion, they had decided they wanted to learn if the baby was a boy or a girl.

I had just locked the front door behind me when I heard the phone. Ted? We hadn't had time to talk that morning. I had wanted to send a message to Annie and Josie, to let them both know how much I wanted all of this to work out.

"Malorie?"

The sound of Steve's voice, his hearty cheerfulness, grated upon me, making me realize how much I had wanted to talk to Ted.

"I thought you might like to have dinner tonight when you get into town. Unless you have other plans?"

"Could we make it breakfast tomorrow? At the Wave Café, nine-ish?"

I hung up. *What am I getting myself into?*

It wasn't just that I might run into Jack. I wondered how it would feel to see the Beech Street house again. What if they had painted it a different color? Or put up window boxes and shutters? I wouldn't be able to see the garden. The fence was too high, for one thing. For another, I didn't plan to stop to take a closer look. I would drive by. At least I would see the tree. That was all. That would be enough.

By now, the sycamore maple's leaves would have filled out the canopy, hiding Annie's tree house from view. Daffodils, Jacob's ladder, Epimedium, lily of the valley, scilla—they'd all be fading, making way for the irises and bleeding heart. Meanwhile, the summer-blooming perennials would be soaking up the rain and sun, anticipating July and August.

In the woods, delicate pinks, lavenders, and greens shimmered in the morning sun. The red fox lay on the top of the stone wall, gazing at the house, ears pricked, alert, yet relaxed. Just as I hung up the phone, it jumped down and ran off into the woods.

I'd always believed that the fox in the reading room fresco was intended as a reminder to live by one's wits. It embodied the unexpected and symbolized the importance of cultivating the skills to cope with it. My idea for what to do if Jack showed up was simple: wait and see. That was as much of a plan as I could muster, under the circumstances.

BY THE time I passed through the Newport Bridge tollbooth at eight thirty that evening, fog blanketed the harbor and town. I could hear the drone of the foghorn. The red hazard lights at the top of the bridge towers pulsed, guiding flights to and from Green Airport. But the bridge itself was nearly invisible, its girders and superstructure shrouded in fog.

Below, Goat Island's green light flashed weakly through the gloom. It was as if I'd been cast adrift. I opened the window wide and strained to hear the sound of the water against the pilings, a hundred feet below, anything to counter the floating feeling. Victims of this illusion had jumped off the bridge on nights like this. I could imagine climbing onto the railing, stepping off into the dark fog cloud. I shivered and rolled the window up.

Just ahead, in the slow lane, brake lights appeared out of nowhere. I followed them to the exit.

At the bottom of the off-ramp, I turned right onto Farewell Street and right again at the stop light on Van Zandt. I slowed at Second Street and turned left, toward town. The street signs looked smeared, as if someone had tried to erase the letters. I knew these streets by heart, whispered their names, and counted the blocks. *Beech Street.*

Only the front light was on. Perhaps Jack and his wife were out for the evening; perhaps they were away, and the light was on a timer. I had planned to drive by, to see what I could see from the car. Wishful thinking. To see the tree, I had to get out of the car.

I closed the car door and pulled on my trench coat. Around me, water dripped steadily from the trees to the pavement. I could see nothing beyond the glow of the front light. The fog concealed everything that had made the house and the garden familiar, everything that made them ours. My fingertips tingled. I needed to touch the tree, to assure myself of its reality.

Inside the gate, on the lawn, wet grass pulled at my ankles; water pooled around my feet in the soles of my sandals. Tendrils of fog swirled around the front light as the air began to shift. The rising breeze brushed my face with mist. Toward the back of the border, a white iris swayed, beckoning to me.

Underfoot, the long grass gave way, not to the pachysandra border I'd planted at the base of the tree, but to recently tilled soil. I leaned over and ran my fingers across the surface. Wet mulch. Why? I blinked away the fog and looked up.

Where I expected to see the tree's arching canopy, a patch of sky yawned open above me. I blinked and looked again. There was no mistaking what I saw. What I didn't see. The tree had vanished.

My knees buckled; I knelt on the ground, too shocked to think. Heedless of the wet, I stretched out, closed my eyes, and imagined the fan-shaped canopy reaching out and up, away from the massive trunk cradling Annie's tree house. At that moment, I couldn't think about what had brought the tree down. All that mattered was that it was gone.

May 5, 1993

At the Wave Café the next morning, as soon as I walked in, Lynn, a waitress I knew from before, waved and took a teapot and mug over to an empty table. "We've missed you!" She looked around. "Where's Ted?"

"He couldn't make it this time. Maybe later in the summer."

"Steve will be happy about that."

As if on cue, Steve appeared and chimed in. "You bet I am. I even got him a T-shirt that says 'local emeritus.'"

After we ordered, we settled into small talk about Newport and Alden, bits and pieces of news that flashed by like billboards on a highway: the real estate market, Annie and Josie's baby plans, my landscaping and garden project at Prospect Hill. And Ted's health. At long last, I could offer a mostly hopeful report.

By the time Lynn served our food, Steve had fidgeted his napkin into shreds. She handed him a fresh one. His eyes flicked from me to the parking lot across the street; he shifted in his chair, as if trying to find the right spot. Or maybe to get away.

"Steve?"

He held up a hand. "That storm in March . . ."

My heart raced. I kept my face still.

"We lost power for almost a week. No electricity. No heat. A half-dozen people died at home in the cold. The newspaper called it 'the storm of the century,' which caused a stir, as you might imagine. As if that made any difference to the ones who died. Anyway, the older trees around town bore the brunt of it." He paused, looked up at the ceiling, then at me. "That tree in your garden came down. Last time I drove by, there was a crew there with chainsaws."

I set my tea on the table and leaned back. Relieved I hadn't told Steve what I knew, I didn't say anything right away. Steve's fresh napkin had gone the way of the first. He was flushed, his forehead beaded with sweat. I let the news sink in that it had been the storm—the same storm that brought down the sugar maple on Prospect Street—not the Nelsons, that had razed the tree.

"When we had it pruned last year, the crew told me it was a miracle it survived Hurricane Bob in 1991." In the aftermath of that storm, we had hauled away a truckload of downed branches, but no major limbs. "They said there was no guarantee it wouldn't go down if conditions were right. A freak storm, like this one, in other words."

Steve nodded. "Well, the Nelsons knew that, of course. They took care of it. No problem."

"Maybe I'll drive by on my way out of town." I checked his face to see how he took that idea. I couldn't talk about the tree anymore. The sense of absence I felt, standing there in the empty space, had left me numb, as if something in me had collapsed. I saw in Steve's eyes that he understood at least something of what I was going through. I squeezed his hand. "I'm not planning to shoot the messenger." It was the best I could do.

He waved Lynn over and paid for our breakfast.

We walked together to his car, on the far side of Washington Square. He was on his way to a closing in Providence. "Good luck today with everything." He opened the car door for me. "Tell Ted I'll be expecting him this summer."

"I'm sure he'll be in touch." We hugged goodbye.

As I backed out of my parking space, I saw Steve's car coming toward me, headlights flashing. He stopped, got out, and came over to me, holding a brown paper bag. "Forgot something." I rolled down my window and took the bag from him.

In it, I found a weathered piece of wood with the words "Annie's Place" burned into it.

"From the tree house." I ran my fingers over the lettering, now faded to a dull beige. The wood had the velvety texture of worn corduroy.

Steve smiled down at me. "I walked by the house a month or so ago when the crew was there cleaning up. This was on one of the piles out front."

Ted had helped Annie trace the letter stencils, guiding her hand as she burned each one with a wood-burning pen. Somewhere, I had a picture of them nailing the sign to the door of the tree house.

"I'd been wondering how to tell Annie. This will make it a little easier." I started to put the sign back in the bag. Steve looked at me, expectant. "What is it?"

He motioned at the bag.

I reached in and pulled out four half-foot-tall seedlings wrapped in plastic and burlap. "Sycamore maple babies!"

He beamed. "I figured you might have a corner where you can plant them, see what happens. One at least ought to make it, don't you think?"

The thought of a sycamore maple growing to adulthood at Prospect Hill made my eyes prickle with tears. I grabbed Steve's hand. "At least one, yes. Thank you!" I waved him out of the parking lot, put the sign and the seedlings back in the bag, and tucked the package under the dashboard on the passenger side.

SANDOR MET me in the parking lot at The Elms. The Garden Club always held its annual luncheon in one of the Newport mansions, each with its own well-ordered and well-tended garden. The Elms had a formal garden appropriate in scale and plantings to the mansion itself.

In the ballroom, Sandor and I set up the projector and found a table for the books I'd brought with me. By the time people began to gather, I was ready. I knew most of them by name. For a moment, as I greeted them, it was as though I'd never left Newport.

Light flooded the room through the French doors that opened onto the terrace. The two allées of chestnut trees bordering the wide lawn already showed signs of summer: in their dense foliage, the pale-gold lobes of young leaves mingled with the rich blue-green of more mature ones. At the far end of the allée on the left side, a gap revealed another casualty of the March storm.

Before we sat down for lunch, several people Ted and I both knew came to ask about him; some asked for advice and for plant suggestions. Distracted, I nodded and smiled. The first few butterflies began to swirl around in my stomach. Would this audience of gardeners, accustomed to their own small gardens, understand what I had to say? Would it have been wiser to do what I'd first suggested to Ethan—give a talk emphasizing practical tips? I would soon find out.

MY NOTES floated in a pool of bright light on the lectern. I took a sip of water and pressed the projector control. An audible gasp followed the sound of the slide moving into position. Had I got the slides in the right order? Or brought the wrong ones with me? I turned to see.

Acer pseudoplatanus. The sycamore maple.

Filling up the screen, the foliage glowed green and gold; the huge trunk, with its rough slabs of bark, seemed a testament to life itself.

I couldn't go on.

I imagined the limbs and branches flailing as the gale-force winds battered the tree. It would have taken more than a single gust to topple it, and when it went over, torn from the earth, it would have left raw root ends splayed out over a void, its glorious strength maimed beyond recognition. I closed my eyes, shutting out the image, remembering that endings and beginnings overlap in a continuous cycle of renewal in nature. That this cycle was often both violent and destructive was a bitter truth.

At least I had the seedlings; perhaps one of them would secure the tree's legacy.

I talked about my first designs, the ones I had done for Luc. Even then, I told the group, I understood how important it was that the garden fit the site, with access to distant and near views, a relationship whose value had become clearer to me as I went along.

I explained how I had begun to revise existing gardens on paper, experimenting with new sight lines, creating new relationships between each garden and its surroundings. As an early example, I showed slides of the garden at the house in Buxy where Annie had had her accident. The cedars that framed the terrace also framed the rolling, oak-studded hills in the distance, with their clusters of grazing cattle. I pointed out how the sight lines led your eye out into the nearby landscape, then pulled you back to the garden at your feet.

I talked about Ellen's planned meadow, describing its development over the last three years. Murmurs, then applause, followed. I could see in the recent slides, better than I had early on, how well it worked. It pleased me that these gardeners responded with such enthusiasm to the idea of "going native." I wasn't surprised. We were all garden designers at heart.

The night before, standing where the tree had lived, then given up its life, I had thought about the morning after the March storm when Ethan showed me the old pond at the potato farm, a discovery that had moved us beyond thinking about the property to designing it.

Endings and beginnings. The tree, downed in the storm, the seedlings in my car, the silted-in pond, soon to be revived. Were they not connected, if only in my own imagination, where I could dwell on them, draw on their energy in my life and in my work?

I FELT Jack's eyes before I spotted him at the far side of the room, at the edge of the crowd. As Sandor and Ellen helped me pack, he remained motionless near the exit. On the way out to my car, I kept Sandor and Ellen talking so they wouldn't notice him following us at a distance.

"Are you feeling all right?" Ellen squinted at me.

"Yes, fine."

"Malorie?" We all turned around to face him.

"Jack . . ."

Sandor stepped close to me and offered his hand to Jack. "I don't believe we've met."

"Jack's an old friend, Sandor."

Jack shook hands with Sandor and Ellen, his eyes on me.

He squared his shoulders, slipped his hand into his pocket, and faced me. "I thought maybe we could have a cup of coffee."

Uncertain what to say or do, Sandor and Ellen waited for me to respond. It was obvious Jack's invitation was meant for me alone.

"I don't have much time."

"A half an hour?"

"Look, Malorie . . ." Sandor took my arm.

"It's okay, Sandor." I didn't want to give Jack a chance to talk about the Beech Street house, or how we knew each other. "There's a place up the street. La Forge. We can walk there."

"I'll be in the office all afternoon," Sandor called after me.

Ellen made a dialing motion.

BY TWO o'clock, the lunch crowd at La Forge had thinned. I headed for a window table. Just outside, a howling toddler lay on his back on the sidewalk beside a scoop of chocolate ice cream already melting onto the concrete. Kneeling next to him, his mother soothed him, wiping his face with a handkerchief. Passersby skirted them, then moved back toward the storefronts, window-shopping.

Jack held a chair for me. When the waitress came with menus, he declined them with a smile. "Just coffee. Two, that is."

"Tea for me."

"Earl Grey, please." The waitress nodded at him.

Jack looked at me and shrugged. "Of course, I remember."

The heat started between my shoulder blades, rising up the back of my neck. I looked down at the paper place mat with its hand-drawn map of Newport's tourist attractions. In the middle, the mysterious stone tower at Touro Park. Was it a Viking artifact? A pre-Revolutionary windmill? I caught myself. It was almost funny. This was exactly the type of detail Jack had enjoyed debating.

How would he react if I told him about the shirt cuffs? Familiar, yes, and too intimate. I didn't want him to know I'd noticed—and remembered.

The waitress set a teapot and cup in front of me, a mug of coffee in front of Jack. He tore open a packet of sugar, stirred some into his coffee, and took a sip. "What is it? Why are you smiling like that?" He tilted his chair back and put his hands in his pockets.

"Remember the time you turned back the bottle of wine? You told the waiter it was corked."

He laughed. "That waiter. Wasn't he something?" The waiter had bridled at the request. Jack hadn't backed down.

When he laughed, his features sharpened; he looked twenty years younger. But his skin, fine-textured and pale, had coarsened. A fine web of broken capillaries sprawled across his cheeks; the flesh along his jaw had softened, already beginning to droop. He would have jowls in ten years. Maybe sooner. His hair, gray and thinning, was carefully cut and styled.

An awkward silence had settled between us. Jack broke it, skimming the surface of his life since we'd last seen one another: his wife, career, children. He fiddled with his spoon; I folded and unfolded my napkin.

"You can imagine my surprise."

And mine? What about mine?

I sipped my tea, waiting him out. I didn't have a plan and I didn't have any expectations. I knew only that our conversation would be like this, like jumping from ice floe to ice floe.

"Of all the houses on the market, yours was the only one Liz wanted to see. I suppose Steve told you she had her heart set on an eighteenth-century house? I wasn't so sure it was right for us." He shook his head, laughing at himself, as if to show me who he was now, a wealthy man indulging his wife's whim. "Of course, I didn't know it was yours. Until I saw Ardis's painting."

Across the street, the toddler and his mother sat on a bench. He held a cup of ice cream, spooning it carefully into his mouth. She'd placed a napkin over his lap.

"But, in the end, even I fell in love with your house." He emphasized "love" with a pat on the table.

I took a sip of tea, giving myself time to think about what the house meant to me, still, and what it meant to him. To him, *your* house meant *my* house. He couldn't possibly understand how much the house had been Ted's, too. It had been ours, really, from the beginning.

"We loved it, too." The knot in the back of my neck relaxed. As long as we stuck to small talk, I would never find out why we were here.

"Your husband restores old houses?" He was doing his best to carry on, in a formal way. Maybe he was having second thoughts about what he wanted from me.

"He started there, but now he designs furniture."

"And your children?"

Of course he would want to know, to check off one more item on the list: husband, children, career. I sensed Annie's presence then, saw her smiling at me, standing with Josie in our kitchen, holding a basket of fresh-picked peas. "I have a stepdaughter."

Jack nodded, distracted, it seemed, as if trying to think of an appropriate response. He picked up a toothpick, turning it end over end, glancing at me from time to time as he talked about the house.

Cool water swirls around me, a pure citrine green where I lie submerged in the lake's shallows.

"What about the garden? Did Steve give you the binder of information I left?"

His lips parted, his eyes darted around the room, as if he'd been startled awake. He straightened up in his chair and leaned forward, folding his arms on the table. "You know, when you didn't come to the closing, I worried it had been a mistake to call you. And then you didn't answer my letters. Until you did." He smiled, trying to turn his veiled criticism into a private joke. "When I found out you were coming down here for the talk, I knew it was the only way." Across the restaurant, side by side on a banquette, a couple shared an early cocktail, two straws, one glass, heads together.

"The only way?"

Jack squared his shoulders and put both hands on the table, as if seizing control. "I think I know why you left Brookton. And me. But I still don't understand why you left the way you did. Couldn't we at least have gotten together to talk? I deserved that much, don't you think? A face-to-face explanation?" His gaze, wide and direct, emphasized his sense of grievance. This, then, was his case against me: he *deserved* an explanation, in person.

"I explained why, in a letter and on the phone. I couldn't wait for you to come back. You didn't accept my explanation." I held his eyes. "That's your problem, not mine. I had to move on. That seemed clear enough to me. Do you remember what you said?"

He shook his head.

"That you didn't get it."

"Well, that's true. I didn't. I loved you, Malorie. I thought you loved me." His eyes urged me to give him this much.

I smoothed the tablecloth and folded my hands. "I'm not sure." Across the street, the child had finished his ice cream. "But I know you had an idea about who you wanted me to be. That's the person you thought you loved, a person who didn't exist."

He shook his head. "You misjudged me. I was trying to help you, you know? You were such an idealist, always so quick to jump to conclusions." His laugh mocked the idea, mocked me.

"You mean *naïve*, right?" Saying it, admitting it, brought me face-to-face with myself at twenty-three. In Jack's view, I'd been blinded by naïveté; it was my naïveté that had kept me from taking advantage of Brookton.

"And that was charming. It was one of the reasons I fell for you. You weren't cynical—at all—like so many of us. I wanted to give you some balance, so you'd survive the whole experience, get your degree, and go do what you wanted to do. You really loved French, the literature and the culture." He smiled, indulgent again, so wise, so aware of my inadequacies.

He was wrong. My näiveté made it possible for me to flee Brookton, but I knew it would be pointless to defend myself now.

"So you went to France. Where?"

"To Flagy, where my grandmother was born. I stayed for five years. If I hadn't, I'm not sure I'd have figured out what I really wanted to do."

"And that is?"

"Didn't you hear my talk?"

"I got there just as you finished. I know it had something to do with plants. I guess I thought you were a scientist—maybe a botanist."

How likely was it he would have understood the talk, anyway? Wasn't this the way it had always been between us? He only heard what he wanted to hear. "Something like that, yes."

I asked him again, "How's the garden on Beech Street?"

His eyes slid away; he ran his hand through his hair. "Liz and I are divorcing." There was a faint snap. The toothpick lay broken on the tabletop. "She'll keep the house in Newport. I'm staying in Brookline."

"Did you know before you bought the house?"

"We'd been having our problems, the kind married people have when they lose interest in each other. Our youngest started college last year. We're bored. We know each other too well. We thought—Liz thought—the Newport property would get us going again."

The Newport property. These words, jargon he was comfortable with, made me shudder.

"She paid for it with an inheritance, just to be clear about that. So, really, it's been her house from the beginning." He looked lost, as if he couldn't figure out how we got here. "You asked about the garden. The big tree . . ." He picked up a piece of the broken toothpick. "It went down in the storm in March. Lucky thing it didn't damage the house. We managed to get some insurance. . . ."

"Insurance? You said the house wasn't damaged."

"To pay a crew to cut it up and remove it. That was an unbelievable pain." His smile implied we could at least agree on that. "It cost a bundle, even with the insurance."

The pain of losing the tree, the pain of dealing with the insurance company. No matter what I said, he would never understand the two had nothing in common. A door slammed somewhere in the back of the restaurant. A gust of air fluttered the curtains in the window next to our table. A seagull had landed on the sidewalk, dipping its beak into the puddle of ice cream.

"I had a miscarriage."

Floating on my back, looking up into the cloudless blue dome, I drift away from the shallows toward the middle of the lake.

He looked at me, his face suddenly blank. "A miscarriage? When?"

"Right after you left for Paris." The drive to Long Meadow, waking to pain and fear in the night, Ardis, my mother, Dr. Stein—it all came back to me.

"You were pregnant when I left for Paris? Why didn't . . . ?"

"Because I knew you would want me to have an abortion. Then it was too late. What would have been the point in telling you after the miscarriage?"

Heading toward the dock across the lake, breathing easily, my stroke strong and sure, I reach it without effort.

"Malorie, wait. Please listen. I have learned that decisions I made then, my thinking about life, my principles—I didn't question them, because to question them would have meant I'd failed at something I believed."

Did he remember advising me to use Danielle's plagiarism as a bargaining chip with Hal Rose? The ends justify the means? Did he remember his lie about the foxes? What principles, exactly, was he talking about? When I lifted the cup of tea, my hands were trembling. I put it down.

"If I had come to you, pregnant with our child, *in principle* you would have expected me to have an abortion? You wouldn't have seen the pregnancy through, if that's what I had wanted?"

He wouldn't—or couldn't—look at me. "I don't know. Really, I don't. But I know I would have wanted to help you." Confusion and something like self-doubt swept over his face. He looked down at the table, then at me, eyes wide, mouth set, and slumped back in his chair.

ON MY way to The Elms to get my car, I looked back once. A reflex. I didn't expect Jack to follow me, but I wanted to be sure he hadn't had second thoughts. However unsatisfied he was with our meeting, I could see in his face as we said goodbye that he had nothing more to say to me. We had nothing more to say to each other. The coincidence that had brought us together again had made clear to us both that what we'd had at one time wouldn't have—couldn't have—lasted.

The mournful sound of a horn signaled a cruise ship's progress out of the bay, heading south into open water. I imagined standing on the bow deck, the wind in my face, as the engines engaged and the boat picked up speed. There would be a slight hesitation as the propellers dug in until, no longer straining, the engines powered the vessel smoothly through the water, the bow wave curling away from it, unfurling as it raced toward the shore.

There were several messages on the car phone: Ted's, warmed by the smile in his voice, told me to take my time, that we'd have dinner together when I got home. The message from Sandor made me laugh: "Who was that guy, anyway? Call me before you leave town."

Ethan's, longer than the others, came at the end: "We got the final go-ahead today, so we can start work on phase three next week. Looks like you won't have much of a break between Newport and Long Island. But everything is just about set: The gravel for the pond came today. The drainage system passed inspection. And another load of plants arrived. How many gardens did you say you were planning? Drive safe." It sounded like he was sorting papers as he talked. "I hope it went well, Malorie."

As I approached the top of the bridge, I slowed and looked back toward town. I found the gap right away. Now, the Trinity Church spire in the background rose in the middle of the space once dominated by the sycamore maple's canopy, calling attention to its absence. As if aware of its new prominence, the spire seemed taller, its brass weather vane gleaming in the afternoon light.

AT EIGHT o'clock I drove up Prospect Street and parked in our driveway next to Annie's VW. Here and there in the early-evening sky, the first stars glittered. Would I ever again look up at the stars without thinking of the tree? Could there be any better way to remember it? The warm air smelled of lily of the valley and lilac.

The back door slammed; Chloe leapt down the steps, calming for a moment to nuzzle my hand before she began to run circles around me.

Ted laughed at her, spoke to her quietly, until she came to stand with us. "Welcome home." His hug fulfilled his words.

Annie and Josie had followed him, holding hands. Something about the way they stood together, shoulder to shoulder, taking each other in in quick, smiling glances, conveyed a new sense of who they were together, and a new sense of purpose.

"Good news?"

"The best." Annie held out a piece of paper. Josie turned on a flashlight. We all gathered around, gazing at it in silence.

The sonogram's swirls of gray and white, cradled in a fathomless space, aligned themselves in constellations—the head, the belly, the curve of the back, the leg, and one arm bent, the hand clearly articulated, the index finger extended.

Annie looked at Josie and Ted, then at me.

"A little girl?" Somehow I knew this, without knowing it.

"We're going to name her Malorie."

Ted squeezed my hand. I felt then the presence of all the people we knew and loved, gathering with us, offering their stories, binding us together into the fabric of this new life whose story was just beginning.

Annie and Josie put their arms around Ted and me; Chloe pushed her way into the middle of our circle, leaning against me, smiling up at us.

Acknowledgments

I AM grateful for the support so generously offered by these friends and family members, whose interest and encouragement helped me in many ways to tell Malorie's story: Ann, Mildene, Beverly, Michèle, Patricia, Mary, Shelley, Jane, Marvis, Carolyn, Susan, Kristin, Daisy, Ebba, Géraldine, Alejandro, Janet, Patsy, Terri, Linda, Sandrine, Kipra, Molly, Claudia, Mary Beth, Mark, Vi, Ilse, Marjolaine, Régine, Françoise, Isabelle, Carol, Signe, Julianna, Kristina, Bay, and Carla.

I wish also to thank the editorial, marketing, and production teams at Hillcrest Media for an outstanding performance, start to finish. Special mention and special thanks go to my editor, Erin Roof, for her eagle eye and guidance throughout the editing process.